AREMAC POWER:

INVENTIONS AT RISK

OTHER BOOKS BY GERALD M. WEINBERG

NOVELS

The Aremac Project
Aremac Power
Mistress of Molecules
First Stringers
Second Stringers
The Hands of God
Freshman Murders

NON-FICTION

Weinberg on Writing, The Fieldstone Method
The Secrets of Consulting
More Secrets of Consulting
Becoming a Technical Leader
The Psychology of Computer Programming
An Introduction to General Systems Thinking
General Principles of System Design
Perfect Software and Other Illusions About Testing
Quality Software Management (4 volumes)
Are Your Lights On: How to Know What the Problem Really Is
Exploring Requirements: Quality Before Design

ADDITIONAL BOOKS AND WRITINGS

see HTTP://WWW.WWW.GERALDMWEINBERG.COM

Aremac Power:

Inventions at Risk

by Gerald M. Weinberg

"Power is not revealed by striking hard or often, but by striking true."
- Honore de Balzac

CHAPTER ONE

Marna sat cross-legged on one of her Grandmother's Two Gray Hills Navajo rugs. ripping her latest equations into tiny paper flakes. She was tossing the flakes into the air and watching them fall like snow when the janitor, *Lapu*, called Luke here in the Laboratory, came around to sweep the cubicle and empty her wastebaskets.

"*Yá'át'ééh*," Luke said.

"*Yá'át'ééh*," she replied, returning the Navajo greeting. "It is good"–but the words tasted like a lie in her mouth, here, today, in this sterile, windowless *Biligaana* room.

The wrinkles in Luke's face told her that he detected the lie, his eyes silently resting on the myriad bits of paper. "I'm sorry if I'm making a mess," she said. "You leave it. I'll pick it all up."

"No mess," he said, smiling. "You make a Milky Way, like when Coyote angry. What made you so angry?"

"I'm sorry," she said. "I shouldn't be angry. It is not the Navajo way."

"Do not apologize. Even small mouse has anger. What ugly thing caused this *iich'aa* to grow in you?"

She glanced down at her black jeans and ill-fitting black top. She wore them loose, not to hide her extra thirty-pounds, but just because she liked the comfort and convenience. And she liked black, Spider Woman's color. Her accessories were all black, too–sensible walking shoes and a digital watch with wide, black leather watchband. The only color she wore was a string of small brown beads circling her neck. She fingered the beads, a gift from her Spanish grandmother, vaguely suggestive of the rosary Marna would never wear.

"It's not his clothes," she said to Luke. He nodded, and her mind returned to the distasteful meeting when Mike in the arrogance of his three-piece manager's suit had laughed at her theory. When he ridiculed her prediction that objects could move instantly from one place to another, she endured his ignorant mockery by reciting her own physics rosary, silently listing all the known isotopic variations of the transuranic elements, one for each of the twenty-four beads. She wasn't listening to Mike's interminable lecture, but she did notice the movement as he gestured out his two wide windows.

Her own little basement office had no windows–an enclosed space that would have been unbearable for her classmates on the Rez. But not for *Maralah* (called Marna by the Anglos) *Shideezihi* Rose, PhD. For her, theoretical physics created an n-dimensional world of symbols and equations, with beauty rivaling the enchanted pinks and browns of her father's mesa country.

No, she didn't envy the windows. She despised them. Windows were bureaucratic rewards for the manipulative political work that always seemed to happen in Mike's second floor office–like his interminable lectures on "the greater good of the Laboratory."

The Laboratory, Marna thought, now looking at Luke leaning on his broom and patiently waiting for her to work through her anger. Here at The Laboratory, Luke was just an invisible janitor. At home, in the Navajo Nation, he was a respected elder. Why should she respect the laboratory's values–values that changed with every new political breeze wafting over Los Alamos Mesa.

Today's zephyr had carried the suspicious odor of the new President's administration. Like Mike's halitosis, which wasn't quite masked by his cinnamon mouthwash, the smell of "national security" hadn't been quite masked by his words. "Theoretical physics is all good and well–I can speak like that to you because we both have our doctorates–but let's face reality, Marna. We're now living in the Age of Terror."

Last month, Marna had thought, we were in the Age of Robotic Warfare. Mike had a way of capitalizing spoken words. Her mind had wandered, then, speculating what next month's capitalized slogan would be. She had missed half of the words before she tuned in again. " … switch your focus. Just because we're a National Lab no longer means we can count on bottomless funding. Models are all good and well, but you could construct models of terror countermeasures just as readily as your obscure quantum effects."

Mike had smoked in his office, probably to get some reaction from her, but she had simply sat quietly twisting strands of dark brown hair between her fingers. She had once made the mistake of pointing out that smoking had been outlawed in the Lab for years. He had simply struck a match and said, "rank has its privileges."

Not that she cared about the Lab's rules. Or ranks. Or privileges. She had just been trying to be helpful, to keep him out of trouble, but nobody enforced the no-smoking rule in the Theoretical Physics Building anyway. And the smoke didn't bother her the way it did some people. She didn't smoke, herself, but at home, her mother and father and brothers always smoked. She didn't care for it, but she was used to it.

While she thought of home in Little Water, her mind half listened to Mike droning a litany of "funding for fascinating projects." He had lit his pipe and was saying something about " … coordinated threats to the infrastructure."

He had puffed two consecutive smoke rings that spun just over her head. "Now, doesn't that sound more interesting than your 'quantum displacement'?" He could also speak quotes around words to make them sound unreal or unimportant.

The Navajo half of her mind had known she should just say something non-committal. Unfortunately, the inner Spanish spark of irritation had suddenly blossomed into a fireball too angry to ignore. "No, Mike, not interesting at all. If you want something really interesting, why don't you allocate an experimentalist to test my theory. If he's competent, he should be able to show results in a year, maybe eighteen months."

He had merely leaned over his desk. Even sitting down, he towered over her five-foot height. "Well, if you want any kind of future here, maybe you should *make* yourself interested."

The unique odor from Luke's hand-rolled cigarette, so unlike Mike's honeyed pipe smoke, brought her back to the present. "What can be more interesting than the greatest paradigm shift since Special Relativity," she muttered, but Luke just tied and tucked away his leather tobacco pouch. "I'm angry because he's trying to shape my mind into his own image."

"He?" said Luke.

"Mike, my boss's boss," she said, but for an instant her mind flashed on Karl, her husband. He wanted to shape her, too, but he loved her, so she quickly rejected that thought. "Mike told me the only reason I was here was because I was protected by EEO, not what he called my 'half-assed' thesis from a second-rate department. He said that HR loves me because they get to check three EEO boxes for me–Indian, Hispanic, and female"

"What is a second-rate department?" Luke asked.

"According to him, the physics department at Cal, Berkeley, where I earned my degree."

"But I heard that you went to the best school. Everyone in the Nation knows that about you."

"And everyone in the world, except for Mike, who has a degree from a fifth-rate department ..." Her voice dropped to a whisper, as if she couldn't bear to tell Luke the next thing. "He says I will never earn a merit raise in this division as long as he is in charge."

She recalled how Mike, having cast his sharpest verbal spear, had leaned all the way back in his executive chair, hands clasped behind his head. When she said nothing, he tipped forward again and said, "Don't you care about the money? Don't you Indians have any ambition? Would you be more motivated if we paid in sheep?"

With that, he had crossed Marna's invisible line. "I own enough sheep already, *télii.*" Only one word had shown her forbidden anger once again, and even though he didn't know she had called him a donkey, an ass, that had been one word too many. Before she completely lost control, she had stood up. "And money is just money. So, if you're through reviewing my work, I'd like to get back to my office."

He had shoved her theory paper across this desk. "This is useless. I'm not going to bother reading it."

Pressing down heavily on her anger, she had taken her theory and walked out of the smoke-filled room, leaving the door open so she could hear him saying something about a conference. Maybe he was going to let her present her work at a conference. She did have some new thoughts she would like to share with somebody who could understand, but it was better not to let her hopes rise too high.

She marched in fury down to her basement cubicle, already thinking of a non-linear correction term in the secondary displacement equation. Nothing, she thought, is more practical than a good theory–but not if nobody appreciated it.

When she reached her office, she scribbled the new term onto the rejected paper. Then, boiling with anger, she sat down and began to shred.

CHAPTER TWO

"Order granted," said the judge. When he banged his gavel, Tess felt like he had driven a railroad spike right between her eyes. *Now I know how pumpkins feel when their faces are carved up. It's a spooky Halloween to be in this Chicago courtroom, a day of betrayal by ghosts.*

Her head already ached from the long, boring hearing. Now she covered her ears, unable to tolerate the noisy chatter echoing off the wood-paneled walls as the hot, stuffy courtroom emptied. "What are we going to do now?" she muttered to herself, then startled when she received a response.

"We appeal," said Arnie, her slightly overweight but impeccably dressed attorney. "We keep appealing. Eventually we'll win."

"I know we'll appeal," she snapped, making her head hurt even more. "We always appeal."

"And we always win." Arnie rearranged some papers on the defendants' table, then straightened the stack by tapping it on the polished wooden surface. "And we'll win this one."

"But now we can't use Aremac *at all*, right?"

"There are a few exceptions, but basically, yes. The authorities are simply too afraid of what can be done with a machine that makes movies of a person's memories."

"Not unless they can use it to extract confessions by torturing people."

"That's not what they say, but it doesn't matter what their reasons are. You can't use Aremac in the United States until we get the TRO lifted."

"TRO?"

"Temporary restraining order," Arnie explained. "But *temporary* is the operative word."

"How long is temporary?"

"With these FDA orders, probably three years. Maybe five." Arnie put the stack of papers in his briefcase. "If you didn't have the best attorney in Chicago, probably ten."

Tess put her elbows on the table and held her head in her hands. "We'll be broke long before that."

"Maybe not, if you're frugal. Or find some other source of income from Roger's inventions." He swiveled around to face her and lifted her chin with both hands. "Just don't get into another contract like this one with Professor Zeng without consulting me. You know you always have to consult me on business deals. Whatever possessed you?"

"It wasn't a business deal," she said, her voice lacking conviction.

"Oh, really? Then what was it?"

"Just scientific research. No money changed hands."

"Well, that was your first mistake." Arnie stood and picked up his briefcase. "Wait here for a minute, then I'll escort you out. I'm going to get a snack. Do you want something?"

Tess shook her head, then stopped when it felt as if her brain would fall out. She didn't think her stomach could tolerate food just now. She couldn't stop her mind from trying to figure out how they found themselves in this mess.

Arnie returned carrying a white paper bag in one hand and a large sugar cookie–minus a huge bite–in the other. "Ready to go?" he asked. "Do you need a ride?"

"No, Roger's meeting me out front. I'll wait for him."

Arnie accompanied her to the courthouse's vast lobby. He signed them out, then pulled up the collar of his cashmere overcoat and headed out into the freak Halloween snowstorm, leaving her to contemplate her mistakes while she waited for her husband.

Everything had been going so well. Denise might be the smartest person of her generation, but with her flat Chinese nose, was always losing her glasses. Her boyfriend, SOS, found them for her by using Aremac to scan her memory back to the last time she had the glasses.

Standing alone in the lobby, Tess smiled to herself remembering how Roger and SOS spent hours trying to repair Aremac's focus. *They're all geniuses, but without me to guide them, they can be truly stupid at times. How embarrassed they were when I pointed out that Aremac wasn't out of focus. It was showing the world exactly as Denise saw it without her thick glasses.* The story was so funny that it had spread at internet speed, bringing them a variety of clients seeking lost objects.

One woman had lost a $65,000 diamond ring. Her husband suspected she had sold it. When Aremac helped her find it, the grateful couple gave their story to the Tribune. Liang Zeng, a visiting professor of neurophysics at Northwestern, wanted to improve his English. That's why he read the Tribune every day, front to back, on the El heading out to his research lab on the Evanston campus. And that's why he saw the story.

Liang showed up at their offices one day in August proposing to use Aremac to map areas in the brain based on errors in remembered pictures. The non-invasive method was such an instant success, Liang's letter was fast-tracked in the November issue of the Journal of Neuroscience Research.

Then someone in the Food and Drug Administration read Liang's paper and decided that Aremac was a medical device, one that had not passed the FDA screening process. *One that had to be prohibited from use on human subjects. One that can no longer produce income, even from finding lost objects.*

A gentle touch on her shoulder awakened Tess from her reverie. She reached behind her neck, expecting to caress Roger's smooth hand. When she felt bristly hairs, she pulled away and spun around. Smiling but concerned, it wasn't husband Roger's spindly six-foot-four. Instead, the friendly rugged features of Agent Don Capitol.

"Dammit, Don, you startled me."

"Sorry," Don said. "I don't know any other way to wake up you eggheads when you're off in brainland."

"This is not a good time for your funny put-downs, Don. Just now, I'm not feeling terribly gracious towards you or your FBI."

He bowed an apology. "I know. I'm sorry. It wasn't intended as a put-down. I was trying to make you smile."

"I'm not in the mood." *Just because you once saved my life doesn't mean I have to smile every time I see you. Especially not a time like this.*

"I heard the verdict. I wanted you to know I had nothing to do with it. For what it's worth, I think it's a dirty trick. I don't think the FDA is behind it. Homeland Security's putting pressure on you, but I was powerless to stop them. I may be Special Agent in Charge here, but the Aremac business has gone way over my head."

Tess felt her anger cool a few degrees. "So you have nothing to do with Aremac now?"

"Not officially. But I came here to offer you an alternative to this TRO."

"So you *knew* we'd lose." The heat of her anger grew back double.

"It's a setup, Tess. Yes, I knew you'd lose, but there was nothing I could do about it."

"Well, thanks anyway." She looked at her watch. "Now can you leave me alone? I'm supposed to meet Roger."

"Of course." He held out his gray calling card, lowering his voice. "You might want to explore some other possibilities. Inga Steinman is coming into town and wants to meet you."

It took Tess only a second to conjure up her image of "the fat lady," the formerly anorexic beauty queen now massive enough to play offensive tackle for the Bears. "I thought she was under investigation for using her government position to make some questionable grants."

"It was worse than that, but the auditors dropped it. Couldn't prove anything. She still has the purse strings, so it might be worth your while to talk to her. The time and place is on the back of my card." He pushed the card into her hand. "I'd understand if you didn't come, but just think about it. It's all I can do right now."

She knew he was a friend. She knew he was sincerely trying to help her. She didn't think Inga would offer a government grant she could accept, but she took his card just to release him before she slipped over the edge of her anger. Without a word, she turned her back and walked toward the concealment of a square marble pillar.

Before she could escape, he laid a hand on her shoulder, turning her around. "One more thing to keep in mind," he said, holding up his hand with thumb and forefinger almost touching. "Homeland Security is this close to putting you–your whole team–in prison. Until they get what they want."

CHAPTER THREE

The anesthesiologist would be in any minute, but Inga had to make this call before undergoing her next liposuction, after which she would be in no condition for this delicate business until tomorrow morning. And if she was to divert Aremac from her government employers to her clandestine partner, this news couldn't wait.

While waiting for her partner to answer, she looked around at the familiar decor of her private room, realizing that these past few years, this clinic had become almost a second home. Certainly the original paintings and the blue and silver matching upholstered chairs and sofa were not like an ordinary hospital room. The hospital's private rooms weren't covered by insurance, but they were worth every penny. They didn't cost much more, really, than the surgeries themselves. Besides, at her weight, no regular hospital would permit her even a single liposuction surgery.

Did doctors really think I would tolerate gastroplasty or gastric bypass–surgeries that will reduce my stomach capacity? Without food, what would make life worth living?

A familiar female voice answered the phone and waited for the code word, then told Inga to hold. This was the expected procedure, but Inga wasn't in a mood to wait. Even here, no matter what she paid, they wouldn't let her have breakfast before anesthesia. She was in a rotten mood.

"Yes?" said a male voice.

She tried to sweeten her tone. "The FBI–that is, the FDA–got their TRO yesterday."

"Why didn't you call me sooner?" The voice sounded accusing.

"I'm in the goddamn hospital, that's why." *How did I ever get involved with this son-of-a-bitch anyway? If it wasn't for the money, I wouldn't put up with this crap from anyone else.*

She didn't expect him to ask what for–he probably knew–or how she was feeling–he didn't care. He didn't disappoint. "So what happens next?"

"Now that they're enjoined from using their brain-camera, they're in a squeeze." He didn't like her to call it Aremac, and she didn't care to displease him. "The FBI is going to make them an offer they can't refuse."

"Then you will make them a better one."

She rolled the idea around in her mind before answering. "That will be difficult."

"We don't want to hear about difficulties. Just results."

"Hear me out." She wasn't used to taking orders, and she didn't care for it.

"I'm listening," his voice snapped, "but I don't have a lot of time. Have you taken all the precautions for this call?"

"I don't have a lot of time, either, damn you. And I always follow procedures, so you don't have to worry about someone finding this throw-away phone while I'm knocked out on the operating table."

"I do have to worry if someone pulls this number from it."

"Then don't worry. I'll erase it." She heard footsteps in the hall. *I'm running out of time.*

"Erasures can be recovered."

"Not if I break it to pieces and put them in with the medical waste. Just listen. No, wait a minute. Someone's here."

Charlene, the anesthesiologist came in wearing ordinary street clothes and carrying a clipboard computer. "Good morning, Inga. I'm here to go over a few things with you."

"Save your breath, Charlene. I've heard your pitch enough times to have it memorized." Inga held up the phone. "I'm on an important call, and I need to finish before I go into surgery."

Charlene tisked and shook her head. "It's not standard procedure, but I guess you're right." She removed a large yellow pill from a plastic container, read the label, and handed the pill to her patient. "This sedative will calm you down before they come in with the gurney."

"I'll take it as soon as my call is finished."

"No, that part of the procedure is not negotiable. I have to see you take it."

Inga knew from experience that Charlene would not yield on this point, but she couldn't have her in the room listening to the call. "Fine," she said, then washed down the pill with some warm water in a paper cup. "Not much of a breakfast."

Charlene patted her on her voluminous thigh. "We'll have a nice meal ready for you this afternoon, don't you worry."

"I won't worry," Inga muttered under her breath at Charlene's back as she left the room. "I'm having a little supplementary meal brought in, with more appropriate portions."

She picked up the phone and turned off the mute. "Still there? She's gone, but I don't have much time before this pill knocks me out. I've managed to work my way onto the negotiating team by convincing the FBI I have more experience in this kind of thing. And I know those children."

"Children?"

"They're babes in the woods. Fixman shaves maybe twice a week, and Myers thinks she's so clever she's an easy mark."

"They don't exactly love you from the last time."

"All they have are suspicions. And I helped them get their government financing when they needed it. I'll play on their gratitude. When it comes to negotiating, they're as naive as banana splits."

"But we don't *want* you to win this negotiation. Make them a ridiculously bad offer from your government position, then steer them to our agents once they turn you down."

"Don't insult my intelligence. I know my job"

"So, what's the problem?"

"It will be too obvious, even to them, if I turn around and make them your offer. I can prevent them from taking the government's deal, but you've got to come up with a really clever agent to close the bargain." *Someone at least half as clever as I am.*

Two attendants appeared at the door with a gurney. "Give me five minutes," Inga said. They looked doubtful, so she repeated herself, this time forcefully. The moment they disappeared, she turned back to the phone.

"Sorry. They're coming for me, but I sent them away."

"All right. I know just the person for the negotiations."

"I don't want to know."

"No, you will have to know, in case they need some subtle steering. There may be others looking to deal, so you'll have to know which one is ours. You'll be informed in good time."

"How attractive will the deal be?" *Damn. I'm beginning to feel that pill, but I have to ask.*

"That depends somewhat on the government's counter-offer, which you will supply."

"Of course. But I meant *your* deal, with your customer."

"That's not your concern, but we have some rather generous customers lined up. Perhaps we shall hold an auction."

"That's fine with me, as long as I get my usual percentage."

"Have we ever let you down?"

"No." *But I'm falling asleep, and I'd better not talk money in this condition.*

"But, of course, you have let *us* down."

There was no mistaking the threat in his voice. "Only once." *Why does he have to keep bringing that up?*

"And that's once too often. We are not paying you to fail."

"I'll give it my best." She yawned.

"No, that's not good enough. You *will* succeed this time."

She heard the click on the other end. She shuddered at the chill in his voice, then gathered herself with the thought of her share of the deal. She hauled herself out of bed, wobbled before steadying herself, then dropped the phone on the tile floor.

After glancing at her soft slippers, she decided they wouldn't do the job, so she hefted up the corner of the bed and dropped it on the phone. Once. Twice. The third time, an assortment of large and small pieces skidded across the floor.

Picking things off the floor was not part of Inga's skill set, so she leaned on the bed and waited for the gurney to return. "I dropped my phone," she said. "I'm kinda dizzy. Could you guys pick up the pieces for me and put them in medical waste. I don't want anybody to get my germs."

CHAPTER FOUR

After five anxious minutes waiting in the lobby, Tess finally saw Roger rushing through the revolving doors, blowing breath steam on his bare hands. She ran to him and threw herself into his hug, the top of her head not quite reaching his shoulder. "We lost," she whispered.

He added a cold kiss to the hug. "I know. I talked to the FDA lawyer on his way out. I think he wanted to gloat."

She grabbed his arm and tugged him into the revolving doors. "Let's get out of this place." They emerged into the snow-covered Federal Plaza, all gray and white and cold except for the brilliant red-orange of Alexander Calder's Flamingo sculpture. "Let's walk under the statue," she said.

"You're amazing." He stood his ground. "You're always ready to play, no matter how awful the circumstances."

"The more awful they are, the more reason to play. Come on."

He hesitated. "We're more likely to catch a cab right here. Besides, I'm freezing."

She towed him by the hand. "A little cold will cheer you up, Darling. Besides, now that we've been hit with the temporary restraining order, we're back among the poor. Where we started. We can't afford taxis. We'll take the El."

She wrapped her right arm around his waist and huddled close against the icy blasts scouring the Plaza. She stopped under the sculpture, then let go of him and spun in a circle, taking in the surrounding buildings. "Okay," she said, satisfied. "Now let's go home."

"I thought you wanted to shop for a while, then try Charlie Trotter's."

"We're poor now. Have you forgotten already? I'll buy some hot dogs at the all-nighter near our El station. Or maybe some cheap noodles."

She could tell from the expression on his face that he couldn't understand why it would make any difference what they ate. *Rich at eighteen, destitute at nineteen, none of it mattered to my genius husband.* They walked in silence, leaning into the wind that whipped between buildings. She rushed him into the shelter of the El station, guiding him as she always did when he lost himself inside his mind. *This time, though, I don't think he's inventing anything.*

Their silence continued unbroken until they boarded their Red Line train and seated themselves. Just as the train pulled out of the station, Roger broke his silence. "It started because Denise was always losing things."

Tess had long ago ceased being surprised by Roger's out-of-the blue pronouncements. She usually knew exactly what he was talking about. Often she was thinking along the same lines. "I thought so, too. The only thing she never loses is Stephen. I'm always surprised any time I see him without her tagging along."

"She's like me with you."

She pecked him on the cheek. "How sweet. But I think we're a bit more independent than those two lovebirds."

"That's because we're an old married couple, set in our ways."

"Sure," she laughed. "We've been married more than a whole year now." As the train slowed for the Addison station, they shared a smile. *I'll bet we're both remembering the same incident.* "The diamond?"

Roger confirmed her suspicion. "I couldn't imagine how a husband could suspect his wife had sold a present he gave her."

"Me, neither."

His face turned serious. "But, I have a confession to make."

"Really?"

"I sold the present you gave me."

"What present?"

"The tie you gave me to wear in court."

She snickered and punched him in the arm. "You did not."

"Yes, I did. I sold it to the court reporter. She said her son needed a tie for his bar mitzvah."

She grabbed him by the neck and kissed him, simultaneously slipping her hand inside his down parka pocket and coming out with the blue striped tie.

"I saw you tuck it away when you were coming through the revolving doors." She waved the tie triumphantly for all the El passengers to see. Most of them pretended to ignore it, but Tess saw a number of half-hidden smiles. *I like making people smile.*

He looked studiously away from the tie. "Well, I'm the inventor of an important medical device." He spread his lapels and stuck out his chest.

The train rattled around a curve, making Tess lean slightly to compensate. "A great one, too. You've already helped more than a dozen people whose surgery would have been impossible without Aremac."

"And what do I get for my troubles? An FDA court order preventing us from saving any more people."

She shook her head. "It's not the FDA, dear. It's the other F-ers, the FBI. Don claims it's Homeland Security, but I think he's fibbing. His FBI has always been looking at a way to pressure us into letting them use Aremac to interrogate suspects. Or anyone they want to interrogate."

"This time they really found a way."

"Cheer up. It's only temporary. Arnie says we'll beat them, eventually. Of course, we're already spending three times as much time in the courthouse as in our lab. And now we have no income until the suit is settled." *I have to cheer you up, because I don't want my despair to contaminate our team.*

Roger took her mittened hands in his. "Now you're the one who needs to cheer up. We've still got those royalties from our other inventions."

"Okay, so maybe we can still eat cold beans out of the can, but no more steak or lobster. And now that they have this restraining order, they'll drag out the case as long as they can. Until we're bankrupt, if possible."

He shook his head. "That won't happen. Liang's department is working to get FDA approval as a medical device. Northwestern really wants it, so they're going all-out."

"Ha. With the FDA, all-out for approval might mean we have to wait only seven years instead of ten." She was distracted for a moment by a crowd around a fire engine down below, then suddenly turned to her husband with another idea. "We could move to Mexico, out of reach of the FDA." *Should I tell him what Don said about Inga, knowing the way he feels about "the elephant woman"?*

Roger went silent again. Tess let him roam around inside his head until the train slowed and rattled to a stop at Jarvis. As she guided him out the door and down the stairs, the wind off the lake was even colder than downtown. It seemed to wake him from his next trance.

"I don't think Mexico is right for us," he said. "Not just now, anyway. I don't want to be that far from my family, and SOS needs to care for his mother. I guess that means we're going to need another brainstorming session. One more stimulating to the brain–hot dogs or noodles?"

"I'll ask Inga. She's the authority on food. Don says she wants to make us an offer we can't refuse."

CHAPTER FIVE

Luke showed no signs of impatience as he sat on the office floor with Marna, both on her grandmother's weaving, picking up the remains of her theory, one flake at a time. "Tell me about this theory," he said, "the one the big man did not value. That made you so angry?"

Knowing Luke had no mathematical education, Marna explained in terms of the holy stories from her youth. "It's like the twin sons of Changing Woman and the Sun, Monster Slayer and Child-Born-of-Water."

He nodded. "They who could travel vast distances instantly, in a single step."

"Exactly. But the *Biligaana* don't believe it is possible to move from one place to another in an instant–"

He furrowed his thin eyebrows. "Of course it is possible. The twins did it."

"But they don't understand–"

"–or don't want to understand. Perhaps you have been too long away from our home." He took one last look around for wayward paper flakes, then stood and walked to the doorway. "Perhaps you must go home for a while, perform the ceremonies to remove this anger poison from your spirit."

When he was gone, she sat on the rug for a while. *I do wish I could be home among family, but, no, dreaming will not solve my problem. I can't put off facing Karl any longer. He's going to be furious that he had to wait so long for his dinner, but I can usually deal with that. The non-raise is a different matter. Money matters always triggers his anger on an altogether different order of magnitude.*

She put aside those thoughts, stood, and left her office. Outside the building, she paused to button her coat against the cold and to look up at the unblemished winter sky. Her earliest memories were of lying on her back in the sand in the dry canyon, all human light from the reservation blocked by the steep sides. The sky was as black as Father's hair, broken only by thousands of silver diamonds crawling slowly overhead until lost below the dark cliffs.

When she went away from the Navajo Nation for the first time to attend college, her entire family was puzzled why she had chosen to major in physics. *To me, it was clear. It was those hours–in summer, sometimes all night–lying in the canyon. Those hours convinced me that somewhere up there, everything possible had already been realized. All I have to do is discover it.*

Here, on the high Los Alamos mesa, the skies were even clearer. *Right now, though, the security guards will come if I lay on the ground, and the autumn wind chills ne too much to stand and stare. Besides, I have to hurry home to feed my husband.*

Her thirteen-year old maroon Subaru was one of only two cars still in the dimly lit parking lot. The familiar late-model Ford four-wheel pickup was always there when she left. *It must belong to Luke.*

After four tries, the Subaru's engine finally kicked over intermittently. As she pulled out of the lot, she noticed how cold the steering wheel was in her hands. *Karl will want something hot for supper. A steak won't take too long, and maybe Albertsons deli will have some soup he likes. He can eat his soup in the few minutes it will take me to broil his rare steak.*

Her first stop was Albertsons. Last stop would be for the McDonalds' fries–he refused to eat warmed-over fries. *Hopefully, Albertsons will have a couple of six-packs of cold Goose Island India Pale Ale so I won't have to stop at the liquor store. If neither store has Goose Island, I'll have to settle for Anchor Steam, but he won't be pleased. Maybe there are still a few bottles of Goose Island left in the fridge from this morning.*

Thirty minutes later, after having settled for Anchor Steam, she struggled up the stairs of their reconditioned World War II four-room duplex, arms loaded with groceries and beer. Not wanting to disturb his painting, she set down both bags and retrieved her key. He wasn't in the living room, so she tip-toed into the kitchen and put away her load before peeking into this studio. He wasn't there.

She loved his studio. His paintings of New Mexico landscapes still took her breath away, reminding her why she loved him so much. There was the stunning picture of lightning striking Black Mesa in a thunderstorm, the serene watercolor of the verdant bosque twisting alongside the brown waters of the Rio Grande, the oil painting of the snow-capped Sacred Mountain of the South–the one the *Biligaana* called Mount Taylor. *rev*

She snapped out of her musing. *I have work to do.*

As far as she could see, nothing had been changed since she'd crept quietly out of the apartment that morning, his breakfast set up to be ready when he awoke. Now, she checked his computer screen for a message, but when the nudie-cutie screen saver disappeared, all she saw was the home page of the Haven Gallery. She squinted at the screen and saw an announcement of an opening today, with champagne and hors d'oeuvres. That must be the message. Karl's handsome movie-star looks were always in great demand for dressing up gallery openings, and he never passed up free champagne.

She resisted the urge to straighten up the mess in his studio, returning to the kitchen, where she glanced at the clock. Eight-forty. She put the beer in the refrigerator. All four bottles of Goose Island India Pale Ale from this morning were gone.

Having no way of knowing when he would be home for supper, she placed the beef-barley soup carton in the microwave, ready to heat. She started the broiler for the steak. The fries were going to be a problem, because the broiling temperature would be too high, and microwaved fries would certainly be unacceptable. She might be able to do the fries in the upper oven while the steak was grilling–if she kept her eyes on the oven every instant.

She spent forty-five minutes dusting and vacuuming the apartment before she decided she couldn't wait any longer to eat her chicken salad. She had barely put her fork into the first morsel of chicken when she heard him clumping up the stairs. She jumped up, punched the microwave's start button, and slipped the broiler pan into the grill. The fries would wait until a minute before the steak was done.

She opened the door just as he was knocking. She looked anxiously at his handsome Anglo face for signs of anger, but he was smiling. As always, his engaging smile always made her catch her breath. She hoped for a kiss, but he brushed past her into the room, rubbing his hands from the cold and sniffing the air. "What's for supper? I hope it's something hot."

She ignored his slurring the words. Her heart gave a tiny flutter at the thought he would be pleased with her menu. "Steak and fries," she announced. "With soup to warm you up first."

"Oh, good," he said, pecking her on the cheek. "What kind of soup."

"Beef-barley. From Albertsons deli. You always like it."

"Yeah, it's okay. Didn't they have clam chowder?"

"I'm sorry. I got there late. They were all out."

He left her side and headed for the fridge. He extracted a bottle of Anchor Steam. "I suppose you got there too late for the good beer, too?"

"I'm sorry. Both stores said they'd been out since the weekend. Their distributor doesn't come til Thursday."

He twisted the top off the beer and took a long swig. "Maybe this weekend you could get there early and buy a case?"

He took another swig and cast a dubious glance at the counter next to the oven, where the fries lay carefully arranged on an aluminum pan. "Even better, what time does the truck come on Thursday?"

"I'm sorry. I forgot to ask."

"Well, call them tomorrow and find out. You can slip out of work and catch the truck. That way we'll be sure to have first crack at the Goose Island."

A seminar on quantum entanglement computations was scheduled for Thursday afternoon–seminar day. *It would have been a good opportunity to share my theory, but I suppose I can slip out for an hour and not miss much. Or maybe I can place a special order on Wednesday. Yes, that's what I'll do.*

Relieved at having solved one problem, she checked the oven timer and picked up the french fries.

"What's that?" he said, pointing with the now-empty beer bottle.

She slipped the pan in the upper oven, checked the timer again, and stepped over to the fridge to fetch him another beer. "It's the french fries. From McDonalds."

He took the bottle and opened it. "You know how I hate warmed-over fries."

"I'm sorry. I picked them up last thing. I thought you would be home."

"So now it's my fault? You could have waited until I was finished with my business at the gallery, then run out and fetched the fries while the steak was cooking."

"I'm sorry. I didn't think of that."

He tasted the beer, making a doubtful face as if it might not be satisfactory, then took a large draw. "If you spent lest time diddling with your quantum crap, you might be able to learn to be a decent housewife. You know, like get a deep fryer and make real french fries. I suppose your mother never had a deep fryer in the hogan."

She felt moisture welling up in her eyes. She turned away. *He doesn't like to see me cry. What's that burning smell? Oh, God, the fries.*

She ran to rescue the fries from the oven. When she saw how blackened they were, she let her hand slip off the hot pad and burned her thumb. *Oh, that really hurts. I should plunge it in cool water right away–but I have to remove his steak while it's still rare.*

Being more careful with the hot pads, she removed the broiler pan and set it on the counter. Using a pair of tongs–he didn't like his steaks pierced, lest the juices run out before he was ready–she put the steak on a warmed plate and served it.

He scowled, probing the meat with his steak knife. "Shit." He held up the plate and thrust it toward her face. "You call that rare? You can't even cook a goddamn steak."

"I'm sorry," she said, but he was already on his feet, steak in hand.

She tried to move away, but he was faster. "Here," he said, pushing the hot steak into her face. "You eat this crap. Where's your damn purse? I'm going out to see if I can find a decent meal somewhere."

After rifling her purse, he grabbed a fresh bottle of beer and left, slamming the door. She was still crying, still worried about his driving drunk, long after she'd picked up the steak, cleaned all the grease off the tile floor, and washed her face. *I can't do anything right*, she moaned to herself. *And I still haven't even told him about not getting a raise.*

CHAPTER SIX

The Limited was scheduled to arrive at eight-thirty, but Tess asked Denise to drop her off at Union Station forty-five minutes early She wanted time in case she changed her mind about meeting Inga Steinman. Denise, her long black hair done up in an elaborate knot, offered to stay and give moral support, but Tess refused the offer. *It's because I need support that I want to do this alone. I need the practice.*

Denise offered her inscrutable Chinese expression in response to Tess's explanation, but offered a supportive hug before driving off. Tess headed for the arrival platform to appraise the lay of the land. Pausing on the way to admire the high curved vault above the Great Hall, she tried to imagine what good could come from this meeting. *If we weren't so desperate for money, I wouldn't be here. Maybe I should have brought Denise–she wouldn't sell out to the torturers at any price, not after what she and her parents endured in Cambodia. For me, torture's merely an abstraction.*

Looking toward the huge American flag, she spotted Don striding toward her. He was dressed in his customary gray FBI suit and a red-white-and-blue tie which Tess thought perfectly matched the flag. *What doesn't match is his black leather briefcase. I've never seen him carry that before.*

They shared a long hug, decidedly non-FBI, but wholly appropriate for two people who had once saved each others' lives. "Hello, Mr. Carrot," she said as they pulled apart. When he replied with a puzzled look, she explained. "I figured it out.

Homeland Security is the stick, and you're their carrot." *And they all think I'm the donkey.*

He didn't deny it. Together, they studied the schedule display and learned that the Limited was twenty-seven minutes late. Not quite enough time to head into the station for a welcoming cup of coffee, so by silent agreement, they decided to avoid the cold grimy platform for as long as possible. The sat side-by-side on one of the polished wooden benches, where Don made small-talk about the landmark and the waiting passengers. "They look like immigrants, like my grandparents, with all that baggage. I thought I saw someone with a goat on a string earlier."

"That's probably why they take the train," Tess said, knowing she should try to match his pleasant banter. "United Airlines doesn't allow goats in the passenger compartment. Does Inga have a goat?"

Don laughed, as she expected, then turned serious. "You don't know, Inga, do you? You were always in a coma when she was around."

"I wasn't in a coma, Don. I was in a locked-in state. I could hear every word and see everything in front of my cameras. I know what she said and did. I don't see much reason to like her. Or trust her."

Don looked studied the schedule board, apparently not wishing to talk business until Inga arrived, but Tess hoped she could steer the conversation to a few useful bits of information. She started off, smiling, with an innocent-sounding question. "Well, Agent Capitol, how does it feel to have a train named after you?"

"The Capitol Limited? About the same as having a building in every state named after you." He broke into a broad smile, then his voice assumed a serious tone. "Well, Mrs. Tesla Bell Myers Fixman, how does it feel to be named after two great inventors?"

"Touché. It is rather intimidating at times. That's probably what my father had in mind when he named me. Intimidation."

"We both carry a large burden of responsibility."

Tess didn't miss the implication. "Like negotiating with me over Aremac? Is that one of the jobs of the newly promoted Special Agent in Charge of the Chicago office? Or were you chosen as carrot because they know we like you?"

"I volunteered. Because I like *you*. And I owe you. Without you, I never would have been promoted."

Too fast, Don. You're not lying, but you're trying to hide the whole story. "And because they think you're the one who can convince me that a little torture is a good thing for national security."

His eyes showed he'd been skewered, but he was ready with his comeback. "It's a trade-off, Tess. Sure, a little torture may cause someone pain, but it might get us information that could save literally millions of lives."

"First of all, how much is 'a little torture,' and who decides. Plus, you're ignoring what torture does to the torturer. And that it's not really effective anyway. People will lie to stop the torture. They just tell you what you want to hear."

He raised his hands in mock surrender. "Let's forget about torture for a moment. There are many circumstances where we want information from a person in pain, someone who's not being tortured at all. Like a person who's been assaulted, and injured, and who wants to show us where the assault took place. Maybe we can work out a system where your anti-torture device could be turned off for a good cause like that. "

"Again, who decides? Who would hold the on-off switch?"

"We have judges for that. Courts."

We've had this argument a hundred times before, and I'm in no mood for another round. Maybe I'm beginning to think his argument had a certain appeal. She checked the glowing schedule display again to give her time to concoct a neutral reply. "Still twenty-seven minutes late. And how did Inga get chosen? *She* doesn't like us."

"Inga knows how to work the system. I don't know how, but she survived all the fuss over the terrorist business. I'm convinced she was doing something illegal, probably working for some corporation, but nobody could prove anything. She's a smart one, that woman. In fact, she got promoted to Chief Administrator for Grants within the Homeland Security Advanced Projects Research Agency. For a big lady, she sure knows how to dance lightly inside the Beltway." He did a little tap dance with his black oxfords.

"But *we* don't particularly like *her*, so why was she chosen?"

"Maybe so we could play good-cop-bad-cop."

"But she's no cop."

"No, but hi-tech negotiations are her job, and she's supposed to be good at it. The best, from what I've seen and heard."

That's what I'm afraid of, Tess thought, but merely stood and started for the platform.

The cold air smelled a little of diesel fuel, yet was rather refreshing after the human smells in the waiting room. When the Capitol Limited pulled in and began to discharge its passengers, Tess thought for a while that Inga wasn't going to be on the train. She was about to say something to Don, when couple of minutes after the flow of other passengers dried up, a porter unloaded four suitcases onto a cart and then, with great caution, helped Inga down the metal steps to the platform. As Inga approached, Tess imagined rather ungenerously that at least two of the suitcases were filled with snacks.

She does look a bit thinner than I remember, and not unattractive–if I wasn't prejudiced against obesity. I should remind myself that I don't gain weight no matter how much I eat, but some people put on weight eating half portions of exactly the same things. It's not a matter for moral judgment. She put on her best smile and offered Inga her hand. Inga smiled back. *I can see how she might have been a beauty queen twenty years ago.*

The three of them exchanged inconsequential chit-chat as the porter followed them into the elevators and up to their meeting room. Tess pressed the button for the eighth floor. "It's the top, but the original plan called for twenty floors. I think they ran out of money."

At the meeting room Inga tipped the porter and gave him an extra twenty dollars to leave the cart with her suitcases. "Come back in two hours," she said. "We'll break for lunch, and you can escort me across the street to my hotel."

Then, as if the porter had never existed, she turned back to Tess. "Well, what about you? I heard about the TRO. Are you running out of money, too?"

Don glared at Inga. Tess exerted great effort simply to smile and motion to the chairs. "Let's sit down." As she had expected, Inga chose the wide sofa. Tess pulled a chair away from the oval oak table and sat a few feet in front of Inga, leaving room for Don to do the same. "I think we can dispense with the table, unless some papers need spreading out."

Don sat, then zipped open his soft briefcase. "Actually, there's only one piece of paper–"

As he pulled out the sheet, Inga completed his sentence. "–but there are scores of spreadsheets backing it up, if you want to see them."

Tess took the paper but set it on the table without even glancing at it. "It sounds like you went to a lot of trouble figuring this out–"

"It's a generous offer," Don said. "Rather surprising for the government, actually. Inga did a good job on your behalf."

"Then I'm sorry you went to so much trouble. With the TRO, the government wouldn't be able to use Aremac at any price. Inga, I'm sorry you had to come all this way, but why? You said you knew about the TRO."

"I do, but I suspect that Agent Capitol's people have ways of ignoring court-issued orders. Am I right, Don?"

Don leaned forward and placed his briefcase on the floor, his gray jacket gaping wide enough for Tess to see his pistol grip. She wondered if that was intentional, but all she said was, "Is she telling the truth, Don? Can the FBI ignore restraining orders from the FDA?"

"I'm not at liberty to say, one way or the other, Tess. But it really wouldn't be any concern of yours. Either we can or can't."

"Well, perhaps it *is* my concern. Right now, we can't use Aremac ourselves, and as Inga knows, that's costing us a lot of money. If you have a way of bypassing the order, we'd expect you to extend that privilege to us, as part of any deal."

She handed him back the paper and stood to leave. "Without that, we don't really care what your offer is. Get back to me when–if–you can take care of the TRO."

CHAPTER SEVEN

Marna liked having all this time alone in the car with Karl so they could talk. However, was been reluctant to say anything that might distract him as he speeded west from Los Alamos around the blind curves of snow-patched State Highway 4 past Bandelier National Monument and Valle Grande. Through the forests on primitive road 126 to Cuba, she was even more fearful, clutching the SUV's passenger hand grip until they reached the wide paved Highway 550. Karl slowed there, alert to the highway patrol until she pointed out the obscure turnoff to the west within sight of Angel Peak.

As usual, there was little traffic on the thirty-five miles of extremely primitive unnumbered road to Little Water, though Karl almost sideswiped a decrepit brown pickup when trying to pass. She relaxed only when she saw that her entire family–minus only her oldest brother Yas, or Yale–was on hand to greet their favorite, their only, daughter.

All that afternoon and evening they visited with her family in Little Water. Marna was thankful that Karl was quiet and polite the entire time. She credited her father's strict Navajo prohibition of alcohol, though some credit could be given to her husband's fear of her brothers. Then, too, when the family broke into Navajo or Spanish, he could only sit quietly and wait for them to revert to their third language, English.

Early this morning as they said their goodbyes, Karl was obviously relieved the ordeal was over. On her part, she was grateful he had sacrificed so she could enjoy the rare visit with her family. He never let her go by herself, saying she wasn't a good enough driver. So now he was driving her all the way to Las Vegas, Nevada, which was the only way he'd let her go to the entrepreneur conference.

Mike had enrolled her in the conference, "for your own good." To her surprise, Karl had approved of the trip, in spite of her qualms. "You should go," he had said. "It will be good for your career. I'll go with you."

Marna felt a tickle of hope that Karl might actually care about some part of her work–something besides the money. He was being so nice to her, even allowing her to choose the more scenic, but slower, northern route through Grand Canyon and Zion National Parks. *He really loves me. This will be a sort of second honeymoon in Las Vegas.*

If he doesn't drink too much.

They had just passed through St. George when she finally mustered the courage to ask, "How are you going to spend your time when I'm in the meetings? Are there good galleries in Las Vegas?"

"I suppose so. I'll check when we get settled."

"We're staying at the Embassy Suites, right at the Convention Center. I'm sure they'll have all that information."

"I suppose I shouldn't complain, because the government is paying, but why did they have to choose a place so far from the big casinos? It's damned inconvenient."

Marna said nothing for a few miles as they cruised down Interstate 15 at over ninety, but finally managed to ask if he was planning to gamble.

"A little. Just for fun. I was meaning to ask you for your ATM card–so I won't have to bother you in your meetings if I run into a bit of bad luck."

Marna stiffened in her seat. The only place she'd been able to resist Karl's charm was banking. She insisted they keep separate bank accounts. Her salary went into her account, from which she paid all the monthly bills, including his car payments and monthly allowance. If he sold a painting–which hadn't happened in more than two years–it went into his account. And since he had no job, he had been unable to hold a credit card, either.

"I don't think that's a good idea," she said, reluctantly. "I might need it during the meetings."

They'd had this conversation before, or perhaps it was her tone that made him back off. "Well, maybe. But I'm a little low on cash just now." He turned his eyes from the highway and kissed her cheek. "Maybe you'd like to stake me–for half my winnings."

She stared straight ahead, struggling to resist his kiss and saying nothing.

"You could be my coach. You know the math. Which has better odds, blackjack or craps?"

He knows he can always hook me by asking my advice. But I have to give him some answer. Just maybe, it will discourage him. "It doesn't matter. They're all stacked against you. The more you play, the worse it gets."

A Cadillac in the left lane was only moving at eighty, so Karl whipped the SUV into the right lane and passed, giving the other driver the finger. "Well, I know that. That's why I'll probably stick to poker. I'm not playing against the house, but against the other players, so it just depends on who's smarter."

"Do you think you're smarter than the players in Las Vegas?"

"Sure. I'm smarter than the players in New Mexico. People are the same all over."

Karl played regularly in small poker tournaments at Camel Rock Casino. About once in ten tournaments, he finished somewhere in the money. Though he had usually managed to drink his small winnings before coming home, he never failed to tell her–and anyone else within range–about his triumphs. She couldn't resist trying to put some reality in his memory, but she couldn't look at him while she did. "The people may be the same, but the Las Vegas games are bigger. Bigger stakes and more players."

"Sure, which is what makes this trip such an interesting opportunity. Bigger stakes and more players means bigger winnings."

And bigger losings, she wanted to say. She didn't want to spoil the trip, so she kept it to herself. She stared out the front window and changed the subject. "I hope you'll have time to come to my session. I mean, it's not really my session, but they have a room set aside where theoreticians can present their work. It's not really technical. Just for the entrepreneurs to discover something they might want to put their money behind. That's why Mike wanted me to go."

"Oh, that's interesting." He honked his horn, repeatedly, then flashed his lights until the white Lincoln in front of him moved into the right lane.

"I think I've made a breakthrough in my theory, but I doubt anyone will think of anything practical to do with it. I guess I have to talk about it anyway, or Mike will be angry. He reserved a fifteen-minute slot for me on Tuesday morning."

"That's nice, dear."

"Do you think you can make it? I could use your support. You know how I am about speaking to groups."

"Sure. What time is it?"

"Eight-thirty. I'm first on."

"Oh. That's kind of early, isn't it."

"I'm sorry. Mike was late registering me. It was the only slot still available."

He pointed to a sign for the Las Vegas city limits. "Well, that was a long drive, but we're here. Look at those billboards. Sin City at last!"

"So will you come?"

"Huh? Come to what?"

"My session."

"Oh, that. Sure. Of course. I wouldn't miss it for anything."

Chapter Eight

Watching Inga stall as they rose to leave the meeting room, Tess suspected the other woman had some agenda besides her official government business–business she didn't want Don to hear. She ignored Inga's hints, telling herself she would pursue the matter next time they were alone–if there was a next time. She wished Inga a delicious lunch, turned down a second invitation to join her, and headed for the El.

For half an hour, while watching large snowflakes whirling around outside the El window, she tried to think what Inga could have meant when she said, "You really should study those spreadsheets carefully, Tess. I know I shouldn't tell you this, but we work under a lot of silly constraints in the government. We may not be able to offer you the best deal. But, of course, it's up to you."

By the time the El reached Jarvis, the snow cover was already an inch deep–pretty, but not enough to impede her progress as she trudged to the brainstorming meeting. Heidi, tail wagging, greeted her at the door, then ran outside to snuffle in the new snow. Roger, Rebecca, SOS, and Denise were already seated in a comfortable circle in the lounge. *They're all geniuses, each in their own way, and all smarter than me. I asked for it, so now I have to be the facilitator, or they won't ever get anything done.*

Denise needed less facilitation than the others, but she was no less a genius and was the hardest one to read when she did need guidance. Regardless of the emotional significance of what they were discussing, Denise always sat, or stood, motionless. Bland facial expression, no nervous tics, yet clearly taking everything into her remarkable brain, processing it, and at rare but crucial moments, speaking her ideas in a soft Chinese accent.

While the rest of the team was settling themselves, Tess studied Denise's remarkable, straight, jet-black, waist-length hair, wondering if there was anything about her appearance that would reveal her extraordinary talent with number and codes. Her inch-thick rimless glasses, long black skirt, sandals, and "Cowgirl Coder" t-shirt might have suggested a hacker, but not the FBI's top computer expert. Denise left the FBI as soon as she learned about the torture, which was unthinkable after her family's experience in a Cambodian prison camp. Hiring her had been an expensive coup, but her contributions to the Aremac team were worth the expense many times over.

Her boyfriend, Stephen Orem Spenser had also been hired away from the FBI. His issue had been with torture, too–the torture of an incompetent manager interfering with his code. Skinny as Denise but as tall as she was short, he was indispensable for his problem-solving under pressure, for which he earned his nickname, SOS. As a bonus, his only salary was a share in the company, so he added nothing to the outflow of cash.

He doesn't cost me money, but he sure costs me anguish in meetings, Tess thought. *I don't know which bothers me more, his lecturing or his tuning into his iPod and tuning out the meeting. He claims he needs the music, but the way he taps and wiggles around, I find that hard to believe. It's getting so I can tell just what he's listening to–like the way he moves his lips when it's country music or drums his fingers when its dixieland.*

Right now, SOS was marching around the room gathering refreshments for their meeting. *Must be a Sousa march. At least his motions give me clues about where his mind is. My dear husband just stares into some galaxy far, far away.*

Rebecca shooed SOS away from the kitchen and made him sit down while she put out the refreshments. Rebecca's pay was less than half of Denise's, but her matronly British sensibility was worth every penny for its steadying influence on the brilliant but immature boys and girls. She didn't know enough science to lead their discussions on technical matters, but when it came to money matters, she was almost equal to Denise, whose father had been a banker before being purged by the Cambodian government.

No, I couldn't save money by cutting anyone off the team. She gave the room a once-over for expense-generating items that could be cut from the budget, but there wasn't much there, either. Maybe her mistake had been moving from the old garage to these new spacious quarters, investing in all these new computers and the lavish sound system that was playing Rebecca's awful Vaughn Williams music, but those were sunk costs. They could save on wood for the fireplace, but the fireplace itself was part of the building, and came with the increased rent. *We could probably do without the popcorn, no matter how tantalizing the smell. But popcorn is just more pennies, like the firewood.*

Just then, Heidi scratched on the door, and Tess considered, then immediately rejected, the idea that her German Shepherd could eat less expensive food. She remembered the day Roger had brought Heidi to her, hoping the dog would be able to sense something from her brain the way Bart's seizure dog, Howler, could do. From the moment Heidi began sensing her brain's simple commands, they'd been like two parts of one person. *I would starve myself before I skimped on food for my beloved buddy.*

No, there was no significant way to cut expenses, and now, with the restraining order, their credit would be zero, so borrowing was out, too. *We just have to find another source of income–and quickly.*

Roger jumped up to open the door for Heidi. He helped Tess shed her down jacket, shaking snowflakes onto the tile floor, where they quickly disappeared. "How'd the meeting go?"

She eased herself into her seat next to the whiteboard, closed her eyes, and concentrated on Heidi's "come" command. Her companion wagged her tail, then trotted over and laid her huge head in Tess's lap. Scratching behind the dog's ears with one hand, Tess happily accepted Rebecca's silent offer of hot chocolate with the other. Rebecca filled her mug, then extended an open tin. "Would you like a biscuit?"

"Thank you, no. I've already been captivated by the popcorn smell." Sipping carefully, Tess gave an exhaustive description of the meeting. "I didn't even look at their offer," she concluded. "Inga actually suggested to me after Don left that we might do better somewhere else."

Rebecca, still fussing over a fresh batch of hot chocolate, asked, "But who besides the government could override the restraining order?"

"That's a problem. It may even be a problem for the government."

Denise's t-shirt of the day read, "Use your head, not your 'nads," in iridescent gold letters on black cotton. She often let her shirts speak for her. She whispered something in SOS's ear– the one without the ear bud. He nodded. "Denise and I agree. We've seen how things work on the inside. We're pretty sure

Homeland Security trumps Food and Drug Administration every time."

Tess drained her hot chocolate and raised her mug to Rebecca for more. They knew the FBI, and were probably right. "Still, it's irrelevant. Much as I hate to admit it, Inga's correct. We can *never* take a government deal, no matter how generous."

"Because of the torture?" Denise asked meekly. As the newest member of the team, she hadn't actually experienced their early clashes with the FBI's use of the Aremac prototype.

Rebecca finished with serving food and slid into her seat in the circle. "Because of the torture. None of us want to be part of that."

That seemed to bring Roger out of his trance. "I've been thinking about ways to improve our anti-coercion safeguards. Studying some recent research about areas of the brain that control fear and pain. By detecting activity in those areas, I think I could do an even better job rigging Aremac to shut down when the subject is coerced or tortured. Our present system is probably ninety percent accurate, but I think we can reach ninety-nine, or better."

"And we could bind it to the software so that any attempt to tamper with it would disable Aremac completely." SOS's t-shirt message for today was a large "73" in white on his usual all-black outfit. Tess wondered what it said on the back. She forced her mind to concentrate on what he was saying."… and Denise and I have a way to do that–"

Denise whispered in his ear again. Tess wished she would stop doing that and speak up for herself. *At least it seems to keep him more involved in their meetings. Maybe that's what she has in mind.*

"–and we already have some ideas for improving it."

"Me, too," said Roger, looking expectantly at Tess.

"That won't really solve our problem. It's not just what they'll do with Aremac, but what they'll do to us. You've all seen what it's like working in a government environment. You might as well say goodbye to our inventing days."

"But you said it yourself," Roger said. "If we don't get some money flowing in, we can say goodbye anyway. SOS is not going to leave his mother behind, and even if she was willing to go to Mexico, which she isn't, we don't have the money for a move like that. Do we?"

"No, we don't. If we don't generate some new income soon, we won't even have a team to move to Mexico, or even Evanston."

CHAPTER NINE

As soon as she mentioned breaking up the team, Tess could see she had everyone's attention, even Denise, who actually crossed her legs at the ankles. Maybe not SOS, but he did touch his iPod, at least changing the music. Rebecca always paid attention when money was mentioned, and Roger was now sitting forward in his chair, both feet planted solidly on the floor in this galaxy.

Tess decided to start the brainstorm informally, by making a suggestion to Roger she knew would be rejected. "You can always go to work for my father, darling. Heck, I could make one phone call and he'd hire our whole team before I had to put in another quarter. Mel would give you the freedom you need–mostly. And certainly all the support." She looked around the room. *At least I can get SOS's attention when I mention the word 'boss.'*

Roger reached across the arm of his chair and took her hand. "Mel's okay as a father-in-law, but I wouldn't want him for my boss."

"Good." She smiled. "That's the right answer. I don't want my husband working for my father, either. In fact, I don't want you on a job at all. You're just not a job kind of person."

She looked around at each of them, feeling a warmth building inside her at the thought of the work they had done together, the trials they had undergone. "None of you are, but especially you, Roger. You haven't a single employee gene in your DNA."

Roger pouted. "Why not? All my inventions are for someone else. That's like being an employee."

"You know what I mean. Stop being silly. If we're going to stay in the inventing business, then we need to invent something that will produce revenue."

"But we already have lots of ways to earn money," SOS said, his fingers drumming on his knees.

Denise started to whisper in his ear, but stopped herself and told him out loud, "But all of them are forbidden by this FDA thing."

"Most of them, anyway," said Tess. "We still get money from the thought-controlled wheelchair and talker, but that's only a trickle. It hardly pays for the electricity for Aremac.–but we're not allowed to run Aremac in any case."

"We can if the FDA doesn't know about it," said Roger. "They have no right to stop me from doing experiments on myself."

"Or on me," said SOS.

Denise simply nodded, but Rebecca slammed her laptop closed. "Those silly buggers cannot keep me out of Aremac if that's where I bloody well choose to go."

"I don't recommend it." She shuddered at her memories of being a zombie for months, unable to move or speak. "Believe me, you don't want to be a living corpse."

"I believe we are well beyond that stage," said Rebecca, who had been the one to formalize their safety procedures when attempting new experiments. "Though of course we can never relax our vigilance. From what I have read, however, we are far more strict than the FDA."

SOS made a rude gesture with his fingers. "But they're the ones who get to say yes or no."

"That may be, Stephen ... ," Rebecca was the only one who SOS allowed to call him by his given name. " ... but when they do check us out, they shall have to say yes."

Tess stopped her handful of popcorn halfway to her mouth. "You have a lot more trust in the government than I have, Rebecca. They may have to pass on our work, eventually, but eventually we'll all have starved to death–" She stared at her handful of popcorn. "–unless we're willing to move out of the country."

Everyone on the team gave some sign of distaste with that idea, and Rebecca put words to their thoughts. "We have no idea what kinds of restrictions we'd be faced in–where did you say? Mexico? I could look into it, but it will take time."

"Do that, but we don't have time. Not with our present burn rate. If we can't move right away, we have to come up with some invention that starts making money and doesn't have to pass FDA scrutiny."

Rebecca reached behind her seat and grabbed a small wireless keyboard. "All right, enough jibber-jabber. Let's brainstorm." She tapped a key and the wall monitor illuminated. "You all know the rules. I shall scribe ... unless someone else wants the job."

Nobody volunteered, so Rebecca started the process. "What we want are inventions for which the world might pay us. You need not have any idea how they will work. We can toss the poor ones in the dustbin later. Just offer things you think someone might want enough to pay for it."

Denise uncrossed her legs ankles recrossed them the other way. "Can they be services?"

"Why not? If we don't want them later, we can pitch them in a crack. For now, no censorship. So, Denise, what service had you in mind?"

Denise looked for someone else to go first, but they all simply stared back at her. "I was thinking that we could offer some real good software consulting, especially in security and cryptography."

Rebecca tapped her keyboard, and "software consulting" appeared on the screen.

"Well, then," Roger volunteered, "hardware consulting."

Up it went. There was a pause. Rebecca glanced at the pile of dishes in the sink. "Dishes that do their own washing up."

After that, the ideas flew non-stop: "Something that moves heavy objects without breaking your back."

"Voice-driven devices. We know a lot about that. And mind-driven devices."

"Data compression algorithms."

Just then, SOS's phone rang, but Rebecca shook her head when he started to reach for it. "I know," he said, "an everlasting cell-phone battery."

Roger: "Something that screens out calls from idiots."

Rebecca: "An intelligent rubber."

"What's that?" SOS asked.

Rebecca wagged her finger at him. "No explanations. That comes later."

"She means 'intelligent eraser,'" Tess said, drawing a disapproving head nod from Rebecca.

The wind outside rattled the windows, and SOS cupped his hand over his ear. "Okay. A robot snow clearer. Which is also a back protector."

More ideas came in rapid succession. "An umbrella-less umbrella. A personal weather shield."

"A mirror that shows how your appearance would be affected by gaining or losing weight?"

"Or by clothes."

"Or makeup."

"Or hair styles."

SOS started to say, "That already exists," but Rebecca shushed him. "Criticism comes later."

Roger yawned. "How about a device that would give you eight hours of sleep in fifteen minutes?"

SOS tried to comment, but Rebecca just wrote "speed-sleeper" and said, "a reverse microwave. Something that cools food quickly, from the inside out."

Heidi heard the word "food" and started wagging her tail. "An automatic dog trainer," Tess said, then tossed a few kernels of popcorn in front of her dog's nose. They disappeared as fast as snowflakes.

"You read her mind," said Roger. "And we know she can read yours. How about a direct brain-to-brain network?"

"That would bring in the FDA again," said SOS, and suddenly the brainstorm degenerated into another discussion of FDA rules and procedures. Rebecca's attempts to stop it failed, so she joined in for a while. She allowed the others fifteen minutes, then cracked down and started up the brainstorm again, giving the recorder's keyboard to Tess, who expanded the list to more than a hundred items.

"I think we can stop now," Tess said. "Roger, why don't you take this list and invent something? Then I'll go to Las Vegas and sell it to someone at the entrepreneur conference. Or maybe find some new ideas."

CHAPTER TEN

When Marna awoke Tuesday morning, she was alone in her king-sized hotel bed. Karl's pillow was unruffled. Shaken and needing support, she skipped the Embassy Suite's free continental breakfast buffet and found a coffee shop in the Convention Center that served real New Mexican food. She treated herself to two large breakfast burritos, which helped her feel better. When she was about to pay, she searched her purse but couldn't find her credit card. Embarrassed, she paid cash, then hurried back up to her room, forgetting to ask for a receipt so she could be reimbursed. She searched all over for the card, but knew all along it wouldn't be there.

She phoned her bank and reported the card lost or stolen, putting an immediate stop on all further transactions. Still unsettled, she washed her face, removing the small amount of unfamiliar makeup she had thought she must wear for her presentation. *It doesn't give me confidence, but only makes me feel unnatural. Uncomfortable. The last thing I need now is to feel uncomfortable.*

Only seven people showed up for the start of her presentation, but two others wandered in yawning five minutes later. Karl, in spite of his promise, was not among them. By the time she finished, the two flip charts were filled with quantum electrodynamic equations, and eight members of the suit-and-tie audience had disappeared like rabbits sniffing coyote. *I must have talked over their heads, exactly what Mike warned me not to do.*

When she looked up from packing away her notes, she saw that one of the audience had hung around. The attractive red-haired woman was dressed casually in blue slacks with contrasting sweater. *No doubt she's here to console me. Try to make me feel good telling me how good my handwriting is. Or something equally trivial.*

Instead, the woman walked up to the right-hand flip chart and pointed to the underlined term in the displacement equation. "This term surprised me. I would have expected it to be negative. If I'd thought of it at all. It's really quite brilliant."

Marna bit her thumbnail and stared at the carpet. "I'm sorry. I really shouldn't have snowed you with all these equations, but I couldn't think of a good analogy. The quantum world is just so counterintuitive compared with the macro scale."

"I agree. I mean, I don't agree you should have left out the equations, but with the quirkiness of quantum phenomena. I suspect that's why so few engineers have succeeded in designing anything useful based on quantum effects. Maybe we'll have to wait for another generation, one that grows up thinking nothing's odd about the Heisenberg effect. The ink still isn't dry on my degree, but I'm still not sure I'm in that generation."

In spite of her miserable morning, Marna looked up and half smiled. "Me, neither. One day these equations make perfect sense to me, then the next morning I wake up and they could be Arabic."

"Oh, not Arabic. That I can read–a little. My husband's half Syrian. More like, maybe, Navajo."

Now Marna's smile spread out over her whole face. "How did you guess?"

"You're Navajo? I didn't guess. That was just the first thing that came to my mind, being out here in the Southwest."

"I'm a half-breed, like your husband, I suppose. My mother's family was one of the first Spanish families to settle in Nuevo México. New Mexico, that is."

"Entiendo un poco español. Pero ningún Navajo."

"Let's stick to English, then, or equations. Otherwise you might retaliate in Arabic."

Now it was the other woman's turn to laugh. "Equations *are* Arabic."

"Touché," said Marna. "Whoops, now I've slipped into French. But don't worry, that's the only word I know. Well, maybe *merci* and *bonjour*."

"English it is, then. May I buy you a cup of coffee? I'd like to discuss an idea I have about your displacement effect. Oh, yes, I'm being so rude." She extended her hand to Marna. "My name is professional name is Tesla Bell Myers, and my married name is Fixman, but my friends just call me Tess."

CHAPTER ELEVEN

After arguing for a full day, Roger thought he was winning, but Rebecca wasn't giving up easily. Older and wiser and non-technical, she had been commissioned by Tess to keep the techies under some sort of control, but the only one she seemed able to control today was Heidi, the dog.

"Just because you can build a fast-sleep machine, Roger, does not mean you *should* build it. We need some cash flowing into our notecase, and flowing in *now*. So let's give this one a miss."

He could hear how angry she was, but he pressed on. "But it won't take long." SOS and Denise nodded hearty agreement. "All we need is a little software."

Rebecca made motions of pulling her graying hair. "Where have I heard that cheeky phrase before? 'Just a little software.' But all right, suppose you could build the software, and you could do it in fifteen seconds–"

SOS straightened up from his slouch, revealing today's t-shirt slogan: "Consciousness: That annoying time between naps." Roger thought it particularly appropriate.

"Now you're being silly, Rebecca," SOS said. "Based on what Roger's told us, Denise estimated one week–less than one of our normal agile iterations."

"We would be finished by the time Tess comes back." Denise seemed to sparkle at the thought of surprising and pleasing her idol. "Then we'd be free to work on whatever she brings back."

Rebecca stood and fetched a bottle of aspirin from the kitchen cabinet. "You nippers are giving me a blinder." She popped two pills in her mouth and swallowed them dry. "No, dearie, she will not be pleased. She'll be furious. You're supposed to be coming up with a way of making money, and even though your estimates always seem to be on target, a speed-sleep machine will not make us a farthing."

SOS didn't give her time to explain. "Of course it will. Lots of people would pay to have seven or eight more working hours in a day. Hey, doesn't Arnie get about five-hundred bucks an hour?"

Rebecca held up her hand and said "Stephen" to stop his lecture, but to no avail. "We could have like a flophouse for lawyers," he rambled on. "You could schedule them in, Rebecca. At a thou per night, that's three thou per hour, for ... " He looked up at the clock. "For ten hours a day would be thirty thousand a day. How's that for cash flow?"

"Wouldn't Tess like that, Rebecca?" Denise asked meekly. Heidi raised her head at the mention of her mistress's name, then dropped back into her own unaccelerated nap.

"Would you kids please stop this fantasy?" Rebecca dropped her voice to a whisper, which usually captured their attention. "I will grant that you can build it. I will grant that you can build it in one week. I will even grant that lawyers will pay a thousand dollars for fifteen minutes of speed-sleep, okay? But how much do you think the FDA, or the court, will fine us if we're caught out violating the TRO?"

"Oh," they all said in unison.

"And that is if they do not simply seize Aremac. Perhaps even destroy it. They do that, you know, to illegal medical devices." She pointed an accusing finger in the direction of Aremac. "Perhaps we shall win our case–eventually–and Arnie will convince the judge that Aremac is not a medical device, but you could not even convince *me* that a fast-sleep machine is not medical."

"Oh," said Roger, then closed his eyes and fell silent. SOS chewed on his already-short fingernails while Denise studied the LOVE tattoo on his forearm.

"Come on, nippers," Rebecca pleaded. "I am not trying to wind you up, just because you cannot make the sleep machine." She stood up gracefully and stepped up to the brainstorm pages, which had been printed in large letters and stuck on the wall with drafting tape. Heidi stretched, and moved to a new napping position under Rebecca's feet as she tapped on the listed items, one at a time. "You have a hundred ideas here. Come on, select another one."

"We've been trying that all day," Roger protested. "The sleep-machine is the only one we know how to build quickly."

"You do not know that, Roger. Not if you fail to try another one. Do you want me to pick one for you? How about this magic mirror?"

SOS shook his head contemptuously. "We're not interested in that one."

Rebecca looked his clothing up and down. "No, I guess you're not. So, which one floats your boat?"

"I love it when you speak British," Roger said. "I kind of like the brain-to-brain network. I have some ideas about how that can be done."

Rebecca slid over and rapped Roger's forehead with her knuckles. "Have you been away with the faeries, Roger? You mess with the brain, and the FDA will mess with you."

"Maybe not," Denise squeaked.

"No maybe about it, dear. Once they have their eyes on you, they're not going to let you get away with human experiments, no matter how safe, until they get their five or ten years of flesh."

"Not if they don't know."

Rebecca's thin eyebrows shot up. "And just how will they not know?"

"We could use the speed-sleeper on ourselves. I would never tell."

"Okay, you're right. If they didn't know, they wouldn't bother us. But that would only get us through the experimental stage. Once we started *selling* the sleep service, we'd be closed down in minutes."

"But we wouldn't sell the service."

Rebecca sat on the arm of Denise's chair. "Darling, you are now trapped in a roundabout. If we cannot sell the sleep service, how are we supposed to make any money?"

Denise stood, eagerly, almost knocking Rebecca to the floor. She skipped over to the first brainstorm sheet, tapped on one item, and read out loud. "Software consulting." Then she used her other hand to tap on "Hardware consulting."

Rebecca frowned, then cracked a smile. "Are you suggesting what I think you are suggesting?"

Denise, put on the spot, clammed up. SOS took over. "I think she's saying that if we built the speed-sleeper, we could use it on ourselves. That would give us an extra eight hours a day, and we could sell our services as consultants. Maybe we couldn't get what Arnie gets, but we've got a pretty good reputation. I'll bet we could get at least a thousand a day apiece as consultants, which makes fifteen thou a week. And we'd still have the same amount of time to work on our own projects. I think Tess would like that."

Roger rose and joined Denise at the wall, "I think people would pay more than that, based on the offers we get every week."

Rebecca looked stunned for a moment, then came to life. "So, children, why are you standing there pissing up the wall? Start building that speed-sleeper of yours."

CHAPTER TWELVE

Tess allowed Marna to lead her to the restaurant where she had eaten breakfast. "It's got paper table cloths–in case we want to write equations."

Tess had difficulty controlling her excitement. *Another real genius.* Marna's enthusiasm for equations was a positive sign that her theory might prove valid. *Still, I can understand why Marna's colleagues rejected her theory out of hand–it would overthrow the physicists' unquestioned gospel. But if Marna was right, then the possibilities for earth-shaking inventions are unlimited.*

Forgetting her financial troubles, Tess couldn't resist the attraction of another genius. She saw her task now to befriend Marna, assess her competence and the plausibility of her theory, and if it proved tenable, then to recruit her to the Aremac team of inventors before someone else realized her potential. Opportunities to gain a colleague like this were as rare as real winners in the casino.

The waitress who seated them in a booth recognized Marna, smiled at Tess, and took their order for two coffees, with Danish pastry for Tess. Tess offered to buy a pastry for Marna.

"Oh, no, thank you. I already had too big a breakfast. Anxious over my talk." She patted the sides of her waist. "Karl says I'm too fat. He wants me to lose weight."

Tess studied Marna's left hand and saw her unusual gold and silver Zuni band on her ring finger. "Karl's your husband?" Husbands could be either asset or liability to Tess's plans. If this

Karl scorned Marna's body image, he was unlikely to be an asset.

She decided to test Marna's relationship to her husband. "Do you have a picture?"

Marna immediately fished a small picture wallet from her purse. "I do," she said proudly, showing Tess a studio portrait with a strikingly resemblance to a young Robert Redford.

So, she's married an Anglo. I wonder what if her family is as insular as mine. Maybe if she sees Roger's picture, she'll open up. Tess laid her husband's snapshot on the table and pushed it over to Marna.

"Oh, he's very good looking. Like Rudolph Valentino, I think."

"That's his Syrian half. I guess we're both blessed with handsome husbands, though my father doesn't think much of Arabs. Does–uh, Karl–does your father get along with him?"

Marna blushed, then shrugged. She handed Roger's picture back and began scribbling mathematical symbols on the tablecloth.

Just like Roger. When the subject becomes uncomfortable, she retreats inside her head. Do I need another one who needs mothering? Maybe it just comes with genius. Let's see how responsive she is.

Tess decided to test Marna again by using another method of bringing her back into the real world and raising her self-esteem. "Well, I don't think you're too fat. I don't think you're fat at all. And besides, Einstein says fat is relative."

Marna giggled at the physics joke and set down her pen. "You're so right. In high school, the Spanish boys said I was too fat, and the Dineh boys said I was too skinny."

"Dineh? That's the Navajo?"

"Sorry. Well, at least now you know one word of Navajo."

Marna smiled briefly, which Tess saw as another little victory over Marna's depression about her talk. "Speaking of Einstein, tell me more about your quantum displacement theory. Your talk was tantalizing, but I assume you simplified it for the suits."

"Not enough, I think." She recovered her pen, ready to write. "They looked baffled. And I was supposed to entice somebody to give us some money to develop practical applications of the theory. Or at least a demonstration."

Tess decided she could be direct with Marna, who didn't seem to have a sly bone in her body. "Well, maybe you enticed *me*. Not that our company has a lot of money right now, but I have some ideas how we might make some use of your theory. But I need to know more. Who else is working on this with you?"

Marna twisted a strand of her gray-brown hair, biting the end. "Nobody, actually. They won't take my theory seriously because they say it violates the First Law of Thermodynamics."

"Aha! That's exactly why I *do* take it seriously."

The coffee arrived, and Tess offered to share her Danish with Marna. "Okay," she said, "but just a sliver. About one-tenth."

Tess gave her a quarter of the roll, then nibbled on the rest while Marna left her piece sitting on the plate as she scratched equations upside-down on the tablecloth so Tess could read them. When she finally paused after fifteen minutes, Tess said, "I'm impressed, and not just by your ability to write upside down. May I keep this tablecloth to show Roger? My husband?"

"Sure," said Marna, then put her hand over her mouth. "Oh! Roger Fixman? The inventor? The one featured in Physics Today? That Roger?"

"You make him sound notorious."

"Oh, no, I'm sorry. I mean, he's so famous. I've read about him–and you–and your 'for peace' inventions. The way you wouldn't let the government use your–what's it called?–to interrogate people. That was so courageous."

Now it was Tess's turn to blush at Marna's guileless chattering. "It's no more than any decent person would do. And we want to be patriotic, but first we'd have to modify the machine–the Aremac, get it? Camera spelled backwards?"

"Oh, right. That's so catchy. I should have remembered."

"Well, we're working to modify it so it can't be used if the person is being coerced, or tortured. Not such an easy problem, though. Not just physics."

Marna's silver-gray eyes sparkled. In spite of her rather ordinary features, the effect of her eyes was a kind of fey beauty. "But I'm sure you'll find a way. Your husband is so brilliant."

"That he is." *But so are we all. Do you know you're one of us?*

Marna gazed down at her napkin. "My husband is brilliant, too, but he's not a physicist. He's a painter. He's sold paintings in Santa Fe."

Okay, a different kind of brilliance. That could be a positive sign. "Now I find that impressive. Most of our friends can do physics, but art, now that's a different matter. Is he here with you? Was he in the audience?"

Marna bit her lip. "Well, not at the meeting. My work doesn't really interest him. He says the math is ugly."

Tess spread her hands over Marna's writing on the tablecloth. "I think it's beautiful, but I guess it's a matter of taste. Like any art."

"I guess so." Marna inclined her head, as if she couldn't accept the compliment, then quickly changed the subject. "Is your husband–Roger–with you?"

"Oh, no. He's back in Chicago, inventing things."

Marna leaned forward and lowered her voice. "You trust him all alone?"

"What do you mean?" Tess thought she knew what Marna meant, and wasn't surprised that someone as brilliant as Marna was probably as socially inept as Roger. Still, she couldn't believe she was asking a total stranger whether her husband slept around.

Marna seemed to be trying to twist off her fingernail. "Well, uh, is he, uh, you know, attracted to other women?"

This Karl is not sounding good. I'd better treat this lightly. "I suppose so. But as far as I know, all he does is look. Heck, I look at men, so why not? Yeah, I trust him."

"But what about when he's been drinking? You know."

"I don't think that would make any difference, but Roger doesn't really drink much."

"You're lucky. Karl needs to drink. For his creativity."

Tess's mental alarms jangled. She studied Marna's face and arms, thinking they might show marks of abuse, but her companion's coppery skin was smooth and unmarked, so she passed her idea off as her own paranoia. "That's funny, because Roger says alcohol *dulls* his creativity. Which is why he seldom drinks. And certainly won't touch drugs. Heck, he doesn't even like to take aspirin unless I insist."

"I guess all men need to be taken care of, don't they? Karl needs my support. Sometimes he's like a little baby. Sometimes …" She seemed to catch herself, and her voice trailed off.

"What is it?"

"Nothing. I was just thinking about my theory. You said you had an idea of how it might be used for something practical. I think that's unlikely, but boy, would my boss drool over that."

"Sure," said Tess. "It's only sketchy, and I'd need to talk it over with Roger and the rest of our team, but it's possible that–"

Tess was cut off by the loud footsteps of a man rushing into the restaurant and shouting Marna's name. A moment later, Karl reached their table, face red, breathing hard, and grabbed Marna by the upper arm, shaking her violently. In his other hand, he held a credit card, which he pushed up under her nose.

She tried to pull back. "That hurts, Karl. Please don't do that."

"You think *that* hurts? How do you think I felt when I tried to get some cash for a fresh buy-in and the card was refused? The cashier tried to take it away, but I snatched it back. I had to leave the casino because the security guards were after me. You'd think I was a criminal or something."

Marna peered up at him, her eyes now large and round, more cowed than fey. "You're not a criminal, but the credit card's blocked now. I thought I lost it, so I reported it to the company."

He slipped into the booth, forcing his wife to slide over to accommodate his large frame. Even across the table, Tess could smell alcohol on his breath. He slapped down the card in front of Marna. "Well, call them back and tell them you found it."

"I don't think they'll do that, will they, Tess?"

The last thing Tess wanted to do was get in the middle of this family dispute. "I don't really know much about credit cards."

Karl laid his phone in front of his wife. "She doesn't know. So you call and find out."

Marna pulled her hand away from the phone as if it stung. "Not now, Karl. I'm having coffee with Tess. She's interested in my theory. Tess, this is my husband, Karl."

He ignored the introduction and seized Tess' cup. "Well, now you're having coffee with me. Your husband." He waved the cup in her face. "See!"

Tess desperately wanted to leave, but just as desperately wanted to stay and protect her new friend. And see how she handled her drunk husband. *When you take someone on your team, you take their whole family, like it or not.*

Marna wouldn't look at Tess, nor at Karl. "Maybe you've had enough gambling for a while, Karl. I can check the credit card later." She seemed to be trying to assert herself, but her feeble assertions sounded like questions.

"That's no good." His voice was hard and bitter. "The longer you wait, the harder it will be for them to reverse their stop order."

Marna clutched her hands, absentmindedly rubbing her wedding ring. "We can get money later, even if they won't honor the card. The casino will still be open later. I don't think they ever close."

"That's *not* good enough. I need to get back into the game *now*. I know those players now, and my luck was about to change. I could feel it."

Marna started to say something to Karl, then turned away from him. Tess could see her eyes glistening with wetness.

Karl grabbed his wife's ear and forced her head around so she was facing him. "Dammit, don't start that crying crap again. You know I hate it. Now give me your purse."

She pulled her head away and pushed her purse behind her on the seat, saying nothing.

People were beginning to stare, but Karl seemed not to notice.

"I said, give me your purse!" He put his hand on her back and shoved her forward against the edge of the table so he could reach around behind her with the other hand. He seized her large brown leather purse. He removed his hand from her back, but held her pressed against the table by leaning his full weight against her side. He dug into her purse and removed her wallet. After pulling out all the bills, he threw the purse on the floor and stood. "I'll pay it all back out of my winnings," he said, then kicked her leg under the table where nobody in the restaurant–except Tess–could see.

When he was out of sight, Tess slid out of her side of the booth, picked up the purse, and shoved in next to Marna, cautiously putting one arm around her shoulder. She handed her a tissue. "Are you all right?"

Marna took the tissue and dabbed at her red, swollen eyes. "Sure. I'm fine."

"How can you be fine. He just robbed you."

"Not really. He'll pay it all back from his winnings."

CHAPTER THIRTEEN

As Roger and Denise drove onto the campus, his first impression was that the Northwestern Evanston campus was very much like his own school, Michigan–though even flatter. Then the lakefront came into view and his impression changed– flat, yes, but the flat shore of ancient water. Lake Michigan dominated his sense of this campus in a way the Huron River never did in Ann Arbor.

Once on Campus Drive, using the map Liang Zeng had emailed, he and Denise had little trouble finding William A. and Gayle K. Cook Hall. Denise explained that in China, the full name of the building might be necessary, another indication that Liang had not fully adapted to American ways–which was primarily why Roger had brought Denise along as interpreter.

Cook Hall was a rather stark gray stone edifice with five rows of windows above the ground floor looking out over the lake. They parked in the visitors' lot below those windows, then walked to the lobby, aided by a stiff breeze off the lake that felt like a giant hand on their backs. While searching the directory for the Department of Neurobiology and Physiology, Roger noticed the listing for the Center for Quantum Devices. He made a mental note to ask Liang what they did, and perhaps for an introduction.

Cook Hall turned out to be even longer than its edifice was wide, and Liang's office and laboratory were all the way at the end of the third floor, with no view of the lake. Peering through the glass window in the office door, Roger doubted that the professor had any interest in looking out at the lake, given the concentration with which he was studying his monitor. When they knocked and entered, Liang Zeng didn't even look up. Only when Denise rattled off a long string of what Roger supposed was Chinese did he snap out of his trance.

Standing, but slightly stooped with age, Liang did not quite reach Denise's four-foot-ten, though his little pot belly suggested he must outweigh her by more than a few pounds. Altogether, he looked like the very model of an ancient Chinese scholar, white goatee, whiter queue tied with a black scrap of cloth, and wire-frame glasses barely held up by the bridge of a flat nose.

After excitedly showing and explaining the latest brain model on his monitor, he paused and apologized for becoming so carried away. "You didn't come all this way to hear about my research, I'm sure. Please, take a seat and tell me what's on your mind. Are we making any progress with your Food and Drug Administration?"

Both Roger and Liang waited for Denise to seat herself, then Roger bowed to the professor to indicate he should choose next. Liang bowed back, and it took a few more bows before they managed to sit almost simultaneously so Roger could answer. "We don't hear much, but I have full confidence in our lawyer, Arnold Danielson. His firm, Foley, Johnson, and Cuddington, is one of the finest in Chicago, so if anyone can find a way to resume your research, they will do it."

Roger offered a short description of the legal tangles, after which Liang said something in Chinese to Denise. Roger realized he must have spoken too quickly with too many new words, but Denise rattled a translation to Liang, and he seemed satisfied. Roger then explained, more slowly, that he was seeking help in understanding the pain and fear centers in the brain. Liang nodded all through the explanation, evidently more comfortable with the medical vocabulary than the legal.

Liang typed a few commands that brought a brain map onto his monitor. "We know more about fear than pain, so I start there." He pointed to a spot on the screen. "Fear is controlled by the medial prefrontal cortex. Once the brain has determined that a potential threat is not truly a threat, the medial prefrontal cortex emits inhibitory signals to the amygdala. You understand?"

Roger nodded and looked at Denise, who was less familiar with the inner workings of the brain. After a quick Chinese exchange with Dr. Zeng, she seemed satisfied and told the professor, in English, to proceed.

Liang explained a bit more about the precise nature of these inhibitory signals, pausing when Roger asked, "So, if I can simulate these signals, like with transcranial magnetic stimulation, the brain will think that there's nothing to fear, even though the person is experiencing something that would otherwise make them afraid?"

"Precisely," said Liang, "but that kind of simulation would be quite difficult to create. It has been done before, but only crudely. Not reliable. Only statistical." He looked at Denise. "Ah, but if anyone in the world can accomplish it, your Dr. Fixman can do so."

Roger inclined his head to Liang. "I hope I can fulfill your confidence in me, professor, but I will certainly need your help. Actually, though, we merely need reliability in the fear."

"In that case, I can certainly provide my help. I am greatly in your debt."

"We can go into more detail later," said Roger. For now, what can you tell me about pain? You mentioned that less is known."

Liang stood. "Come with me to my laboratory," he said, then said something to Denise in Chinese.

"What did he say?" Roger asked as they followed Liang down the hall.

"He asked me if I was afraid of rats."

"What did you tell him?"

"I said that if they were in cages, I'd have no problem. He assured me that they were all securely confined."

The lab itself reminded Roger of their Wyatt's lab in Ann Arbor, where Tess had accidentally locked herself into a persistent vegetative state. He was glad Tess wasn't along. She had lost her enthusiasm for animal studies, never wanting to put an animal through what she had experienced for several months. Now, she and Roger often fought to be first to volunteer as a human subject in new situations, neither willing to risk anybody else before they had demonstrated safety.

Roger tuned out while Liang gave Denise a brief tour of the lab in Chinese, breaking into his thoughts of Tess only when the professor started to speak English. "Of course, our use of rats is quite limited, giving only the first crude approximations that fear could be regulated in the rostral anterior cingulate cortex. We then moved to human subjects and confirmed this result. When pain increases, blood flow in this area also increases, indicating a growth in neural activity. The correlation is clear, but so far we can see only gross results. If there are finer distinctions, we would need an instrument like Aremac to isolate them."

"What kind of pain?" Roger asked, but Denise had to translate, followed by Liang's long explanation in Chinese.

"He says that the effect is independent of the source of pain, but the most common stimulus is a heat pulse, because it can be most accurately measured."

"We'll have to look into that," Roger told Denise. "I doubt they ever use pain as great as a torturer would use."

"I do not understand," said Liang. "Torture?" He seemed upset until Denise explained that they were trying to *prevent* torture, not administer it. Then he nodded his approval, making Roger wonder if he was reacting out of personal experience.

Roger decided not to inquire about Liang's experiences in China, asking instead about experiments to negate the pain.

"Some experiments have shown that subjects can control pain by visualizing biofeedback from the cortex, which confirms the general possibility. But nobody has yet succeeded in controlling the pain externally, as with transcranial magnetic stimulation."

"But it's theoretically possible?"

"With more research, yes."

"Good," said Roger. "Then will you help us with that research?"

CHAPTER FOURTEEN

Marna left the coffee shop table mumbling some excuse, and Tess found herself alone. The truth was that she was relieved to be away from Marna's horrid marital problems–and ashamed to be relieved. Marna was a genius, no doubt, and Tess would give almost anything to add her to the Aremac team. But Marna mumbled, played with her hair, and was utterly naive about the real world. No doubt she would would require even more facilitation than SOS, which made Tess tired just thinking about it. But worst of all, Marna craved male attention at any cost short of learning how to dress, walk, talk, and generally make the most of her hidden attractive female qualities.

Tess sat for a few minutes, then decided a tour of the conference exhibitors might help wash away the ugly incident she'd just witnessed. When she went out on the observers' balcony overlooking the exhibit hall, she wasn't prepared for the enormity of it. More than two stories high, it still had insufficient space to absorb the maelstrom of noise generated by hundreds–no, thousands–of attendees and vendors circulating below.

She left the balcony and rode the escalator down the the main floor. At the door, she put on her admission badge, then hesitated for a heartbeat until she felt herself pushed into the stream of humanity by those behind her. A few feet inside the door, she stopped and allowed the crowd to split into two streams passing around her. She tried to ignore the lights and colors and motion so she could focus on why she was here: to find backers for Roger's inventions.

Hardly any of the booths looked promising. Most seemed to be signing up would-be entrepreneurs as franchisees for food, fun, and fakery. Others displayed inventions for which more ingenuity had gone into marketing than into creating something useful. Some booths, she couldn't figure out why they were there at all. At one spot, a booth bimbo in a skirt almost up to her navel thrust a plastic bag into her hand. She detested being forced to carry advertising gimmicks, but rather than create a scene, she took the bag. As she strolled among the exhibits, subsequent vendors filled the bag with free keychains, calendars, pens, and gadgets whose functions she could not imagine. *At least Roger will have fun trying to figure them all out. If I can't dump them somewhere first.*

Most of the booths were selling, not buying. Tess was looking for a buyer, but she kept distracting herself with thoughts of poor Marna. Just as she decided to leave this circus and check up on Marna, she passed a quiet booth labeled "Justice for Africa." Curious, she backtracked and studied the three posters decorating the booth, trying to figure out whether this organization was buying or selling.

One poster showed a scene of starving, fly-infested black children. Another, a naked man lying in the dust, crunched into a fetal position while ten or twelve other men beat him with sticks. The third showed no people, just the facade of a symmetrical white building with broad steps leading up through a colonnade–perhaps a courthouse or some other government building.

A thin lady in a well-worn but stylish tweed suit watched her from one of the booth's two folding chairs. Just as Tess was

AREMAC POWER • 74

about to move on, the woman stood, focused on Tess's badge, and addressed her in an accent that was distinctly British, though different from Rebecca's. "Hello. If I'm not mistaken, either you're Tesla Fixman–" She laughed softly. "–or else you've stolen her badge." Smiling, she extended her hand, glancing down at Tess's plastic bag. "My name is Alicia Silsbury. I'm sorry I don't have any free gifts to offer, but I'm glad you've come by. Ever since I saw your name on the participant list, I've been hoping to meet you, but with this crowd, I was beginning to think it wouldn't happen."

"Meet *me*?" Tess asked, her curiosity rising in parallel with her suspicions. "What are you selling?"

"Actually, I was hoping *you* could sell *me* something. I believe you'll find it an interesting business proposition. Do you have a few minutes to sit down and talk about it?"

Her eyes scanned the gargantuan room as if seeking some other place to talk. For a moment, Tess thought this was suspicious, but then Silsbury explained, "I must apologize for our booth. We registered late for the conference and had to take whatever they offered. I know it's noisy, but I'm not supposed to wander too far from the booth." She let her eyes follow the crowd passing the booth without hesitating. "Not that we have many visitors."

Tess lowered herself slowly into the nearest of the two chairs. *Well, maybe she's another one who wants to make immoral use of Aremac, but I can't be suspicious of everyone. Why not hear what she has to say? At least it's a chance to rest my feet.*

Silsbury slid the second chair a few inches closer to Tess, still at a respectful distance, then sat with her legs crossed at the ankles and her hands folded gracefully in her lap. "I know it's terribly inhospitable not to offer you tea, but Justice for Africa is really not a very rich organization. And the prices these conferences charge for simple tea service are outrageous." She touched her lips as if trying to take back her words. "No, that's not accurate. We are fairly rich when it comes to supporting our cause, but we don't waste money on frivolities."

Tess stuffed the bag under her chair. "I was hoping you had a wastebasket, so I could dispose of this rubbish."

"You may leave it there, if you wish. To African children, much of it would make valued toys."

What an excellent solution. "So what is your connection with African children?" *But now comes the charity pitch.*

Alicia smiled knowingly. "You think I'm going to give you the sob story now–the you're-so-fortunate-why-don't-you-give-a-little-to-these-starving-children spiel."

Tess could feel herself starting to blush. "That did occur to me, looking at your posters."

"Then you're as perceptive as I thought you'd be. We do make that spiel, and I certainly would not turn down a donation. But the type of help we want from you does not involve money–at least not money passing from you to us."

She's very good at this. A lot like me, only more experienced. I should leave, but I can't resist seeing how she turns this around. Besides, it's nice to be sitting. "Okay, so what is it you want from me? And I warn you, my company is not really in a position to donate help. Or money."

"I know."

"You know?"

"I read of the recent court decision, the restraining order. You seem surprised that I know about your case. Perhaps you don't appreciate how famous you–and your invention–are. And how much that restraining order interests us."

"*Temporary* restraining order," Tess corrected, not wishing to be seen in a weak negotiating position. "We don't expect it to be sustained."

"But temporary could be many years, could it not? I do know about court procedures–you've noticed the word 'Justice' in our name."

Tess resisted conceding the other woman's point. "We may not have to wait so long. Local police want to use Aremac again to interview cooperative witnesses, and local politicians are beginning to sense an anti-crime issue here they can hang their hats on." She stopped to see if Alicia was following. "You do know what Aremac does, I presume."

"Oh, yes, we know very well. Aremac's powers are why we want to do business with you."

"All right, you have me at a disadvantage. You apparently know a great deal about my company, but I know nothing about you. Why don't you tell me just what sort of business 'Justice for Africa' does?"

"Of course. How rude of me." Alicia edged her chair even closer, then adjusted her skirt. Tess tried to remember the last time she herself had worn a skirt to a business event.

Alicia nodded toward her posters. "You may be aware of the many emerging countries in Africa–Benin, Simbara, Zezanika. And perhaps you've heard of some of their problems."

"Yes. I read the news."

"Certainly, though the American view of African news is often rather distorted."

"I have lots of experience with distorted news," Tess said, allowing some bitterness bleeding into her voice. "I can well imagine."

"Specifically, then, you may not know much about justice systems in Africa, which are rather different than your

American systems. Some ways better. Some ways worse." She pointed to the fetal man being beaten. "And some ways, simply different."

"Give me an example."

"Yes, that would be good. What has happened to your Aremac–the reluctance of courts to accept eyewitness brain-pictures into evidence–would not happen in most of the chiefs' courts in West Africa. They place high value on eyewitness testimony. Whenever there are reliable eyewitnesses, justice is swift and sure." Again, she pointed to the fetal man.

Tess was beginning to get a glimmer of what Ms. Silsbury had in mind. She no longer thought of leaving. *Too many questions.* "Swift justice can easily be injustice."

"Indeed, though I believe your own Constitution guarantees the right to a speedy trial–a right not always honored in practice. And in unstable countries of Africa, if a trial is not speedy, the eyewitnesses may not live long enough to testify. That is why, in the interests of improving justice in these countries–justice for the raped, the robbed, the tortured, the murdered–our organization wishes to purchase one of your Aremacs for a Simbara court. If it works as we believe it will, then we would want to purchase many."

Tess hoped Ms. Silsbury couldn't see or hear her heart thumping in her chest, which wouldn't help her negotiating position. "That sounds promising, but Homeland Security tends to think Aremac is critical to national security. My contacts strongly suggest they will stop us from exporting an Aremac, if we could even build and test one without violating the FDA order."

"Couldn't you build it in one of the African countries we serve? We could provide all the support you'd need."

Tess studied a chip in her nail polish, not wanting to show weakness by revealing the source of her hesitation. "That could be very expensive."

"Not a problem. We have the money." She raised her thin eyebrows. "Does that mean you'll do it?"

"We might." Tess decided she might as well tell Ms. Silsbury her real reason. "But my team doesn't want to leave the United States."

Silsbury spread her hands as if the answer was obvious. "You're their leader, dear. Persuade them."

CHAPTER FIFTEEN

Marna had been in casinos before. Though the Dineh had long voted against casino gambling in Navajo Nation, opinions were changing. Her father had been ambivalent. He could visualize the Dineh taking limited advantage of *Biligaana* foolishness to finance new hospitals, schools, and to care for old people, but he wasn't sure they could maintain limits, preserve the *hozho*, the harmony of Dineh life. He had been cautious, asking his college-educated daughter to study the economics and sociology of the casinos of other tribes.

First, she had eased into the task by studying the mathematics of all the games–blackjack, craps, keno, and each of the slots. She read the surprisingly vast literature on the social side of gambling–the design of casinos, the problems of gambling addiction, the endless scams and cheats. Then she had visited Isleta's Gaming Palace, the Mescalero Inn of the Mountain Gods, San Felipe's Casino Hollywood, Santa Ana's Star Casino, and Acoma's Sky City Casino. She never gambled herself, gambling being for the mathematically challenged. Instead, she observed the behavior of gamblers and casino workers. Then she spoke with the management of each casino, learning the subtleties that never appeared in the literature.

It was during these studies that she met Karl, who was supporting his art by dealing blackjack at Casino Hollywood off Interstate I-25 midway between Albuquerque and Santa Fe. The management had kindly offered him as a guide, and for three days she had the full attention of this handsome, flattering

Anglo artist. Nothing in her prior experience had prepared her for such attention from a man, and two months later, he persuaded her to marry him without consulting her family. "Better to ask forgiveness than permission," he had said. Knowing she would never receive permission, she accepted.

She wrote down all her gambling observations, to be used later in the public debate, but also made a three-day verbal report to her father, the entire time gathering courage to tell him of her secret marriage. In the end, he had accepted the accomplished deed, saying, "If he makes you happy, that is all that counts."

But now, as she searched for Karl in this crowded casino, he was not making her happy. *But it's my own fault. If he needs money to gamble, it's not my place to refuse him–and certainly not to cut off the credit card without his permission or knowledge.* She might legitimately attempt to steer him away from the tables–that was a wife's duty–but ultimately, a man must make his own decisions. So now she would find him and apologize, and tell him that she had reinstated the credit card. He would forgive her, and harmony would be restored.

He had said he was playing poker, so she first sought him there, in the poker room where a large tournament was in progress. The tournament filled the poker room and even overflowed to extra tables set up in the main hall. There must have been at least a hundred tables. Marna examined each one. No Karl.

Perhaps he had cashed out, or gone broke, but she couldn't find him among the spectators. She asked the tournament director if there was a private poker room, but he didn't want to allow her inside. She asked to see his manager, and eventually worked her way up to the casino's assistant manager. She told him she was representing the Navajo, studying for a possible casino vote in the future. It was hard for her to lie, but at least her story was partly true–and less embarrassing than revealing she was searching for her wayward husband.

He escorted her into a private room where two high stakes games were in progress, neither of which involved Karl. There were other casinos in the complex, with other poker rooms, so she thanked the manager and tried to leave. But, having bought her story, he insisted on leading her on tour of the rest of the facility. Caught by her own lie, and feeling the irony of being guided through yet another casino by another good-looking Anglo, she maintained the pretense and continued her search at his side, pretending interest in his monologue.

Had Karl been this full of himself? Had I been so naive I didn't see through it then, the way I do now? No, Karl was different. Karl was an artist, not an inflated bureaucrat.

As they approached the roulette tables, she thought she saw Karl's full head of blond hair. Her first impulse was to leave her guide and run to her husband, but something made her hesitate. Having worked in casinos, Karl was rarely silent about his contempt for roulette and all those who played. *Why is he playing now?*

"Do you know what time it is?" she asked her host. She rarely wore a watch, and the casino, of course, had no clocks.

He checked his Rolex and told her the time. "Oh, my," she said. "This has been so interesting, I've almost forgotten. I'm due at a meeting in the convention hall in five minutes. I'll have to run to make it. May I come back later for the rest of the tour?"

"Of course," he said, and she took off in the direction of the convention hall. She slipped behind a row of slots where her guide couldn't see her, but from which she could observe the roulette table. And her husband.

She watched the assistant manager disappear up the stairs leading to the casino offices, then moved behind another row of slots, closer to the roulette table. She knew she couldn't just stand around watching–that was a no-no in any casino–so she took some change from her purse and began playing a nickel machine called "Sizzling Sevens." She could hear the machine clanging out the payoff from a winning spin, but her attention was focused on the view between her machine and the one on her right.

There were only two people besides the croupier at the roulette table, not unusual, even when other games were crowded. What *was* unusual was that Karl was betting small stacks of black hundred-dollar chips. *Where did he get so much money? He can't know I've just reactivated the credit card. Maybe he won at poker after all? But then he would have stayed at the poker table, or come up to our room to brag about his winnings. And maybe pay me back. So where did the money come from?*

A moment later, she saw the answer. She could tell from his body language that Karl had just lost a big bet when the other player at the table put her arm around him and handed him a pile of chips from her stack. Marna couldn't see her face, but from the rear view of the wrinkles on her neck, she could see that the woman was at least fifty. And, if the thick diamond necklace that almost covered those wrinkles was genuine, she must have been a well-heeled fifty.

Karl took the chips, placed a bet, then kissed the woman on the cheek. Marna's heart pounded with shame. Shame for distrustfully spying on her husband, and shame for what she had just discovered.

Maybe it isn't what it seems. Maybe they're just gambling friends, working the wheel in concert. People did that sometimes. Karl loves me. I shouldn't be so suspicious.

Five minutes later, Karl and the woman had a short discussion that Marna couldn't hear over the casino noises, then left the table holding hands. Marna started to follow, but was caught by an elderly woman dressed in a powder blue polyester suit who had been playing the machine on her left. "You forgot to cash out, honey. I wish my machine was that lucky."

Momentarily disoriented, Marna recovered and said, "Why don't you take over for me? I have to … " She couldn't say what she was really doing, and she was sure the woman wouldn't accept the money. " … I have to go to the toilet. Would you play for me until I come back? If you win, I'll split with you."

"Sure, sweetie," the woman said. "I can play both of these. You hurry back. I'm not going anywhere."

Marna could no longer see Karl and his companion. *Where could they have gone? They weren't carrying any chips, so maybe they're going to the cashiers' cage to buy more.* A dozen steps later, she had a full view of the cashiers. No Karl.

Where else could they be? They had been heading in the general direction of the hall connecting the casino to the convention center, so she slipped off that way, checking all the possibilities on both sides. When she reached the doorway, she could see all the way down the long hall to the convention center entrance. Nobody. *Can they have gone that far already?*

She heard a child crying on her left and turned to see a mother and father trying to placate a five-year-old girl carrying three balloons. They had just come around the corner, from the hotel wing. *Maybe Karl and his friend went to one of the hotel restaurants.*

She moved quickly but carefully into the wing, realizing suddenly that she was acting as if she were stalking a deer on the Rez. She looked around, but nobody was watching her. She continued her hunt, so intent that she almost exposed herself to Karl as she turned past a souvenir shop into full view of the lobby. He was standing with his woman, just about to board one of the elevators.

Marna took a quick step backwards. As soon as the elevator doors closed, she moved into the lobby. She hadn't seen if any other people were on the elevator, so she watched the lighted numerals above the door. They didn't stop until the twelfth floor, then they reversed and started down.

The elevator to her right was open, and empty. She stepped quickly inside and pushed twelve. A young man in a gray business suit approached and called for her to hold the door, but she pressed the "close" button. The door shut in his face. He said something, but she didn't hear it.

Much too slowly, the car began to ascend. *By the time it reaches twelve, they'll be gone–wherever they were going.*

Three. Four. *Was there a restaurant on twelve? I can't remember, but there must be.*

Six. Seven. *Yes, that's it. He'll be in the restaurant. I'll join him and his friend for lunch.*

Nine. Ten. She saw a directory on the elevator wall. She was still checking for restaurants when a bell rang and the door opened on twelve. She didn't see any restaurant listed on twelve.

Holding the door with one hand, she peeked out into the long hallway. It was empty on her right, but far down to her left, she saw them. At least she thought it was them. Even with her glasses she couldn't be sure, but she could be sure that it was a man and a woman, and they were locked in a clinch.

Then they disappeared. Into a room.

She rushed down the hall, tripping once on a seam in the carpet, not quite falling to her knees. She wasn't quite sure if she had the right room, but she stood quietly listening at the door. Her eyes might be weak, but there was nothing wrong with her hearing.

She made out a woman's voice inside, then heard giggling. Then everything was silent for a moment–and then a man's voice. Even through the door, she recognized Karl's distinctive baritone.

Trembling, she braced her back against the door, but her legs failed and she slid to the floor. In her mind, she was eight years old watching helplessly as brother Gaagii kicked apart her little dam of rocks and sticks. All the water had drained from her tiny pond, leaving gasping fish flopping helpless on the drying mud. Now, *she* was the pond, empty and drying, with all her carefully nurtured fish dying.

She sat, empty of all feelings, until awakened by sounds of animal pleasure from behind the door. She stood, steadied her resolve, then stumbled back to the elevator.

CHAPTER SIXTEEN

Tess cut short her visit with Alicia Silsbury, went to her room, promising to return later if she could. She had so much to do, but she needed time to gain an overview so she would know what to do first. Standing at the window, she tried to inspire herself with the overview of Las Vegas. There was the dominating Stratosphere Tower–like Justice for Africa, drawing her eye, but not first on her list of important things to attend to. The manicured park below was an attractive oasis in the desert, reminding her that she would rather be in Chicago. But the distant mountains were like the vast but distant potential for the application of the quantum displacement theory.

The mountains won. She had to stay in Las Vegas until she could talk with Marna. Karl was looking like a huge barrier blocking the way to the mountains. *If he's likely to show up, I'll have to try to get the poor woman to a private place.*

Part of Tess's mind caught her thought. *Listen to you. All you're concerned about is getting Marna on the team, so you can exploit her theory.*

You're not being fair to yourself, the rest of her mind responded. *We would be the best thing that ever happened to her. Sure, we'll benefit if it works out, but it will be a mutual benefit. Right now, nobody's listening to her. Especially not her husband.*

Sure. You're concerned about her husband, but for your sake, not for hers. With him around, she's not likely to keep her mind on her work. Why don't you help her stand up for herself, for her own sake?

Dammit, I'm no psychologist.

Come on, girl. You're the world's greatest manipulator. If you put your mind to it, you could help her stand on her own two feet.

All right, she thought, yielding to her altruistic instincts, *but first I have to check out my conjecture about inventions based on her theory.*

She hooked her Mac to the hotel's internet connection for a chat with Roger, thinking that its moderate bandwidth would probably result in herky-jerky transmission delays. The conference center had a meeting room with a much faster line, but under her new budget, the meeting room was a luxury.

Besides, she thought as she keyed the connection codes, *I'm not sure of the security there. Not that this is any better, but it's a bit more private, and I can establish my own encryption.*

But she didn't have time to set up the encryption, for a moment later, Roger's face appeared on her computer's screen, one sluggish stripe at a time. "Sound check?" he said, ready as always to take her call. "Alpha, Beta, Gamma, Delta–"

"Not so great," she interrupted. "Let me try my headset." She fitted the tiny device, wishing it were as comfortable as the Aremac snood. This might be a long call.

"Okay, try again."

"Epsilon, Zeta, Eta, Theta, Iota–"

"Enough. It's better. Not bad, in fact. Who else is there?"

"Everybody," he said. Three more voices said hello so the sound-activated cameras could focus in on their locations. The audio quality for each was adequate, but there was a noticeable delay before her screen split into four quadrants showing

Rebecca, Roger, SOS, and Denise. She smiled when she saw that the lovebirds were so close together that they both actually appeared in two quadrants, one centered on his face, one centered on hers.

"Hi, everybody. I miss you all. How about an update?"

"We got two royalty checks." After a brief delay, the quadrants disappeared and the screen filled with Rebecca's face. "Enough so we can survive another two weeks, if we don't put butter on our popcorn. I hope you've won a bundle in the casino."

"I haven't even smelled the casino. Not that I'd want to. It's bad enough in the exhibit hall."

Suddenly the screen rolled over to the pen in SOS's hand, tracking the sound of tapping on the arm of his chair. "Stop that, SOS," Tess demanded.

"Stop what?"

"Tapping on the chair."

"Was I tapping?"

"You're always tapping on something. Denise, why don't you hold his hand? And, incidentally, how are you doing?"

Denise made an incoherent sound, sufficient to cause the camera to switch to her, but telling Tess only what she already knew about the programmer's introversion. If she wanted Denise to respond, she'd better ask a specific question.

"How did your visit with professor Zeng go?"

"Uh, pretty good. We think we can access fear and pain centers. I mean, Roger thinks so. We're working on the software."

Before Tess could ask another question, SOS's face took over the screen. "Denise and I have made some progress on the pain guard software, but we're having trouble with the fear guard."

"How come?"

"We can't figure out how to scare Roger."

"Try lions."

"No fair," said Roger's voice, followed by his smiling face on the screen.

"Fair has nothing to do with it. If you want more ideas, watch one of those so-called reality shows."

"I'd rather watch a Stephen King movie."

"That won't work. You've seen them all ten times."

"At least I'm a better subject than Rebecca. Nothing scares her."

"Nothing you'll ever know about." At the sound of Rebecca's voice, the screen started to switch to her face, but stopped halfway and replaced the stripes with Roger again.

"I rigged up that speed-sleeper."

Tess could see the pride in his face. "You did? It really works?"

"So far. One hour in it, and I'm fully rested."

SOS's face appeared. "Works great. We all tried it. I can work twenty-three hours straight before I start yawning."

"I think we can do even better," said Roger. For now the eight-for-one ratio is good enough to let us implement Denise's idea."

"What idea is that?" Tess said. "Denise has a million ideas." She could imagine Denise blushing, but as long as she remained quiet, the screen wouldn't show her face.

"Consulting," said SOS, and Tess could see Denise's profile as she whispered in his ear. "We've each got an extra seven hours a day now, so we figured we could take on extra work. Right now, we have an offer of $20,000 for a bank job Denise can do in eight hours."

"That's $2,500 an hour." Denise's face came on the screen with her hand over her mouth. "I'm not worth that."

Tess watched Denise being pulled off the screen, then the screen switched to SOS, who seemed to be hugging her. "You're priceless. But we'll settle for $2,500 an hour."

Tess was still smiling when Rebecca finished her check-in of pending issues, all of which could be postponed. "So, Roger, did you have a chance to work with the equations I sent you?"

Roger started to say something, but suddenly the screen switched to SOS shouting "Dak! Dak! Dak!" Then silence, and the screen went blank.

Hearing the Klingon warning, Tess instinctively yanked the cable, ripped off her headset, and slammed the lid on her Mac. She shuddered and looked around, then stopped herself. Of course the eavesdropper wouldn't be physically in her hotel room. Though they might well be in the hotel. Even next door. She would have to find a pay phone outside of the hotel.

It took her more than an hour to find a working pay phone outside a 7-11 a mile from the hotel complex. Part of that time was attempting to make sure she wasn't followed, but eventually she acknowledged her amateur status and resigned herself to the possibility that she'd been tailed by a professional.

When Roger answered, Tess had a checklist ready on a PostIt™ stuck on the glass. "Let's do this quickly. I have no idea how secure this call may be. I may have been followed, so tell me quickly. Maybe we have a few minutes of grace while our eavesdropper sets up again."

"We've done what we could at this end." SOS's voice rebounded with speakerphone echo. "Wait until you hear what we came up with."

"Shush, Stephen," said Rebecca's voice. "I want to hear Tess first. Did you have something specific in mind?"

Tess cupped her hand over the mouthpiece. "I did, but I didn't want to bias you. I was thinking of a power source, drawing on Earth's gravitational field."

"Aha!" said SOS. "Great minds running in parallel. The basic idea is to use instantaneous displacement to send a mass upward, then let it accelerate under gravity. If it's a magnet falling through a coil, it will generate a current."

Tess scratched one item off her list. "Exactly what I had in mind. "But I couldn't get a grip on how *much* power. Did you?"

"No," said Roger. "The equations say it will work, but the size of the effect depends on whether relative velocity is preserved in the displacement. The equations you gave don't cover the dynamic case. If velocity is not preserved, it would take a rather large device to produce a useful amount of energy."

"What's the scale? Like a power plant?"

"Maybe like a single family dwelling power plant," said Roger.

"That could be quite a viable product, but it would put us squarely up against Big Corporate Power. They wouldn't like that at all."

"I suppose we might make a car battery, for electric cars." Roger spoke slowly, as if his mind was already altering his design.

Rebecca cut in. "That's a dodgy scheme that would put us up against Big Corporate Oil. I don't give a toss for the corporations, but they would bury us in barristers. How about inventing something that would keep a cell phone running without ever needing to be recharged?"

Tess heard Denise's high-pitched laugh. She might be an off-scale introvert, but she did speak up when her feelings ran high. "Let's do that one. I'm sick of reading thrillers where the plot turns on someone's cell phone battery running out of juice at a critical moment."

"That, too," said Tess, smiling to herself. "But I was thinking more of the marketing. A small device that's cheap and a direct replacement for something consumers already buy. The marketing channels are in place, and there are already dozens or hundreds of small competitors, so we could slip right in as soon as we had a product."

Rebecca picked up the thought. "And because it's small, we wouldn't need a huge production facility–"

"–so we wouldn't attract a lot of attention until we had a toehold in the market. And we could start generating cash rather quickly."

"We need to do this on the quiet," said Rebecca. "Once we make it work, everyone will want it, and try to pinch it, like that Inga person."

Alerted to the outside world by Inga's name, Tess turned to see a black Lexus with dark tinted windows pull up the the 7-11. "Then we'd better get off this phone. Any last words?"

"Sounds perfect," said Roger. "You ladies have done the hard part. All I have to do now is invent it."

Tess sounded a kiss into the phone. "I have full confidence in you, darling."

"Maybe that confidence is misplaced. I need to extend the equations, and you know that's not my strength."

Tess pulled her PostIt™ list off the window. *The rest can wait. I think I know just the person who can do it.*

CHAPTER SEVENTEEN

Locating "just the person" who could extend the equations proved to be more difficult than Tess had predicted. Marna wasn't in her room, nor was she in any of the session rooms. Tess searched the exhibit hall, but the crowd was so large and active that she couldn't be absolutely sure she hadn't missed her target.

Tess was pretty sure Marna wouldn't be in one of the bars, and the casino seemed unlikely. After six months of lying on her back in a persistent vegetative state, she loved to be outside in the sweet, clear, warm air. But walking all the way around the complex yielded no sign of Marna, so she forced herself back inside to continue her search in the artificial-smelling air of the Center. Inquiries at all the restaurants yielded no clue. In desperation, she roamed the casino.

Tess had just about given up when she spotted her quarry sitting in the sports betting area. Unlike the four others spread around the seats, Marna didn't seem to be playing. She had pencil and paper, but wasn't even watching the results or the videos. In fact, when Tess came around to face her, Marna didn't seem to be doing anything but weeping, but the backs of her betting sheets were filled with Greek symbols and integral signs. *Oh, oh. She's in denial about something.*

Tess took the seat in front of her, swiveled around, and propped her bare forearms on the padded seat back. "I've been looking all over for you. I didn't know you gambled." She knew

Marna wasn't gambling, but trying to bury her feelings in her equations.

"I don't," Marna said sullenly. "Gambling is for people who can't do math … People like my husband." She scratched a theta from her papers and substituted an epsilon over two.

"Amen to that. Fortunately, my husband's math is excellent. Is that why you're here in the casino, waiting for your husband to finish gambling?" *Of course she's not, but I'm not going to do her personal work for her.*

Marna ducked the hint and held up a page for Tess to read. "No, I'm here because my boss thinks it would be good for me."

"Gambling?"

"No, this stupid convention. He thinks I'm too theoretical, so I should meet people who put theory into practice."

"Well," Tess said, pointing to herself with both forefingers, "now you can tell him you've met one of those practical people. And that we don't have horns."

Marna looked horrified. "Oh, no, I didn't mean you were a bad person. It's just not me, that's all. I'm all theory–but I'm really no good in the lab. I break things–that's if I don't blow them up or electrocute myself."

"So maybe we can help you with that part of it. I spoke to my team. They think we might be able to develop your quantum displacement theory into a practical device of some sort. We'd need your help with the equations, though.

Marna's rubbed the wetness from her eyes.

That caught her attention. "I copied the equations from the tablecloth, and printed out a copy for you." Tess handed a single sheet to Marna. "I hope you don't mind that I simplified the notation a bit."

Marna scanned the sheet quickly, then perused it carefully. "These are terrific, Tess. Can we go somewhere else to talk about them?" She looked around at the other players. "It's getting noisy in here, and it's depressing me. And I need my computer."

"Sure. Let's go to your room and get it. We can work there."

Marna stiffened. "Not my room."

Oh, oh. She doesn't want to run into her husband. "Okay. We'll stop there and fetch your computer, then we can go to my room. It's probably not as fancy as yours, but it has good light and a worktable."

"Can we just use your computer?"

"Yes," said Tess, and led Marna out of the casino and down the corridor leading to the Travelodge, the least expensive hotel in the complex. Neither woman spoke until they were inside the room, then Marna started an irrelevant conversation about Tess's computer, which Roger had outfitted with a few bells and whistles.

As Marna positioned herself on the chair in front of the computer, her pants leg pulled up and, to her horror, Tess saw more than half a dozen bruises on her calf–old yellow ones, young purples, and even several crusted red scabs.

Tess was fed up with Marna's inability to face her marital problems. *If Marna's going to work with us, she has to learn to stop this abuse. It's time to take a risk. If I push her away from us, then it just wasn't meant to be.*

Tess put her hand over the trackball, preventing Marna from using it. "Marna, I saw your husband kick you today, and just now, when you sat down, your pants leg pulled up and I saw old bruises. What's going on?"

Marna tugged down her pants and tried to move Tess's hand away from the trackball. "Nothing. It's not important."

Tess clamped down firmly on the trackball. "It's important to me, Marna. If you tell me it's none of my business, I'll stop asking." She paused until Marna looked up and into her eyes. "And I'll also stop working with you on your theory. I can't work with someone who tolerates torture."

Marna studied the carpet for a long time. "Yes, sometimes he kicks me. But–"

Tess tried to cut off her excuses, but Marna was too quick. "–it doesn't hurt very much. And it's not torture. It's just a kind of love tap when I've been bad."

Love tap? Bad? She's totally out of touch with reality. Tess reached over and tried to pull up Marna's pants leg, but Marna pulled her leg away. "And it's only when he's been drinking too much."

"You mean when he's drunk? Like this morning?"

"That doesn't happen all the time. Only when he's having trouble with his art." She paused, but Tess simply raised her eyebrows to ask for truth.

"Or when he's short on cash. Things like that. His life is hard. He doesn't have the university education like we do."

"So he never went to college?"

"Well, he went ... but he didn't finish. He's not good at taking tests."

Tess took Marna's hands in hers and spun her around to face her. "So he gambles, spends all his money–money you've earned–, drinks heavily, and kicks you so it leaves bruises where it won't show. What else, Marna? What else happened today since we had coffee?"

It was only an intuitive guess on Tess's part, but when Marna began trembling all over, she knew she'd hit the mark.

Now she would have to deal with the damage she might have caused.

Little by little, and ever so gently, Tess extracted the story of Karl's roulette partner. Finally, she asked, "And what are you going to do about it?"

"I don't know," Marna sobbed, a tremor racing through her body. "What *can* I do?"

"You could go back to him and tell him you know he only screwed that woman because you were a bad girl and didn't give him all the money he wanted. Are you that kind of woman, Marna?"

Marna sat up and dried her eyes with her knuckles. "Maybe. Part of me wants to go back, but I can't. Not now. He's crossed the line, and I don't think I can cross to his side. But he has my credit card, and all my money, and his car, so what can I do?"

"How about you go spend some time with your family? On the reservation?"

Marna shook her head violently. "No, I can't do that."

"Why not?"

"Because if my brothers find out, they'll kill him."

She's still protecting him. "Do you care?"

"I don't know, but I do care about my brothers. If they harm him, they'll go to prison–red men beating up a white man is not an honored activity in New Mexico."

So I was wrong. She thinks she's protecting her family. That's an improvement, at least. "Probably not anywhere. Do you have a friend you can stay with in Los Alamos?"

"Not that kind of friend. And I don't think I can face people at work. I need to get away somewhere. I have lots of accumulated vacation time, but I have no money."

Tess hesitated for a long time. Marna started crying again, but Tess was busy silently arguing with herself. *If you rescue her, it's only for your own selfish reasons. And he'll probably come after her, so if she doesn't learn to deal with him herself, it's going to mess up your whole team.*

But she's got to start somewhere. And I'm risking our company, so is it entirely selfish if it could cost me everything?

You're right about that. The odds are great that such a revolutionary theory has a flaw.

But I've listened to her thinking and studied her equations. I think she's the real thing—one in a billion.

Tess looked up as if to check her impression of Marna. For a change, she wasn't fiddling with equations, though the faraway look in her eyes showed she might be doing them in her head.

She seems to be arguing with herself, too.

Maybe she's finally going to do something for herself.

Does she have it in her? Does she —

Marna's audible swallow broke Tess's internal argument. "Could I ... Could I come work with you? Maybe help your husband use my theory to invent something practical?"

It was weak and uncertain, but it was the first step Tess had been waiting for. "What about your husband?"

"I don't know. I'm trying to control my anger, so I need to get away from him, at least for a while. Should I forgive him?"

"That's not my decision, Marna." *I'm going to help her help me, but I'm not going to rescue her.*

Marna corrected her posture and faced Tess squarely. "Then I won't decide now. I'll give myself a month before I think about it again. I want to experience life without him— among people who are willing to give me a chance to prove myself."

"All right, that's good enough for me. You come to Chicago with me. I'll put you on salary, and I'll pay your expenses."

Marna held up her hands in protest. "But I couldn't take your money. How would I pay you back?"

"Don't worry. If my gamble pays off, neither of us will have reason to worry about your credit."

CHAPTER EIGHTEEN

With Marna under her protective wing, Tess was eager to vacate Las Vegas, but she felt obligated to speak to Alicia Silsbury about her offer. By the time she returned to the Grand Hall to say goodbye, at least half the exhibitors had packed up and abandoned their booths. The Hall wasn't exactly quieter, but the noise was different. Fewer people were chattering, but large display cases screeched across the floor, shouted orders echoed from the bare walls, and hammers pounded packing crates into readiness for shipping.

All the posters were gone from the Justice for Africa booth, so at first Tess thought Alicia had already left. But there she was, two booths away, talking quietly with a young blond man wearing a green-ribboned badge identifying him as a conference official. She saw Tess, waved to her, and shook hands with the young man before returning to her own, now empty, booth. Tess noticed how smoothly she had set him moving away with a well-timed touch on his back. *She's used to handling people. A pro.*

"Oh, I'm so glad you could make it back. I was hoping I would have a chance to tell you more about our mission."

"I'd love to hear about it," Tess said. "However, I don't want to encourage you. I've just committed our company to an important project, so I'm afraid we won't be able to take on anything new for the foreseeable future."

For just a moment, Alicia's face showed appropriate regret, then her smile reappeared. "Well, I'm disappointed, of course, but I wish you luck in your new enterprise. If you can spare the time for me to treat you to lunch, I'd still love to have the opportunity to tell you more about us and our mission."

"There's really no chance I'll change my mind."

"I believe you, but who knows the future? When you've completed your important project, you might be able to find time for us. We truly are a worthy cause."

Somehow, Alicia's words touched a tiny guilt nerve in Tess. Looking at her watch, she said, "Sure. I've been so busy, I've forgotten about eating. I'm all packed, and I don't have to be at the airport for a while, so okay. But I'll pay. I don't want to take money from those starving kids."

Alicia laughed politely. "No, I insist. It won't be any place expensive. I was thinking of the salad buffet restaurant down near the Hilton. I do adore salads. Would that suit you?"

"Sure. That sounds great."

Alicia started walking and beckoned Tess to follow. "Let's go, then. I don't leave today, but I know exactly what you mean. The restaurant should be quiet by this time, and I've had quite enough of this horrid, noisy place."

The indoor walk to the restaurant took almost fifteen minutes, but the two women kept their conversation to neutral comments about the decor that lined the corridor. Halfway there, Tess finally identified Alicia's accent. Watching *Masterpiece Theater* one night, Rebecca identified it as "pukka voice"–the perfect, socially acceptable voice of the British upper class. When Tess said she liked the sound, Rebecca said, simply, "I loathe it."

The restaurant smelled of chives and garlic, arousing Tess's appetite. They took plates and grazed up and down the four long three-tiered buffet tables, confining their talk to the quality of the produce, skipping the meats. Only when they were seated with full plates of fresh vegetables did Alicia begin her pitch. "I believe I sketched out our mission for you this morning."

"Yes, you did. Something about legal systems in developing African nations. But I don't truly understand what that means, exactly."

Alicia made a small rearrangement of the veggies on her plate. "You're not alone. Even people like you who have obviously spent some time in courtrooms don't notice all the expensive equipment that comprise the infrastructure. Some of it is behind the scenes, like photocopiers, file cabinets, desks, pens, pencils, and paper. They're ordinary things we take for granted, but most of these countries just don't have them."

Tess looked at her heaping salad plate. *Yes, I even take this bounty of food for granted.* "I can imagine."

"And then there's the things you don't have to imagine, if you've been in courtrooms. Like steno machines, chairs for juries and spectators, even judges' gavels. Then there's sound equipment and recorders, video equipment, and in many places, equipment for simultaneous translation. And metal detectors– they're rather expensive, you know."

I don't know, but I can believe it. "I suppose you need reference books and computers and networking gear."

"Absolutely. And don't forget software. That's often the most expensive, though we work hard to negotiate deals with the software vendors."

Alicia picked up a pimento olive with her fork and nibbled a tiny bite of it. Tess had hardly touched her food, either, so she ate three forkfuls of greens before asking, "Do you equip jails and such?"

"Yes, jails are a huge expense, though we rely mostly on local builders. It helps the economy, building jails–sad but true. And we do have to import some special confinement equipment, though we try to keep it simple. It's difficult for some of the locals to cope with complex electronic systems, while at the same time, they can afford to throw more personnel at the problem of guarding prisoners. Still, they don't generally keep people in jail as long as we do, and not for such minor offenses."

"What's considered minor?"

"Oh, it varies from culture to culture, but, for example, they don't jail people for using narcotics."

"For dealing?"

"Sometimes, but most of their narcotics are home grown."

Tess watched two security guards pass by the restaurant's interior glass windows, looking in with a serious air. "What about police?"

"Most people don't realize the enormous number of things needed to support police work. Vehicles, uniforms, radios, dispatch stations, fingerprint gear, handcuffs and other restraints–"

"Weapons?"

Alicia pushed a cucumber slice to one side of her plate. "Well, yes, that's one of the unpleasant realities of justice, isn't it? But that's not our main emphasis. Most of that sort of expenditure–for things like batons, chemical sprays such as pepper spray, … "

Her voice trailed off. Tess felt as though she were being studied for a reaction, but said nothing.

"And then there are bags and belts and holsters to carry all this stuff. We just paid a bill for over $24,000 just for equipment bags. At least they were made with local labor. We did supply the special cloth. And the zippers."

"I'm impressed," said Tess. *I truly am.* "Okay, I'm sure there's more, but where did you figure we would come in?"

Alicia started to explain again about the importance of eyewitnesses in local courts, but Tess held up her palm like a traffic cop. "No, I understand that, but what did you expect our people to do? Build a turnkey Aremac for you?"

"That, of course, but more. I didn't tell you about our consultants who come over to Africa to train the locals how to use, maintain, and repair things. We'd want some of that kind of help–and, of course we'd pay for it and provide transportation, housing, and amenities."

"What sort of amenities?"

"Oh, I don't mean our people live like colonial barons or anything. Simple comforts commensurate with the surrounding culture. We don't like to stand out."

If Alicia thinks she doesn't stand out, the only one she's fooling is herself. Perhaps she thinks that Prince Charles doesn't stand out, either.

"And, of course, we provide guides and translators."

"Sounds like quite an adventure."

Alicia tore off one tiny end of a breadstick, then held it on its way to her mouth. "I shouldn't make it sound like a fairy tale. There can be hardships, though I guess if I can survive–and thrive–anyone can. I was brought up in rather comfortable surroundings." She put down the breadstick bit and raised her teacup. Tess could picture her raising her cup to the Queen.

Alicia sipped her tea, then set it down gracefully. "Believe me, I never drank tea from an old tin can before I was forty years old."

I'd like to ask how old she is now, but there's an even more delicate matter I need to raise. "It sounds like a wonderful, humanitarian cause, something I've never really thought about. Unfortunately, as I told you, we're just not in a position to undertake any new projects at the moment. Or in the foreseeable future. I will tell the team about it–though the adventure might prove tempting to the boys–and I'll definitely keep your organization in mind should our situation change in the future."

"As I told you, I am disappointed, but I do understand. And, look, you've hardly touched your salad. You need to prepare yourself for your flight."

Tess smiled and said, "No, I'm the one who's kept *you* from your meal." After that they sat silently eating, Tess cleaning her plate while Alicia selected four or five choice morsels from hers.

Finally, Tess checked her watch, and picked up the bill. "It's been very interesting meeting you, Alicia. Perhaps sometime in the future … "

"Of course," said the older woman, standing as Tess stood. "From time to time, my business takes me to Chicago. May I call upon you some time, perhaps to witness a demonstration of this marvelous Aremac?"

CHAPTER NINETEEN

Inga had spent far too much time walking around this damned Conference Center. A uniformed guard had noticed her difficulties and offered her one of the motorized wheelchairs, but she refused. She never could admit to herself she was no longer the athlete she had been as a college beauty queen. Now she was paying the price for her pride.

She needed time in the hot tub to take the weight off her ankles, knees, and hips. The tub in her suite was too small, so she had engaged a private tub in the fitness center–more walking to get over there. Given the difficulty of reaching her muscles, the masseur had done an acceptable job relaxing her, and now the jacuzzi was hot and reasonably quiet. She wasn't happy with the security, though, even with the locked door. She was accustomed to listening through walls, so she didn't trust that others might not eavesdrop on her.

Well, it would just have to do, because I have to make this call, and the walls in my room next to Tess's are even thinner than the spa's. She hoped the white noise of the jacuzzi would provide some extra protection, but her contact had complained that he couldn't hear, so she shut down the pumps. *At least now I have a chance of hearing if anyone approaches outside my door.*

The familiar rough male voice on the other end of her cell call had asked her about Tess's actions at the conference. "Did you speak with her?"

"No. Of course not, but I was prepared to say hello if I bumped into her. I don't think she was aware of me, or if she was, she didn't recognize me or attach any significance to my presence. Of course, I couldn't watch her all the time, but I thought I kept pretty good track of her comings and goings."

"She didn't know you were staying next door to her?"

"I'm not stupid. I left after she left, and arrived after she arrived. I doubt if she looked up her neighbors at the front desk. She's not the suspicious type."

"Don't underestimate them. You made that mistake before."

Inga felt chilled. She forced her body down until the hot water was up to her neck. "And don't you lecture me. You weren't so clever yourself. Do you want to hear what I found out or not?"

"Go ahead."

"She visited a lot of booths, but didn't spend much time at any of them. Except, she talked a lot with a woman from some organization called 'Justice for Africa.' I don't think anything came of it."

Inga was having trouble holding her body down in the water. "Just a minute," she said, slipping around to a deeper part of the tub.

"What's that noise? It sounds like water. Where are you, anyway?"

"That's not your concern." *I'm not drowning, as if you'd care.* "Do you want to hear about this Justice for Africa?"

"No, I know about them. They're not a problem. Did she make any other contacts, outside of the booths."

Inga's hair had gotten wet moving around. She couldn't reach her towel and didn't want to climb out of the tub. Her annoyance infected her voice. "I noticed she was spending a lot of time with one particular woman, so I tried to drop one of your devices on her." *It never hurts to show him I'm earning my money, especially when I'm not making much forward progress.*

"On Fixman? Not a good idea."

"No, the other woman. But I didn't succeed, so all I could do was check her out. She was from Los Alamos. Maybe you could find out more."

"Los Alamos?"

"Yes, the National Laboratory."

"Interesting. Do you think they're into weapons?"

"You're misinformed. There's virtually no weapons work at Los Alamos these days–"

"That you know of."

"If anyone knows, then I know. Most of the weapons work is done elsewhere, like Sandia Labs. Besides, I told you I investigated her, this Dr. Savron. Marna Rose Savron. You can probably find out more than I did."

"She's a doctor?"

"Everyone at Los Alamos has at least one doctorate. Hers is in theoretical physics."

"What would Fixman want with a theoretical physicist? She and her husband are physicists themselves."

"Maybe they want her speciality, quantum displacement."

"What's that?"

"You wouldn't understand," Inga snapped. *I wish I could quantum displace that damned towel I can't reach.*

"And you do?"

Damn, she cursed to herself. *Did I give uncertainty away?* "In a general way, yes. I downloaded a copy of her thesis. I'll need more time to study it."

"Good. I'll have my people look into it, but make the time to do it at your end, too. And get back to me quickly. They're up to something. We want that interrogation device before they make a deal with someone else."

"Yes, that's what I told you. They're up to something, and they think there's money in it."

"That's the bottom line, so why don't you know more?"

"If your people hadn't taken so long to crack their encryption, I could have heard more of their internet conference before it was over." *I'm sure as hell not going to tell him that I think they detected my tap and called out some sort of signal. I just hope they couldn't trace the tap back to me.*

"Even so, you should have picked up something."

"Of course I did. I don't understand the details–yet. It sounds like a new source of revenue, if it works. She wasn't sure it would work."

"How soon will they know?"

"Fixman sounds confident, and based on her husband's track record, I wouldn't bet against him. But it sounds like it will take a while to develop an income stream, so we have a short window of opportunity to obtain the interrogation device before they're flush again."

"Then we'd better move quickly. Either we buy them off, or we do something a bit more drastic."

CHAPTER TWENTY

Within a day of Marna's arrival in Chicago, she was having doubts. She had met the team, but they seemed more interested in their fledgling inventions than in her theory of quantum displacement.

Tess is still interested, but she's always busy with Rebecca, or out of the office on some business or other. Stephen listened at first, but he doesn't really understand physics. And, when I tried to show him some FORTRAN code, I could see from his facial expression that I had fallen from his good graces.

Denise seemed friendly enough, though she was out of the office most of the time earning money at some bank. Rebecca helped me set up a workplace and was always available to answer questions, but she didn't even know Newton's Laws of Motion. That wasn't her job.

Which left Roger. He's definitely a physicist, and brilliant enough, and he tried hard to understand my theory. But there seemed to be a communication gap between us. He could understand my equations, but he seemed more comfortable translating them into hardware. The trouble was, he couldn't make the hardware work.

Day by day, as they kept failing to construct an experimental demonstration, Marna began to regret ever coming to Chicago. *I shouldn't have accepted Tess's offer so quickly. It's going to be the same old thing. They don't believe my theory, and they don't accept me as a worthy colleague.*

One morning, while they sat in the lounge, Roger reviewed all their failed attempts for the team. "I just can't make it work," he summarized. "Maybe it's like the Michelson-Morley experiment."

"What's that?" SOS asked.

Denise knew. Denise seemed to know everything, about everything. "Two physicists who set out to measure the velocity of the aether. You know, the imaginary fluid that was supposed to fill up empty space."

"That doesn't sound like these experiments," her boyfriend said.

"The point was that they never found *any* velocity, which led to the conclusion that there was no aether. The theory was false."

"Oh. So you think there's no such thing as quantum displacement?"

"Well, I've set up the experiment the best way I could, and I don't see any displacement. Unless you can think of something else, what else can we conclude?"

It was all Marna could do to hold back her tears until she escaped to the bathroom.

* * *

To make Marna's loneliness worse, one of Arnie Danielson's law partners had taken on her divorce case, reminding her how much she missed Karl. Tess took her to a photographer's studio to have the bruises on her legs photographed before they faded. The procedure was tedious and embarrassing, and her state of mind was not improved when Tess said, "Too bad you didn't snap some pics of the brute with his lady friend in the hotel."

"That would be overkill," the lawyer explained, waving the fresh packet of incriminating photographs. "These will do the job quite handily. Still, pictures at the hotel couldn't have hurt."

Marna greeted this news with ambivalence. Part of her feared Karl would find her and come after her, while another part still loved the only man who had ever paid any attention to her. The closer they approached a legal end to the marriage, the more her heart of hearts glowed with the faint hope she could reform him. Until Tess suggested Marna use Aremac. "We can capture pictures of Karl and his lady friend in Las Vegas."

Marna was curious about Aremac. All the other members of the team had tried it, so maybe it would be some sort of initiation rite. "But with the TRO, we wouldn't be able to use the pictures in court, would we?"

"Probably not," said Tess, "but they might be used to intimidate Karl."

Instead, recalling Karl's infidelity intimidated Marna, reminding her that there was no hope of returning to her comfortable nest of illusions. *Whether the experience makes me more of a team member, I have no way of knowing. If Roger can't demonstrate my theory, there's no place for me on this team.*

* * *

To his credit, Roger kept trying, but Marna's time was running out. She had told her boss in Los Alamos she was using up some of her accumulated vacation weeks. She refused to tell him she was in Chicago, half-hidden in the home of Roger's

Uncle Nazim and Cousin Addie. However, when she told her family where she was, two of her brothers–Ahiga (called Al) and Tse (called Tom)–both ex-marines, had insisted on driving to Chicago to protect her from Karl until the divorce was final.

They had refused to listen to Marna's objections, and now took the precaution of driving her everywhere. Sitting between them in their faded red Ford pickup, she felt safer than she had in years. *Maybe I should just go back to the Rez, be with my family. Forget this physics nonsense.*

After two weeks, Marna still blushed when Al and Tom walked her through the sewing rooms of Nazim and Suhayb's lingerie factory. The battery lab was hidden in a long-idle workshop in the back. It was an effective location for hiding the team's secret development activities, but when Al snatched up pairs of crotchless pink panties or Tom exchanged suggestive remarks with one of the sewing machine girls, Marna wished Tess would allow her to use the locked back entrance.

Most days, Marna had been working at home–Nazim's home–but now Roger wanted her to come to the battery lab to supply some physical constants for a key trial. At the newly-installed steel lab door, Marna buzzed and Tess and Heidi trotted out through the double doors to meet her. Leaving Heidi outside to guard the door while the brothers bantered with the workers, Tess led Marna into a large room with bare, yellow brick walls and solid but worn plank floors. Despite having no windows, the room was well lit at this time of day from three skylights twelve feet above their heads. When Tess bolted the door behind her, Marna could still hear the whirr of sewing machines from the other room. *Lapu would it was the sound of ghosts of past sewing machines in this hundred-year-old room. I think he understands more than any of us.*

They walked across the room, weaving their way among half-unpacked boxes and half-constructed machinery, to a waist-high workbench where Roger tinkered with an aluminum-frame bristling with wires. About the size of a loaf of bread, it was the latest working model of a device that was supposed to displace a small graphite sphere one centimeter from point A to point B in zero time with no measurable expenditure of energy. If Marna's theory was correct.

SOS didn't look up from his computer, which Marna saw was cabled to the apparatus, ready to enter her quantum constants. She set the printout she had labored over for several days in front of him. He squinted. "What's this?"

"The constants for graphite."

"I know that," he said impatiently. "But why do you keep giving me all these digits? They must have fifty digits each."

"Thirty-four, actually. They have to be accurate down to the Plank length."

SOS shook his head. "No way. My floating point fraction is only fifty-two bits. Maybe eleven or twelve digits. You can save all this effort, because I just trash the rest."

Marna looked to Roger for help. "You mean you haven't been using all the precision I've been giving you?"

"Hey, I coded the equations exactly to your specs."

"Not if you're using only fifty-three bits. No wonder the device doesn't work."

That got Roger's attention. He walked over, took Marna's paper from SOS, and gave him a curious look.

"Hey, that's the IEEE standard." SOS impatiently grabbed the paper out of Roger's hand. "Sure, your FORTRAN can print out as many digits as you want from its floating point, but anything after twelve digits is just meaningless noise."

Marna's brain was whirling with the implications of the loss of precision. "Not true. I use FORTRAN with the ARPREC package. Or, in this case, where I had to work out n-dimensional LISP."

"I thought you said that FORTRAN was the only language you knew."

"No, it's just the language I use for simple, approximate calculations. For calculations involving the nature of space-time at quantum dimensions, I use ARPREC or LISP. How else would I get all these digits of accuracy?"

SOS pivoted on his chair, facing Marna for the first time, his eyes opened wide, giving her his full attention. "You did these in LISP?"

"That's what I just said."

"Can I see the program?" Marna thought he sounded like her brothers on the night before Christmas.

CHAPTER TWENTY-ONE

Now that her LISP expertise had won her SOS's acceptance, even admiration, Marna should have felt she belonged to the Aremac team. *But Roger seems to be holding out. I suppose he likes me. He's not the kind of person who really likes or dislikes people. To him, people are worth his attention or not, and I'm useless if he can't demonstrate my theory. But it's still not happening.*

The job of recoding SOS's embedded software to handle greater precision was straightforward. Straightforward but tedious. SOS said, "I simplified the task by trading code space in memory for speed. Until we proved the theory, we'll use as large a memory as we like. Later if the theory proves out and we want to make a small, cheap device, we're going to have to reduce the memory. Extra work then, but this tactic would simplify things now."

Maybe they'll never have to do the extra work, if my theory is fallacious. By this time, that's what everybody thinks. But SOS did say "until we prove the theory," not "if we prove the theory."

Roger, though, is not so positive. He keeps saying that there must be something wrong with his apparatus, but I don't believe him, for two reasons. First, he's probably just being kind to me, hiding the fact that he doubts the theory.

Second, we all know that the hardware isn't that critical, and it's well within Roger's skills. If something is wrong with the apparatus, it's in the software.

She knew it was the team's practice to review each other's code, but this approach was new to her. People in her section of the Lab guarded their codes jealously. She would have loved to have some expert review her codes, but she had no experience at code reading, or being read.

When SOS read her LISP program, she learned some excellent tricks. He seemed impressed that he could find only inefficiencies, but no actual errors. "You have a natural talent for this," he said. "You're wasting your time in physics. You should have been a programmer."

She felt it was the highest compliment he could pay, but a moment later she found out she was wrong when he said, "I want you to read *my* code. Maybe you can find the bug that's crisping Roger's experiment."

Marna's face grew hot. "You're teasing me, SOS. You know I don't really know C++."

He made a dismissive gesture and reached for his bookshelf. "For someone with your brain, it's trivial. Here, read these."

He handed her two eight-hundred-page paperback volumes: *Thinking in C++*. "Skim these tonight. Tomorrow, first thing, we'll review the code."

* * *

The C++ books were fascinating reading, but there was no way Marna could work through sixteen hundred pages overnight. She tried, but fell asleep with Volume One in her lap sometime after three in the morning. At five, Addie found her sleeping, woke her, and made her undress and crawl into bed for some real sleep. Instead of sleeping, though, she thrashed around, tangling her sheets and dreaming of polymorphic stacks of character array literals swimming in a soup of syntax.

When she arrived at the factory, two hours late with a scorching headache, SOS had everything set up for a small walkthrough of his code, with Marna, Denise, and Tess as reviewers. For the first hour, Marna watched how the other women questioned every assumption SOS had made, but she was too busy struggling just to understand the C++ language to contribute anything herself.

They broke for lunch. Marna walked over to Wendy's with Al and Tom. Al was spooning green chile onto his cheeseburger from his personal jar when a skinny white kid wearing a tie and a badge reading "store manager" stopped at their table and shook a finger at him. "That's not allowed, sir."

"What's not allowed?" Al asked.

"You can't bring your own food into Wendy's."

"This isn't food, pal. It's a religious ceremony."

"It looks like food. You're going to eat it, aren't you?"

Al handed the plastic spoon to the manager. "Here. Taste it. Tell me if it tastes like food to you."

The kid backed away. "That's all right, sir. I'll take your word for it."

Marna was embarrassed, but had to bite the insides of her cheeks to keep from laughing. Tom kept his face buried in his napkin. Al tried to look serious but failed. "I think he was afraid it was some kind of hallucinogen."

"Worse than peyote for him," Tom said. "I wanted to see him light up when it burned his mouth."

When they stopped laughing, Marna tried to explain the review process to her brothers. "It's not like fixing trucks, or Roger's experimental apparatus. With hardware, you're dealing with real, physical things, like a truck part is broken and you have to run over to Napa to get a new one,"

"And maybe wait a week while they have it shipped in," Tom added.

"Exactly. In hardware, there are delays like that all the time, but software is more like theory, where your own mind is the only limitation."

"Denise found a tiny bug in SOS's code this morning, and he'll have it fixed by the time we're all back from lunch."

"That's more your style, isn't it, *Shideezhi*?" Al asked, studying his calloused fingers. "You never were very good with your hands–"

"–but she types like her hands are in a stick race," Tom said, laying his large hand gently on his sister's.

"But she still can't keep up with her lightning brain."

Marna hid her face in her hands, peeking out between her fingers. "Stop it, you two." *But I do love it.*

To change the subject, she started to explain the general concept of SOS's program, which was difficult to do in terms her brothers would understand. "It's like when we were in the arroyo at Elk Creek and thought we were in Lonely Wash–"

"It was an easy mistake," said Al. "They're so similar."

"Exactly. So if the program can make two patterns similar enough, in different places, the little ball can't tell which one is which, so it can jump from one to the other in less than …"

Her voice trailed off. *That's it! It's not some little bug, but SOS has the whole concept wrong. It's right step-by-step, but he doesn't get it.* She stood, pushing away her meal.

"Aren't you going to finish this," said Al, picking up her half-eaten burger. "You're going to be nothing but skin and bones, like those Spanish girls."

"You can have it. I've got to get back."

* * *

Marna ran all the way back, but Denise, Tess, and SOS had already restarted the review. "We thought you weren't coming back," Tess said. "You didn't seem to have your heart in the process."

Marna laid her hand on her chest, trying to calm her breathing so she could talk. "No, no, I loved it. I'm learning an enormous amount, but I just don't know enough about C++ to add anything sensible. But I have a question."

SOS urged her on with the usual hand gestures. "Questions are the best. Especially from reviewers who don't know a whole lot. Their questions usually upset a whole apple cart of assumptions."

Marna put her fingers to her lips. "And that's all right?"

"Oh, no, I hate it–for ten seconds. Then I let go of my ego and love discovering where I went wrong."

"You're sure you won't mind if I spill your apples?"

He put up his hands in mock defense. "Give it your best shot."

Marna looked to Tess and Denise for any sign of objection, then swallowed three deep breaths. "You're sure?"

He nodded confidently. "Sure. What's wrong with the code?"

One more breath, then it all came out in one long stream. "The coding's fine, but the design is all wrong. You've missed the concept entirely. I can see why you misunderstood, but I can't figure out how to make it any clearer. It's not like one single thread, but like a great weaving, with cross threads all moving back and forth in parallel–"

Her breath ran out, but she kept weaving her hands back and forth as if she were facing a loom. She gulped in another breath. "You see?"

Her words rattled on, but the others weren't getting it. "Can you slow down a bit?" Tess begged. "Are you saying the specs are all wrong?"

"Not *all* wrong, but kind of inside out." Marna stamped her foot on the wooden floor in frustration. "No, that's not it, either. I can see it all in my head, but it's hard to explain in words. In English words, anyway."

"Try Spanish," Denise suggested.

Marna kneaded that idea in her head for a moment. "No, that doesn't feel right, either." She rattled off a few quick sentences in Navajo, but the others returned only blank looks. She wrung her hands and switched to English. "I just can't do it."

"Sure you can," Tess said patiently. "Come on, sit down. We'll go through it slowly, as many times as you have to until we understand it."

Marna tried again. After fifteen frustrating minutes, Roger joined them. "I can't work anyway, with the way you guys are carrying on. Maybe I can help."

But he couldn't. More than an hour later, Tess called a break. Roger went back to fiddle with his apparatus, while Denise helped SOS brew a pot of his double-caffeinated coffee. Tess took Marna's hand and led her on a slow stroll around the lab, saying nothing. When they'd complete circled the room three times, Marna stopped next to Roger's workbench and stared at his wired aluminum frame. "It will work, Tess," she sobbed. "I know it will work, if only SOS can make the program right. But I just can't find the words. I can see it in my head, but–"

Roger put down his crimping tool. "You can really see it in your head?"

"Yes. Sure. That's always my problem, getting it out so someone else can understand it. I just–"

Roger raised his hand to silence Marna's babbling. "If you can really see it in your mind, then all we have to do is put you on Aremac."

CHAPTER TWENTY-TWO

When they finally finished slapping their foreheads for overlooking the most obvious solution, Marna let them drive her over to the Aremac office. She was more than a little nervous, and would have liked the walk to calm down and compose her thoughts. But everyone else was so excited, she didn't want to disappoint them.

They posted Rebecca as indoor guard, with Tom and Al and Heidi patrolling the outside for FDA agents. Roger fitted Marna with a snood, then let her fret while he calibrated the system for her brain patterns. She knew the story of Tess's persistent vegetative state, but by now she was so eager to show the internal pictures of her theory, there was no room left for anxiety in her emotional cupboard.

Finally, Roger ramped the superconducting magnet up to full power. SOS started the video recording, then they all sat enthralled as Marna narrated the flowing display of the workings of her mind, myriad rainbow butterflies, the *ho no gaille*.

To save time, Roger initially skipped color calibration, but Marna said the colors on the screen were not matching the colors in her model. Roger couldn't see how precise colors would matter, but when he finally adjusted them properly, SOS emitted a long, loud, "Ohhhhh!" Roger, Tess, and Denise still didn't see the difference, but SOS said he was now ready to design the program properly. "I can salvage most of the code, but I have to cast it into parallel threads."

Marna brow wrinkled in puzzlement as she worked the snood off her head, not bothering to straighten her hair. "But your processor isn't really parallel."

"Oh, don't worry. I can simulate the parallelism. Come on into my office. You can watch me do it right here. Then we'll test it on the simulator and ship the code over to the factory. We'll have the experiment running in no time."

* * *

In spite of SOS's optimism, it was after midnight before they unlocked the doors to the empty factory and rushed to their secret laboratory in back. Marna, suddenly anxious again, proposed that they wait until morning until their minds were all fresh. Before she finished her little speech, she knew from the eager expressions on their faces that there was no way they would allow her time to brood over the possibility of another failure. *At least now they all want me to succeed, but I don't want to let them down.*

Minutes later, the code was transferred to the experimental apparatus. Tess checked all the recording equipment. Denise double checked it, while SOS drummed his finger on his padded wrist rest and Roger poised his finger over the red start button. Finally, there were no more excuses.

"This is it," Roger announced. "An historic moment in the history of physics."

They all pressed close to the monitor that showed a magnified picture of the graphite ball resting at the right-hand end of the evacuated tube.

Roger pressed the button.

The ball didn't move.

SOS broke the disappointed silence. "Well, back to the drawing board."

* * *

Marna sat with her head heavy in her hands. *I was so sure it would work this time. Maybe I'm truly chasing a phantom, beautiful, but never to be caught. Just like the* ho no gaille.

Tess's voice dragged her out of her funk. "I guess we should have taken a break. There's probably a dozen bugs in the code."

Denise looked up from the video recording screen. "Not just in the code. I even screwed up the video."

"How could you screw up the video? It's idiot-proof," SOS said.

Marna had never heard him use that impatient tone with his girlfriend, but Denise simply responded with one of her rare smiles. "Then I must be an idiot. Look at this."

She transferred the image of the tube to the wall monitor, where they could all see there were two graphite spheres, one at each end. "Somehow it's reversed the image and overlaid it on itself."

SOS's tone softened. "Hey, maybe you didn't screw up. Maybe it's the real picture. It could have moved, then moved back. If it was fast enough, one frame would look like the ball was at both ends."

Denise shook her head. "That can't be it. All the frames look like this, not just one."

Tess, finger-traced the path between the two spheres' images. "Besides, there's no transition smear on the picture. So, the sphere did not pass from one end to the other."

SOS didn't give up. "Maybe it was fast enough not to register."

Marna couldn't hold it in any longer. "You're both wrong. And both right."

They looked at her, puzzled, waiting for an explanation.

"There's nothing wrong with the video. The sphere did not pass from one end to the other, not in the usual sense. *It was never in between.* And, yes, it was fast–faster than any instrument could measure. It's actually in both places at the same time."

"Like quantum entanglement?" Roger asked, fascinated.

"I call it quantum displacement," Marna's said, slowly and tentatively. "It's on a macro scale, so it's not quite the same thing as entanglement."

Tess jumped up and threw her arms around Marna. "That's wonderful. Incredible. We just proved your theory."

Marna's whole body remained stiff. Tess drew back, confused. "So why aren't you jumping up and down for joy?"

"Because we can't use it."

CHAPTER TWENTY-THREE

Marna hadn't wanted to stun them into silence, didn't want to lose their respect, but what could she do but tell the truth? They simply could not make the device they had in mind. *And it's totally my fault that I didn't anticipate this.*

As usual, SOS was the one to break the silence. "What do you mean we can't use it? Why not? Is it going to explode or something?"

"Don't you see? When we create the correct matching pattern of quantum space at both ends of tube, the ball can be at either end with equal probability. We can't send it to the upper end and know it's there. Before it can start to drop through the gravitational field, it will wind up back at the lower end. It's impossible. There's no way to extract energy–"

Frowning solemnly, Roger held up one finger. "Spoken like a true theoretician, Marna. But Rule Number One is this: Don't ever tell an inventor that something is impossible. In ten seconds or less, he'll prove you wrong."

Marna allowed a sliver of hope to slip through her misery. "It's not impossible?"

Roger jumped up and erased a corner of the nearest whiteboard. With a red pen, he sketched the tube in an upright position, then used a black pen to draw one graphite ball resting at the bottom and another all the way at the top. "When the fields are on, we don't have any way to know where the ball is. Right?"

"Yes, that's exactly the problem."

He began tapping on the board with the pen, alternating between the two black balls. "Someone call out a number."

"Five," SOS barked.

Roger stopped tapping. The pen rested on the top ball. "You see? If we cut off the fields at random, half the time we'll catch the ball at the top. With the field off, it will start to fall, inducing the current."

Marna was skeptical. "Okay, that will give one burst, but then how will it get back to the top."

"We'll just alternate rapidly on and off, at random, so half the time we'll catch it in the up position."

"Why does it have to be random?" Tess asked.

"If it's regular, we might set up a stable condition."

Tess persisted. "Yes, and that would be good. It would generate twice the power output."

"Only half right. It would either generate twice the power or no power at all, depending on which stable cycle it locks onto," said Roger, in a loving, not a critical, voice.

Marna's eyes teared up in envy, but she was pretty sure the others were to engaged to notice.

Tess quickly typed something into her laptop, then looked up. "Aha. So by randomizing, you guarantee that on the average it will generate half the power. Of course, you'll have to smooth the output, but that's trivial." She turned to Marna. "Do you see it? It *will* work."

Roger bowed to Marna. "I believe we've not only confirmed your theory, but designed at least one practical application."

Marna felt her whole body tingling, almost as she imagined an orgasm might feel. "Can you really make it work?"

"It may take a while," Roger explained, "but there's no doubt in my mind."

Marna studied the experimental setup from one side of the workbench and then the other. "Then my theory works? Really works?"

"I suppose there could be some other explanation," Roger said. "But within the range of experimental error, it's confirmed. We can reduce that error with more refined measurements, but the instruments are pretty expensive. I know you want definitive experimental proof of your theory, but for now our goal is to make a practical application. Your Nobel Prize will come later. For the moment, I think our measurements are close enough to make something practical."

"How close?" Marna asked.

"I'd say we're about ninety percent there–"

Marna clapped her hands as the erotic tingling grew.

"–but with most inventions, the first ninety percent takes only ten percent of the effort."

Marna looked at Tess, puzzled for a moment, then said, "So if this took two weeks, then the last ten percent will take eighteen more weeks."

Tess clasped her friend's shoulder. "It doesn't quite work like that, Marna. "The next nine percent of the work takes ninety percent of the effort. But the last one percent may take an infinite amount."

"What she means," said Roger, coming to Marna's rescue, "is that most inventions never actually make it to the market. Once we have a working model, we still have to make tests and design changes so we can be sure it's safe, even when broken.

We've also got to human-engineer it so ordinary people can use it, and then re-engineer it to standards so it works with existing systems."

"And doesn't interfere with them," Tess added. "Since this battery–battery charger, really–is based on a moving magnet, it's going to generate electromagnetic waves, and they could raise havoc with all sorts of other devices–"

"Like pacemakers?" Marna asked.

"That's the worst case scenario," said Roger.

SOS shook his head. "Except for explosive devices."

"So why not just shield it?" Marna suggested.

"Oh, we'll quite likely wind up doing that," said Tess. "But we can't have it weighing a hundred pounds, or even one. And it has to be able to be manufactured for a reasonable price, so we certainly can't use a diamond as the moving part, even if it were magnetic, which of course it isn't. And–"

Marna raised both hands in mock surrender. "Okay, okay. You see why I'm a *theoretical* physicist. I have no experience with these things, but is there any way I can help from now on? Other than by staying out of the way?"

"Oh, no," Tess said. "That's the last thing we want you to do. We can solve all these other problems, I'm sure, but all we've done so far is move the ball one time from A to B."

"But it went back and forth, many times," Marna objected.

Tess picked up the entire apparatus, which currently weighed about eight pounds, and stood it on one end on the workbench. "When we run it like this, with B above A, then with Roger's random on-off, it will drop back to A again, which will induce the current. But we still don't know what happens when it falls back to A and hits the bottom with a velocity. It has to bounce, at least a small amount and that will mess up the quantum effect. We have to catch it in precisely the right position–and that's a huge assumption right now–in order to send it back to B."

"But … " Roger's voice trailed off as he took the apparatus from Tess and turned it over in his hands for more than a minute. "But, Marna, when it gets back to B, will it have retained its velocity or not?"

"My theory doesn't say–so far at least. Why does that matter? It will generate electricity either way."

"But how *much* electricity? There's the rub." He rubbed the shaft of the device as if to bring his words home. "From the point of view of theory, it's a great breakthrough already. But, if it's going to be a practical device, we'd like to have the velocity retained. Otherwise, we could wind up trying to market a cell phone battery that's at least eight feet tall."

CHAPTER TWENTY-FOUR

Marna had seen Roger only once in the three weeks since their first quantum displacement. He had refused to leave the lingerie factory, except for a daily trip to his fast-sleep machine, striving to finish a working prototype of the cell phone battery charger in less than Marna's predicted eighteen weeks. Trying to beat Tess's prediction of running out of money in fourteen weeks, he was sleeping one hour a day in the modified Aremac and working twenty-three hours–minus junk-food snacks and bathroom breaks.

Marna stayed home at Nazim's residence, trying to work out the theory behind the velocity problem. Some days, Tess came over to the house to help out, but most of her help was supporting her friend through the nitty gritty of the divorce proceedings.

Karl wasn't making the divorce easy, either, though he still didn't know where she was. He had reached her cell phone once, but when Tess saw her crying, she took the phone away, then canceled the phone contract. Karl must have known from the court filings that Marna was somewhere in Illinois. He kept prying the attorneys for her phone number, if not her address.

The morning after the first real winter storm raced in off Lake Michigan, Roger insisted Marna's brothers fetch her to the battery lab. When she arrived, Roger had come through the sewing rooms to meet her at the front door. "We're stuck, Marna. We need your help."

"What's wrong? Things were going so well. Three weeks ago, you said we were ninety percent there."

Al was parking the pickup, but Tom stood next to Marna and urged her inside. "You two would stand out here and freeze if I let you get started. Besides, you're not supposed to talk about this stuff outside of your lab."

"Sorry," said Roger, yielding as Tom grabbed each of them by an elbow and rushed them past the sewing machine ladies.

Marna could barely wait until Roger locked the steel lab door behind them. "What happened to ninety percent done? I don't have vacation time forever."

"Well, we also told you that more than ninety percent of the work lay ahead. But we were wrong about the first statement, so we were definitely wrong about the second. We've got a lot more than ninety percent ahead. We might never make it work."

"I don't understand. What's the problem?"

"The problem is that we don't know what the problem is."

"Can we sit down?" Marna asked. "I think better sitting down."

"And take off your coat," Tess said, standing up from her computer monitor. "You're going to sweat to death, or I'm going to die watching you. I do *not* want to be running a sweat-shop."

Marna took off her coat and gloves, and all three pulled up brown steel folding chairs facing the whiteboard. Marna tossed her coat on another chair and took the lead. "Start by telling me what happened."

"What didn't happen would be more like it," Roger said. "We can't get any magnetic material to work as the displaced object. So, we won't be able to generate any electricity."

"What materials have you been successful with?"

"Beryllium worked fine, but that was about it. That and the graphite."

"Carbon, in other words. Beryllium and carbon." Marna stood and wrote Be and C on the board. "Low atomic weights."

"That's what you told us to try."

"Yes, because the theory says they'll be most susceptible to the displacement effect. Hydrogen would have been the best candidate, but obviously a gas wouldn't do the job. Same for helium." She wrote H and He on the board and put a line through each of them. "What about lithium?"

"Too reactive," said Tess. "Tarnishes right away as soon as it's exposed to air. We might use it if we could seal it with something."

Marna waved off that suggestion, wrote Li on the board, and crossed it off. "What about boron? That should be stable enough."

"That's just it," said Roger. "We tried a boron sphere, but it disintegrated in the device. And of course we couldn't use nitrogen, oxygen, fluorine, or neon–"

"–not unless we were going to run it super-cooled," Tess added. "Which would be impractical commercially."

"Okay, I understand," said Marna. "And I suppose you didn't want to handle raw sodium. So what about magnesium?"

"Broke up, just like the boron."

Marna's round face broke out into a huge, toothy smile.

"What's so funny about magnesium?" Tess demanded, not feeling amused.

"Isotopes."

"Isotopes?"

"Yes. Did you try aluminum?" Roger and Tess both nodded, and Marna raised her hand. "No, don't tell me. Aluminum worked fine, right?"

"Not exactly," said Roger, but there was a questioning look on his face.

"What does that mean, not exactly?"

"It was very hard to calibrate the software to make it work. Much harder than the others. We had to increase the precision, and the calculation was much slower."

"Of course. That fits perfectly."

"Fits what?"

"The theory. I mean, the refinements I've been making. It's basically why I recommended you start with the low end of the periodic table. Heavier elements are much more complex– you could see that in the equations I gave you, right?"

"Yep," Roger nodded, discouraged. "At the rate the complexity grows, aluminum may be the most complex we'll be able to compute in real time. Maybe silicon. Which means–"

"Let's worry about that later. You did succeed with aluminum, didn't you?"

"Yes, we did."

"Well, you probably won't succeed with silicon, but that remains to be seen."

The buzzer sounded. Someone was at the door. Tess and Heidi got up and checked, then came back with a message for Marna. "It's your brothers. They say you shouldn't skip lunch."

"Oh, darn. They always break into my best thinking. I don't have any trouble skipping meals when I'm working, but they think I'm too skinny as it is." She clasped her hands on her waist. "Not by Anglo standards. Okay, tell them to bring me something."

"What do you want?"

"I don't want anything, but don't tell them that. Bring anything, because I won't eat it anyway, but they won't know."

Tess returned to the door and passed the message. "I told them you wanted a one of those New Mexican green chili cheeseburgers. They laughed and said you'll have to settle for a Whopper. No green chili in Chicago. They'll bring some for all of us. And two without buns for Heidi." Heidi's tail slapped the floor a mile a minute.

"Heidi can eat mine," Marna said. "Do you want to hear my theory, or do you want to wait for the food?"

"You're kidding, right?" Roger laughed. "If you know what's going wrong, you'd better tell us now or you'll never eat another burger."

"All right." She started scribbling equations on the board. "You know the main equations, so I'm just writing the new ones, in a kind of shorthand."

Tess waved her off. "Just give us the bottom line. What's going on?"

Marna reluctantly put down the marker and sat. "Okay, let me ask one more thing. When you did the graphite, did you weigh the sphere before and after?"

Both her listeners looked puzzled, and Roger said, "No, why would we do that?"

"Okay, then did you happen to notice if there was any carbon residue somewhere inside the chamber after the displacement?"

"No," said Tess. "It was perfectly clean."

"Not the first time," said Roger. "You weren't there the first time. I remember having to wipe out the inside of the chamber, but I thought it was just some dirt we hadn't noticed."

"I don't think it was dirt. I think it was carbon-13 that got left behind when the carbon-12 was displaced. Might have been some entrapped nitrogen, too, but you wouldn't have noticed that."

"It looked just like dust."

"Carbon looks like that. Both isotopes."

"But I never saw it," said Tess.

"Then I'll bet Roger always used the same graphite sphere every time."

Roger frowned. "I guess so. I never thought about it."

Tess nodded with understanding. "So after the first time, the carbon-13 was removed from the sphere, so I never saw its dust. If that's true, we can test it."

Tess started for the test bench, but Marna stopped her. "We can do that later. Let me tell you the rest. I didn't see this implication of the theory, but when you told me about the boron, I started to suspect. You see, the carbon-13 isotope is only about one percent of natural carbon, so if it was left behind when the graphite displaced, the sphere would remain intact. But boron is about an eighty-twenty mixture of B-11 and B-10, if I remember correctly. So, leaving behind one or the other–I don't know which one you were tuned to–would likely shatter the sphere."

Now Roger was nodding, too. "And magnesium? Same thing?"

"I think so, though there's three isotopes, about eighty-ten-ten. You were probably tuned to Mg-24."

"And," Tess added, "I'll bet aluminum has only one isotope, so it didn't shatter."

"Actually, it has about half a dozen, but all the others are radioactive. I suspect those didn't exist in your sample–except possibly in minute trace amounts. Not enough to matter."

"And silicon's the same?" Roger asked.

"Not exactly. It has three stable isotopes, but one of them makes up more than ninety percent of what's found in nature. I'm not sure what effect separating out the other two would have on the structure of the sphere."

"But we could purify the material, like the first pass of the carbon did," said Tess. "It would be another manufacturing step, but that would solve the problem."

Roger shot out of his chair and stomped up to the whiteboard. He grabbed the red marker and started scribbling all over Marna's notes. "It won't solve anything," he growled. "Nothing. Silicon isn't magnetic, and neither is aluminum or any of the lighter elements. If even chromium is too big, then we don't have a magnet to move through the coils. And we can't use alloys, because they'll separate. The whole idea won't work."

He threw down the marker and strode away, accompanied by the ever-guarding dog. Over his shoulder, he called, "I'm going to the toilet to throw up."

Tess looked at Marna and raised her eyebrows. "He's not usually like that. I think he's really crushed. But he'll calm down and come up with some other invention."

"He's already come up with another invention."

"What do you mean?"

"The device separates out one specific element mixed with others, so–"

Tess's eyes widened. "So it could make us rich. Like, there's plenty of gold in the world, if we could only separate it from its natural medium–like seawater. And with this device, we can–"

She stopped, suddenly, noticing the severe frown on Marna's face. "What's wrong? You should be ecstatic. Is there something wrong with my idea?"

"No, the idea is perfect. It's just too perfect. The device could be used to separate isotopes of uranium or plutonium. Every country in the world could build nuclear weapons for pennies. I've created a monster."

CHAPTER TWENTY-FIVE

Marna's brothers knocked on the door with lunch. Tess said to Marna,"Chase Roger out of the bathroom, then go in there and hide your tears. Maybe wipe them off if you're finished crying. For now, anyway. If your brothers see you crying, we'll have to stop and explain, so let's wait until we update Roger before we cry some more."

Once Marna was out of sight, Tess opened the door. Tom handed her two large bags of burgers, fries, coleslaw, and root beer. Heidi sniffed each bag and wagged her approval.

"How are things going?" Tom asked. "Not that I'd understand anything you're doing."

Tess winked, feeling he would recognize the meaning of what she was saying. "Marna's in one of her thinking moods. I'll try to make her eat something, but no guarantees. If she doesn't eat, I'll let you know so you can stuff her tonight at supper."

"If she's finished thinking by then," he said, laughing as he closed the door.

Tess locked the door, then returned with the food to the whiteboard area. Marna had already returned from hiding and was explaining their biggest problem to Roger. "I don't get it," he was saying. "Why would we worry about uranium or plutonium when we can't even work with chromium, which is a fraction of their atomic weight?"

"Because maybe with enough resources, or maybe when computers get much faster, people will be able to quantum-displace uranium. Right now, the only thing that stands in the way is the inability to compute the quantum states fast enough."

Tess slipped over to her worktable to retrieve her computer. "But Marna, that's exactly what makes us safe. Look."

She tapped a few keys and held out the computer. Marna stared intently at the screen. "What am I seeing?"

"Those are the computation times, in cycles, for each of the quantum states that succeeded. See, here, look at the ratios."

"Ratios to what?"

"The time for beryllium. Carbon took about twenty times the cycles needed for beryllium."

"That's not much."

"No, but look at aluminum. Sixty-five *million* times the cycles. We haven't worked it analytically, except in a rough way, but we suspect it's exponential."

Marna's twisted a lock of hair between her fingers. Her face went blank. Tess allowed her to remain inside her head for five minutes, then started opening the lunch bags. She found the bag with the naked burgers and broke off half a patty for Heidi.

Fifteen minutes later, the humans were wiping their faces with little soap-soaked papers when Marna finally emerged mentally into the real world. "Could be. Yes, it could be. I'll have to work it out in detail, but it could be."

Tess handed her the one uneaten hamburger. "Eat this while I show you some more numbers."

Marna accepted the burger unenthusiastically. She nibbled while Tess wrote on the board, reading aloud as she wrote. "If it is really exponential based on atomic weight, then

AREMAC POWER • 142

the uranium calculation will take more than ten to the hundredth power more cycles." Tess starting writing zeros on the board, then gave up and wrote, "googol." "That's not the search engine, but the number."

Marna fed Heidi a finger-pinch of hamburger. "I know."

"So you know this uranium calculation is beyond any computer, past, present, or future. Or any combination of computers."

"Of course I know, but maybe someone will optimize the calculation. Find a new algorithm."

Tess wrote three more zeros on the board. "Actually, it was the one-hundred-and-third power, but I left off these three zeros for simplicity. And the contingency you're talking about."

Now Marna was fingering her grandmother's brown beads. Tess sighed. *Not again.* "What is it now?"

"Uranium's not the only problem. It could be hydrogen, and there's no calculation problem there."

"You're talking about heavy hydrogen, right? Deuterium and tritium? Like in bombs?"

"No, not really. I mean, sure, you *could* build a device to separate hydrogen isotopes, but they're not that hard to separate with existing technology. No, I'm talking about separating hydrogen from anything–water, for example. And using it for fuel."

Roger spread his hands, shoulders raised. "That's a great idea. I'll invent that next. Nothing wrong with low-cost fuel."

"You're wrong, darling." Tess sat down next to Marna and putting an arm over her shoulder. "Marna's thinking about the economic disruption that abundant cheap fuel would cause. Am I right?"

Marna nodded, biting down on her upper lip.

Tess stroked Marna's hair. "You're right, of course, but eventually, someone else is going to find out about quantum displacement. At least we can release these effects to the world slowly, to give societies time to adapt. It's the best we can do."

"I suppose. But I'll have to quit."

Roger did a double take. "You can't quit. We need you."

"She doesn't mean this job, darling." Tess gave him a pitying look. "You're being fat-headed. You shouldn't have had all the fries. Marna has to quit her Los Alamos job."

"Oh. Hey, that would be great. But why?"

"Because eventually someone there will pick up her theory and realize the implications, and then the government will take over. And she'll never be able to publish. Marna, is that going to be all right?"

"Yes. I mean, no, but yes. I never wanted to be famous–"

"–but you would give up a sure Nobel Prize. A lot to ask."

Marna gave up on her burger instead, holding it out, bun and all, to Heidi, as if to say she wasn't interested in material things. "Not if it's necessary to avoid hurting millions, or billions, of people. But won't everyone know when they see your first patents?"

Roger looked at Tess as if to say, "you tell her."

"There won't be any patents. Everything about this project has to be what's called a 'trade secret'–precisely because even one patent would let the cat out of the bag."

"But people could just reverse engineer any invention, so they'd know anyway."

Now it was Roger's turn. "That's why we have to engineer the invention so it can't be reverse-engineered." He looked around at the brick walls as if suddenly thinking they were too flimsy. "If we can't do that, we can't allow it out of this lab."

Chapter Twenty-Six

On Saturday, Tess had SOS bring Denise to the battery lab. The storm from earlier in the week was long forgotten. Temperatures had risen twenty degrees and the snow was gone except for a few dirty piles in the shadows between the brick apartment buildings. SOS was back to wearing short-sleeved t-shirts. Today's read, on the front, "There are 10 kinds of people in the world." On the back, it said, "Those who read binary and those who don't."

Like SOS, everyone was dressed in their usual more-than-casual clothing–excepting Denise, who was wearing her banker's blue suit with white shirt. Tess had put Heidi outside to patrol the sidewalks with Tom and Al, hoping to save Denise's suit from a coating of dog hairs, but with Heidi's shed undercoat all over the lab, it hadn't helped much. Denise was already picking stray hairs off her sleeve.

Denise had been generating the cash flow that allowed the rest of the team to keep experimenting. She worked overtime at the Fourth Federal Bank of Illinois, building a system to protect their customer files from identity theft. One of the bank's clerks had taken home a laptop containing unencrypted account files for their premier customers. The laptop had been stolen, the accounts invaded, the press alerted, and the bank almost broken. They were willing to pay almost any price to assure their customers there would be no more identity theft. For them,

Denise's FBI experience was a godsend, not just for what she could do, but for the public relations value.

The bank wanted Denise to work on Saturday, to make up for time lost in Monday's storm, but even though they were willing to pay time and a half, Tess turned them down. "That was a lot of money," SOS said as he brought Denise through the steel door into the lab. "Given our financial condition, this meeting must be really important."

Tess motioned them to the kitchen wall. "Nothing could be more important, Find something to drink and come sit down while Roger finishes checking the room for bugs."

"Bugs?" SOS looked suspiciously at the ceiling. "Not that again."

"That, always," said Tess ruefully. "From now on."

"Until?"

"Until forever. That's what we're here to talk about. Security."

SOS emitted a long, sharp whistle. "More than we have already?"

"Much more. We're onto something huge–beyond huge. We can expect lots of people to be after our secrets."

"Bigger than Aremac? What could that be?" SOS popped his can of Jolt Cola.

"I'm not going into that now, because the less you know that you don't need to know, the better. But if you need a comparison, think of the Manhattan Project."

SOS tried to whistle again, but all that came out was a bluster of dry air.

Once they were all seated–excepting Roger, who was still scanning the room–Tess stepped over the the white board. Her picking up the marker pen was their sign that the meeting was officially open. "After need-to-know, our first line of defense is to keep this group as small as possible. Ideally, we wouldn't add anybody. I can trust all of you, at least if you're not tortured or threatened, but remember Bonnie."

"Who's Bonnie," Marna asked.

"She applied for a job when we were building Aremac. She was well qualified, but she turned out to be an industrial spy. A very nice woman, actually, but they threatened her child." Tess looked at each of them. "In a way, we're lucky that none of us have children that anybody can threaten." Nobody commented on her voice's sad echo of her lost baby.

Roger put his bug detector back in its case and returned it to its place in an upper cabinet. "All clear, as best I can tell. But we can never be perfectly sure."

Marna looked around at the painted brick walls. "At least we have no windows. I hated that when I first came here, but now I'm glad." She looked up at the three skylights. "And my brothers are watching the roof. And around the building. Keeps them out of trouble–" She inclined her head towards the door, behind which some forty young women were busily sewing underwear.

Roger raised his hand, but didn't wait for Tess to recognize him. "If we can't hire anybody new, then I think it's time for the rest of you to try out my sleep machine. I've been super-productive for weeks, and no harmful side effects."

"There's *always* side effects," said SOS. "You know that better than anyone. You just haven't noticed them yet, unless it's those headaches. But sure, I'm willing to try."

Denise nodded. So did Marna. Tess acknowledged them with a nod. "That's great, but I'm going to hold myself out for a while. One of us should, and I'm the least useful."

SOS started to boo and hiss. "No false humility, Tess. You're the most important person around here–and *that's* why you shouldn't be experimenting on yourself. Same conclusion, opposite reason."

Tess stuck her tongue out at SOS, but she was smiling. "No, Denise is the most important person around here now."

"Me," Denise mouthed, pointing to herself with her fist.

"Yes, you. Your first and foremost assignment will be head of security."

Denise swallowed hard. "Me? What about Rebecca? She's the one who can shoot people."

"You can use her for that kind of physical security if you wish." Tess looked up at the skylights. "And Marna's brothers, if you want and if they're willing. But your principal job will be to oversee all aspects of security, the way you're doing at the bank. There can't be any holes–physical, technical, human, or otherwise. Can you do that?"

"I, uh, guess I can try, but you'll have to help me." She looked around at each of them, making eye contact the way she rarely did. "I mean, all of you will have to help me."

"Anything you need," Tess assured her. "I know this is a total surprise, but I've heard about the job you're doing at the bank. You're clearly the best qualified among us. And, oh, by the way, you're going to have to terminate the bank job as soon as possible. Security is going to be a full-time job."

"Don't we need the money?"

"We do, but we're going to have to find other ways to finance ourselves. That's my job–though as usual, I'm open to suggestions. Right now, I'm thinking of looking into this Justice for Africa business. Maybe we can sell them a few Aremacs to tide us over."

CHAPTER TWENTY-SEVEN

Tess had worried for days whether Denise could truly lead their security effort. *She needs to be assertive, but she always seems to defer to her lover boy. I've thought of a million ways to encourage her, but the very best idea is still to throw her in the middle of the lake and see right away if she can swim. If she needs to be rescued, this was the best time to find out.*

Roger had his hand up, and Marna looked at Tess as if she also had something to say. Tess waved them away. *Time to sink or swim.* "I'm stepping down and turning this meeting over to Denise, so she can get started."

Denise hesitated for five seconds, then ten, and Tess began to contemplate who would be her next best alternative. Before she had her first name, however, Denise was on her feet, straightening her skirt and moving to the board. She extended her tiny hand to Tess for the marker, then waved her boss to her seat and calmly erased the variety of notes on the board.

"There are probably a thousand people in the world who know more about security systems than I do—" Denise paused and looked at each of them for a long moment, Tess first, then Rebecca, Roger, Marna, and, finally, her one true love, SOS. "—but none of them are in this room, so I guess it's up to me."

Tess had to keep her mouth from gaping. In the twinkling of an eye, Denise had transformed herself from a virtual shadow of SOS into a confident, well-informed, clear communicator. Thinking back, Tess realized that Denise had done this before, any time she was describing technical matters in which she was immersed. Evidently, her bank assignment had immersed her in security problems, and not just the cryptographic aspects. *And I was so anxious, I didn't notice.*

" … everything starts with *physical* security," Denise was saying. "If we can't protect our computers and our persons, we'll always be vulnerable to theft and kidnapping. All the encryption in the world won't protect an ATM if someone jackhammers it from the sidewalk."

A shadow crossed one of the skylights. SOS pointed upwards. "Well, I definitely feel better with Marna's brothers on duty, but there's only two of them."

"Plus Heidi," said Tess. "No stranger gets past her unannounced."

"I have five more brothers," said Marna, counting on her fingers. "And my father and lots of cousins. … though we'd probably have to exclude a few of my cousins."

Denise waited for Marna to finish, then wrote "threat" and "response" on the whiteboard. "That's a good thought, Marna, but numbers aren't enough. If the threat was just your husband after you, I'm sure *Tse* and *Ahiga* could handle it nicely–"

Tess was surprised Denise knew the brothers' Navajo names. *Maybe I should stop being surprised by anything Denise knows.*

"–but if some large organization was after the five of us–" Denise acknowledged each of the others with a slight nod. "–how many people would it take to guard us, twenty-four-seven?" Tess thought it was a rhetorical question, but Denise paused, waiting for an answer.

"There's no answer," said Tess. "Not unless we know how big the organization is, and what they're willing to do."

"Exactly," Denise said while writing something on the board. She stepped back, revealing the words "potentially infinite" under the word "threat." "At some point, there's a physical threat that's just too big to defend against. We need to decide what our cutoff is going to be, and what we'll do if a bigger threat comes along."

Roger bent his neck in puzzlement. "But if we can't defend against it, then by definition, we can't do anything,"

"Not true. For example, we can booby-trap our hardware to destroy itself if tampered with, and if our secrets were more important than our lives, we could all carry suicide pills."

Suddenly everyone was talking at once. Denise didn't try to shout over them, but stood quietly with her arms crossed defiantly until they all noticed and calmed down. "Let's not deal with *that* issue now, not before I've gone over the whole security concept. There may be other ways to deal with that eventuality, so let's wait."

This was simply too disturbing for Tess, who obviously hadn't thought this through as deeply as Denise. "I'd like an example of those other ways, before I can continue."

Denise shrugged, a slight show of impatience. "Okay. One basic line of defense is to ensure that no one of us has all the information needed to understand our inventions."

"So they'll just kidnap two of us. Or all of us."

"Yes, but at least that reduces the probabilities. I didn't say it was a perfect solution. I don't believe there *is* any perfect solution, but there are ways of making an opponent's task so expensive they may give up before they start."

Roger, who had been sitting with his elbows on his knees and his head in his hands, looked up. "Like by making public what they're trying to do to us? If they want to keep their own behavior secret from the public?"

"That's one way, and we'll consider that as part of our plans. But can I go on now, to some other issues?"

Roger put his head back in his hands, but SOS raised his index finger. "One more thing. There's only one Aremac to protect–"

"So far," said Tess.

"Okay, so far. But if–when–we start selling battery chargers, there will be thousands or millions out there. How can we protect them?"

Denise lowered her eyes a fraction, as if in deference to her lover. "I believe that's a solvable problem. The bank wanted to protect some proprietary software–like their algorithms for currency exchange decisions–so I learned that there are several companies who will seal a loaded chip in a ceramic block. The block acts as a dongle, plugged into their mainframe when they're processing currency deals."

Rebecca coughed into her hand. "Dongle? Is that like a dangle?"

Denise looked blank. "What's a dangle?"

"It's English. I'll explain later, in the ladies. So what's a dongle?"

"It's a hardware device that authenticates software. When the dongle isn't present, the software won't run. Or at least won't run some of its features. So if there's only one dongle, you can only run one copy of the software at a time, on one computer. It's kind of like a key."

"Any half-soaked scrote can copy a key."

"Not these keys, Rebecca. The chip can't be removed from the dongle without destroying it, or in some cases, destroying the chip's contents."

"Doesn't that create problems of heat dissipation when they run the software?" Roger asked, looking up but blinking his eyes as if he'd just awakened from a stupor.

"Yes. The bank dealt with that by limiting the amount of computation–the algorithms themselves were pretty simple, so they used a rather primitive chip. But if you wanted more speed, you could use a powerful chip and bathe it in a coolant."

"We can do that for Aremac," said SOS, "but cooling wouldn't be practical for the charger, not if it's going to be portable."

"That depends on our algorithms, doesn't it? It's a software engineering problem, and that's *your* department."

Tess was about to respond when her phone tickled her hip. Roger and SOS started discussing algorithms the instant she started listening. They stopped the instant she put her hand over the phone and spoke to Marna.

"Let's take a break. Your husband is outside, trying to force his way in."

CHAPTER TWENTY-EIGHT

The first thing Tess noticed when she reached the outer door of the lingerie factory was the chill in the air. The temperature outside must have dropped fifteen degrees while they'd been in the windowless lab debating security.

The second thing she noticed was Marna's husband, Karl. When she saw the expression on Karl's movie-star face, she realized that not all the chill in the outside world was caused by the weather.

Two uniformed police officers stood with Karl. Behind them, Tess could see Heidi keeping an eye out, looking threatening. Al was also keeping an eye out, but without the intimidating look, unless you imagined the portent behind the perfectly neutral expression. She suspected Tom was watching the back door.

On Karl's left, a petite policewoman with a heart-shaped face and stray wisps of dirty blond hair escaping under her officer's cap held a clipboard with poised pen. On his right stood a much taller man with bushy black eyebrows and a pot-belly hanging over his equipment belt. He held nothing at the moment, but seemed ready to grab from that belt whatever tool the occasion demanded. Tess had heard how cops were often killed when intervening in domestic disputes. Given the expression on Karl's face, the cop's readiness seemed appropriate.

"What's the problem, officers?"

The clipboard seemed to be the blond's badge of leadership. "This gentleman claims his wife has been kidnapped and is being held hostage here." She peered past Tess through the open door. "What is this place? Some kind of sweatshop?"

"Not at all, officer. Would you like to come inside out of the cold? We have nothing to hide."

Once they entered the outer sewing room, Tess turned to face the group. "Would you like to see the factory permit? That's in the office."

The blond, blew on her bare hands, then looked at Karl. "Later. Sir, do you see your wife here?"

"Over there," Karl pointed, indicating the far corner. Tess was surprised to see Marna sewing at one of the industrial machines, on which was stacked a foot-high pile of baby blue cloth panties waiting to be hemmed. *Good work, Marna. Maybe they'll not look into the back room.*

Marna didn't look up from her work, though the other women in the room kept taking peeks at the police, or perhaps at the good-looking man between them.

Karl made a break for Marna, but didn't get five feet before the policeman grabbed his arm and stopped him dead. "You'll stay here with me while my partner checks out your wife. If she is your wife."

Karl struggled vainly to free himself. "Oh, she's my wife all right. I've got papers to prove it." He reached for his inner pocket, only to be stopped by the cop's ominous raised eyebrow.

"Well, let's see what your wife has to say for herself."

The policewoman had reached Marna and was exchanging words that Tess could not hear. Marna's body language seemed unusually calm and controlled. After three or four minutes, the policewoman returned to where Tess was standing and Karl was being held. "She admits they're married, but she says she's filed for divorce and that she's here of her own free will, trying to avoid him. She also says she has a restraining order, but from Mexico."

The lady cop stepped close to Karl, and though she was at least six inches shorter, it looked to Tess like a controlling position. "She says you hit her. That you stole her money. That you were screwing some rich lady in a Las Vegas casino." She sounded like she was reading criminal charges, which, Tess thought, perhaps she was.

"I never hit her, and the money was mine. And she never saw me screwing anybody."

Tess wondered if the police could see through Karl's evasions. *What a skilled liar. He'd kicked her, not hit her. Though they were now in Chicago, their official residence was New Mexico–a community property state. And, as far as I know, Marna couldn't actually see through hotel room doors.* "Ask him if he kicked her."

"Let us handle this, Miss," said the policeman, releasing his grip on Karl and herding Tess some distance away. "And who are you, and what is your role here, anyway?"

"I'm Dr. Tesla Fixman, and I'm … her boss. I gave her a job here so she could support herself away from her husband where she'd be safe." Tess looked around and saw Roger's Uncle Suhayb standing in the open doorway of his office. She decided to take a chance. "Many of the women here are avoiding abusive men. Would you like to interview them?"

"Not right just now, but I would like to see their papers."

Tess suspected this was a bluff to intimidate her into staying out of the dispute. All she said was, "Fine." She escorted the giant cop over to introduce him to Roger's uncle. She left him there and returned to support Marna who had now been brought over to confront her husband. *She doesn't really need me, though. She seems to be handling the situation perfectly well all on her own.*

Karl kept glancing around apprehensively, first at the policewoman, then at Heidi, as he sweet-talked his wife. "You know it's all a misunderstanding, darling. I've got a nice room just a few blocks from here where we can talk this over and get it all cleared up. Everyone misses you. All your friends."

Marna looked at him in disbelief. "Everyone? You don't even know who my friends are."

"You're being modest. Maybe you don't know how many people love you and miss you. Like I do."

Tess thought she might vomit if he went on in this cloying tone, but Marna put a stop to it. "I'm not going anywhere with you, Karl. If you're lonely, invite one of your girlfriends to your nice room."

"But you're my wife. You *have* to go with me."

Out of the corner of her eye, Tess could see Heidi stiffen as his syrupy tone turned aggressive.

Karl started to reach for Marna's arm, but the policewoman slapped his hand away. "It's up to *her*, Mister. Whether you're married or not, she can come and go as she pleases."

"We'll see about that," Karl snapped.

Heidi growled, which caught Karl's attention for a moment. He inched backward, then regained his offensive attitude toward Marna. "My lawyer says that if you leave me, he'll take away everything you own. And half your earnings. At least."

"Look around, Karl," Marna said calmly. "Do you think we make that much money sewing underwear? Maybe you should get a job and give *me* half."

Tess bit the inside of her cheeks, knowing that Marna wasn't even making the piddling wages of these sewing machine operators. And that, if plans worked out, after the divorce, she might be one of the richest women in the world–richer even than J. K. Rowling. But she couldn't give any hint of that, or Karl's lawyers would be all over the money like paparazzi on Princess Di.

"You can't fool me," Karl hissed. "You've got lots of money hidden somewhere. And we'll find it."

"Right, Karl. It's under the floor mat in my car. By the way, where *is* my car? One of my brothers wants to fetch it for me and drive it to Chicago."

"It's not your car. It's *our* car. Part of our community property, according to New Mexico law."

"Come on, Karl. Don't be mean. You've got your own car. You don't need two."

Karl looked away. Tess thought Marna didn't see it, so she said, "Where's *your* car, Karl? It's community property, too. According to New Mexico law."

"I don't have a car. Just the one."

"You sold it," Marna said. "Didn't you?"

"I have expenses," Karl said defensively. "What was I supposed to do when you left your job without even telling me?"

Tess noticed the policeman over by the office, smiling at Uncle Suhayb, shaking his hand. "Do you need anything else?" Tess asked the policewoman. "We have orders to fill, and all this drama is distracting. I need to get my girls back to work."

The policeman returned. He bent down and scratched Heidi behind the ear while he gave his partner a nod.

She turned to Karl. "I think we've got what we need. Let's go, Mister. These ladies have work to do."

Karl didn't move until the policeman took hold of his elbow and steered him toward the door. Heidi followed.

"I'll be back," Karl called over his shoulder.

The policewoman stayed with Marna until her partner was out the door, then said in a confidential tone, "You might want to ask your lawyer to get you a local restraining order."

Restraining order? Tess thought. *No way. They work fine against struggling young companies like ours, but they're useless against abusive husbands.*

CHAPTER TWENTY-NINE

Even after Tess watched Denise skillfully herd the team back to the lab and sit them down with the door locked, she noticed that everyone else continued chattering about Karl's intrusion. Marna looked as if she were pulling off her fingernails. "He suspects, doesn't he?"

"Suspects what?" asked Roger.

"That we're on to something that might make a lot of money. He's going to try to get his hands on some of it. A lot of it."

Tess took Marna's hand between both of hers. "Let's leave that to the lawyers. We'll get this divorce over, nice and clean and quick, then he'll have no basis for a claim."

SOS, oblivious to any need to calm Marna, volunteered his opinion. "I've heard that lawyers can *always* find some basis for a claim."

"That brings us back on topic," Denise said quietly, making a slow gathering gesture that seemed to hypnotize SOS into closing his mouth and sitting down. "Spies can always find some basis for cracking secrets. I suggest we take advantage of this experience with Karl and see what we can learn by pretending he was a spy trying to find out what we're doing in here."

SOS fiddled with his iPod, having trouble making his earbud stick without catching his long hair. "Why pretend? He *was* trying to find out what we're doing in here."

Roger looked up from writing notes in his engineering book. "I learned something. I saw what Marna did out there, with the sewing machine. It was brilliant. They never even thought of looking in this room. Didn't even know it existed. And it gave me an idea of how to solve all these security problems. Maybe we should drop this invention business and go into the lingerie business with my uncle."

SOS finally had his earbud in place. "Way cool. I could tell everyone I was in ladies' underwear." When he saw the look Denise gave him, he sealed his mouth with his index finger.

"Well, darling," Tess said to Roger. "If you invent things, you change the world. If you can't deal with that, then, yes, you'd be better off in bras and panties."

SOS choked. Rebecca smiled knowingly. Tess thought Marna and Denise were blushing, but with their dark skins, she couldn't be sure. Roger, however, was definitely high pink. "All right. I know this is getting tough, but it's only going to get tougher. So who wants out?"

Nobody moved, and Tess was about to ask Denise to move on to the next security topic when Marna's hand rose tentatively. "I do."

I thought she was starting to feel part of the team. What did I miss? "You do?"

"Yes, but first I want out of this building. Right now it smells wrong, like it was contaminated by Karl's presence. Not safe. Can we please go somewhere else?"

Tess knew better than to attempt a rational argument to talk Marna out of something she didn't arrive at by rational thought, especially on the subject of Karl. "Let's take you home to Uncle Nazim's. I don't think Karl knows where that is."

"But if he follows us, then he'll know."

"Can your brothers deal with a shadow?"

A tiny smile crept through Marna's sorrowful face, a smile that immediately turned to apprehension. "I'm afraid of what they would do to him."

Is she concerned for her brothers, or for Karl? Tess thought, but she said, simply, "We'll tell them to restrain themselves. Now, grab your coat. We're going out."

It was still cold outside, but the sun had made an appearance and the air was clear, so they decided to walk to Uncle Nazim's, stopping at Millie's Vienna Red Hots, which was only two blocks out of their way. Tess thought it was a bit early for lunch, but the stop would give Tom and Al a chance to check out any suspicious followers.

All the way to Millie's, Tess kept looking over her shoulder to see if anyone was following. She saw nothing, not even Tom and Al. But before she had taken the first bite of her "with-everything," Al came in and ordered four take-outs. While he stood waiting at the counter, he sent Tess a subtle nod.

He doesn't want to upset his sister, she thought. She excused herself and slipped up to the counter to order extra fries which she had no intention of eating.

"There are two of them," Al said quietly. "But it's not Karl."

"You think he's hired someone?"

"He couldn't afford it, but he might have steered them onto Marna."

"Can you tell who they are? FBI?"

"No, I'd recognize FBI. We see their type snooping around the Rez. These are reporters."

Tess's fries arrived. She paid with a twenty-dollar bill so the server would have to step away and make change.

"How do you know?"

"We asked them. They say they heard Maralah was fired from the lab for mishandling classified information."

"Oh, shit. Who told them that?"

"Could have been Karl, but they wouldn't say. If you want, we can persuade them to say."

I'll bet you can. "Best to have nothing to do with them. The last thing we want now is publicity. Can you lose them?"

"*We* could, but you probably can't."

"I'd rather not have any violence, Al. Can't we just ignore them?"

"If they find out about Uncle Nazim's, they'll never leave our sister alone. Better to get rid of them once and for all."

I don't think I want to know about this. "Reporters. Jeez, they creep me out."

"All the more reason to send them packing." With that, Al took his sack of hot dogs, paid, and left without waiting for change.

CHAPTER THIRTY

Tess looked around Millie's, the posters and bumper stickers plastered on the walls, the neon beer signs, and the windows that offered a clear view of the neighborhood. She sniffed the delicious odor of garlic, and decided that this was as good a place as any to clear up Marna's desire to leave. The six of them had the only large table, and all six smaller tables were on the other side of the dining area. Any conversation would be masked by the clatter from the open kitchen behind the counter, but still she warned the others to keep their voices down.

She opened by assuring Marna that Karl wasn't following them, omitting the information about the reporters. *I'll tell them later when Marna isn't so upset.* "Marna, can you clarify what you meant by wanting out? Do you want to leave the team?"

"Oh, no." She seemed genuinely taken aback by that idea. "I want *all* of us out. Out of the country, that is. Or out of Chicago in any case."

"Oh, my." *That's the last thing I expected.* "Because of Karl?"

"Not just Karl. If we chose the right place, we could make it much harder for any others to intrude on our space."

Tess wiped a piece of pickle relish from the corner of her mouth. "I don't know. If we chose the wrong place, we could make it much *easier* to follow us." *But the reporters are another reason to try to find the right place.*

SOS waved toward a travel poster on the far wall. "Some Pacific island would be perfect. Somewhere with monster surf."

Before Tess could stop them, everyone started calling out favorite vacation spots–Switzerland, Sweden, New Zealand, Costa Rica–until they noticed Marna had her hand up, waiting for them to slow down. "I was thinking of the Navajo Nation. On the Rez, I have a large clan and many sister clans, and no Anglos could sneak up on us unnoticed."

Denise jotted "Navajo Nation" on her notepad, adding a question mark and holding it up so all could see. With a scissors gesture, she cut off further suggestions. "That's an interesting idea, Marna. If we do decide to move, though, we can't go right away. So, for now, our best security for the charger is that nobody knows about it."

"For now," said SOS. "But if we produce an energy source that lasts forever, then everyone will have one and everyone will know."

Tess, her hot dog finished, sat back, laced her fingers across her belly and tapped her thumbs together. "Who says it has to last forever?"

Three teenaged girls with bare midriffs opened the door, letting in a blast of cold air. SOS leaned over the table toward Marna, but waited until the girls reached the counter before whispering. "That's the theory, isn't it? Marna?"

Marna matched his quiet tone. Tess could barely hear her. "Yes, that's what the theory says. The device produces energy, and all it consumes is a trickle for the chips. So it *could* last forever."

Tess joined in on the whispering. "We don't have to *let* it last forever."

Denise slammed down her pen, bouncing a couple of Tess's fries out of their basket. "I *hate* planned obsolescence. Are we losing our moral sense already?"

Tess had not seen Denise so angry since she told the story of her family being tortured as 'Chinese spies' in Cambodia. "I hate it, too, Denise, but that's not what I'm talking about. Not exactly."

"Then what *exactly* are you talking about?"

"Keeping our technology secret, which we all agreed on. If we sell a battery that *never* wears out, you can be sure the whole world will be trying to crack its disguised technology. So, we can limit its lifetime, but make sure it's still a bargain."

SOS picked up one of the scattered fries and stuffed it in his mouth. "But infinite life is our big selling point,"

Table manners aren't your big selling point, you oaf, Tess thought, smiling to herself. "No, our big selling point is *longer* life than our competitors' batteries. Not infinite, but lots longer."

"Oh." Denise sounded a bit more relaxed. "I can see where planned obsolescence is a necessary part of security, but I still don't like it. Besides, won't limiting life mean extra technology in the device? Extra cost?"

"Good point," said Tess. "But it shouldn't be that much trouble to put in some kind of life-limiter, should it, Roger?"

She could see her husband was already creating something in his head, but he had a pained expression on his face and took more than a minute to answer. "And destroy it beyond recognition once its time is up? Yes, we can do that."

Denise wrote "limited lifetime" and "self-destroying" on her pad, then waited while the bare-midriff girls left with their take-out orders. "But even if it just lasts longer, some people are going to try to reverse engineer it. There are ways of extracting software without accessing the hardware directly. How do we prevent that?"

"We can see if there's a cryptoprocessor available for our code," said SOS. "Or I can port it to some other cryptoprocessor."

Roger stopped rubbing his eyes. "A cryptoprocessor can be violated. Some university people have even built special code-breaking hardware for that purpose."

SOS started to reply, but stopped when Tess put her finger to her lips. Two well-dressed men had entered and taken a table across the room. They seemed to be listening to SOS and Roger's voices. *For all I know, these could be the reporters.* "Let's not get into that now. Denise can record it as a TBD."

She rose, laid a tip on the table, and suggested they take Marna home. They left the restaurant, but the walk along the old-style three-story brick apartments didn't seem to slow down their animated back-and-forth conversation. They were barely out the door when SOS said, "One advantage is that we don't have to modify the software once it's in the device. So, we can make it a closed system."

Roger didn't buy it. "No system can be entirely closed."

Tess nodded agreement. "And, we'd better not make mistakes. We'd have to recall every device and ship a new one to correct even a tiny programming error."

Denise was walking quickly to keep up, but it didn't seem to affect her breathing. Or her thinking. "So, we need a very high level of quality. That's a good idea anyway. Most successful code-crackers work their way in through some bug, like allowing buffer overruns. But I'm getting ahead of myself." She slapped her own wrist. "I think I should note that, on Aremac, we don't have a problem with recall to fix bugs. I doubt there will ever be more than a few hundred Aremacs ever built. Am I right, Tess?"

Tess had to grab Roger's coat sleeve to keep him from walking into the oncoming cars on Albert street. "Well, you never know, but we can take that as a working hypothesis. For a hundred or so Aremacs, we can ship new dongles for software upgrades. It's quite different than the charger situation."

They hustled across the street through a break in traffic. Denise dragged SOS behind her. She was breathing normally, but he was puffing. "We can do like the big software vendors and sell meaningless upgrades every three months for big bucks. In fact, we can program the dongles so they won't work after ninety days, so people will have to buy the new ones."

Denise held him to a halt just over the curb. "You're kidding, right? You'd better be."

SOS dropped his chin to his chest. "Yeah, well, sort of. But it would be a good idea even if we gave the upgrades away for free. That's not planned obsolescence, is it?"

"Then what's the point, lover boy?"

"Everybody would have to check in with us every so often to get the new dongle. Then we could see if they were misusing Aremac."

Tess sighed and began walking again. They reached Uncle Nazim's house, and she didn't want to linger out in the open. "I'd rather you put your effort into building the software so Aremac couldn't *be* misused."

"We're doing that, Tess, but everybody makes mistakes. There could be loopholes we didn't anticipate. The expiring dongles would at least limit how long they could be used before they had to be fixed with an upgrade."

Tess noticed how quiet Marna had been and decided to try stopping the conversation for now so they could get out of sight. "All right, I'll concede that. Denise, can you make that part of your overall security system for Aremac–a kind of planned obsolescence? We can hire some company to ship the new dongles, so we stay out of the upgrade business."

Denise wrote a note on her pad. "I can probably do that, but what I'd really like is to find a way to stay out of these technical sidetracks. Maybe the two boys could head back to the Aremac office with Rebecca and work on some of these loopholes there. We three can probably finish up this security overview inside with Marna, where it's warm."

SOS didn't question his girlfriend's suggestion. *I think I've just seen a glimpse of who gives and who follows orders in their private relationship. Hmm, Roger didn't express any opposition, either. What does that say about us?* She watched thoughtfully as SOS led her husband and Rebecca back the way they had come.

Inside the house, Denise locked the door behind them. Marna led them into the kitchen, put water on for tea, and laid three mugs and spoons on the table.

Tess sat down and took paper napkins from an ornate brass holder. "Do you really think we need to discuss this now? Aremac is sort of dead in the water right now, at least not high priority."

"It's a matter of security by disinformation," said Denise. "If we stop working on Aremac, people will know we're onto something really big somewhere else. Like at the lingerie factory."

Tess studied her reflection in her teaspoon. "So we might want to go with those African people, as a diversion. And we could use the money."

Denise wiped an imaginary smudge off her tea mug. "That's not a bad idea. It shouldn't mean much more technical work. We can use the same security for Aremac's software that we design for the charger. It might be overkill, but more security never hurts."

"I'll look into it. I have that woman's card somewhere."

"Okay, that's good. I'll write up some notes for this meeting and read them all to you at our next security meeting. But then I'll burn them."

"Of course," Tess laughed, and Marna, setting the teapot on the table, laughed with her. *That's the first time she's really laughed since Karl's visit.*

Denise started to pour tea, then stopped after the filling Tess's cup. "And Marna, I'll have some things for you to do, but for now, ask your brothers about your idea of moving to the Navajo Nation. Maybe ask your father, too, but do it from a pay phone somewhere."

CHAPTER THIRTY-ONE

Three hectic days had passed since Denise assigned Marna to investigate the possibility of moving operations to the Navajo Nation, but Marna had been too busy with technical matters to pursue the subject. Roger had produced his first sample of carbon nanofoam, only to learn that this pure carbon substance retained its magnetism for just a few hours after it was made. Unless they could find a way to stabilize the magnetic field, the nanofoam cylinder couldn't reliably generate electricity by moving through the coil of wires.

This discouraging discovery led to furious round-the-clock brainstorming. After the first day, the team generated the idea of placing a piezoelectric crystal as a stopper at the bottom of the tube, where electricity would be generated whenever the moving cylinder struck. Roger, Tess, and SOS spent the next two days experimenting with different crystals being struck by beryllium and magnesium spheres.

Meanwhile Marna worked out the new parameters needed in her equations, so she hadn't given a thought to the idea of moving to the Rez. Denise, who was winding up her work at the bank, hadn't bugged her about it. Nonetheless, Marna was feeling guilty about not doing her share, so when brother Al buzzed, even though she was deep in her quantum universe, she resolved to make time to bring up the issue.

When she met Al in the sewing room, all the workers had gone home. He told her it was time to take a break. "You wouldn't ever eat if we didn't drag you out of there. And it's not just eating. You never do anything but work, work, work, so tonight both of us are taking you to a movie."

"A movie?"

"Yes. After dinner. There's a Western at the Orpheum. It's a classical movie palace, and it will be just like the old days in Gallup when we used to sit in the balcony and cheer for the redskins to beat the cowboys."

Marna couldn't help smiling at the memory. "All right. I need to talk to you boys anyway. Let me get my coat."

"Keep the door open so I can watch you. Otherwise you'll go off into la la land again."

They decided there wasn't time for a fancy meal before the last show, so they parked the pickup near the theater and walked to a nearby joint that sold fish and chips by the pound. Standing at the chest-high counter, they ordered a six-pack of root beer and three double orders of shrimp and chips. It was too cold to eat in the pickup, so they took one of the three tables that tried, but failed, to hide worn spots in the green linoleum floor. They spread out their feast, with the pint of cole slaw in front of Marna, who knew she was the only one who would eat anything resembling a vegetable. Chips, of course, didn't count.

"So what do you want to talk about, little sister?" Al asked.

Cold air swept across their table as a two well-dressed middle-aged couples rushed into the restaurant, rubbing and blowing on their hands. "Speak Navajo," Marna said, in Navajo. "This is clan business."

Tom swore a mild Navajo curse. "I thought you were going to give us a raise."

"It might turn out that way. Don't eat all the shrimp while I explain." She then explained the possibility of moving Aremac's operations to the Navajo Nation for security reasons. The *Biligaana* couples listened to her while they waited for their order, speculating loudly in English what language they were hearing. Neither Marna nor her brothers took the bait, and the couples left just about the time Marna wound up her explanation.

"It's possible," said Tom. "If it would provide jobs on the Rez, the elders would be for it—"

"—as long as what you were doing was clean and wholesome," his brother added. "You've never told us what you're doing in there."

"Well, you know about Aremac, and that would be moved, too."

Tom rolled his eyes. "I have no idea what the elders would think of that machine, but it would be interesting to find out."

"Roger and SOS are working on making it abuse-proof. The People might be able to help with that."

"And what are you doing in the back room, *Shideeezhi*? You side-stepped that question."

"Basically, it's another invention, but that's all I can tell you now. And you'd better not tell anybody else even that much."

Al put down his bottle of root beer. "If you want us to find out about moving some new invention to the Rez, we'll have to say something."

He reached for the shrimp bag, but Marna grabbed it away. "Hey, I haven't had my share." She took three shrimp, then slid the bag back to her brother. "Okay, I'll have to clear it with Tess and Denise. Then you can ask around."

"As soon as you give the word, we'll get the family working on it."

"So you think it's possible?"

"Very possible." Tom looked at his brother. "And I'm not complaining, but I wouldn't mind leaving Chicago to the Cubs' fans."

Al, chewing the last mouthful of chips, agreed with a nod, then swallowed. "If you're finished, *Shideezhi*, then let's get out of here so we don't miss the teasers."

Marna had heard of old movie palaces like the Orpheum, but this was the first one she'd ever seen up close. Not that anything was close on the grand scale of the lobby. The ceilings were four stories high, corresponding to the three levels of balcony reached by the maroon-carpeted grand staircase with ornate, symmetrical golden balustrades. Two pear-shaped crystal chandeliers dropped halfway down from the dark recesses of the domes in the vaulted ceiling, bathing the lobby below in a golden light.

She pulled her eyes away from the glitter long enough to tell her brothers, "I'm all greasy. I need to wash my hands before the movie starts. I don't want to miss the cavalry coming to the rescue, so save me a seat."

"Tom will find us seats, but I'll have to stay with you. I'll be right outside," Al said, leaving her to find her way through the crowd into the ladies room, a huge space that matched the opulence of the lobby.

As she was washing her face, admiring the Egyptian bas reliefs framing the mirror, a woman stepped up beside her. "You're a difficult woman to reach, Dr. Savron. Do you have a minute? I'd like to talk to you about your theory. I believe I have a way for you to achieve the recognition you deserve."

Marna studied the woman in the mirror before turning around. She was her own height, with an ordinary face, neither pretty nor plain, the kind of face you wouldn't remember or be able to describe if you did. She was neatly dressed in gray, with gray accessories that somehow gave her an ominous look. Marna wished she had made Al risk coming into the restroom.

Marna turned around. There were women in the stalls, but otherwise she was alone with this stranger. *Who is she? How does she know me?* "What do you know about my theory?"

"I know that you've been unjustly ignored, denied your proper recognition for your brilliant work."

There was that recognition word again, Marna thought. *I don't care about recognition, or do I? No, I have to get rid of her. Something's not right.* "If you want to talk to me about my theory, you can come to my office during working hours."

"That might not be a good idea. May we meet for tea, perhaps tomorrow at the Regency coffee house? You know where that is, I believe, about a block from your workplace?"

"I know where it is, but I don't think you and I have anything to discuss that can't be discussed at my office. Obviously, you know where that is."

Two of the women exited their stalls and went to the sinks to wash. Marna's visitor said nothing, apparently waiting for them to leave while standing between Marna and the door. As the first woman finished, Marna nudged her visitor aside. She matched pace with the departing woman and said, "Did you read any reviews of this show?"

They walked out together, discussing the movie. Marna wanted to look behind do see if the gray woman was following her, but she didn't dare. When her walking companion turned into the auditorium, Marna stood in the doorway peering inside but unable to see a thing while her eyes adjusted to the dimness.

I can't tell Denise about this, or she'll think the boys didn't do a good job of guarding me.

A hand clasped her shoulder.

She wanted to scream. She felt as if she were about to faint.

Then she heard Al's voice speaking Navajo. "Hey, *Shideezhi*. We've got seats in the balcony."

CHAPTER THIRTY-TWO

For days now, SOS had been working around the clock with
Roger, using speed-sleep to help them crack the code security
problem. They had tested several manufacturers' chip-
embedding systems and felt the hardware protection solution
was within reach. All that remained was choosing among three
different systems, based on initial equipment cost and cost per
dongle. Protecting the software itself, however, was proving
much more difficult.

It was now just before noon, and they had been working
all night. SOS's pacing echoed throughout the Aremac room
whenever he reached a wall and about-faced like a soldier. "I
think we've got a secure approach, but how can we be sure?
How about black-boxing some software on the web and offer a
prize for anyone who cracks it."

Roger blinked his eyes, as if trying to concentrate on the
suggestion. "They could just download the code."

"We'll have the code on our server, Roger. That should be
obvious."

"Oh, right. I wasn't thinking."

"Are you okay?"

"Sure. Except for these damn headaches. Sometimes they
distract me."

"What headaches?"

Roger squinted as if the soft laboratory light was too
intense. "Oh, I've been having them for a while. When the
light's too bright. Or some perfume or other sets me off. I

thought it might be the speed-sleeping, but it doesn't seem to bother you. Does it?"

"Not a bit? Are you taking anything?"

"Aspirin. It doesn't help much."

"So they really hurt?"

"Like a railroad spike between the eyes. Maybe it would help if you stopped marching back and forth."

SOS's eyes roamed the room. "That's terrific."

"What?"

"I said, 'that's terrific.'"

"I mean, *what's* terrific."

"That you've got these painful headaches. They're just what we need."

"What the hell are you talking about. The last thing I need is a headache. Half the time I can't think straight, and the other half the time I'm not sure."

SOS stopped walking and looked down at Roger. "Don't you see? It's just what we've been looking for. To test the latest version of Aremac's anti-coercion feature."

Roger squeezed the bridge of his nose between his fingers. "Oh. The pain. You want me to try using Aremac when my head hurts."

"Right. I'm not satisfied with those hot little pinpricks." SOS emphasized his statement with little finger-jabbing motions. "I mean, they're okay, as far as they go, but with your headaches, we've got some real pain to work with. This is super cool."

"That's easy for you to say. You're not wearing my head."

"Yeah, right. Sorry about that." SOS pulled his earbud and tapped it on his palm. "How's the pain now?"

"Nice of you to be concerned."

"Sure I'm concerned. You know I can't make a test unless the pain is ramped up. Are you taking aspirin now?"

"Not for a couple of hours. I was thinking of taking some more."

SOS laid his hand on Roger's shoulder, preventing him from rising. "No, don't. Let's get you on Aremac first. It won't take long."

"And I'm supposed to believe a programmer's estimate?" Roger sighed, but went to Aremac and lay down while his partner fetched the snood.

Fifteen minutes later, SOS had his data. No matter what he tried, the anti-coercion mechanism kept preventing Aremac from extracting pictures from Roger's brain. "This is great. I'm going to try one more thing."

Roger sat up and tore the snood off his skull. "No more, buddy. Not today anyway. Why don't you check over your data. I'm going home to see if Tess has any stronger medicine."

"Okay. Yeah, you get something for your head. But don't take anything tomorrow, so we can do some more tests."

Roger left without responding. SOS worked over his data for a while, backed everything up, then decided he was hungry. And lonely. Denise and the others were over at the lingerie lab. Rebecca was out in reception, but she waved him away when he invited her to lunch, saying she had to catch up on her bookkeeping. Not wanting to eat alone, he put on his coat and headed for the Red Star China Buffet, four blocks away. At this time of day, people routinely shared tables. Denise didn't like to dine with strangers, so this would be a rare opportunity to talk to somebody interesting.

After heaping his plate with crab rangoon and pot stickers, he found a table for four just being evacuated by a group of teenage boys. He pushed aside their plates, set down his own, selected "Hey Ya!" on his iPod, and started drumming on the edge of his plate with his chopsticks. Before long, a waiter cleared the rest of the table, leaving SOS alone with a clean table with space for three other diners. Moments later, a lady in gray approached. Curiously, she carried no food.

"May I share your table?"

He turned off the iPod. "Sure. I'll hold a place for you while you load up."

She sat. "No need. I'll be hungrier if I wait until we've finished talking."

He thought that was a rather strange thing to say, but if she just wanted to talk, that was magna cool with him. "What are we talking about?"

"How about your academic career?"

"My academic career?" *This is one weird lady, but okay.* "You won't find that very interesting. I dropped out after getting my masters. Too boring."

"How did your mother feel about that?"

"My mother?" *Maybe this old broad is a friend of Mom's. She's about the right age.*

"Yes. Your mother. Susan Margaret. Didn't she want you to earn a PhD?"

How do you know that? Must be a friend. "Yeah, she was pretty upset. She wanted me to continue in Dad's footsteps. Be a university professor. So you know my mother?"

She ignored his question. "And you didn't want to be a professor?"

"No, I did. I'd like that, but graduate school was too boring, so I didn't get a PhD. So I can't have an academic career. End of story."

"Maybe not."

He stopped a pot sticker halfway to his mouth. "Huh?"

"You don't necessarily have to have a PhD to hold a university chair. Not if you have made a name for yourself in research or publication."

"Well, there you are. I'm no writer."

"But you are involved in some fascinating research."

A tiny warning alarm went off in SOS's brain. "What research?" *Mom must have told her something about Aremac. It's been in all the papers.* "The Aremac? That's really Roger's baby. I'm just a grunt programmer."

"Yes, the Aremac was interesting, but now there's this battery business. To me, that's much more interesting."

The warning alarm was screaming. "What do you know about that?"

"Not a whole lot, but I'd like to know more."

SOS stood up. "I think I'd better leave."

She laid a hand on his arm. "No, please don't go. Your mother would be very disappointed if you didn't hear me out about this opportunity."

He let her hand guide him gently back into his seat. "What opportunity?" *I might as well find out what she's up to. Denise will want to know.*

"It's not been announced yet, but there's about to be a new endowed chair in Computer Science at Stanford, a very generously endowed chair."

Stanford? Now that's interesting. But suspicious. "And if it's not been announced, how do you know about it?"

"The endowment has been provided by some friends of mine, friends who will have the final say in who gets the position. And they're not looking for the usual fusty academic. They want someone young with startling new ideas. Based on new theory, but with real practical applications. Like your battery."

This can't be what it looks like. He studied a swirl of plum sauce on his plate, as if it might hold an answer.

"Do you think your mother would like to say her son was a full professor at Stanford? Wouldn't that please her enormously?"

It sure would. But is that what I want? Or would I rather work in secrecy, inventing great things, but never able to talk about them?

She sat quietly, allowing him to ponder her offer, then said, "This is not a pipe-dream. I could make that happen."

"It sounds too good to be true." *And what's that rule? If it sounds too good to be true, it probably is.* "I'd like to think about it. Do you have a way I can contact you?"

She handed him an engraved card. He glanced at it and saw that all it held was a phone number and an email address. "I don't even know your name."

"Better to keep it secret for now. This is a very delicate matter, and the university would be very unhappy if they knew I was doing this for my friends."

She stood and offered her hand. "My friends are willing to wait, but not too long. If I don't hear from you, say, in three days, I'll assume you aren't interested. But talk it over with your mother. I think she'd like to know that this once-in-a-lifetime opportunity has opened up for you."

He watched her leave the restaurant, ignoring all the delicious food. Suspicious, but if she was a spy, he now had a way to track her down. He would back-search the phone number. Then he would surprise Denise. She would be proud of him. Either way.

CHAPTER THIRTY-THREE

Rebecca was beginning to resent that everyone else was inside having fun. On the other hand, she was spending most of her time out here in the reception area fending off snoopy FDA bureaucrats, snoopier reporters, and exasperating lawyers with their niggling requests for documentary evidence. It was all she could do to maintain her British manners when a mature woman in gray came through the door and stood before her reception desk.

"I'm seeking some information."

The woman was flawlessly polite, but something aroused Rebecca's suspicion. Maybe it was just paranoia. "About … ?"

"Well, I understand you have a new project going that has something to do with long-lasting batteries."

Oh, no. Another reporter. But how does she know about the project? "I'm sorry, you must have the wrong address. We have nothing like that here."

"No, I'm sure it's the right place, but I understand that you might be reluctant to give information to a stranger. That's why I'm willing to offer you something in exchange."

Exchange? You mean bribe? "I'm sorry, I don't know what you're talking about. Now, if you don't mind, I'm extremely busy."

The woman didn't budge. "I think you understand me, Ms. Solomon." She spread her arms as if displaying herself as a mannequin. "Like me, you're not getting any younger, and as far as I know, the Aremac company doesn't have a retirement plan.

I thought you might be interested in earning a little extra money so you might fund your own Keogh plan or something similar for your old age."

Well, at least she's not wasting any time getting to the point. I do appreciate directness. Maybe that's what she needs. "Perhaps you're right, but at least I'll have an old age."

"What do you mean?"

Rebecca put on her most gracious smile. "In my right hand, under my desk, I'm holding an automatic pistol. In case you don't know that about me, I am trained and willing to use it."

"What?"

Rebecca raised her left hand as if directing traffic. "Please don't interrupt. It's not polite."

"But–"

"No but. If you are still standing in front of me by the time I count to three, let's just say you won't need your retirement plan. One."

The woman was gone before Rebecca said "Two."

CHAPTER THIRTY-FOUR

Early the next morning, waiting in the anteroom for the nurses to finish their work with SOS, Tess's tired brain struggled to understand what had gone wrong. *It was just another software test, so nobody was concerned about safety. But the software was attached to hardware–albeit small hardware–so I should have known better. In fact, I did know better, and if I had insisted on doing what I knew we should do, SOS wouldn't have lost his ear.*

As soon as I know he's all right, I'll get to the bottom of this. We can't afford to harm anybody, let alone our own teammates.

The nurse said that SOS's room was now open to visitors. She followed the rest of the team inside, pleased to see that this exclusive private hospital had pleasant rooms. When she had seen the room rates, she was glad Aremac, Inc.'s expensive insurance policies covered the major share of the costs in case of accidents. The three vases of signature roses were a nice touch to the room, and she was sure the sight and scent would help SOS recover quickly. But perhaps the fifty-six-inch flat-panel television's curative powers did not exceed, say, a thirty-six-inch display.

In any case, Arnie had recommended Rose Haven for the discretion of its doctors, something Denise thought was essential if their lab was not to be swarmed with inquisitive OSHA inspectors. SOS had been registered as the victim of an unfortunate household accident, which was easier to sell given that it had occurred at three in the morning when nobody else was in the building.

Now, half a day later, Tess, Marna, Roger, and Rebecca reclined in upholstered chairs on the patient's left, his right ear being thoroughly bandaged after the operation. *I wonder if his iPod earbud is inside the bandage*, Tess thought, then mentally kicked herself for being so callous.

Denise sat on the edge of the bed on his right. Everything she had to say to her boyfriend was evidently being said in code, by squeezing his hand. As usual, despite his condition, SOS was doing all the talking. "Shouldn't some of you be guarding the store?"

"It's been taken care of," Tess said. "You just worry about getting well."

"Hey, I'm not sick. I'm just broken. I may wind up looking like Dr. Frankenstein's creation, with big stitches and all, but they say the ear should stick. It helps that it wasn't quite fully detached, but just hanging–"

Rebecca inclined her head towards Marna, whose face was looking rather pasty. "We probably don't need that much detail, Stephen. Besides, with your hair, stitches won't show."

"What hair? Oh, you mean when it grows back." He ran his hand over his smooth scalp. "I don't know. Maybe I'll keep it shaved."

Denise shook her head.

"Well, maybe not. They asked me if I wanted them to leave the other side unshaved. Wouldn't that have been something?" He looked again at Denise. "Well, maybe not."

Tess refused Roger's silent offer of his chair, instead gripping the foot rail and leaning toward SOS. "Can you tell us what happened."

"Well, they shaved my head, and then they put me out with some cool stuff in a needle. Then–"

"Not the surgery. The explosion. What exploded? I didn't think we had any volatiles in the lab."

"Oh. I don't really know what happened. I was hoping Roger had some ideas. You looked at the lab, didn't you, Roger?"

"What was left of it, yes." He waved his comment away. "Just kidding. There really wasn't much damage outside of the immediate area."

"So what do you think happened? All I was doing was testing my latest modifications to the charger software. You know, the optimized algorithm. There were no functional changes at all–at least there weren't supposed to be. All that should have changed was the speed."

"I don't think there were any functional changes. We were pretty careful reviewing the new code."

"Then what happened?"

"My best guess–" Roger stopped when a nurse entered and clipped a blood oxygen monitor on the patient's finger. He said nothing until she made a note on the chart and left. "My best guess is that it was the change in speed."

"Couldn't my program keep up?" SOS winced as he started to turn his head.

Roger's head wagged a "no." "On the contrary. Your program was too fast."

"How could it be too fast?" Marna wanted to know.

"Every time the core drops back to the bottom under gravity, the program computes the new quantum field, which sends the core back to the top, where it retains its downward velocity."

Marna tapped her fingers together impatiently, as if she were matching the back-and-forth of the cylinder. "So it goes faster and faster. We know that, Roger."

"Okay, so the speed builds up until the program can't keep up any longer. Then it hits bottom and stops, and the cycle starts over again."

Rebecca shrugged. "So? Isn't that the way it's supposed to work? I thought I understood at least that much."

"Supposed to, but didn't."

Rebecca looked to each of the others as if seeking help. "Why not? How about an easy-peasy explanation suitable for an old bird?"

"I puzzled over that for a long time until I figured it out." SOS said.

"So?" said Rebecca.

"So, the velocity kept building up. The speed. I don't know how fast it was finally going, but in theory, it could reach escape velocity. Maybe more, Marna. You'll have to check the theory."

"Escape velocity?" Rebecca said. "Like a rocket? Isn't that 25,000 miles per hour."

"Right. Over 10,000 meters per second."

Rebecca unconsciously placed her hand on her large leather bag. "That's faster than a speeding bullet."

Roger nodded, confirming her assessment. "Maybe ten times as fast. One thing a cell-phone battery should not be is dangerous. But if I'm right, this model would serve better as a World War III weapon."

A cluster of people passed by in the corridor. Tess leaned forward again and lowered her voice. "So you think the core became a projectile that went right through the crystal at the bottom?"

"The way the damn thing was shattered seems to confirm that theory," Roger said. "Or, it could just have been the crystal itself, unable to keep up as the oscillations became too rapid. I'll have to check the relaxation time. Maybe we can just use a different piezoelectric crystal. There are lots to choose from."

"Why not just slow down the program?" Rebecca asked.

SOS had the fastest answer, beating Tess by a quarter-second. "That would limit the power output."

"We have to limit the power anyway," Tess said. "Marna, you work with us on this. We can trace backward from the desired power level, then you can tell us how slow the program has to be."

SOS laughed.

Tess was glad to see him laughing. "What's so funny?"

"It's a new one on me, making a program slower."

"That is pretty funny. Can you do it?"

"Of course. I'm thinking I can make the speed adaptive, so I don't have to fiddle with it every time we make some program change."

"You work it out." Tess stood. "Come on, gang. The doctor said we should let him rest."

"I'll stay," said Denise. "I won't bother him."

"Right," said Tess. "But if you do work on this problem, don't let anyone hear you. And for sure don't write anything down about this weapon business."

Denise put both hands behind her head, stretched, then pulled her hair back tightly. "Don't worry. That's all we need, for the military to know we've accidentally created a super gun."

CHAPTER THIRTY-FIVE

SOS was out of the hospital in two days. When he entered the office, Tess smiled as Heidi jumped up, put her paws on his shoulders, and sniffed his bandage and the shaved head. Finally, she decided he was still the same old SOS. SOS evidently thought so, too, because he had insisted on coming back to work so he could attend Denise's meeting, which she had delayed until everyone else could attend.

They held the meeting in the Aremac office. Rebecca locked the front door, closed the shades, put some candles in the window, and posted a sign saying they were closed for Santa Lucia Day. When everyone was seated, Denise went to the emergency door, disabled the alarm, and opened it to admit a mature lady dressed in gray. Instantly, the lounge resonated with three separate gasps, but Tess noticed that Heidi didn't even bother to check out the stranger. Heidi always scrutinized strangers, so Denise must have already introduced them.

"Some of you have met already, but I'd like to introduce you all to my former colleague, Ethel Vandervelde. Before she retired into private practice, she served in various undercover roles in ... well, you don't have to know where she served."

Tess didn't know what was going on, but she sat observing the others, sure that Denise would explain. Roger looked equally puzzled, but Rebecca could barely restrain a knowing smile. Marna's face was inscrutable, but SOS's agitation was quite clear. "What is this, Deni? That woman followed me the other day and tried to pump me for information."

"Yes, she did, and quite well, too." She held up an ivory-colored cell-phone sized box. "And recorded it all in here. She was working for me, testing some of our potential security leaks."

"You had her spying on me?" SOS sounded more hurt than angry.

"You weren't the only one," Rebecca said. "She visited me, too." She looked at Marna, who was studying the non-existent floor dust. "I suspect she visited Marna, too."

"Yes. All three of you. It's a standard way of testing, used by all the agencies. And it's not a test of loyalty. It's a test of competence–how you deal with potential security attacks."

Tess found herself nodding her head. "You continue to amaze me, Denise. Where did you learn all this security stuff?"

"You know I was at the FBI."

"They trained you in espionage?"

"Not really. I came to the FBI on loan from NSA–the National Security Agency."

"The code breakers?"

"That's what we did, and that's what I was trained to do. But that's not really where I learned this trade. Did you know that NSA has a digital library that contains essentially every espionage book ever written–fiction or non-fiction, as well as everything in between of dubious veracity?"

Roger whistled. "You're kidding."

"No, it's true."

Roger whistled again. "Why would they have that? I mean, I can understand the non-fiction, but why fiction?"

"For a couple of reasons. First of all, spies get lots of their ideas from novels–from anywhere, really, but what better place than spy novels. But even more important, lots of field codes are book codes. Secure, simple codes based on numbers that point to words in a code book–page, line, and word. We have much more sophisticated cryptographic schemes now, but the book codes are fast and easy to use. You don't need a computer to code or decode, but they're virtually impossible to crack unless you have a copy of the right edition of the code book. And you want the book to be something common, a best-seller, for example, that won't attract any attention when an agent carries it."

"You mean not like *The Sins of the Fathers*?" Tess asked.

Denise laughed, and she and Tess had to explain the joke about Good Soldier Schweik, who delivered the wrong volume of *Sins* for a book code. Then she turned serious again. "Well, if you have a computer–a very fast computer with the ability to index vast texts–"

"Like Google?" asked Roger.

"Very much like Google, but different in some critical ways. Anyway, if this computer has a database with all these spy books' words indexed by page, line, and position, you can input a coded numeric text and quite readily identify the code book that was used."

"That's fascinating, but how did that train you?"

"Oh, it didn't, but the agency still kept paper copies of all those books around. I read them all."

"All?" *Actually, I'm not surprised, now that I've watched Denise read text from her computer as it scrolls by at high speed.*

"I'm a fast reader. And I skimmed the worthless ones. You soon learn which authors know something about espionage and which don't."

"And so you learned to test the competence of all your operatives." Tess surveyed the others. SOS was clumping around the room, pouting. Rebecca was no longer trying to hide her smile. And Marna was chewing an extra-thick strand of her hair.

"Among other things, yes," said Denise. "I hope you all understand why I had to do it?"

"I understand," Marna squeaked, hair still in her mouth. "Still you scared me half to–well, you know. Now don't be offended, but what I want to know is who tests *your* vulnerability."

Denise spread her arms, palms open. "That's the sixty-four billion dollar question, which no security system ever completely solves. Basically, you all have to trust me. Make a test if you can, but it's not easy. And no test of this kind guarantees anything–just like software tests. Maybe you don't pick the right weak point to exploit. Maybe your actor isn't convincing enough." She looked at the gray lady. "Ethel is very good, though, isn't she?"

Rebecca nodded. When the others made no move to speak, Denise pressed on. "Maybe your operative weakens if the offer is repeated often enough, or maybe her circumstances change. But at least the test can expose things your operatives have to learn."

"For example?"

"You, Marna, did quite well, but you did several things wrong. One, you should *never* have left your brothers' protection."

"But they couldn't go in the ladies room."

"Well, they could, but that's another story. They could have waited right outside, not two-dozen steps away."

"You're right. I won't make that mistake again. I'm afraid to ask, but what else did I do wrong? I thought I handled it pretty well, other than being so scared."

"Scared isn't wrong. In fact, it would be wrong not to be scared–or to pretend to yourself that you weren't scared. No, your biggest mistake was confirming that you had a theory."

"Did I do that?"

She held up the ivory box. "Do you want me to play the recording? Right away, you said 'What do you know about my theory?' And you repeated the mistake a minute later."

Marna's hand covered her mouth, as if she could go back in time and trap her words. "Oh, my. What should I have said?"

"Ideally? You should have given the woman a puzzled look and simply walked away. Don't confirm that you have a theory. Don't confirm who you are. Don't confirm *anything*. Don't engage, even to tell the person they're wrong. Everything you say might give them information."

"Whew. That's hard, but I think my father and some of the old men in the Nation know how to do this. Especially when dealing with outsiders."

"Then learn from them. Yes, they're probably experts."

"Could she have said something to the woman in Navajo?" SOS asked.

"No, best to say nothing, even in a language they're not likely to understand. For you, my dearest one, that means you've got to learn to keep your mouth shut. Mouth shut!" She faced him, reached up to place on hand on top of his head, then placed the other hand under his jaw and squeezed her hands together. "Mouth shut! Get it?"

He pulled his head out of her hands. "But once I guessed she was be a spy, I tried to pump some information out of her."

"That's *another* mistake. Never try to beat them at their game. Ethel is a professional spy. You're a professional programmer. What do you think would happen if she tried to beat you at, say, debugging a program?"

"I guess I didn't do very well. She really got me when she talked about my mother."

"Yes, you're a sucker when it comes to anything your mother wants. I prompted her for that. But your biggest mistake was *not reporting the incident to me*."

This is beginning to sound like a lovers' quarrel, Tess thought. *I don't like the tone, but I know I would only worsen matters if I interfere. They have to work this out for themselves.*

"I didn't want to worry you. I would look her up from her phone number and tell you when I had more information."

"That's stupid, or maybe just incredibly naive. If you don't report these contacts to me *right away*, you didn't take care of them. You'd *all* better understand that. If I'm missing information, I won't be able to see any pattern. I mean, it's hard enough even if I have all the information. Let Rebecca teach you. She reported to me right away, and she gave me every detail, few as there were."

SOS slumped back in his chair, head down. He seemed to have had enough, so Rebecca slipped in. "I've had some training, but I couldn't have been perfect. What were my mistakes?"

"None, according to what I know. Ethel, did you see anything?"

"No, she had me out of there almost before my feet touched the floor. But there is one thing, for the future."

"What's that?"

"Try not to shoot anyone. It attracts too much attention."

CHAPTER THIRTY-SIX

The next day had been quiet for a change, with no more security tests. Tess was working with Rebecca in the business office, trying to squeeze a few more pennies out of the budget, when out of the blue she turned to Rebecca and asked, "Do you think I'm putting too much emphasis on security? Since Denise has stopped working at the bank, I'm feeling the difference her extra income made."

"You're asking the wrong person," said Rebecca. "As far as I'm concerned, an operation like this can *never* have enough security. You won't get the government protection to which ordinary citizens are entitled. And the government itself is trying to pinch your secrets."

Heidi growled and stood suddenly, ears fully erect. A moment later, the entry buzzer sounded. Tess swiveled halfway around and saw three overcoat-clad figures standing at the glass front door. Rebecca threw up her hands. "Speaking of the devil."

"You know them?"

"Too well. They're our friends from the FDA, though I think at least two of them are actually FBI agents."

Tess stared hard at the three figures. "How can you tell? They all look like bureaucrats."

The buzzer sounded again. And again. Heidi now stood at the door, eyes fixed on the visitors.

"I'd better let them in." Rebecca pressed the button under her desk to release the front door lock. "Heidi, sit!" Heidi sat. "Heidi, stay!" Heidi looked unhappy, but froze.

Rebecca stood and headed for the door, pausing to answer Tess's question. "You can tell because they're packing heat. I don't think FDA agents are generally issued firearms."

As the three entered, Rebecca unlocked the door to the Aremac room. "Hello boys. What mischief are you making today? Would you like to see the room where we dissect the little human babies?"

Heidi watched, but didn't move, as the tallest and heaviest of the three flashed an ID badge at Tess, then quickly pulled it away. "I'm agent Flowers, Ms. Fixman." Then, to Rebecca, "We know when you're running your machine, but that's not why we're here."

Rebecca offered a shallow bow. "Oh, would you like some tea?"

Tess wondered if Flowers really knew when the Aremac ran, and if so, *how* he knew. *Maybe they monitor power consumption. We'll have to change to a backup battery.*

"Actually, we've learned that you are operating another laboratory. We'd like to inspect that one."

And how do they know that? "You'll have to wait while Ms. Solomon notifies our attorney."

Flowers waved a piece of paper. "We have a warrant."

"You'll still have to wait. We're entitled to have our attorney present." She took the paper and studied it.

"No, you're not, but we'll extend you that courtesy if he arrives at your other laboratory before us."

Tess read the address on the warrant. "Fine. Let me get my coat. Rebecca, you keep Heidi here. If you can't reach

Arnie, get *someone*. We have more than enough attorneys. One of them should be available."

She turned to the FDA men, trying not to sound hostile. "If you gentlemen will wait outside while I take a nature break, I'd like to ride with you." She cast them what she hoped was an embarrassed smile. "If I may. Because of some litigation or other, we're trying to save money on gas these days."

Flowers mumbled something to the others, then left. As soon as all three were out the door, Tess grabbed her coat off the rack and whispered to Rebecca, "Go find a pay phone and call a rental company and get us a truck. Have them deliver it to you, but put the company name on the rental agreement so any of us can drive it. You know the size we need?"

"I can guess, but I'll need to tell them where you're taking it."

"New Mexico. Maybe Arizona. On second thought, tell them California. Suggest it's going to be Northern California. If we decide to stop in New Mexico and they're looking for us in San Francisco, well, too bad for them."

"If that warrant is valid, you won't be able to remove anything until they've combed the entire laboratory." She pronounced it "lab-*or*-atory."

Tess buttoned her coat. "Don't worry. I'll take care of it. Just have the truck ready when I call."

The ride to the lingerie factory in the FDA car was short but silent. When they pulled up in front, Tess looked in vain for signs of Arnie's Cadillac. She took as much time as she could climbing out of the car and leading the three agents to the entrance. Inside, she took them immediately to the office and introduced them to uncles Nazim and Suhayb, letting each one read the warrant. One of the secretaries took the men's coats, then Tess led them out into the first factory room. *Still no sign of Arnie.*

The men swept quickly through the room, opening a few cabinets, pulling out some fabric or spare sewing machine parts, then leaving them out as they slammed the cabinets shut. Suhayb followed them around and meticulously replaced each item. After about five minutes, they proceeded to the second factory room and repeated the procedure. When they finished, Tess said, "There. Are you satisfied now?"

Agent Flowers looked at the door to the laboratory. "What's in there?"

"Oh, that's another building."

"I don't care." He grabbed the door handle and tugged. It was locked. "Open up."

"Oh, but you can't go in there."

He waved the warrant in her face. "This little piece of paper says I can."

She looked around one last time for Arnie. *I guess I'll have to handle this myself.* "No it doesn't."

"You read it. You know what it says."

"It says you can search the premises at 1223 Lexington Street."

"Right. So open the door."

"But I told you. That's another building. It's on Wallace, not Lexington. Different address, and I don't see *that* address on your warrant."

The leader sent one of his men out the front door to check. On his way out, he passed Arnie Danielson on the way in. As usual, the attorney was impeccably dressed and looked as if he was fresh from his barber and manicurist. As soon as Tess explained the situation, he took control. "Well, gentlemen, you may search these premises as much as you like, but please don't disturb the girls and make them have to tear out their stitches. As for the other building, as I'm sure you know, you'll need another warrant."

"We'll be back," said Flowers as he stomped out, almost forgetting his coat.

Arnie started to tell Tess something, but she waved him off while she phoned Rebecca. "Lock up there and bring the truck." She hung up, then immediately said, "Darn, I should have said to the back entrance." Then she turned to Arnie. "What were you saying? I'm sorry, but I had to get the move started."

"You're leaving, then? For the Navajo Nation?"

"As we discussed."

He studied his copy of the warrant for a moment. "Don't kill yourself rushing. There's no way they can get a warrant still today."

"I hope not, but I'm not taking any chances."

"Can I help you load?"

"Thanks, but we've got lots of help, and you need to protect your back. Besides, we have a few legalities to discuss."

He tucked the warrant in his inside jacket pocket, then showed his empty hands. "I don't have much more to tell you, Tess. The FDA does have jurisdiction on the reservation."

"Aren't they an independent nation?"

"As a general rule, any statutes that apply to everyone in the United States are presumed to apply to Indian reservations. It's a general rule, but it can be altered by specific treaties with individual tribes. Unfortunately, you couldn't afford to have me analyze the hundreds of treaties to see if we can find a loophole. Most of them apply to things like cigarettes and native medicines, but sometimes we lawyers can twist things in our favor."

"Sometimes?" Tess laughed.

"Don't make me blush. Anyway, from the case records my associates have found, your biggest protection will be the indifference of the FDA to native affairs. Most problems on the reservations are handled by the Indian Health Service, and they're more on the natives' side than the FDA is–when they're interested at all. As long as nobody's shipping hallucinogens off the reservation, the FDA usually thinks they have better things to do than travel out in the dusty desert where they can't get their Starbucks White Chocolate Mocha Frappuccino."

"Let's hope you're right."

The front door banged open and Rebecca came running in with keys in her hand, followed by Tom and Al. Arnie took one look at the two ex-marines and said to Tess, "Besides, your best protection is to have friends among the natives. They seem to have learned ways of dealing with unwanted Europeans."

CHAPTER THIRTY-SEVEN

"Texas," said Tess, tracing the route she thought the entire battery charger lab was taking to the Southwest. "The convoy should be led by Al's red pickup somewhere around here on I-40." *Half of my team has been on the road for less than twenty-four hours, but I already feel an empty space in my heart. I wanted more than anything to be with them, but somebody has to stay behind to clean up matters here in Chicago.*

SOS leaned over her shoulder and laid his finger on the map. "Tennessee."

Rebecca, studied the Rand-McNally map from across the table. "My US geography isn't that complete, Stephen, but I don't think the lorry will pass through Tennessee. Not from here on the way to New Mexico."

"Not the truck–uh, lorry," said SOS. "The dongle."

"Oh," said Tess. "Okay, but we packed the dongle-maker on the lorry, didn't we?

"Not the machine. The software."

The frustration in his voice tore Tess's attention away from the map, across which she imagined a tiny truck and pickup creeping slowly toward safety. "What about the software?"

He set his laptop on the table next to the map. He pointed at the screen. "More bad news. Some students in Tennessee cracked my security scheme."

Tess studied the email. "Cracked? How?"

"Actually, shattered would be a better word. They started with a crack and pried it wide open."

"Is it really a problem?"

"I can't see anything wrong with what they did, the little snots."

"Can you fix it?"

"No problem. Except you're going to have to send them the five grand in prize money."

Tess knuckled her forehead. "I don't know if we've got $5,000. Rebecca?"

"We can cover it, but just barely. Are there going to be any more prizes?"

"That's the good news," said SOS. "Out of more than a hundred hackers I know are working on it, these are the only ones that found a flaw. So far. I actually love the smart little snots."

Tess reached up to grip his shoulder. "So don't be so depressed. That proves you've done an *almost* perfect job. If you want a reason to be depressed, have Rebecca show you the checkbook."

"Are we really and truly running out of money?" SOS asked, suddenly serious. Having become rich from stock options when a previous employer had gone public, he usually took the financial side of the business for granted. "I can sell some more of my stock."

Tess stood, turned around, and gave him a hug. "Thanks, pal. But hold on to your money a little longer. It's just the monthly operating budget that's going to be depleted. We still have some reserves–though God knows how much this move to New Mexico is going to cost. Anyway, this woman I met in Las

Vegas is coming today. She could be the answer to our financial prayers."

"Oh, yeah. Do you want me to stay and meet her, or can I get to work on this stupid dongle?"

"No, you can hide in back and do your thing. Just be ready in case she has some technical questions. I may want to impress her with the genius of our researchers."

"And maybe you want to change your t-shirt, Stephen." Rebecca traced the writing on his electric-green shirt that read, "FAILURE IS NOT AN OPTION. (It comes bundled with the software.)"

He looked down at his shirt, puzzled, then shrugged. And sighed. "It's back to the drawing board. Anyway, I have nothing else to do now that Denise is on her way into the Wild West."

In his voice, Tess heard a tone of delight harmonizing with an undertone of disappointment. "So it's not a problem?" she asked, but SOS had already disappeared into the lab, trailed by Heidi. *The real problem is going to be moving the hobbled Aremac.* Shipping the huge and rather delicate magnet was a much more complex job than moving all the smaller items from the battery lab. She doubted they could transport it to the Navajo Nation and operate it there without interference from the FDA.

She heard a door opening and looked up, but it was only SOS returning, pulling on a brown t-shirt that read, "24 Hours in a Day, 24 Beers in a Case–Coincidence?" He pointed to the lettering. "Is this better?"

Tess cast a resigned glance in Rebecca's direction. "It will do. I was asking you if the cracked code was going to be a problem. I know you said it was no problem, but I've heard that before."

He let out another sigh, proportionate to his size. "It's the kind of problem I can sink my teeth into."

"So you're sure you can solve it?"

"If anyone can, I can."

"That was evasive, Stephen." said Rebecca.

"Denise says I shouldn't be so cocky. Know my limitations. I'm trying."

"Have you finally convinced your mother to come to New Mexico?"

Before he could answer, Heidi alerted. The buzzer sounded. Alicia Silsbury had arrived.

Tess made sure that the Englishwoman was okay with Heidi's presence, then introduced her to her two colleagues. She allowed Alicia and Rebecca a few minutes to exchange reminiscences about their common homeland before asking Alicia what she would like to see.

"See? No, that I can do with pictures. If possible, I would like to *experience* this Aremac of yours for myself."

SOS rubbed his hand over the stubble from his recent surgery. "You'll have to shave your head."

"If necessary," said Alicia, before Tess could explain that it was a joke, perhaps intended to discourage her.

Hearing Alicia's unhesitating acceptance, Tess's estimation of her rose several degrees. This was a person to be reckoned with. "He's kidding you. We used to have to shave our heads, in the early days. If you want really detailed pictures, you may want to do that. But in practice, it's no longer necessary."

Rebecca smoothed her own hair. "The worst that can happen is you'll need to touch up your perm. I've tried it myself. You won't feel a thing."

"Then I can do it?" Alicia asked, more eagerly than Tess expected from an English gentlewoman.

Tess shook her head. "I'm afraid there's a problem. If I recall correctly, you know about the FDA injunction?"

"Yes, I do."

"Well, unfortunately, the TRO is still in effect. We're legally prohibited from using the machine on human subjects."

"Even for a demonstration?"

"I don't think the FDA makes exceptions for demonstrations."

"Who would tell them? Not I, certainly."

Even though the Feds might not detect Aremac running on internal power, it's too big a risk. But we desperately need the money Alicia might bring. Even without needing the $5,000 of unplanned expense we've already lost this morning, even before the mailman's here with the bills. Then there's the convoy, burning up gas and heading into who knew what expenses. If we keep the session short, and remove her immediately, we should be able to get away with it. We've powered it up before, for testing, and it was never detected. And if I don't keep us in business, who will?

She made up her mind. "All right, let's do it. But Alicia, you understand this can only be a very short session? Rebecca, lock the front door and put up a sign. What holiday is it today?"

Rebecca examined her calendar. "The best I can find is St. John of the Cross. Patron saint of mystics."

"Fine," Tess said. "Most people think Aremac is mystical. Print it up and put it in the window. Come, Alicia, let's do this quickly, in case the FDA is monitoring today. SOS, put Heidi in her crate and get things set up for us, will you?"

Tess led Alicia into the lab and made her remove her earrings, necklace, bracelets, and rings. They tried on several snoods before Tess found a good match, surprised to notice how thin Alicia's hair was. Her hairdresser had done a clever job of concealing several almost bald spots. "I think this one fits you best," she said, carefully slipping on the mesh of carbon nanotubes. "Come over to the gurney and lie down, then I'll hook you up."

Tess helped Alicia sit on the gurney, then tip over onto her back. While she hooked up the cable from the snood, Alicia modestly smoothed her skirt over her knees, even though SOS was behind the operator's console, facing the other way.

"Ready?" asked Tess.

"I believe so," said Alicia.

"Oh, sorry. I was asking the operator. Are you ready, SOS?"

"All set. We're hooked to monitor two."

"I don't feel anything," said Alicia.

"The magnet isn't powered yet," said Tess. "But you won't even feel anything when it's on. Well, some people say they feel a sort of tickling in their head, but I never did. If you do, don't worry."

"Okay. What am I supposed to do?"

Tess showed a few simple calibration pictures while SOS adjusted Aremac's parameters for Alicia's unique brain patterns. When the output matched the sharp lines and colors of the pictures, she told Alicia they were ready to start the real work. "Did you have breakfast this morning?"

Alicia's voice echoed slightly from under the magnet's gap. "I did. It's not going to make me ill, is it?"

Tess laughed. "Oh, no. Nothing like that. I was just suggesting something recent to visualize. Close your eyes and picture your breakfast sitting in front of you. Or, any other still scene if you wish. We could do movies, but we don't have time."

"I'll do breakfast. That's okay. All right, I'm ready."

"SOS will turn the machine on now, and you'll hear a slight hum. Just keep the picture in mind."

The lights dimmed momentarily, then the hum began. The monitor's screen broke into a rainbow tessellation of pixels which gradually swirled into recognizable shapes. A blue-and-white china plate with two eggs, sunny-side up with one yolk leaking a bright yellow stream onto the plate, just touching a rasher of deep brown bacon. To the right of the plate, a silver knife and spoon materialized, matching a pair of forks on the left. Tess recognized the flowing floral pattern of Narcissus 1900. Either the flatware was an imitation, or Alicia had taken breakfast at a seriously upscale restaurant or hotel. *Hmm, not quite the impoverished charity organization.*

When the picture stabilized, SOS clicked off the magnet. Tess wheeled Alicia out of the magnet's gap and helped her sit up so she could see the monitor.

"How's that?"

"Incredible! Such detail. It truly is mystical. I had imagined some crude computer drawing, but this is beyond what I'd hoped for. Pictures like this should hold up in any court."

Tess was caught up in Alicia's enthusiasm. "If they're true. If you'd like, we can show you what happens when you try to lie." *This could cinch the sale.*

"How would I do that?"

"Just make up a picture. Like fix the broken egg, or take away the silverware. Can you do that?"

"I can try."

Rebecca checked her watch, then the wall clock. "Tess, are you watching the time?"

"Oh, yeah. Sure. This won't take but a minute, then we'll shut down."

"We really ought not risk it."

"Leave it to me, Rebecca. I know what I'm doing."

Tess wheeled Alicia back into the magnet, the hum started, and for a moment, the monitor showed nothing. Then an image appeared–the bacon and eggs without the silverware. By the time Alicia was out of the machine and watching, the word "FABRICATED" flashed on and off over the picture.

Alicia started at the flashing message. "Impressive. But how do I know you didn't just put that there because you knew I was making it up?"

Tess smiled. *This woman is no dope.* "If we had time, we could do a double blind test." She looked at her watch. "But we've already been–"

From her crate, Heidi started barking rapidly. With a loud crack, the lab door swung open and hit the wall.

In rushed agent Flowers, followed by a horde of men and women in dark blue FBI jackets.

A camera flashed, then flashed again.

Flowers walked over to Alicia and grabbed the snood's cable. "And what's this? The latest hair net?" He held out his hand and posed for the camera. More flashes.

He dropped the cable and directed the cameraman to photograph everything and everybody in the room, then put his hand on the magnet and faced Tess. "I guess you couldn't move this baby as fast as you emptied that other lab."

"It was just a storage place, not a laboratory. Yes, we had a few things there. We brought them over here, to save on rent."

"I'm sure that's what you did." He waved over one of the FBI agents. "All right, cuff them all. When you're done, take them to the van and seal this place. That should put an end to their tricks."

The cuffs were too tight, but Tess didn't really care. *I should be kicking myself. This is all my fault. My greed.*

But all I care about now is whether SOS had time to hit the SECURE ERASE button for all our development files.

CHAPTER THIRTY-EIGHT

They had driven the two trucks non-stop for just over twenty-four hours on Interstate highways, alternating drivers among the five of them–Roger, Denise, Marna, and her two brothers. They felt the air soften as they moved south and west, but here in the high desert of New Mexico, it was still winter, with remnants of snow on any patch of ground shaded from the intense sun. Now they were finished with the Interstate system and about to enter Navajo Country. As they pulled off I-40 and down the exit ramp to State Highway 56, Roger stretched and yawned. "How far is it from Thoreau to Crownpoint?"

Marna, who sat in the pickup between Roger and Al, the driver, corrected him. "It's pronounced 'Threw.' And it's not named after the author, in case you were thinking that."

"I wasn't," he fibbed.

"Sorry to correct you, *Shideezhi*, but this might be the only subject where I know more than a PhD physicist. One version of history says the Mitchell brothers originally named the town Mitchell, but after they left, it was changed to the name of their bookkeeper. Others say it was named after Henry David, but the real name is–"

He said something Roger couldn't catch. "–in Navajo. Means 'little prairie dog,' Roger. So don't let my little sister intimidate you with her vast store of knowledge. She's been away too long."

Roger felt somewhat vindicated. "At least I got Crownpoint right, didn't I? I'm looking forward to Crownpoint, with a nice motel room with clean sheets and a hot shower."

"I'm afraid that's not going to happen," Al said. "There's no motels in Crownpoint."

"Okay, I'll stay in the hotel."

Al guffawed. "What hotel?"

"No hotel, either? Bed and Breakfast?"

"Nope."

"Then where am I going to stay? In a tepee?"

"That's Plains Indians, dope," Marna said. "Even after being away too long, I know *that*."

"Okay, I give up. Where do I sleep?"

"We'll be staying at Yale's," said Marna. "That's Yas, my oldest brother. He has a large house in Crownpoint. My niece and nephew are away at college, so we'll use their rooms. Denise and I will share. And, yes, you'll have your own room– clean sheets and everything. But you'll have to make your own bed. Nellie–my sister-in-law–may be a neat-freak, but she's nobody's servant."

As they rolled down the long main street of Thoreau, Roger paid attention to the succession of commercial buildings. Half the buildings looked like any other street in the country, the other half being trading posts, Indian jewelry stores, and souvenir shops. Plus motels. "That place looks nice. We could stay here and not bother your sister-in-law."

"If you stay here, your rudeness will bother her much more than an unmade bed. Just be quiet and accept the local hospitality. And other customs. You're not in Chicago any more. Besides, you probably couldn't get a room in Thoreau now, because we're just in time for the rug auction, day after tomorrow. This month is usually the biggest, with people Christmas shopping. Look at all the 'no vacancy' signs."

Roger wanted to ask about the rug auction, but he didn't want to make any more ignorant mistakes. He kept quiet for the next twenty-five miles, acquainting himself with the myriad shades of brown and green on high desert buttes and shrubbery. As they approached Crownpoint, he first thought it looked like any American suburb, without hotels and motels, but the houses perhaps a bit smaller and farther apart. There didn't seem to be a recognizable downtown, but there were lots of cars parked in the lot at Basha's supermarket, where both vehicles stopped to buy groceries to bring to Yale's.

Basha's, too, looked like a normal American supermarket, though certain aisles contained foods Roger had never seen in Chicago, like huge sacks of Blue Bird flour that Marna explained were for making fry bread. He didn't notice any liquor department, but the meat department had a large assortment of mutton, which made his mouth water remembering his mother's kebobs and lamb pies.

At the checkout counter, he received a shock. On a photocopied job opportunity sheet taped to the gum rack, the headline caught his attention: "LIVE AND WORK IN FRANCE."

He read that Disneyworld Resort in Paris was hiring "real Native Americans" to be part of their shows. *The paper looks old and tattered. I wonder how long it's been there. Did any "real Native Americans" take up their offer? It would be offensive to me, but I don't think I'll ask Marna how she feels about it.*

As they stood in Basha's parking lot waiting for Denise to finish her checkout, Roger looked over the few scattered large buildings in the distance. After a while, he decided to dare

213 • GERALD M. WEINBERG

asking Marna another question. "There doesn't seem to be much in the way of industry, does there?"

"This is a small town. I don't think even two thousand people."

As if to confirm Marna's statement, a pack of five scraggly dogs emerged from behind Basha's dumpsters, making Roger think of Heidi, then Tess. "Do you have any idea where we can put our laboratory?"

"Yale says he's located an empty garage that should be suitable, in size at least. It's not likely to be very fancy."

"We've been in a garage before. If it's got electricity and running water, we'll be okay." He hesitated. "Does it?"

"Yes, Roger, it does. But first we'll have to receive permission to run a business here."

"I wouldn't think that would be a problem. The town doesn't look that prosperous, and we would bring employment. They should be happy to have us."

"Spoken like a true *Biligaana*. To be acceptable here, you have to produce something that will benefit the people here, not just bring in money. Money is okay, but *just* money is not."

Interesting. Marna seems more confident, more authoritative, now that we're on the reservation. I suppose I should have expected that, given how much less confident I feel here than in Chicago. "So what kind of cell phones do the people need?"

"What they *don't* need is cell phones. Most places on the Rez they don't work anyway, and where they do, the people who need them already have them."

"We could build a better system of cell phone towers."

"That would take money, lots of money, Roger. Maybe not a good thing," Marna reminded him.

"And maybe something we don't have now. What about hospitals?"

"We have the PHS Indian Hospital here, and three hospitals about an hour away, in Gallup and Grants. And there's the helicopter to take really major cases to the University Medical Center in Albuquerque. So we don't really need another hospital. Many of our people won't even use the ones we have when they're sick. What we need is less sickness."

"What would help that?" Roger took a deep breath of the cool, clean air. "It seems so much more healthy here than in the city. I haven't had any headaches since we got west of the Mississippi. So what do you need that you don't have?"

"What *you* need is to stay off your sleep machine. It's not natural."

"Sure," said Roger, not willing to argue the point right now. "So what do people here need?"

"Better heat in the winter." She pointed to the water tower. "Cleaner water, and more of it."

"Water, huh?" He slipped inside his mind for a few moments. "Marna, we could do molecules, couldn't we?"

She clearly knew he was talking about using their separation process for purification. "I think so, if they're simple enough, and tightly bound."

"So could we do water?"

"I suspect that would be one of the easiest. The total atomic weight is down in the range you've done so far. Still, I suspect it would require a rather different program to shape the quantum field. Or maybe not." Her face glowed with excitement. "We'll have to work that out."

"So a water purifier would be almost as valuable as perpetual power."

Just then, Denise emerged from Basha's with Marna's father, Hastin Rose, who was pushing a fully laden shopping cart. Roger thought that except for his slight limp, Hastin looked no older than his sons. He dressed like them, too, dark hair pulled back in a queue, and wearing worn jeans, Western boots, and a heavy black-and-red plaid shirt.

Marna watched her father approach, her eyes shining, while she continued speaking to Roger."Not really, Roger. With unlimited power, you could purify water with ordinary distillation."

Hastin joined them, picking up on their conversation. "And provide heat in the winter. But what we have to do right now is get you accepted in our community. For that, you have to provide something of value."

Roger began unloading the grocery bags into the pickup. "What do people use for heat now, Mr. Rose?"

"Wood. Coal. Dung."

"What about electric?"

"Too expensive, and outside of centers like Crownpoint, there's no electricity anyway. At my house, we have a generator that we can use in emergencies, but otherwise we do without."

"But *Azhé'é*, what happened to the government project to electrify 18,000 non-electric homes?"

"You answered your own question, Maralah. It was just another government project–a so-called demonstration. Once they demonstrated that they could provide some solar or wind power to a few homes, the *Biligaana* lost interest. I should not disparage them. They did help a few families get some power some of the time. Not enough for heating, though, and that's our biggest need. And even those systems are breaking down and cannot be fixed. Seems they don't know how to make small reliable stand-alone power units."

"But we know how to make reliable stand-alone electricity, don't we Roger?" Marna said, pride in her voice.

"Well, yes, but you wouldn't get much from a cell phone battery," Roger said.

"Our people don't live in massive houses, do they *Azhé'é*? Many of our hogans have only one room. Probably most of those 18,000."

Roger returned Denise's cart to the collection rack, stepping aside for a young Navajo young woman pushing a twin stroller. "But Marna–or should I call you Maralah here? You couldn't even heat one room with one of our devices. Not even a one-room doghouse."

Denise pointed an accusing finger at Roger. "I think you're missing the point. Up until now, your specialty has been small devices–nano-tubes, micro-sensors, miniature embedded computers. You're a genius at that level, but sometimes your greatest strength becomes your greatest weakness. Or your biggest blind spot."

"I grant you that, but what does it have to do with this problem?"

"You've been fixated on a small, portable cell-phone-size power source. They don't have much need for cell phones here. Anyway, we've just figured out that our method produces far too much power for a cell phone unless we slow down our quantum field-generating software. And many of our difficulties come from the miniaturization–like shielding without adding weight. If you designed a generator to heat and electrify a house, you could shield it with lead bricks if you wanted."

"But a house-bound generator is of zero interest. A trivial project. Once we have the lab set up, I could build one in a day."

Marna inclined her head toward an old, stooped couple emerging from Basha's, trailed by a boy carrying their two small bags of groceries. "Maybe it's of zero interest to you, Roger, but to that old couple, snowbound in their hogan for weeks at a time, it could be a lifesaver. And, it could be your ticket to acceptance in our community."

Denise climbed into the pickup's cab, then leaned out for a last word. "Besides, if it will only take you a day, why not just do it? We'll employ some people to copy it and sell it to the local people."

I never thought of it that way.

I'm going to need some time to rethink this whole project.

CHAPTER THIRTY-NINE

Tess had never been in jail before, but if this room was a jail, it didn't fulfill her images one bit. It was more like a hotel room, moderately priced, except there were no windows. And, as she quickly learned, the door was locked from the outside. *I guess that makes it a jail, but I doubt very many people know about it.*

There was a minibar, with no lock and no alcohol, but holding a dozen different snack foods, some of which she would even have deigned to eat had she been the slightest bit hungry. There was even a telephone, but her attempts to dial even Arnie's local number merely provoked an irregular, annoying beep.

There was a TV set with all the usual hundred meaningless cable channels. She watched the local news for a while, but there was no mention of the raid on Aremac. She turned it off and tried the small stack of magazines–*People*, *Time*, and *TV Guide*, all current but of zero interest.

She tried to follow the advice she had once read somewhere: "When you are trapped, try to escape. When you can't escape, seek information. When you can't get any more information, sleep." She had tried the door, looked in vain for windows, and removed the ventilation grilles only to sneeze from dust up her nose. Once she stopped sneezing, she saw that the ducts were blocked by bars just behind the grilles.

She pounded on the walls and screamed for help, just in case this room was part of an otherwise legitimate motel. By the time she calmed down, she had searched every inch of the room and its tiny bathroom. *I think I'm still in Chicago, but for all the clues I found, I might be in Arkadelphia or Zanzibar.*

She laid down on the pink bedspread and tried to sleep. She was so angry and agitated, she didn't think she could sleep, but she must have dozed off because the sound of the door opening came as an awakening shock. Agent Flowers stood in the doorway scanning the room as if he thought Tess might not be alone. "I hope I didn't disturb your nap."

For one fuzzy moment, Tess thought of making a dash past her captor into the corridor. When she saw Flowers was backed up by at least two FBI clones, she switched tactics. She sat up, ran her fingers through her red hair, and demanded, "I want a lawyer. I'm invoking my constitutional right to counsel."

He took two steps into the room and eased the door closed behind him, leaving his escort out in the hall. "Sorry, we didn't bring your constitutional rights in here. But you're going to be here for a while, so we do want you to be comfortable. Do you have everything you need? Different toothpaste? Nightgown? Tampons?"

She ignored his innuendoes. "What do you mean, no constitutional rights in here? Where am I? What gives you the right to hold me here?"

"Possible terrorist conspiracy, but I think you knew that already." He pulled up one of two faux-leather armchairs. "Want to talk about it? A little information might get you out of here sooner, rather than later. Or never."

"I have no idea what you're talking about. If you want, I'll confess to a small violation of a temporary restraining order. I thought a little demonstration for a potential customer might not be covered by the TRO. Evidently I was wrong. So, I apologize.

I'll pay the fine." She held out her hand, palm down. "Slap my wrist if you like."

"Oh, we don't really care about your little demonstration, but it did give us a perfectly valid excuse to lock up you and your co-conspirators."

"Co-conspirators?"

"Listen, Ms. Fixman, you can save both of us valuable time by not playing dumb. You have been using your interrogation device to pick the brains of two former Homeland Security employees–employees with access to information so highly classified I'm not allowed to tell you the name of the classification. And now you've been consorting with an agent who regularly trades with foreign governments, many of which harbor members of known terrorist organizations. So you're in deep trouble, trouble you can magnify if you don't cooperate with us."

Tess's head spun, trying to process the twisted logic of her captor. She stalled for time to recover her senses. "And just who are *you*?"

"You know my name, but names are not important. It's enough for you to know that we are legally constituted members of the Office of Homeland Security of the United States of America–a country to which you supposedly owe your allegiance. You saw my badge earlier, when you were arrested."

"The FDA is now part of Homeland Security?"

He laughed. "Not a bad idea. I'll pass that on to the President." He leaned forward. "But enough chit chat. If you want to get out of this comfortable room, you need to answer just a few questions."

"Like what?"

"Like where is the source code for the Aremac's operating system?"

Tess felt a wave of relief coursing through her. *SOS did manage to erase our working files before we were dragged away.* "There *is* no source code. We work directly in binary." *Actually, the source code is encrypted and backed up in several secure places, but I'm certainly not going to tell him that. He probably knows, but doesn't know where those places are.*

"All right. I know that's a lie, but let's pretend it's true. Where is the binary, the object code?"

"Plugged into the machine, of course. In the dongle."

"Don't mock me, young lady. You won't like what happens if I get angry."

In spite of his words, she could already hear the anger in his voice. *Good. He's threatening me, which meant he doesn't really have the power he needs.* "I'm not mocking you. The binary code is in the dongle. Where else would it be? In the magnet? You know Aremac can't operate without it–"

"Stop! You know that we know the code is in the dongle, but you also know that there's no way to read it from there. Not without destroying the little bugger, and it's the only one."

She shrugged. "Well, since that's the only copy of the code, then I guess you're stuck."

He stood. *Oh, oh. Did I go too far? Is he going to hit me?* Instead, he reached out and tapped her forehead with two fingers. "Ah, but it's not the only copy of the code. I'm guessing it's all right in here, and we have just the machine to extract it."

"Oh, no," she squeaked, real fear in her voice. *If they screw up, I could be a vegetable again.* She let him see her hands shaking. "You're not going to put me on Aremac?"

"Oh, yes," he said, holding her hands together so he could apply handcuffs. "Since you won't cooperate any other way, that's *exactly* where I intend to put you."

CHAPTER FORTY

Yale's garage candidate was a mess, but to Roger's eye, a workable mess. It was bigger than the original garage where he and Tess had built Aremac, and it didn't smell of old cooking grease. It had never been a restaurant, having spent its entire life as the home of Western Stage, which had outgrown its confines and moved to a brand new, larger building next door. The predominant odor was good, honest automotive grease, which neither helped nor hindered Roger's plans, but provided a sense of a solid working environment.

The other leftover from Western Stage was the elaborate gray steel shelving still used to store miscellaneous parts for autos, trucks, and farm equipment. In bargaining for the rental, Roger had allowed Norton Begay, the owner of Western Stage, to keep his parts on the shelves in return for reduced rent and possible future services.

Less than four hours after moving in his own equipment and parts, Roger took advantage of those "future services." The rental truck had brought everything he needed to construct the guts of a prototype portable heater-generator. What he lacked was a housing that would radiate quantum-generated heat safely into a dwelling while hiding the true nature of the source of that heat. Roger himself was not used to inventing devices on this scale, but in Norton Begay, he found a true inventor's soulmate. They spent their first two hours together swapping inventor tales. After the first hour, Marna and Denise left in disgust, muttering something about "inventestosterone."

Norton was somewhere on the far side of fifty, though his thick black hair showed not a single strand of gray. He wasn't as tall as Roger, but must have outweighed him by close to a hundred pounds. Most of those pounds were hanging over a large silver belt-buckle in the guise of a belly–not a beer-belly, because Norton's only drink seemed to be infinite quantities of iced tea. Like all of the men in his employ, Norton dressed in a wool shirt, blue jeans, and sturdy brown work boots. The only difference among them was the color of the shirt and the amount of grease it sported. Norton was clearly the leader in the lubrication race.

Though the air temperature was almost freezing, the high desert sun warmed Roger and Norton enough so they could sit on a split-log bench out front of Western Stage's new building. They ate fry bread and sausage, gulped iced tea, and discussed Roger's problem.

Once they got down to business, Norton needed less than five minutes to understand what Roger needed, "I think I can rig up something. But you're sure you don't want to tell me how this little heater-generator of yours works? I can understand pretty much anything."

"I'm sure you can," said Roger, sincerely convinced after talking with Norton. "Which is why I'm not going to explain it to you. But I will tell you why."

"All right. I'll accept that for now. I'm all ears."

Which he isn't, Roger thought. Norton's small ears were actually disproportionate to his large head. "The device is based on a theory thought up by Marna Rose."

Norton held his hands shoulder-width apart. "I've known Maralah since she was this big. It's hard to believe she's grown up, let alone inventing new theories."

"Is Maralah her true name?"

"I don't know. We always called her that. It means, 'born during an earthquake,' which she was. And she's always been a little earthquake herself, shaking things up, like by going to California to college and then working at Los Alamos with all those geniuses."

"Well, I'd say she's a genius herself, when it comes to physics, but not–"

To Roger's surprise, Norton completed his sentence correctly. "–in her personal life. I mean, she was a good girl, but then she married that slimy *Biligaana*–" He clasped Roger's shoulder, almost painfully. "No offense, friend, but I'm not one to smooth over the truth."

"No offense taken. Karl Savron is definitely one of the slimiest … *Biligaana* I've ever met. Did I say that right?"

Norton picked up a large rusty nut and bolt from the ground and began trying to work the nut loose. "Close enough for a *Biligaana*, What did he do?"

Roger wondered if the bolt was a metaphor, but let it slide. "Well, I'm not going to give you details of what he did–I saw the shotgun in your office–but Maralah finally realized it was time to dump the creep. The problem is that if we patent her device so she can earn royalties, and if we do it before their divorce is final, he's going to get half of everything. You know, community property."

"No way! Not unless it's stuffed up his ass. And there would be lots of us standing in line to do it." He demonstrated in the air with the bolt. "Wait a minute while I get some WD-40 to loosen this up."

Norton returned in minutes carrying the red-yellow-and-blue can in one hand and his super-sized iced-tea glass in the other. "Want some? I've got more?"

"No thanks. About the heater: we have to keep the mechanism a trade secret–"

"–until after the divorce. I understand."

"I'm sure you do, but there's one more complication. Once we start selling the device, the patent clock starts ticking, and we have only eighteen months to file our claim."

Norton drained his tea in one long draught. He set down the glass and began working WD-40 into the bolt. "That shouldn't be a problem."

"With Karl contesting the divorce, it probably will be. So, we may never be able to get a patent, which means we'll just keep it as a trade secret as long as we can."

"All right, I understand, but you're naive if you think someone like me won't bust one of the heaters open and figure out how it works."

Watching Norton's determination to bust the nut loose, he could believe it. "There, my friend, is one of the ways you can help me. Help Maralah. In two ways."

"All right, I'm still all ears."

"First way you can help is by testing the security of the innards of this device. I'm going to give you one–just for your eyes only–and challenge you to figure out how it works. You can try anything. If you destroy it, I can make others. I made two this morning, though they won't be calibrated to actually work until Maralah figures out the new parameters."

Norton's thick fingers moved the nut about an eighth of a turn. "Has it got anything dangerous I need to watch out for?"

"It could be dangerous, but there's nothing toxic in there unless you eat some of it."

Norton held up the tail end of his left-over sausage. He didn't seem concerned about touching it with WD-40 on his hand. "Tasting this, you might think I'd eat anything, but I do have my limits."

"Well, nothing inside will look appetizing, I think, even to those goats." Roger nodded toward the pair of white goats Norton kept tethered in the weeds between the two garages.

Norton tossed the sausage to the goats. The smaller one stared the larger one away and kept the sausage for herself. "Okay. So the idea is to see what secrets I can learn, no holds barred."

"Right. But you have to promise that if you do learn anything, you'll keep it secret."

The nut turned another eighth. "I suppose I should ask what's in it for me."

"I think you'd do it for the fun of it. I would. And for Maralah. But I'll pay you just like for any other job."

"Hourly rates?"

"What you've got posted in your office is fine with me, but you may have to give us credit for a while, if you're going to run up a big bill."

Now the nut had moved a full half turn, but Norton kept working it back and forth. "Any limit on the hours?"

"Nope, just so you tell me every time you run up another thousand."

"That much? You must figure your security is a hard nut. Not like this one." He waggled the bolt back and forth.

"Denise says I'm not supposed to be cocky when it comes to security, but I'm pretty confident. Do you know anything about computers? Software?"

Norton raised his hands in surrender, but the bolt and nut were now separated. "Not my bag. I can handle simple electrical problems in cars and trucks, but when these new cars with chips go broke, I've got a nephew that helps me out. He's pretty sharp. Not in Maralah's class, but pretty sharp."

"All right, but if you get to the point where you want computer help, don't call your nephew. I'll lend you Denise, and she'll do her best to play hacker. She's good at that stuff. The best there is."

"She's the Oriental girl you were with, right? Chinese? Japanese? I can never tell them apart, but she's pretty. You're sure she's not still working for the FBI? I'd like to run my toes through that long hair."

"How do you know about Denise and the FBI? You only met her once, and I was with you the whole time."

"This is a small town, my friend. News of strangers gets around to the neighbors in, how do you say, picoseconds."

"Actually, I'm counting on your neighbors as part of our security."

CHAPTER FORTY-ONE

It's not often, **Tess thought**, *that eidetic memory is a liability, but if they can force the program out of me, this could be one of those times. But I think I'll be all right–if I'm not too scared to bring off this deception. So, calm down.*

Two hours ago, she'd been taken out of the motel-room prison, brought here to the Aremac lab, and strapped down on the gurney by two female agents. *I have no idea what they're planning to do to me, or why they're waiting so long to do it. Maybe Flowers is concerned about a possible lawsuit when this was over. If so, it's the only thing he seems concerned about. He's scary. No, I'm scared. Maybe that's why he's keeping me here so long, strapped down–to scare me.*

I have no idea where SOS is. Or Rebecca. Or Alicia. Surely this escapade will slaughter any chance of acquiring Justice for Africa as a customer. Put that out of your mind, girl. That should be the least of my worries right now.

Flowers wouldn't answer any questions about the others. *No, of course he won't answer any questions about anything. It's one of his psychological tricks. But I need information. If these government agents–if they really are government agents– manage to extract the Aremac code, that will be the end of all our efforts to avoid misuse of Roger's invention.*

She thought she had made some progress with her Br'er Rabbit approach. At first, she hadn't realized what effect it would have when she begged not to be placed in Aremac. "Please don't throw me in the briar patch"–the briar patch in this room being the Aremac–had induced them to put her on the gurney. After lying here alone for the first thirty minutes, she began to conquer her fear enough to make a plan for fooling them. *But I'm still afraid of what might happen, because I'm not sure they knew enough to operate the machine safely. Or whether they knew too much for me to fool them. I need to do more, to be sure.*

At long last, she heard the door open. She couldn't see who had entered, but she guessed. "Listen, Flowers, how about letting me sit up. I can't think too good this way."

"You don't really need to think that much. Just tell me where to find the source code." It was Flowers.

"You've got the wrong person. I just do marketing. I don't know anything about the source code, as you call it. I just know how to demonstrate the machine."

"That won't work. Your friend Stephen told us you were the one who knew all the code. He wanted to tell you he was sorry, but he couldn't help himself."

He wouldn't have done that, would he? "He was just telling you that so you'd leave him alone. He's a big coward."

"Sorry, but your little lie detector here would have caught that. We asked him to show us the people who knew all the code, and your picture came up. And there was no FABRICATION warning."

So Stephen has been in the machine already. Probably didn't give anything away or they wouldn't have me here. Unless they just want to check up on what he revealed. "He must have disabled the lie detector somehow." *If I tell them that, they're less likely to suspect that he really did.*

"Nope, we caught him in some lies, so it was working all right."

"What lies?" *Could it really have been working?*

"Why would you need to know that? It's *your* lies we're concerned about."

"Why would I lie? I have nothing to hide." *Now, if you'll just believe I'm lying now, the trap is set.*

"That's good, the right attitude. But we'll just check anyway, just to be sure."

She heard more footsteps entering the room. *They're getting ready.* "You can't put me in that machine." *Don't throw me in the briar patch.*

"Why not?"

"You just can't." *Will this trembling convince you? I don't want to overplay my hand.*

"But you said in court it can't hurt anybody. Were you lying then?"

"I wasn't lying. It can't hurt just anybody, but I'm different. I was trapped in there for six months. I couldn't move. I couldn't talk. It was the most horrible thing that could happen to anybody. If you don't believe me, go to the FBI office and ask Special Agent Capitol. Donald Capitol."

Flowers moved toward the gurney, to where Tess could see the annoyance on his face. "We've already spoken with him, and we know what happened to you. But you're still going to have to go into the machine. And this time you'll be able to talk, so why don't you just do some talking now? Maybe you won't have to go into the machine."

So far, so good. "Please don't put me in there. I'll tell you anything you want, if you just don't put me in there." *I hope Don didn't tell you what kind of talking I could do through Aremac.*

"Oh, excellent. So, tell me where we can find the Aremac source code."

"But I told you, there isn't any source code."

Flowers touched the gurney, moving it an inch or so into the magnet's maw. "Then tell us the object code. Stephen says you have it memorized."

"You know that's a lie. Nobody could memorize all that code. There's more than a million lines."

"He wasn't lying. He says you have an eidetic memory. You remember everything perfectly."

She couldn't lift her arms, but her hands made a dismissive gesture. "That's a myth. Sure, I have a good memory, and I know some tricks, like the number of the badge you flashed at me was 12128."

His eyes widened just a fraction. "Pretty impressive."

"It's just a memory trick, see. 121 is eleven squared. Eleven is seven plus four, and 28 is seven times four. So I can remember it. There's no way I could remember a million lines of code. Especially binary code. It's just a bunch of ones and zeros." *I wonder if I could. I know I can do source, but binary? Maybe I'll try, if I ever get out of here.*

"Well, we'll see, won't we." He turned to the two female agents standing back against the wall. "Check her straps, ladies. Not too tight. She says she doesn't like it when she can't move at all. Just make sure her head can't move after you put on that hair net. We wouldn't want to give the machine any trouble."

One woman moved to each side of the gurney. Tess squirmed as they tightened the straps. "Don't do this, please! If you can run Aremac, why do you need the code anyway?"

"You never know, do you? We might want to make a few slight modifications to the programs."

I'll bet you would. Well, you might be surprised at some of the modifications we've made already.

I just hope they work.

CHAPTER FORTY-TWO

Roger was pleased it didn't take long before Yale's wife, Nellie, adopted a motherly approach to Denise and Marna. They were not that much older than her own daughter, and she quickly learned that Roger was actually younger than her own son. Her son was away at college in the East, and she obviously missed him. *Well*, Roger thought, *she reminds me of my mother, too, so if it makes her happy, we'll play mother-son for a while. The important thing is to get to work on this heater-generator so we can afford to move Tess out here.*

He hadn't heard from Tess in two days. Her voice mail had answered his calls. He might have worried, but she usually let her voice mail take all her calls so she could work without interruption. *She was hoping to close a deal with the Silsbury woman, so she must have been busy. Hey, I'm busy with my own project, but I do miss her.*

While Denise and Marna worked on software problems at Yale's, Roger explained Denise's workplace security plans to Norton. "She says she wants double doors for security."

Norton appraised the existing doors. "I can do that, but maybe we should just replace the garage door with cinder blocks."

"No, we have to keep the large door open for other projects."

Norton's eyebrows shot up. "Other projects? I thought you worked with small stuff."

"Oh, yeah, but we've got a magnet that's as big as a car. Vertical." Roger stood on his toes and raised his arm as high as it would go.

"A magnet that big would be something to see. When's it coming?"

"We don't know yet, but anyway, we have to keep the big door. Can you make it more secure?"

Norton looked the existing doorway up and down, then paced off the space. "I can do anything, but I'll tell you in advance it won't keep someone out if they're determined to get in."

"I know, but it will delay them and cause a commotion. Some of the people who want to break in here will not want the publicity."

"All right, Roger. Give me two minutes while I get the boys started on the doors, then meet me out back."

Out back was an auto graveyard bigger than a football field, sloping upwards from the garages, allowing Roger to see all the cars and trucks from one spot. Closest to the buildings, the ground was littered with unidentifiable machinery as well as old appliances, rusting in the sun. Roger saw a pile of what looked like perfectly usable solar panels.

He was examining one for flaws when Norton emerged from the back door of the larger garage. "You won't find anything wrong with them."

"Then how come they're sitting out here? They must be worth thousands."

"Oh, the weather won't hurt them, and if someone wants to steal one, he's welcome to it. Government surplus. Left over from that collapsed Sandia electrification project. I got them for two cents on the dollar."

Roger took out his handkerchief and wiped a corner of the coating on the window-sized panel. "Wow. What are you going to do with them?"

"Nothing, not until you came along. Now I think we could use them for security."

Roger set the panel carefully aside and tilted up another one for inspection. "Security?"

"Kind of a disguise. Make most folks think that's where the heat is coming from, rather than your little black box."

"Makes sense. Denise will like that."

"Of course, disguise won't prevent someone from eventually trying to peek inside, but the fewer people who try, the better your chances of keeping the secret."

"That's probably the best we can do."

Norton motioned Roger up the slope among the junkers. "Oh, I can do even better than that. I figure the device has to have a radiator and a fan to distribute the heat through the house." He reached into the open hood of a fairly late model Chevy and tapped on the radiator cap. "We have a few hundred of these here, and thousands littering the Rez. We could even take trade-ins to lower cash costs. That will be appreciated."

"So you would circulate heat inside just like in an internal combustion engine?"

"Anti-freeze and all. Some of these stoves will be left in empty hogans for weeks."

Roger unscrewed the radiator cap and peered inside. The antifreeze reached within an inch of the top. "We could keep empty hogans warm."

"Too obvious, and too much against the culture. Even though it wouldn't be wasting anything, people might think it's wasteful to leave the heat on. So, they'd turn off the heat."

Roger fiddled with the radiator cap. "Fine. I bow to your knowledge of the culture."

Norton took the cap from Roger and replaced it. "It's not just culture. It's kind of universal humanity. I'm sure you have Anglo skinflints."

"We do," Roger conceded.

Norton walked further in among the car corpses and picked up a loose chrome Buick grille. "Another universal is kids. And stupid people. So we have to put some kind of grille in front of the radiator. Something like this, plus a mesh screen inside to stop inquisitive little fingers."

"I can picture it. It's getting to be quite a kludge."

"And I'm not finished yet. We'll stick a car battery inside as part of the disguise–" He motioned Roger back down the slope to the appliances. "Then we'll salvage one electric stove burner for the top. People are used to cooking on their wood stoves."

"Nice. How about baking?"

"Some people will want to stick with their traditional outdoor ovens, but, yes, we could make a deluxe model with an oven box. We'll need a thermostat on those. We can probably pull quite a few from these junkers, but lots of them are ruined, like the burners. So we might have to buy new once we use up the scrap."

"What a contraption we're going to have." Roger was grinning while he scanned the junkyard for other ideas. "You know, we could make our black box cool as well as heat."

"Maybe save that idea for later. I don't think there's that much demand for air-conditioning on the Rez. Besides, people who want air-conditioning can use the electricity to run a window unit. It doesn't get that hot up here, and it's a dry heat that people like."

"But it's such an easy feature."

"Easy for you, but it's another complication that could go wrong. These house batteries may not be perfect, but you've got to learn that good enough is good enough. In effect, good enough equals perfect. After all, what's the problem we're trying to solve? To make a perfect heater-generator, or to help people who lack heat and electricity?"

"Still ... " Roger's voice trailed off.

"No, you've got to have a sense of where to stop. And you don't want the device to seem too sophisticated or it will attract more attention. What we've got now is something that looks like it's been cobbled together out of a junkyard, which it will be–except for your little secret inside. Just the sort of thing ignorant savages would build, and of no interest to sophisticated *Biligaana* tourists."

"All right," said Roger, who was testing a Mercury grille with the toe of his boot. "When can I have a working model of a stove?"

"As fast as you can get me a working black box for the inside."

CHAPTER FORTY-THREE

Tess closed her eyes so she could think without being distracted by Flowers and his flunkies. *I'm not going to have much time to work this out. Thinking is all I can do, strapped to this gurney. I can't believe SOS told them anything useful. If he did that, he could have given them the software, and if he gave them the software, they wouldn't be strapping me into Aremac.*

Or would they? Maybe they want to confirm what he told them? But if he's given them the software, it doesn't make any difference what I do. So I have to assume he hasn't, in which case, he found some way to foil the machine. And to make them believe him.

They're taking a long time getting started. Maybe they don't even know how to operate Aremac. Were they bluffing me with the threat of throwing me into the briar patch?

Over by the operator's console, Flowers was talking to someone she couldn't see. She strained to hear, but Flowers must have been facing away from her. She couldn't make out his words.

She heard another person replying to Flowers. He must have been facing her because she could make out a few words. More importantly, she recognized his voice: Willard somebody-or-other, a police technician who had assisted her two or three times when the locals had rented Aremac to extract pictures of crimes from eyewitnesses. *So, they do have someone who knows something about operating Aremac.*

Hopefully, if Willard knew just enough and not too much, she could turn Aremac's features on and off mentally and fool him into thinking it was working flawlessly under his control. *That must what SOS did. At least I hope so.*

She heard Flowers's heavy tread approaching the gurney. "We're not going to hurt you. Willard has explained that pain shuts down the machine. And we're not going to frighten you, for the same reason. But we don't know how easily you frighten, so we're going to give you a little shot to calm you down."

Now he's playing good-cop. A little shot–sure. Damn. Nice, friendly drugs. There goes my brain.

Think, girl. They don't want to knock you out entirely or they won't get anything from you.

Can they keep me awake, unable to think for myself?

She couldn't turn her head, but just at the edge of her peripheral vision, she thought she could see one of the women preparing a needle. *Maybe I need to shut the damn machine down right now. Permanently. But I can't do that until I'm inside.*

She prayed that they would put her inside and turn on Aremac before the injection. She felt her sleeve being rolled up, then a patch of skin on her inner elbow cooling. She smelled alcohol. *I have to do something now, or take my chances being drugged.*

"Wait! I can't–" Before she could finish the sentence, she felt the needle prick her arm. She strained to detect the effects of the drug creeping up her arm. Nothing. She fought down panic. *I won't even know if they've affected my brain.*

But if you're afraid of losing control, won't that give you control? Won't that trigger the fear cutoff?

I don't want that. I want them to turn on the machine and believe what I give them.

Unless I can't resist giving them the truth.

Double damn.

She felt a slight vibration as the gurney was wheeled about a foot into the maw of the magnet.

"I hear it's better if you keep your eyes closed," Flowers said.

Then I'll open them, she thought defiantly. *If I can't see the monitor, I'm not going to be sure whether I'm in control or not.*

She heard the slight hum of the magnet starting up. Her mind soared back to the memory of the efforts Roger had made to reduce the magnet's noise for the comfort of the subjects. Of her, initially. *Oh, oh. My mind is starting to drift. Is it the drug or just wishing Roger was here to rescue me? Not that Roger could do much against the likes of Flowers. Rebecca would make a better rescuer. At least she can shoot straight. She may even have killed people in her former life. She would never talk about it.*

"Comfortable?" asked Flowers, his voice oozing with fake concern.

Oh, God, I was drifting. And he's only going to give me his voice to focus on.

"I'd like you to picture the overall system diagram of the Aremac software."

I'll bet you would. "Screw you, Fowler. I mean, Flowers."

Heidi barked.

What's she doing here? I thought they took her away when they took me.

"We have your dog here. Heidi, that's her name, isn't it? Did you hear?"

"Have you fed her?"

"Don't worry, we wouldn't want to hurt her. You wouldn't either, would you?"

Tess suddenly realized what Flowers was trying to do. Her chest tightened as if caught in one of her father's band web clamps, which wasn't far from the truth, strapped as she was on the gurney. "Leave her alone." Tess was barely able to breathe the words.

"We'll leave her alone–as long as you cooperate."

"You harm her and I'll kill you. Someday, somewhere. Count on it." *Damn. He can hear my voice trembling, and I can't control it.*

"That won't be necessary. Just give us what we want and she'll be fine. Why don't you start with that system diagram?"

"It's too hard. I can't do it if I can't see the monitor."

"Which monitor?"

"Any one. One is on an arm, so it can swing in front of my face. But I have to see Heidi, or I won't do it."

Flowers issued some orders. The monitor appeared about two feet from her face. "All right, there it is. Give us the picture."

"I have to see Heidi."

"You'll see her. We're moving a table so we can put her cage on top."

"It's not a cage. It's a crate." *Now where did that come from. Get hold of your brain. This is the hard part.*

Heidi's crate appeared to the right of her feet. Tess and her German Shepherd studied each other. *They don't know she can read my thought commands–that she can be my hands now that I'm here in Aremac again. She can't do much while she's in the crate, but maybe later–.*

"There, are you ready to go to work?"

Tess thought hard. *Down, Heidi. Down.* Heidi shook her fur, gave Tess a distraught look, then, slowly, lay down. *Maybe that was just a coincidence. Maybe she was going to lay down anyway.* "Okay, I'm ready. Do you know how to put my picture on two screens?" *Now I have to concentrate. This isn't easy.*

"Just a minute," Willard's voice called. Ten seconds later, Tess's screen illuminated with a rough sketch of a system diagram.

It's a true system diagram–but one from more than a year ago. Not a lie, because Flowers hadn't specified a date or asked me for the most recent diagram.

Focusing her mind, she sharpened the image. When it was sharp enough to make the words in the boxes legible, she closed her eyes and conjured up the word, "FABRICATION." *Now comes the first test. I have to make them believe the lie-detection is turned on. Concentrate!*

She spelled out the error message, then opened her eyes and saw "FABRICATION" overlaid on the diagram. *Just don't hurt my dog*, she prayed.

CHAPTER FORTY-FOUR

"We should really have the garage door open," Roger warned, remembering their accident back in the lingerie lab. "You never know what's going to happen when you give the smoke test."

"I agree," Norton said, "but its freezing out there. More than freezing."

"So what? This is a supposed to be a heater."

"Supposed to–those are the operational words. What if it runs backwards or something?"

They had been cautious. Both had plenty of experience with initial trials gone wrong. The very first Hogan Stove–that was the name they'd chosen for their contraption–sat cobbled together in the middle of an emptied garage bay. Norton's entire crew had spent half the morning removing all breakables and combustibles. Norton himself had laid up concrete blocks to make what he called his duck blind–a half-shelter behind which he and Roger now crouched. *We've reviewed all possible contingencies. All we had to do now is screw up the nerve to press the start button.*

The prototype lacked the dummy solar panel, and the on-board starter button had been bypassed for a cable running to the duck blind. Both men knew that the greatest danger of something unexpected was in the first half-second after the button was pressed–much too fast even for agile young Roger to jump out of the way. Now they were a dozen safe feet away, protected by two layers of cinder block with a three-quarter-inch steel plate sandwiched between. And still they were nervous.

"Maybe we should do this outside," Norton conceded. "If this baby blows, I could lose half my new building, but I'd still have the whole mortgage."

"If it blows that big, you won't have to worry about the mortgage."

"My widow would."

Roger stood up, exposing his upper body above the top of the blind. "Okay, let's move the whole thing outside."

"What about security?"

"Nobody will notice what we're doing."

"Ha. Typical dumb *Biligaana*. Two days on the Rez, and you think you understand who's watching what. Believe me, we take this outside and the reporters will be discussing it with the feds over supper tonight in Tuba City."

"That's a hundred miles away–"

"Right, *Kimosabi*. We redskins use smoke signals." Norton grabbed Roger's shoulder and pulled him to the floor. "Get down," he said unnecessarily, then punched the start button. Instantly, the Hogan Stove began to hum. Two seconds later, it began to emit a clinking sound.

Norton slammed the button with his palm. The clinking stopped. "Something loose. Let's go look."

Roger reached the stove first. Glancing at the thermometer wired to the radiator, he let out a deep whistle. "How long was this on?"

"Maybe three seconds. Five, tops."

"It's already up to operating temperature. You should have let it run to see if the cutoff worked."

"Let's find out what's loose first, then we'll run it again." Norton laid his hand tentatively on the Chevy grille. "Maybe we *should* install a cooler. I was just joking before, but it's too bad you can't run your contraption in reverse."

"But I can, more or less. There's lots of ways I could use the energy for cooling–"

Norton laid his forefinger on Roger's lips. "Not on Model I. And certainly not today. Right now, we still have a chance to have this beast ready to demonstrate at the Rug Auction tonight. If we miss that deadline, we have to wait another month for another opportunity. The bells and whistles can wait a while."

Watching Norton check each possible source of a loose connection, Roger could not keep his mind from imagining a dozen potential bells and whistles. He was deep into the virtual design of his second refrigeration unit when Norton broke his revery by pulling his hair.

"Wake up, kid. I found it." He was holding up a blackened piece of wire twisted beyond Roger's recognition. "This little bugger was too close to the heating element. Burned right through, then the long end started vibrating. Get your mind off that refrigerator and start thinking of a new path for this wire."

"How did you know–" Roger started to say, then realized that Norton must have wanted to design a cooler himself. *He's just like me, but older. And, I suppose, quite a bit wiser.* "All right," he said, but his mind had already tossed him sketches of three more solution candidates.

Maybe one of they wouldn't explode and kill us.

CHAPTER FORTY-FIVE

"It's working," Willard's voice called out across the Aremac lab.

"But *she's* not," shouted Flowers. "She's lying to us. Get that dog out here!"

"No, wait," Tess cried. "I'm not lying."

"Sorry, but your own machine caught you."

"No, look at the diagram. It's a real system diagram. What you asked for." *I hope Flowers is studying the diagram.*

There was a pause. "How would I know if it's real?"

"Look at the date. In the box on the lower right."

"The damn thing is more than a year old–"

"But it's a real system diagram. You didn't say which one you wanted. So don't hurt Heidi."

"Clever bitch–and I don't mean the dog. All right, no more games. Give me the most recent system diagram."

"It's more complex. A lot more complex. It will take a few minutes to get it exactly right. My brain doesn't seem to be working really well." *Maybe you won't drug me next time.*

"That would be a very good idea, getting it exactly right. Take your time."

Tess scoured her mind for pieces of obsolete Aremac diagrams and diagrams from other systems that had nothing to do with Aremac. She had to close her eyes to weave over a hundred of those pieces into a superficially plausible diagram that she hoped would fool Flowers and anybody he had in the room. *For a while at least.*

When she had the diagram ready, she held it in one part of her brain and accessed the Aremac program in another. This was the next critical test. The lie-detector had to be off, with Flowers thinking it was on so she could lie without detection. But she was not absolutely sure that SOS had disabled the detection function. The FABRICATED she had composed on the first picture may actually have overlaid the real word that would have been on screen if the lie-detector was on. After all, it was supposed to look exactly like the real message.

The lie-detector switch would be in the emergency escape program in volatile memory, not on the dongle. *That will narrow my search, but there are still thousands of instructions to scan. She felt dizzy. Is this from the drug, or just the hard job?*

It must be the drug. You lived in this machine for six months, so this task should be child's play.

But parts of the program kept going fuzzy.

She willed herself to concentrate, but she had to keep flipping back to the memory of the bogus system diagram. Searching and remembering at the same time was just too much. *It shouldn't be. It must be the drug. I'm not going to be able to pull this off. The way my brain is working now, the system diagram takes just too much memory.*

In the back of her mind, she heard Roger's voice. "If at first you don't succeed, try shortstop." *Don't just try again. Try something different.*

Why are you trying to hold onto both tasks at once anyway? Aremac has terabytes of spare memory.

Piece by piece, she reconstructed a bogus system diagram, saving the vectors and labels in spare Aremac memory. If Willard understood what the operator's console could do, he could watch what she was doing, but he would have to ask the right question. *I hope he's never seen the boys doing this, or if he did, he doesn't remember.*

There, the whole diagram is safely in Aremac's memory.

She wanted to sigh in relief, but she kept her breath sounds consistent. Now that the diagram was coded in a shorthand computer graphic language of vectors and labels, she could devote her entire mind–all but a link to the stored diagram–to the search for the lie-detector switch.

And there it is! Oh, God, it's on. Stephen must have turned it on in case Aremac was used on Rebecca or Alicia, because they can't operate the machine mentally. Sure. Being ignorant of technical details, they had no reason to hide their lies. But SOS did, and so do I. I still didn't know if Aremac classified my original diagram as a fabrication. I'll have to look into that later–if there is a later. Interesting. Can someone fool it with truthful lies?

With a jolt, she realized her mind was wandering again. She set the lie-detector switch to off, then pushed the program to a corner of her mind while she accessed her phony system diagram and reconstructed it for the monitor. When she was done, she fell asleep, exhausted.

The next thing she knew, someone was pinching her thumb. "–given her too much," Flowers was saying.

A female voice told him the drug would wear itself down in a few minutes.

He pinched her thumb again. "I guess we can wait, now that she's cooperating."

"Ouch. That hurt," Tess said, coming fully awake.

"The machine just shut off," Willard shouted. "The pain indicator is on."

"Shit," said Flowers. "I didn't pinch her that hard."

And you don't know I can control that pain indicator, Tess thought, hoping her inner smile didn't show on her face. *Well, I guess it's time to give you the whole program, all million lines. Maybe I'll throw in a healthy dose of Wyatt's old spaghetti code. That will keep them busy. But what will they do when they find out it's bogus?*

I've got to find a way to escape before they start torturing Heidi.

Chapter Forty-Six

The sky was still light, but the first weavers were already standing in line at the main entrance to Crownpoint Elementary School. There were five Navajo ladies whom Roger thought ranged from about twenty to eighty, each holding a carefully folded rug. Or perhaps it was one rug wrapped in a larger one. Roger couldn't tell.

Two of the women's weavings were bundled in plastic, though the sky was only partly cloudy. *It's too cold to rain anyway*, Roger thought, shivering in his light coat. All of the women wore heavy wool or down jackets. They chattered away seemingly oblivious to the cold. *If the cold doesn't bother them, will they care about the Hogan Stove?*

The parking lot was already about one-third full, half with fancy passenger cars that belonged to tourists and serious buyers, the other half with dented pickup trucks. Many of the truck beds were being used as tables for what looked like standing picnics for Navajo families. The tourists mostly milled about, not knowing what to do, though some seemed to have found their way to the drive-in across Main Street. Roger was too nervous to eat, and besides, he wanted to wait for one of the famous Navajo tacos. Norton had pointed out the food stand when they were inside setting up the stove in the lobby.

"Do you think they'll like it?" he asked Norton.

"They'll be too spicy for most of the tourists."

"Not the tacos. The stove." *Oh, no, he was pulling my leg again.*

Norton wasn't doing a good job of hiding his grin. "They'll be cautious at first, but they'll love it."

"We should have put it in the gymnasium where the auction takes place. It was freezing in there."

"It was, but it won't be. The principal doesn't keep the school at full temperature for the auction. Wastes money." He looked around at the gathering crowd, which was starting to cluster near the latched door. More than ten weavers were now in line. "It's cold now, but when that room is packed, everyone will be sweating. It would make them hate the stove."

"But then they won't see the stove out in the lobby."

"Oh, they'll see it when they come in, and they'll appreciate the heat there. And when they're bored with the auction, or don't have any rugs of interest coming up, they'll be wandering around the lobby and the hall, looking for something to amuse them. Why do you think all those jewelry and souvenir vendors are set up all along the hall? They're not doing it as a hobby."

The school doors were opened from the inside, right on time. The weaver line stood disciplined on the right side of the opening, while disorderly tourists pushed in on the left. Roger started for the door, but Norton guided him to his left, where another entrance stood at the far side of the gymnasium. This door brought them to a wide space, a twin to the main entrance hall. The walls were lined with student artwork, including some posters mocking Columbus Day. Mostly, though, the paintings were positive and colorful, with lots of rainbows, flowers, and birds. Some had English printing, others had what Roger assumed was Navajo.

On the right, in the middle of the hall, was one end of the low-ceilinged vendor corridor, lined on one side with more student art. They could see the tourists at the other end swarming in to examine the dozen or so tables with their carefully arranged rings, necklaces, bracelets, Kachinas, pots– and a variety of souvenir junk that probably came from Hong Kong.

The two men made it halfway down the long hall before encountering the crowd, then knifed their way forward to the lobby where the weavers were checking in their wares. Each rug received a number on a yellow ticket, half of which was given to the artist, the other half stapled to the rug. "Doesn't stapling damage the rugs?" Roger asked.

Instead of answering, Norton steered Roger into the back door of the gymnasium, where incoming rugs were being piled on four large folding tables for examination by bidders. "See for yourself."

"Can I touch them?"

"Of course you can touch them." Norton rolled his eyes at Roger's ignorance. "I thought you Syrians knew all about rugs."

"Roger flinched at the stereotype, but said, "That's my uncles. And my cousin Bart. I know diddly about rugs."

"Well, rugs don't break." Norton demonstrated by holding up a three-by-four Ganado and yanking two ends apart. The rug didn't even stretch. "See. That's your first lesson. Now you stay here and play with the merchandise, while I go demonstrate the stove."

Roger put down the corner of a small Storm pattern rug he was beginning to examine. "I'll go with you."

"No, you stay here. We want to give people the impression that the stove is a Navajo product. They'll know already that you have something to do with it, but it's better if the selling is done by me. And Maralah, when she shows up."

"Okay, whatever it takes to sell them. You're costing me a fortune with all the chips you've destroyed in your experiments."

"Don't worry. The stove will sell. You just enjoy the auction."

And Roger did enjoy it, even though the heat swelled to over ninety as the rugs piled high on the examination tables and the room filled. Following Norton's advice, he raced to the front of the rows of steel folding chairs to stake out four chairs for himself, Norton, Marna, and Denise. He laid his coat across three chairs and his cap on the fourth, something he never would have done in Chicago. Here, it seemed that nobody would think of stealing anything, though he couldn't say why.

Their places secured, he went back to examine more rugs. Bidders were pushing and shoving to get their hands on specific rugs. After a few minutes in this tussle, Roger stepped back and watched from a distance, noticing how the weavers themselves sat against the gymnasium walls around the tables, eyes on the bidders, probably noting their preferences. *Maybe they're choosing the size and pattern of their next month's project.* He smiled to himself. *Tess would call it market research.*

He was almost glad he carried only small change. Otherwise, he would have bid on every third rug as a gift for Tess. He tried to imagine which rugs she would like best, regretting that he hadn't paid more attention to her explanations of why she had chosen each weaving in her collection.

Eventually, the tables grew so crowded, he left to scout the vendor tables in the corridor. On one table, alongside some delicate silver chains, he found a book on Navajo weavings. He bought a copy, then waited in line at the Navajo taco stand to buy a taco and a lemonade. He returned to his seat inside the gym, and was halfway through the book when Marna arrived with Denise.

Marna showed Roger a white bidder's card with the number thirty-three. "Just in case I see something cheap that I really love." She made him move their reserved spaces to the left side of the room, so they could see all the other bidders as well as the raised stage. Roger had never been at an auction before, but as the ceremonies moved along, he began to see her logic.

Though fascinated by the auction, Roger couldn't keep his mind off the stove sales taking place in the reception area. When the last rug was sold to a Santa Fe woman who seemed anxious to come home with something, Roger elbowed his way through the crowd to find Norton surrounded by more than a dozen potential buyers. Eager as he was, Roger had the sense to stand to one side while Marna signed up one after another, flashing a smile at Roger after each sale. He was pleased that she seemed to have forgotten the threat of Karl showing up.

By the time the last of the buyers had evaporated, Roger was convinced that Norton had done well, but asked anyway.

Norton gave him two thumbs up. "I even sold five to the Anglos. They didn't really believe the heaters would work, but they wanted Navajo art objects for their Santa Fe homes. One of them owns a gallery and wants me to make twelve of them for a show. I told her I'd have to talk with my partner."

"Sure. Why not? If we don't have to put the workings inside, your own crew can make them without involving me."

"Oh, I'll make them myself. Works of art, you know. She said I'd have to attend the opening, on Canyon Road, no less.

Big time!" Norton raised both hands and wiggled his spread fingers.

Marna and Denise giggled behind him, and Roger laughed out loud. "So how much did we get, altogether?"

Marna checked her notebook. "Not counting futures, like from the gallery, we sold forty-five stoves. I haven't counted the promises, but it's many more."

"We're going to need a bank account," Marna said, "My brother Shilah's wife's sister is a teller at Wells Fargo, in Shiprock."

"I don't trust banks," said Norton. "And if the federals are after you, Roger, you shouldn't either. They can clamp down on you like a roadrunner on a rat snake." Norton paused to let the image sink in. "Besides, we don't have that much in actual cash."

"What do you mean?" said Roger.

"Come back in the gym, and I'll show you."

Roger and the two women followed Norton to the stage, where volunteers were sorting through the unsold rugs. "See those two piles of rugs? We own them–in trade for the stoves."

"In trade?" Roger's head was in his hands. "And how much money, in actual cash."

Norton held up a small roll of bills. "If you mean Benjamins and such, $4,200."

"That's all? For forty-five stoves?"

"*Down payments* on forty-five stoves. And about twelve thousand in checks. Those are from the Anglos." He lowered his voice, though Roger saw only Navajo in the vicinity. "I charged them double–works of art, you know."

"Norton!" Marna squealed. "You didn't, really, did you?"

"Hey, they do it to us, so why not? Anyway, they thought they were stealing–and they looked like they could afford it."

He stepped over the the piles of rugs and lifted a three-by-five Wide Ruins, stroking it between his thumb and forefinger. "But this is where all the money is. Not that all of them are the quality of this one. After all, these didn't make their minimum bids–but we don't have to take the ones we don't want. These are just place holders. When we deliver the stove–" He read the identification tag. "–to Vera Calley–we'll look over what she's got and pick enough to cover the value."

Roger still looked dismayed. "So all our money is tied up in rugs?"

"Oh, no," said Norton, digging in his jacket pockets and pulling out handfuls of silver and turquoise. "We've got jewelry, too."

CHAPTER FORTY-SEVEN

Though she was still bound helplessly to the gurney, for the moment Tess felt safe. *But what will happen when my captors discovered my code was bogus. And it's only a matter of time before they will discover it–at which point Heidi and I will be in danger again. I just can't guess how long it will take.*

She could hear people somewhere else in the building. Quite far away, *That probably means they have a way of checking right now. No doubt they're in the offices trying to hack our personal computers. Or maybe they're in communication with their experts.*

She hoped they couldn't see her deception just by reading the code–she had tried to make the algorithms look plausible. *As soon as they do find out, they'll have me back in Aremac. This time, they might not spare Heidi. Even if I can fool them again, how often can I get away with the same trick?*

And, nobody knows I'm here, so there's no reason for them to let me go. Maybe they'll let Rebecca go, or Alicia, even if they hold SOS as a backup. Rebecca and Alicia don't know anything about the code ... Oh, but they do know who held them captive. If you can believe Flowers's identity card.

She could lift her head far enough to see Heidi whining. *She must have seen my movement. She used to whine when we first crated her, then she learned how to open the door by herself.*

Tess could see that the door was closed. It might have been locked, but the corner of the gurney blocked her view of the latch. If it was locked in some way, there wasn't anything she could do about it, but she'd learned never to underestimate Heidi's resourcefulness.

"Heidi, come!" she whispered, knowing Heidi's huge ears could pick up sounds that would not register with the people down the hall. The sounds of Heidi pawing at the latch would be a different story. She willed her dog to paw quietly, if that were possible, but to open the latch quickly.

The trouble was that Heidi didn't know exactly how to open the latch. She had simply learned to paw at it furiously until it opened. Tess could hear that she was doing that now. *It could take a long time before she hits the latch just the right way–or forever if the kidnappers have added a lock.*

Tess heard footsteps approaching. To her relief, Heidi stopped scratching. A gruff woman's voice from the doorway said, "What's the commotion in here?"

"It's my dog," said Tess, thinking quickly. "I think she needs to go out. Or maybe she needs water."

"Too bad. She's got water." The speaker stepped into Tess' line of sight. A short, wiry woman with chopped bleached haircut and dark eyes with too much liner. Tess recognized fear in her voice. She wouldn't have been the first person to be afraid of the large German Shepherd.

Tess decided to test her observation. "Then you need to take her out."

"Not me. She can crap in her cage." The door slammed. *That woman is definitely afraid to deal with Heidi outside of her crate.*

Tess could not hear footsteps leaving. Maybe it was the door muffling the sound, or maybe the woman was standing outside listening. She would have to take a chance.

"Heidi come!" she whispered, as softly as she could. Tess held her breath as Heidi began scratching again.

A moment later, Tess heard the crate door bang against the wall. In two seconds, she felt Heidi's wet tongue all over her face. Strapped down as she was, she couldn't escape until Heidi decided her face bath was complete.

"Good girl," she said, trying to think through the hard part. Each of her wrists was individually strapped to the table, but she could turn her hands slightly and move her fingers. She had designed the straps that way so the person on the table couldn't interfere with Aremec's operation, but would feel as little constraint as possible. *I wish I had a targeting stick, but hopefully, Heidi will recognize my signals. A stick would be faster, but I have what she have–nothing but my fingers.*

"Heidi, hit it!" she whispered. Heidi knew that command from her earliest training, but she wouldn't know what to hit with her paw unless Tess could guide her by increments.

"Hit it, Heidi!" she whispered, wiggling her fingers. "Hit it!"

Heidi pawed her face, a good first step, but she had hoped the dog would see her fingers and paw there. Heidi wasn't close to the ultimate target, but had the right behavior. Good enough to be reinforced, so Tess made a clicking sound with her tongue against the roof of her mouth. It was not quite the sound of her little clicker, but she hoped Heidi would make the association.

Heidi pawed her face again. Tess clicked again.

Another paw. This time, Tess didn't click. Withholding the click told Heidi that she was not getting closer. Instead, she said "Hit it." She wanted Heidi to continue pawing, but to try some different behavior to earn the click-reward. For a moment, nothing happened. "Hit it," Tess repeated, wiggling her fingers again.

Heidi pawed Tess's forehead. No click. "Hit it."

Heidi pawed Tess's mouth. Click. The finger-wiggle wasn't working, but Heidi was at least moving in the right direction.

Mouth again. No click.

Neck. Click.

Inch by inch, click by click, Heidi moved her paw strikes down Tess's arm until she bumped the back of her hand. But then she moved past the hand and began pawing Tess's thigh.

Tess stopped clicking. Heidi paused, then bumped her thigh again. No click.

After what seemed like endless paws and clicks, Heidi had the general location firmly in mind, but now Tess couldn't reinforce with a click until Heidi found the emergency release of the hand strap. To make matters worse, the drugs seemed to be slowing her reaction to Heidi's attempts.

She dozed off for a moment—or was it longer? She awoke to the sensation of a large German Shepherd paw pressing different spots on her hand and wrist. Each time she moved closer to the release, Tess blinked her eyes awake, then started responding to Heidi's attempts. Heidi had been clicker-trained from puppyhood, so she was quick at this game, but Tess kept dozing off. *It's taking so long. I'm going to hear the lab door open before Heidi finds the right spot.*

Click. For a moment, Tess thought she had made the sound. *No, it was a different click. The door?*

No, stupid. She swore at herself, lifting her forearm. It was the click of the emergency release. She was free!

But she wasn't ready yet. Her drug-dazed mind tried to think of all the work she had to accomplish before someone came into the room and saw her loose. "Heidi, good girl. Crate!"

Reluctantly, her dog slunk back into her crate. *If someone comes in, they might see the crate door open, but that's just a chance I have to take. I mustn't be caught off the table until the rest of my work is done.*

She reached across and released her other hand. Stretching over her head, she pressed both hands against the inside faces of the gap in the huge magnet. She pressed outward as hard as she could, trying to increase friction because there was nothing on the smooth faces to give her a grip.

Hoping the gurney's wheels were not obstructed, she tensed her shoulders and pulled, keeping the outward pressure against the magnet. At first the gurney didn't move, but knowing that starting friction was greater than rolling friction, she clenched her teeth and strained harder.

The gurney began to roll. With only a foot or so to go before her head was fully in the gap, she had to switch quickly from pulling to stopping, but she was a little late. Her head was too far inside.

Now she reversed the procedure, inching back out a hair's breadth at a time until she could look straight up at the black reference mark on the white ceiling above her eyes. *Great. I'm in position.*

She forced herself to take three deep breaths and think through her plan one more time. Then she slid her right arm down to the side of the gurney, letting her fingers guide her to the emergency on-off button.

One more breath, then she had no more excuses. She pressed the button.

Now Aremac was on, and she was inside.

CHAPTER FORTY-EIGHT

For a couple of days, Roger's manufacturing and delivery of Hogan Stoves went without a hitch. Norton's crew was assembling four or five stove housings a day. One of his men, Louis Tsoh, was a skilled tool-and-die maker who had chosen to be underemployed on the Rez–where his type of precision work was scarce–rather than move to a city like Albuquerque where he could have made five times the money. Roger showed the tall, stringy expert what he needed in the way of precision parts, which freed him to work on the delicate electronics. He worked in Nellie's basement, the cleanest venue he could find while waiting for the completion of his clean room at the garage.

He was winding wire with Denise's help when Norton and Marna descended the wooden stairs shivering off their coats along with the end-of-November cold. "You have a problem," Norton said, coat in hand.

"Me?" shrugged Roger. "Not we?"

"I don't think they're after me," Norton said. "Or Maralah. Maybe Denise here, but mostly you, I think."

Denise finally looked up from her magnifier. "Who are we talking about? Who's looking for Roger? And maybe me?"

"My cousins say federal agents are snooping around the Rez asking suspicious questions. Reporters, too."

Roger was inclined to ignore the rumors, but Denise took her security post seriously. "I suppose you can recognize reporters by their flunkies with their video cameras stuck in your face, but how do you recognize federal agents?"

"They were Anglos, they wore suits, and they weren't here for the rug auction. November isn't really tourist time. These two looked like federal agents."

Roger was skeptical. "*Looked* like federal agents? What does that mean?"

Norton started to respond, but Marna restrained him with a raised hand. "Listen to him, Roger. Our people are sensitive to this sort of thing. It's a matter of survival, like recognizing rattlesnakes."

Denise was rapidly scribbling notes on a palm-sized yellow pad. "That's good enough for me. If we're going to make a mistake in our security, we'll err on the side of caution. Any ideas about what we should do?"

Norton was ready with his answer. "Roger has to lie low. You, too, Denise. You have a lovely pink complexion. It makes you too conspicuous."

Denise touched her cheek. "Hey, my grandmother was your grandmother's sister–thirty-thousand years ago, back on the other side of the Bering Strait. I think I'm darker than you. To them, I'll be just another squaw."

"Maybe if you dressed differently," said Marna, pointing to the red-letter slogan on Denise's t-shirt: *I'm sorry. Did I make you think?*

"She's right," said Norton. "Your t-shirts have got to go. And either you wear a bra or something that will hide your ... well, you know."

"A disguise? Cool! Maybe you've got some shirts with Navajo slogans?"

"I don't," said Marna. "But we'll look in my niece's closet."

"What about me?" said Roger, turning his head to show his profile. "An Arab could pass for Navajo, couldn't he?"

Marna ran her finger along his cheekbone appraisingly. "What do you think, Norton? He's got the nose for it, and his hair is black enough."

"He'd have to shave a lot better."

Marna laid her hand against his cheek. "His skin is about as dark as mine."

Norton cocked his head to one side. "I suppose if he wears dark glasses and keeps his mouth shut, he might pass–to Anglo eyes, anyway."

"Hey, why do I have to keep my mouth shut? I'm fluent in Navajo." He rattled off a string of syllables that left the other three looking at him strangely.

"That ain't Navajo," said Norton. Marna nodded her agreement.

"What do you think, Denise?"

She shrugged. "Could be Navajo as far as I'm concerned."

"See," said Roger, triumph in his voice. "It was Arabic, but Denise doesn't know the difference."

"The agents might," said Denise. "Better to keep your mouth shut."

"And stay out of sight," Norton insisted. "As much as possible."

Roger showed his palms in surrender, but Denise wasn't satisfied. "People have already seen us, and they know who we are. Won't someone give us away?"

Norton exchanged looks with Marna. "Our people are not enamored of giving information to federal agents. Or reporters. But, of course, you never know who might be tempted by something they have to offer, like turning the other way to some violation or other. Better you stay inside as much as possible."

"I have to go out to install stoves."

"Maybe, until some of my boys are trained. We'll put you in back of the pickup and wrap you in blankets. No self-respecting *Biligaana* would ride around the Rez like that."

"But it's freezing out there."

"See," said Norton, a grin spreading across his broad face. "A perfect disguise."

CHAPTER FORTY-NINE

Tess mentally checked Aremac's internal clock. *Twenty-thirty. Maybe my captors will quit for the night, leaving me alone in the lab. Probably not. If they take me back to my prison motel room, there goes my plan.*

Twenty-thirty-two. She had to act now, but her cowardly mind kept wanting to run through the risks. *Maybe I could just wait until they release me–or maybe they never will.*

Twenty-thirty-five. I don't usually have this much trouble acting. Maybe being here again, flat on my back in Aremac, immobilizes me. I can't let that happen, but what if Heidi gets hurt?

Twenty-thirty-eight. She was about to put her plan in motion when the door opened. She immediately recognized the blonde's rough voice. "We're going to call it a night. We'll leave the dog here, but we're taking you back to your room. I'll just wheel the gurney into the–. Hey, who moved you?"

Blondie started toward the gurney.

Enough waffling. Now or never.

Tess shut out the woman's voice and sent her mind into Aremac.

Back when she had been a vegetable, she had practiced this fire drill a hundred times, but that was in the old building. She'd never personally tested the new, supposedly improved, fire suppression system, but she knew how it worked. How it was *supposed* to work.

She felt the woman's hand on her knee. Now. No more time. Her mental finger touched the fire alarm.

Before the alarm even sounded, she heard a mechanical clunk from the doorway. "What the–" said the blonde, the rest of her words cut off by the clanging alarm. She hesitated for no more than five seconds, but that was too long. She ran for the door, but the steel fire-limiting door had dropped with a thunk, trapping her with Tess as the colorless fire-suppressant gas hissed into the room.

Blondie froze, staring at the hissing gas jet in the ceiling.

She doesn't know it's harmless. I've got a few seconds before she figures that out.

Tess pushed herself upright, but her legs were still strapped to the gurney. Before she could put her hands on the strap's buckle, Blondie had turned from the door with a drawn pistol. "Just stay right there, Ms. Fixman. My colleagues will be here in a moment to straighten all of this out."

Tess hoped that only the fire department would be able to open the sealed room, but that still left the problem of the pistol. *Well, it's been a couple of years, but they say a Schutzhund - Three dog like Heidi never forgets. Let's find out.*

"*Fass!*," she said in her sharpest German command voice, releasing the leg strap and rolling heedlessly off the gurney, just in case Blondie should get off a shot. But Heidi was out of her crate in an instant, snapping her massive jaws down on Blondie's gun hand, then shaking violently until the pistol clattered to the floor.

Dazed by her fall, Tess tried to stand, but stumbled to her knees. She crawled as fast as she could, racing toward the dropped pistol.

When her hand touched the cold steel she looked up to see the woman frozen to the same spot where Heidi had first bitten her arm.

Where Heidi still held her arm.

Tess picked up the gun, knowing she wouldn't be able to use it if the woman challenged her. She was still wondering if her bluff would work when she noticed the spreading wet spot on Blondie's slacks. Looking up, she saw the look of utter fear in those darkened eyes and knew that as long as Heidi was in the room, there would be no need to use the gun.

Now the waiting began, giving Blondie plenty of time to plead for Tess to call off her dog. Tess didn't know how long it would take the fire department to arrive, so she called Heidi off the woman's wrist with a crisp "*Aus*!"

More German commands: "*Platz! Bleib!!*" Heidi lay down and stayed still, watching attentively as Tess strapped a compliant Blondie onto the gurney.

The main power had been cut off the instant she had touched the alarm, leaving only the emergency lights and a single phone. The room was almost dark, but Heidi would let her know if Blondie tried to get loose. She wanted to call Arnie. She picked up the phone, but it was dead, probably killed by the kidnappers.

There isn't anything I can do until the fire department lets my captors into the room. By now they've probably discovered that my code is bogus. She tried to ask Blondie some questions, but either she was too well trained to answer or too frightened of Heidi. All Tess could do was sit and wait. She hid the gun in the back of the supplies cabinet, knowing she couldn't shoot anybody when they finally came through the door.

After about ten interminable minutes, she heard the sirens and braced herself for what would come next. She need not have worried. When the firefighters came through the door, they were alone. She wasn't prepared for that.

When firefighters saw that Blondie was strapped to the gurney, they gave Tess a questioning look.

Tess thought quickly. "She's a mentally ill patient. She believes she's some kind of secret government agent. We had her here for an experimental treatment but somehow she managed to set off the fire alarm before I could subdue her."

"So there's no fire?"

"I'm sure there isn't, but you can check. Just keep her strapped to the gurney until your ambulance can take her back to Read Mental Health Center. And don't listen to any of her pleas. She can be violent, and she hasn't taken her meds."

Tess was not sure they would entirely believe this story. She reassured the firefighters' captain that she and her dog were okay, then quietly slipped out the front door. She noticed a sign on the door that the offices were closed by the Department of Homeland Security. There was some small print under the notice, but when she leaned over to read the words by the flashing red lights of the fire truck, Heidi emitted a low growl and a female voice said, "It's just legalese. It doesn't give a clue as to who they really are."

Tess turned around. "Alicia. How did you know I was here? How did you get away? Where are Rebecca and SOS? What–"

Alicia raised her mittened hand. "Whoa! One question at a time–but after we get you away from here and out of this nasty wind. You're not dressed for this, and the others are waiting down the street, in the car, near the coffee shop. Are you hungry?"

Tess wanted to know how Alicia freed herself, but she started walking as directed. Heidi stopped to relieve herself, then ran to catch up in a heeling position. Tess wished she was as free as Heidi to use the curb, but she wasn't concerned about food. Not for herself, though Heidi needed to be fed. "What others? Is Roger here?"

"No, but as soon as we got free, we told him what happened–"

"He's not coming here, is he?"

"No, he wanted to, but your attorney was worried they would kidnap him, too. So your husband is still in New Mexico, hoping you'll join him soon. Very soon."

CHAPTER FIFTY

Riding in the back of Norton's truck, all Roger could think about was the news that Tess had been kidnapped days ago, but was now free. He didn't notice the passing countryside, but as soon as the pickup was two miles out of Many Farms, Norton pulled onto the shoulder and rapped on the back window, motioning Roger to come up front. Roger happily shed all three of his blankets and climbed over the railing.

When he opened the cab door, Norton said, "Better keep one of those blankets. The heater's not that good. And put a rock or two on the other blankets so they don't blow away."

"Where am I going to get a rock?"

"Gee, I don't know." Norton stretched his neck, peering over Roger's shoulder at the side of the highway. "Do you suppose anyone would miss one of those?"

Roger turned and felt himself blushing as he gazed upon the millions of rocks among the prickly pear and chamisa lining the roadside. "I was thinking about something."

"Maybe you should learn to think with your eyes open. It's an old Indian trick."

"You're making fun of me," Roger said, smiling. He jumped down from the cab and found two football-sized salmon-colored rocks. He heaved them into the truck's bed, then climbed in after them. He took the cleanest blanket for himself, shook it out, then folded the other two and pinned them down with the rocks.

Inside, the cab seemed warm enough without the blanket, maybe in contrast to the slate-gray overcast day outside. Roger wrapped himself in the blanket anyway, carefully aligning the stripes vertically as Norton had instructed–otherwise, according to the Dineh, he would go crazy. Roger didn't believe that, but someone who saw him might.

There wasn't one chance in a thousand that anybody else would be using this road just now, but Norton looked both ways before pulling the pickup back onto the barely paved surface. "About what?" he said as soon as their speed was up to a bumpy fifty-five.

"About what what?" said Roger.

"What you were thinking about."

"Oh. I was thinking about Tess. I want to go to Chicago."

"I understand, but all you'll do there is expose yourself to the same risk. Better she should come here."

"I know that, logically. But I'm not sure she'll be safe anywhere now."

"Didn't she say she has a record of her kidnapping? She can blackmail the government with that."

"If it *was* the government. We don't even know all the people who might be after us, and that made me think how vulnerable we are. Maybe we should try Marna's idea of putting the company in her father's name."

"To protect the assets from her husband?"

"That, too, but also to give us another level of anonymity. And so we can get some credit cards."

"Why credit cards if you want anonymity? Besides, they're a rip off. I always pay cash. Or a check, if I want a receipt."

They passed a small hogan set in a patch of trees about a hundred yards off the road, the first dwelling Roger had seen since leaving Highway 191. "If we had cash, I'd pay cash, too. We're running out of parts. And cash to pay for more. I figure we can float some money on credit cards until we figure out how to get more cash for these stoves." He turned and looked back to see if both stoves were still in place, though he knew Norton had securely roped them down.

"I don't need cash for parts. I've got lots of things to trade." Norton patted the toolbox on the seat between them. The real tools were in the back. This one contained a selection of jewelry they had received as down payments.

Roger wasn't convinced. "I'm running out of beryllium and crystals, Norton. I don't think I can trade a squash blossom necklace for a shipment of piezoelectric crystals. But I'm pretty sure I can charge them to a credit card. Up to our credit limit, anyway."

"And pay an arm and a leg in interest."

They passed a turnoff for Rough Rock. "Isn't that where we want to go?"

"It's not in the town. That's just the closest address. About three miles ahead, we start looking for a dirt road off to the left."

Roger began looking, but it was hard to tell what bare patch among the rocks might be a road. "I hope we can pay them off before we start having to pay interest. Tess may have some more money in Chicago, but I don't know if she can get at it safely."

"Didn't she send you an email?"

"No, we agreed to minimize communication because we might be monitored. That's why I didn't worry when I didn't hear from her. Then Rebecca called to say they'd been released. Or escaped."

"They could be tapping phones, too?"

"Yes, they could." Roger pointed out the window. "Hey, is that the road?"

Norton shook his head, but slowed down noticeably. "I think it's the next one. Keep looking."

Roger would have missed the next one, but Norton whipped the pickup left into what looked like bare, rocky ground. Only when they were out of sight of the road could Roger see the two parallel wheel tracks clearly. No building was in sight, though there was only low scrub to block the view. About two bone-jarring miles in, he saw that the road dropped off into a shallow canyon with a small hogan perched on a broad shelf above a dry wash in the bottom.

After a precarious ride down the road that hugged the face of the canyon, Norton stopped about a hundred feet from the six-sided hogan. Roger counted eight sheep in a wire-enclosed pen. He noted the neat white picket fence around a modest garden with dry stalks and leaves from last summer's vegetables. Seeing no people, he started to open the car door, only to be restrained by Norton's hand on his shoulder. "You should know better by now, *Kimosabi*. Wait for them to check us out and greet us."

After what seemed like five minutes, an ancient, stooped Navajo woman emerged from the blue door. She exchanged some words with Norton. The only one Roger understood was *Ya'at'eeh*, a simple hello. Norton then opened his door and walked over to greet her. He continued talking, motioning towards Roger, until the old lady nodded. She went inside while he fetched Roger from the truck.

"I explained to her that you don't speak the language. You must look like one of the People to her."

"So, my disguise must be pretty good, if I can fool her."

"Well, Grandmother Black is half-blind, and I don't think she's seen a *Biligaana* for the last forty years. She probably thinks you're a mute, so it's best if you don't talk–if that's possible. We should have this routine down by now."

They went to the back of the pickup. Roger climbed up and began to untie the smaller of the two stoves. "She must have seen some of us at the auction."

"She wasn't there. Her granddaughter bought the stove for her. She's worried about grandmother living alone out here, but she looks like she's doing okay. Her sheep look healthy, and it's been five or six years since grandfather died."

Roger put his shoulder against the stove and slid it towards Norton. "I don't suppose her granddaughter paid cash."

"Actually, grandmother's going to pay. Evidently, she wouldn't hear of her relatives paying."

Roger looked at the scraggly spread. "I guess it won't be cash then."

Norton tipped the stove on the edge of the tailgate. "Better than cash. Grandmother is one of the master weavers on the Rez. The cheapest of her *Teec Nos Pos* rugs would bring twice the price of a stove–the *Biligaana* price."

Roger jumped down and helped Norton lift the stove and carry it into the hogan. Inside was one large room with a few pieces of plain furniture, but dominated by a huge loom in the center containing a three-fourths finished weaving in a dozen vegetal-dyed yarns. Roger stood staring at the intricate pattern, mouth hanging open in admiration and fascination. He could see patterns within patterns within patterns, and would have stood there forever without Norton kicking him in the shin and inclining his head towards an empty corner.

To Roger, the inside of the hogan felt even colder than the November day outside. *For good reason*, he thought. Grandmother Black had obviously been anticipating them and their stove. Roger could see from indentations in the floor that she had moved furniture that looked too large for her frail frame to budge. *Or maybe she had help, though the narrow bed reinforces the idea that she lives alone.*

They spent several minutes discussing the proper location for the stove, Roger thinking it would be more efficient more to the center of the room, but Norton insisted it go close to the wall so nobody could run around it—which, according to Dineh lore, would cause the hogan to burn down.

Once the location was settled, installing the stove was mostly a matter of ensuring that it was level, then attaching the inoperative solar panel to the south wall of the hogan. They would have been out in fifteen minutes and driving to their next stop, but Grandmother Black insisted that they stay while she tested the stove by making them coffee. The stove worked perfectly, and she had no trouble understanding its operation. While they sat on low stools and sipped bitter coffee, she chattered away, apparently explaining the rug pattern in words that Roger didn't understand. Even so, from her elaborate hand motions, he felt he understood something of what she was trying to say.

When they were finished with the coffee, she went to a pile of carefully folded rugs on a wooden table on the east side of the hogan. After a short discussion with Norton, she opened one of the rugs for their viewing—another vegetal-dyed *Teec Nos Pos*, if Roger recalled his book correctly. Norton examined the rug carefully, but Roger could see it was just a courtesy. After the inspection, Norton nodded and accepted the rug, showing both sides to Roger before folding it carefully and taking it outside.

A few shreds of blue were just breaking through the gray sky. In the sunlight, the colors of the rug were even more striking. Though the sun had been visible for mere moments, Roger realized that the inside of the hogan had already heated appreciably above the outside temperature. The stove worked. Grandma Black would now be able to weave her rugs with less pain in her obviously arthritic hands.

While Norton wrapped the rug in a black plastic trash bag, he asked Roger what he thought of it.

"It's beautiful–but I liked the one on the loom better."

"It's for a museum. Not for us. What did you like about it?"

Roger climbed in the cab, saying nothing until they were safely over the loose rocks on the narrow road out of the canyon. "I can't explain, exactly. The colors were about the same, and it was the same type of pattern. But it had something else, something ineffable."

"That's just a fancy word that says you can't explain it."

"Maybe what I'm talking about was my reaction to it. It was breathtaking."

"She saw that. She asked me if you were a weaver."

"She did? What did you tell her?"

"I said you were. She said she could tell."

CHAPTER FIFTY-ONE

Traffic was almost non-existent, so Tess crossed the first street against the light, desperately wanting to move far away from the Aremac office as quickly as possible. Heidi hesitated for a moment, then seemed to decide it was better to break the law than leave Tess unguarded.

It was difficult to talk with the cold wind in their faces, but as soon as they were out of sight of the office, Tess couldn't contain her questions to Alicia. "You said the others were waiting. Which others?"

"Rebecca. SOS. Your attorney, and mine."

"Did Arnie–my attorney–get you all out?"

"No, Arnie didn't even know we'd been kidnapped. Neither did my attorney, but when I didn't show up for a meeting yesterday, Wendell started asking around. He has influence in the right places, but it still took twenty-four hours to get me and the others released. These people, whoever they are, claimed they didn't know anything about you, but somebody in the government obviously did."

Tess's eyes were teary from the wind, but she could now see the distinctive red and yellow blinking of the coffee shop sign. She stopped asking questions and hurried her pace. Maybe a warm room and hot food would stop her shivering, though she suspected the cause was dread, not cold.

Arnie, Rebecca, and SOS rushed out the front door to meet her, their faces taut with worry. A short, round man wearing a fur hat lingered in the background–Wendell, Tess assumed. Arnie hugged her tightly, then dragged her inside without releasing the hug. "Are you okay? Did they harm you?"

"Not physically." Suddenly, she stiffened. "Wait. Where's Heidi?"

"I put her in the car with a chew stick," said Rebecca. "Come sit down. We have a table over there in the corner."

After Tess assured and reassured everyone she was okay, Alicia introduced her attorney. Tess, still shivering, anxiously scanned the other people in the restaurant. "Are we safe here?"

Arnie removed his cashmere coat and draped it over Tess's shoulders. "I assume your captors don't want to be seen in public, so we're better off here than anywhere else."

Tess tried to see out the windows, but all she could make out were shadows of cars cruising the neighborhood. "They did disappear quickly when they heard the firefighters arriving. All but the one I had captive."

"Where is she?" Alicia asked.

"Hopefully on the way to a mental hospital. I didn't want her around to see where I was going."

Arnie stopped studying the menu. "Is she injured?"

Oh, Arnie. Always thinking of lawsuits. "Just some bruises where Heidi made her drop her gun."

Arnie shut the menu decisively. "So, now it's guns. If they're that desperate, they'll no doubt try to kidnap you again."

Even bundled in Arnie's coat, Tess felt cold shuddering through her body. "Who are these people? Are they really government, or was that a disguise?"

Wendell blew on his hands. "They are definitely from some government agency, or agencies. I discovered that much, but beyond that, I don't know. I assume they're some sort of secret counter-intelligence operation."

Tess sighed. "That makes sense–in a nonsensical sort of way all these people have. The FBI has been after Aremac right from the beginning. But can they just kidnap American citizens and hold them in secret prisons?"

Arnie tried to wave down a waitress carrying dirty dishes, but she kept her eyes focused on the kitchen door. "Under present laws, they can do pretty much as they please, though the legal justifications are rather shaky. I suppose the last thing they want is publicity."

SOS removed a thumb-sized gray device that was clipped in his pocket protector. "They may not want publicity, but we can sure give them the whole load. Aremac recorded everything, everything they said or did in the lab. I guess they didn't realize what it could do."

The waitress emerged from the swinging kitchen doors, carrying a tray, still ignoring Arnie's attempts to catch her attention. He stopped trying and turned back to his companions. "That recording won't do you any good, SOS. They've taken over your building, claiming you violated the FDA injunction. So they have Aremac. And your recording."

SOS held up the gray flash drive. "Not to worry, Arnie. Aremac transmits its logs to two of our remote servers in real time. And yes, I've backed it up already. They won't find all the copies–including this one."

"That may be," said the lawyer. "But I don't think we can use those recordings. Maybe later, but for now, I think they're going to keep after Tess–and maybe Roger–until they steal what they want."

Wendell nodded his agreement. "These are not nice people. I was lucky to get Alicia out. You, Tess, I don't think I could have gotten out, no matter what strings I pulled."

Tess wondered what strings he had pulled to get the others out, but the waitress finally arrived to interrupt her thoughts. Everyone ordered hot drinks, which Arnie supplemented by asking for a selection of desserts.

Tess was hungry, but really didn't want to think about food right now, so she let Arnie order her broccoli-and-cheese soup. When the waitress left, Tess reached across the table and placed her hand on Alicia's. "I'm so grateful for what you and Wendell did for us, but would you two mind sitting on the other side of the room for a few minutes? We have some confidential matters to discuss."

Alicia stood immediately. "Of course, dear. Come, Wendell, we should leave."

"Oh, no, don't leave the restaurant. Please. We should be finished by the time the food comes, then I'd like you to sit with us again. Okay?"

"Certainly," said Alicia, and led Wendell to the farthest booth, passing four senior citizens as they paid their bills and left the restaurant.

In spite of their distance, Tess leaned in and lowered her voice. "I think, Arnie, that you and Wendell are right about these people. From what I've just been through, I'd guess there's not much that would stop them."

Tess paused. The other three signaled their agreement. "We've got to get to someplace safer. I propose we immediately move *everyone* to Navajo Country–"

Arnie shook his head vigorously. "There's still a risk there. The FBI–or pseudo-FDA–could come in any time. It may be safer than here in Chicago, but it's not safe enough. In my opinion."

"I trust your opinion. In that case, will you negotiate a contract with Alicia's organization? I think they have some clout."

"Maybe," said SOS, "but how will that help us? I mean, I know we need money, but unless we use it to hire a private army, how are we going to keep these bozos away?"

The waitress arrived, followed by a younger waitress carrying a second tray. Arnie directed a portion of the order to Alicia's booth, dismissing both waitresses. "He's right, Tess. Under ordinary circumstances, a JFA contract would be a smart business move, but now ... ?"

"Aremac will be our distraction. We'll take the contract. We'll assemble Aremac II on the Rez, but nobody will know about our other projects–like the fast sleeper or the charger."

SOS looked up from his bowl of chile. "You're a few days out of date, Tess. I spoke to Roger and convinced him to lay off the sleeper until he figures out where his headaches are coming from." He lowered his voice. "And the charger is kaput. Now it's a stove."

A stove?

Tess wanted to ask a thousand questions, but Arnie interrupted her thoughts. "Assembling an Aremac on the reservation may distract the bad boys from your other projects, Tess, but that's not going to stop them from kidnapping you again. Or Roger."

"Then we'll both go to Africa for a while. We'll install the new Aremac."

"Africa?" Rebecca and SOS said in chorus. "Why Africa?"

"It's far away. And safe."

Rebecca shook her head so hard the dishes on the table rattled. "That's naive, Tess. Africa is a huge continent, and half of it is at war. Where in Africa did you have in mind?"

"If Alicia's organization has the influence she says they do–and Wendell's success at freeing us seems to support that– they should be able to find some African country where we can continue development without American interference."

Movement near the front door caught Tess's eye. Since the seniors left, the Aremac group had been the only patrons, but a man and woman in overcoats were now entering. They were middle-aged, possibly even retirees. Tess watched them seat themselves at a booth off to one side. Though it was quite warm in the restaurant, they didn't take off their overcoats. The way they kept themselves so carefully wrapped, Tess imagined that they might be naked underneath. Or hiding something else.

Rebecca whispered, "Don't they look a little like Lucille Ball and Desi Arnez?" SOS looked puzzled, so she explained. "They were old TV comedians, Stephen. Very famous before your time."

"Maybe in the Middle Ages," he said.

Everybody but Tess laughed. *They may look like comedians, but all of a sudden, I don't feel safe.*

Rebecca must have noticed her reaction. "They're probably nobody, Tess, but from now on, we do have to suspect everybody. Arnie, can you negotiate a contract without Tess and Roger?"

Arnie pushed away his empty pie plate. "No problem."

"All right. I'll stick with Tess until I've got her safely out of the country, then Stephen and I will head for New Mexico to do the same for Roger."

Tess wanted to say something, but Rebecca was digging in her purse and didn't look up. Tess feared Rebecca's hand would emerge with her gun, but instead she extracted several bills and dropped them on the table. "You stay here, Arnie, and start working with them." She inclined her head towards Alicia's booth, then stood. "Let's go, Tess. To O'Hare. We may still be able to get you on a late flight to Europe."

"But I have no clothes. No passport."

"I have your passport, and it's not safe to go to your house. I'll pack some scanties later and ship them to you. Or you can go commando. We need to do a bunk. Now."

CHAPTER FIFTY-TWO

It was a risk, but Roger insisted on driving with Norton to Gallup to meet cousin Bart's train. It had been just after they left Grandma Black's with her rug payment that he'd thought of bringing out one of his uncles, Qasim or Zahid, to handle the job of exchanging cash for their rugs–and for the jewelry, if that was possible. The uncles ran an import/export business, with a retail shop in Chicago's Merchandise Mart, plus a wholesale trade that took them all over the world.

They had never been to the Navajo Nation, but he knew they handled some Navajo rugs because Tess had one from them as a gift. He'd called Qasim with a phone card from an anonymous pay phone, asking if one or the other could come out and appraise rugs for them–maybe taking some into their shop and selling them. Qasim had readily agreed to handling the rugs, but said neither he nor his brother–who was now on a buying trip to the Middle East–could come to New Mexico.

Instead, Qasim proposed sending his son, Barakah. Bart, as he was called, was almost Roger's age and just entering the business. He might be inexperienced, but his father, who didn't bestow praise easily, called him a "fast learner." Roger couldn't very well refuse the offer. Also, he was truly pleased with the idea of having his cousin with him in New Mexico. Even so, he had his misgivings about what kind of salesman Bart would be. *Maybe I just can't picture little Bart as a grown-up.*

Anyway, it was too late now for doubts. The pickup cruised toward the station down Coal Avenue–old Route 66, as many signs proudly announced–between the tracks on the right and the myriad pawn shops, taverns, and hotels on the left. Sitting in back, Roger stopped worrying about Bart and assessed the effectiveness of his blanket disguise. The dozen or so people who were outside seemed far more intent on surviving the cold than in looking through disguises to find Anglo inventors on the run. When Norton parked at the almost deserted station, he decided to risk exposing himself on the platform so he could greet his cousin personally.

He was only exposed for five minutes. They were three minutes early, and the train was two minutes late. During that time, he saw nobody suspicious in the arrival area. In fact, he saw hardly anybody at all until a uniformed trainman came out to meet the arriving Southwest Chief.

Roger expected to see Bart standing on the open stair, waving the way they always did in the movies, but it wasn't until the train had glided and squealed to a complete stop that his dark-skinned cousin appeared. He was the only passenger descending from the first-class car–if you didn't count Howler, his black-and-tan German Shepherd wearing his orange seizure-dog vest.

Norton grunted as he lifted both of Bart's huge suitcases. "What have you got in here? I hope it's money."

Bart seemed to take him seriously. "There's a lot of paper, but it's not money. My father always pays in gold." Then he broke into a big grin.

Norton laughed, dropped the suitcases, and extended his huge hand to Bart. "I'm going to like this cousin of yours, Roger. I already like his dog. Does he shake hands, too?"

"He's a working dog," Bart explained. "He's not supposed to interact with other people while he's watching after me."

Norton picked up the suitcases again. "Guarding all this gold? I couldn't run very fast with it."

"Actually, he's sort of guarding me. In case I have a seizure. He warns me when I'm about to, so I can lie down safely."

"A seizure. Is that where you twitch all over and see visions?"

They reached the pickup. Norton unlocked the cab and hefted the two cases behind the seat. "We have a holy man over near Sand Spring who has visions like that. Well, we *had* one. I don't know if he's still around. I don't think he had a special dog, but maybe he did."

Bart ordered Howler to jump in the truck bed, then climbed into the cab. "People have told me I twitch, but I'm not aware of it. And I don't know if you'd call what I see a vision. Maybe."

Roger climbed inside, squeezing Bart over against Norton. He was glad to see how casually his inventor friend accepted his cousin's handicap. but he worried that Bart might get sick on the Rez and not be able to do the job he'd come out for.

It was just after seven when their pickup pulled out of the station, with barely enough light to see the red sandstone cliffs in the distance. Roger wanted to have dinner somewhere and talk about what was going on in Chicago. He was starved for news, but Bart said he wanted to see if some of the pawn shops were open so he could study prices and quality of rugs. Roger thought that was a good sign, but didn't think many shops would be open.

"That's not a problem," said Norton, making a u-turn and parking in front of a red-and-yellow false front brick building with glass blocks for windows. An overhanging red sign plugged Coca Cola, but the sign on the face of the building said "American Bar." "There'll be some owners in here, wrapping up their day. The ones I know will be more than happy to open up for a big-shot rug dealer from back East."

Roger and Bart waited outside until Norton came out a few minutes later with a coatless, flabby fellow who went right next door and unlocked Arbuckle's Pawn Shop for their inspection.

Bart spent more than an hour examining every rug in the store–at least fifty by Roger's count. He chatted knowledgeably with Mr. Arbuckle, occasionally turning to discuss prices in Arabic with his cousin. Arbuckle probably thought they were speaking some Navajo dialect. Norton kept up the pretense by looking as if he understood.

Afterwards, Arbuckle shook Bart's hand and invited him to come in any time to buy or sell or just talk. Bart said he'd come back in a few days to discuss jewelry, once he was settled. When Arbuckle had locked up and returned to the American Bar, the three men piled back into the pickup. "He definitely thought you were Navajo," said Norton. "Or maybe some other tribe. With your dark skin and big nose, we won't need to disguise you, like Roger."

"You think we can get away with it," Roger said, appraising his cousin's profile.

"Sure, to the *Biligaana*, all Indians look alike–even if they're Arabs."

Roger laughed, then saw that his cousin wasn't laughing. "What's wrong, Bart?"

"It's not about what he said. I think it's funny, too, but I have a message for you, something they couldn't send by email or phone. I should have given it right away, but I couldn't think how to break it to you."

"What's wrong?"

"Tess was kidnapped–"

"What?!" Roger grabbed his cousin's shoulders and shook him, hard. "What are you talking about?"

Bart pried Roger's hands away. "Don't worry. She's all right now."

"All right? Where is she?"

"She's headed for Africa, and you're supposed to join her. Right away. With your Aremac."

Chapter Fifty-Three

The moment Rebecca stood, Tess noticed "Desi" hit one button on his cell phone and put the instrument to his ear. Then he turned his face away from her and began talking. "Lucy" turned away, too, but took something from her purse. She seemed to be checking her makeup in a small mirror, but Tess could see her eyes. *She's not looking at her face, but at me.*

Tess tugged at Rebecca's sleeve and whispered, "Don't leave. Just go over and fetch Alicia and her lawyer."

When Alicia and Wendell sat down with them, Tess saw Desi close his cell phone and begin intently stirring his coffee. Lucy put away her mirror, but when she turned her head for a moment, Tess noticed she was wearing some sort of earbud. Tess asked Wendell for a piece of paper, but when he hesitated about tearing out a page, SOS handed her a three-by-five card and an orange pen from his pocket protector.

On the card, she carefully printed, "I THINK WE'RE BEING WATCHED. MAYBE LISTENED TO. DON'T LOOK AT THEM."

Nobody questioned to whom she was referring, or whether she was being paranoid. SOS took out another card and wrote, "WHAT DO YOU WANT TO DO?"

Tess thought a while, then wrote, "WE THREE WILL GO POWDER OUR NOSES. YOU MEN PLAY SENTRY."

Alicia and Rebecca nodded, then all three women rose and headed for the toilet. It was a small room, dimly lit, with two stalls and one sink, and smelling of heavily scented hand soap. Crumpled paper overflowed the single wastebasket, but other than a quick exchange of disapproving glances, none of the women commented on the lack of tidiness. Rebecca put her back against the door, listening for any sound outside. "I think we're secure in here, but keep your voices down."

"Am I being over cautious?" Tess asked.

"Considering that you've just escaped from kidnappers," Alicia said, "I don't think so. What do you want to do?"

Tess asked Rebecca for a copy of Alicia's written offer. "If this is still open, we would like to accept your request to buy one or more Aremacs. We thought we'd let the lawyers work out the details while Rebecca and I escaped to the airport. We figured we might catch a flight to Africa–or at least to Europe if there's no direct flights. But it looks like we're being followed."

Alicia took the small folder from Tess, looked it over, then handed it back. "Yes, the offer is still open, and that's wonderful news. I mean, not about being followed–"

"We may be listened to, as well. That's why I came in here. I think that woman, the one that looks like Lucille, has some kind of listening device. Is that possible?"

Rebecca moved away from the door and herded the other two toward the stalls. "Not only possible, but quite likely with modern spy technology. Probably can hear through that door, too, so let's start flushing toilets. Tess, you flush that one–" She pointed to the right. "–and Alicia, you flush the other, but alternately, so there's always noise. I'll stand here where I can talk to both of you and watch the door at the same time."

It took a few tries to coordinate the flushing, because the toilets refilled too slowly so there was dead space. Rebecca turned on both of the sink's faucets, but they still had to stop speaking during the quiet intervals. When Rebecca was finally satisfied that their white noise screen would suffice, she told Alicia she could speak, but as softly as possible.

"I'm extraordinarily pleased at your decision, Tess, but I think you're foolish to imagine you can escape by commercial airline."

"Why?"

"These people are connected to the government somehow. All they have to do is give your identifying information to airport security and claim you're a terrorist suspect. You'll be caught before you ever get near a plane, and you'll be right back in their hands."

"She's right," said Rebecca. "I wasn't thinking."

"I didn't think of that, either. If I can't leave the country after all, where can I hide?"

Alicia started to speak, then paused for the dead space between flushes. "Oh, you can leave the country all right. Just not by plane."

"You mean drive? Like to Canada? Won't they check that border, too?"

"It's a big border, so you might get through, but I have a better idea. JFA has several charter ships carrying equipment and supplies from the US to Africa. I think there's one due to leave later this week. I don't know the exact date, but I know the dock we use in New Jersey. We can drive there and hide out until the next ship leaves."

"Are you coming with us, then?" Rebecca asked.

"You want to go, too?" Alicia asked. "There's nice cabin space on board the ships, but it's quite limited. And some of it might be reserved already."

"No way Tess is going without me." Rebecca removed her pistol from her purse, checking the clip as if to emphasize her point. "Do they check passengers for weapons?"

"Not on freighters, as far as I know. You'd basically be treated as crew, but I'll need to make a few phone calls." She waited again for the next flush. "On an absolutely safe phone."

What kind of phone does she have? She sounds so confident. Tess wanted to ask, but all she said was, "So how do we get to New Jersey?"

"I figure we'll shake Lucille and Desi, then just drive. There are dozens of directions we might take out of Chicago, so as long as they don't know where we're going, we should be all right. But no credit cards or phone calls along the way."

Tess handed the JFA offer back to Rebecca, then showed her empty hands. "I have no credit cards. Or money."

Rebecca put her gun and the folder back in her purse, then inspected her wallet. "I have less than fifty dollars."

Alicia checked her purse. "I'm about the same. That won't be enough."

"Arnie always carries a lot of cash," said Tess. "Does Wendell?"

"I don't know. We'll take all he can spare. I can use an ATM if we do it close to here, so we don't show them which way we're going."

Rebecca tucked away her wallet. "Me, too, but maybe we should go a mile or so west or south, get the money, then turn towards New Jersey. It will take a little longer, but it might be worth it."

"There's some cash in the office, and probably some checks," Tess said, then hesitated. "But I suppose we can't risk that. But maybe SOS has some cash."

"I hope so," said Alicia. "We're taking the boy with us. And the dog."

CHAPTER FIFTY-FOUR

When Tess's next message arrived, Roger imagined a young brave in a loin cloth and moccasins running hundreds of non-stop miles through woods and mountains, splashing through streams, canoeing across lakes, tiptoeing across sharp black lava fields, and falling exhausted into the arms of the next runner who took the leather pouch and began the next leg without a word.

Norton did confirm that the single sheet had come in a leather pouch, but Roger hadn't seen the pouch and suspected Norton was kidding again. According to Norton, the message had been carried by a hand tools salesman making a regular call on the garage. It had been hand-addressed to one "Rogger Fissmen." Assuming Tess still knew how to spell his name, he knew the message must have been transmitted orally at least once.

The message was simple and unlikely to make much sense to anyone else: "MAKE SNOODS QUICK. MAGNETS COMING. JUSTICE MONEY." To Roger, however, it was clear. Tess must have signed a contract with Justice for Africa. Since magnets, plural, were coming, the contract must be for at least two Aremacs, which meant plenty of money, though he had no idea how it would be delivered. And since he was to make snoods, that meant the supply of snoods in the Chicago office was either destroyed or inaccessible. Hand-building the carbon nanotube snoods would be on the critical path. Since he was the only one who had the skills to make them, he had to push other projects aside and start right away.

The inventory of carbon nanotubes in Crownpoint, New Mexico was zero, other than the small cache they had brought from the lingerie lab. It might be enough for one snood, but certainly no more.

Mr. Arbuckle had said his pawn shop had just about anything valuable somewhere in stock, but he'd never heard of carbon nanotubes. In all of Gallup there were none, and Albuquerque wasn't much better. Marna was sure there were some in Los Alamos, but none they could access, so Roger dispatched Denise and Bart to Phoenix to purchase as much of the rare material as they could find. Denise would stand guard, but Bart would make the purchase, since Denise was too easily recognized.

Once the others were gone, Roger set to work in Nellie's basement to make the first snood. At first, his only audience was Marna, who volunteered to be his gopher if he would explain the theory as he worked. He liked that. He also liked the intense halogen light she brought downstairs after she watched him straining his eyes. Her nephew's school microscope, which wasn't exactly a laboratory-grade instrument, was ten times better than his naked eye for part of the work.

Even with these aids, his eyes could only take about two hours of snood work at a time. On his second break, he saw that Norton had come in unnoticed, watching the work with interest while waiting for Roger to finish. "You got a big package waiting for you at the garage. What do you want me to do with it?"

Roger spread his hands, measuring the space in front of him. "How big?"

"Your arms aren't long enough. It's about the size of a car, but taller. And marked fragile."

"The magnet. It must be the magnet."

"Well, then it's the goddamn biggest magnet I ever saw. Bigger than the junkyard down in Gallup."

"I'll get my blankets. Did anybody see it arrive?"

"You're kidding, right? No, I'm sure nobody took any note of a two-ton magnet. We get eight or ten dozen every day here in Crownpoint."

"Right," said Roger, starting up the stairs. "Are you coming, Marna?"

"Wouldn't miss it for the world. I'm still a physicist, you know. We're attracted to magnets."

Roger was surprised at Marna's little joke. *Maybe she's starting to feel comfortable back in her own home.* On the ride over to the garage, he decided to explain to Marna and Norton about some improvements he'd dreamt up for the snood. "I can't wait to try them out."

Norton reached across Marna and punched Roger's arm. "Maybe you ought to wait at least until you have more of that carbon stuff. Make one the old tried-and-true way so you'll be sure of that, at least."

"Where's your pioneer spirit, Norton?"

"Hey, I'm one of the Indians, remember? Not the pioneers. I want to see this Aremac thing working, otherwise what would I do with that super-size magnet?"

Roger agreed he would restrain himself until the first snood was finished and Aremac 2.0 was in operation. Norton appointed Marna to be his enforcer.

At the garage, Roger opened a large envelope taped to the box and took out the specs. He was delighted to see that the magnet was the finest, latest, and most expensive model, not the old reject they had cobbled together for their first Aremac. He gave Norton's men instructions about removing the crate and setting it up, warning everybody not to attempt to turn it on until they had scoured the premises for loose magnetic materials. Then he would inspect everything and supervise the initial power-up. For now, since the magnet was useless without a working snood, he rode back to Nellie's.

Nellie was home and in the basement studying his work, hands securely grasped behind the back of her embroidered vest. "Mind if I watch?"

"Not at all, but it's got to be more boring than watching ice melt."

She pulled up a leather-covered bar stool. "I love watching ice melt. It's so beautiful. And so is your work."

He took up the half-finished section of snood, holding it under the light, searching for flaws. Finding none, he began the delicate process of attaching the next piece.

"You know," he heard Nellie whisper to Marna, "making snoods is just like weaving miniatures, but without a loom. He's definitely a weaver."

It was the second time this week someone had called him a weaver, but he still didn't understand. He was even more puzzled when, on his next shift, he found four wrinkled Navajo women standing by his bench inspecting his work.

CHAPTER FIFTY-FIVE

Before leaving the restaurant's ladies room, Tess prepared notes for each of the men. She seated herself at the table, trying to look nonchalant while they read. She noticed that while they were holding their toilet conference, a young couple had entered the restaurant and taken a booth next to Desi and Lucille.

In spite of the weather, the boy was wearing a t-shirt which showed part of an elaborate paisley-like tattoo running up the back of his neck. The girl had spiky vermillion hair with gold loop earrings and a matching nose ring. *I wonder if you had to be at least eighteen to be a federal agent, even if you didn't have to follow dress codes.*

If these teenagers were indeed agents, her plan was moot, but there was nothing she could do about it now. She looked at each of the men and received a nod of understanding. Arnie emptied his wallet into Rebecca's hand. Wendell did the same for Alicia. Tess told them not to count it, but she estimated at least two thousand dollars. *Clearly, I'm in the wrong profession.*

With the money safely tucked away, Tess took three deep breaths, then tapped the table with her spoon. Arnie and Wendell stood and walked over to Lucille and Desi's booth. Wendell sat down alongside Lucille, and Arnie wedged his considerable bulk next to Desi. "Hey, man, I noticed your cell phone. I've been thinking of getting a new one, and yours looks like the latest model. How's the service?"

Desi gave Arnie a blank look, then stared helplessly past him as Tess, Alicia, Rebecca, and SOS rose quickly and headed for the front door.

Desi shoved against Arnie's huge bulk. "Excuse me, but I have to leave."

"Oh, stay a while," said Arnie, holding his position against the smaller man. "Help me out. It won't take a minute."

That was the last thing Tess heard as she backed out of the door, watching to see if the young couple followed.

They didn't.

By the time she reached Alicia's car, the others were already inside. Alicia was at the wheel with the motor running, and SOS was in the passenger seat. Rebecca was in back with Heidi, who was whining to go out. *I don't have time for this*, Tess thought, but when she tried to push her way inside, Heidi jumped out and began sniffing the rear tire. *Don't pee on her car*, Tess wished, *but do get it over with.*

Tess got her first wish, but not her second. Heidi just kept sniffing the rear tire and whining. Rebecca crawled out of the back seat and came around to see what was wrong. Heidi began to bark loudly, running back and forth between Rebecca and the tire.

"Heidi, stop that," Tess yelled, but Heidi paid no attention. "I think she's gone nuts. Help me get her in the car."

"I think she's trying to tell us something," Rebecca said calmly. "And I think I know what it might be." She removed her glove and reached under the fender, feeling along the edge. "Yep." She held up her hand in triumph. Heidi stopped barking, sniffed the object Rebecca held, and wagged her tail furiously.

"What is it?" Tess asked. "And may we go now, Miss Heidi?"

Rebecca wrapped her hand tightly around the object and motioned Tess to wait. "Just a minute. Heidi, find another. Find it, Heidi."

Heidi just spun around, chasing her tail. "Come on, you silly dog," Tess said. "In the car! Inside!"

Heidi jumped in the car with no further fuss. Tess slipped in after her, then let her climb over her lap to sit by the window. Rebecca put her finger over her lips, then handed the object forward to SOS, showing him how to fold his hand around it. "I think it's a bug, or a tracking device. Can you tell?"

As Alicia drove off, SOS switched on the overhead light and studied the object. Enclosing it again in his hand, he said, "It could be. I can't tell for sure without equipment, but why would they put anything else there?" He started to roll down the window.

"What are you doing?" Rebecca said.

"I'm going to toss this piece of crap."

Rebecca held out her hand. "Not yet. Let them track us for a while, then I'll stick it on another vehicle."

CHAPTER FIFTY-SIX

The weather in Crownpoint had turned unseasonably warm. Roger and Norton were resting on the bench enjoying the afternoon sun, discussing their plans for testing and shipping Aremac 2.0. They had just begun to discuss their finances when Denise and Bart drove up in the red pickup, raising an unwelcome cloud of dust.

Coughing, Roger stood to greet them. "If you've brought back some cash, Denise, I'll forgive you for the dust. But next time, would you kind of roll in to a slow stop?"

Denise jumped down from her driver's perch. "As soon as Norton fixes these brakes. Or Bart gets a driver's license." She reached back into the cab and slid out a steel strongbox. "When you see how much Bart earned for us, I think you'll forgive our dust."

Bart let Howler jump out of the truck bed, then came around to join Denise, visibly proud. "I sold a few of the best ones in Sedona and some of the lesser ones and most of the jewelry in Phoenix. But most of them, I shipped to my dad. He's going to have a special show, but he wants more product before he sets it up. You do have more product, don't you?"

"We definitely do," said Norton.

"What about the nanotubes?" said Roger.

Norton took the strongbox from Denise and peered inside, mouthing a low whistle. "I'd better put this in the safe." He disappeared into his office.

Denise handed him a small, securely wrapped box. "I think we've got enough for at least two more snoods, if the quality is as promised."

"Any other news?"

"Wait until you hear. When we were in Sedona, I received a call from Mrs. Silsbury."

Curious. Denise still refuses to call Alicia by her first name. Is she suspicious?

"She and SOS are driving out here to help assemble the Aremac," Denise continued. "It will take them a few days after they get Tess and Rebecca safely on a boat to Africa."

"That's great news, but Aremac 2.0 is already together and working. We're going back to building stoves, but I guess SOS can help–with deliveries if nothing else."

Bart's eyes widened. "You've already got it on the truck? That's incredible."

"What truck?"

"I told you before. It has to be built on a truck."

Roger shook his head in disbelief. "You never said anything about a truck, Bart. You're kidding, right?"

"No, that's what Mrs. Silsbury told me originally. And this time she asked if you had the truck yet." Bart lowered his gaze to the dusty ground. "I thought I told you about the truck before, but I guess I didn't. Did I?"

Roger's voice softened. "It wouldn't have made any difference, Bart. There's no way we have the computing power to compensate for the jolting and vibration."

"I think she meant it has to be easy to move, not that it has to operate while the truck is driving around."

"You think?"

"I'm pretty sure."

Norton emerged from the office with a wrench and opened the hood of the pickup. Denise walked over to watch what he was doing.

Roger ignored them. "All right, even supposing that it doesn't have to operate while moving, we still have a difficult problem. It will probably have to be retuned after every trip. Maybe even repaired. At least it won't have to carry its own power."

Bart studied his shoelaces.

"What's the matter, cousin? What else aren't you telling me?"

"It *does* have to carry its own power."

Roger covered his ears with both hands. "I don't want to hear this. Okay, what else does it have to do?"

"That's all. I think."

"You think? And we can't just call Alicia." Roger sighed and looked heavenward. "All right, *why* does it have to carry its own power?"

Bart turned around, gazing at the hills that gave Crownpoint its name, then at the horizon to the east. "If you were going to operate Aremac out there, how would you power it? I've never been to Africa, but my impression is that it's not much different than this–and probably less developed."

Norton called over from under the truck's hood. "So the roads will be like here, too. Full of ruts and rocks and rodents. So you'll need four-wheel drive sprung so it rides like a Rolls Royce on new pavement. but capable of carrying a two-ton magnet, another ton of delicate electronic equipment, a best-in-class generator, and a crew."

"I guess so."

Norton laid his wrench on the cylinder block and sauntered over, leaving the hood open. "And don't forget fuel. If it's like here, they probably don't have gas stations on every corner. Heck, they probably don't even have corners."

"It doesn't matter," said Roger. "I don't know a damn thing about trucks."

"You don't know a damn thing about security, either," said Denise. "How come you're standing outside here in plain view?"

Roger bowed to her. "Have mercy, Oh Mistress. We've been inside all day. Besides, now we're talking about trucks, so we need to go out back and see if there's a suitable truck in the graveyard."

Denise shook her head in disgust. "Maybe you'll get away with it this time, but it's an unnecessary risk. At least stand in the shade. You can see the trucks from there."

Norton led Roger inside. "I don't need to see trucks. I know about trucks, so you can let me take care of this. You don't have to do everything by yourself, Roger."

"I suppose you know where we could buy a truck like that? And where we'd get the money to pay for it?"

"Mrs. Silsbury will pay for it," said Bart. "I'm sure." He started to walk to the door.

"You don't have to leave," Roger said. "I'm not angry with you."

"I'm heading to the house to talk to the ladies about a rug."

Roger knew he was talking about the weavers who'd been coming regularly to watch him make snoods. "Okay, but how fast can you get the money if we do find a suitable truck?"

"Fast enough. Just find the truck."

"So, Norton, can we?"

"I can find more than one."

"One will be hard enough."

"Not really. I know they have at least three over in Chinle that are not being used any more. We can have them for a song–but don't tell this Silsbury person that."

"I suppose you're going to tell me that one of your cousins owns them?"

"Not actually a cousin, but he belongs to a sister clan, and we did go to school together. Your customer seems to have deep pockets, so what's the harm in getting Charlie a reasonable price?"

"How reasonable?" Roger's eye caught sight of Norton's pickup, hood open with wisps of steam rising from the radiator. "Never mind. I suppose they're in the same kind of shape as *your* truck–which wouldn't be big enough, by the way."

"It would be a nice feature if they had brakes that worked," said Denise. "And see if you can throw in air-conditioning. It's supposed to be hot in Africa."

"No problem," said Norton. "Actually, they're practically brand new. Hardly been used at all." He scowled at Roger. "And there's nothing wrong with my truck except for the paint job."

"Sure." Roger thought he was beginning to recognize when Norton was pulling his leg.

Norton raised his right hand and grabbed his crotch with the left. "I swear, Roger. They're those movie trucks they customize over in Pecos. The HollyNav company used them to make a couple of those Hillerman movies, then they sold the lot to Charlie for scrap. And they're not just sitting outside in the weather. He's got all three in a rented barn, on blocks and all covered with tarps. I've seen one of them. It's a beauty. A hybrid. The large batteries are probably ruined by now. They'd be costly to replace, but I'm sure the diesel engines are in fine shape."

"What's a movie truck?" asked Denise.

"You know, they keep their cameras and lights and crap on it for location shoots. It's got its own generator, with extra large fuel tanks and lots of padded compartments for small equipment. Jimmy Gardner explained it all to me."

"Who's Jimmy Gardner?"

"His mother is Little Deer Clan. He's always hanging around making movies for his classes at UNM. He'd sell his soul for one of those trucks, but nobody'd give him five cents for his soul."

Roger was beginning to believe, just a little. "Could it carry the magnet?"

"I might have to augment the shocks and springs, but it's definitely got the power. You should see that gorgeous engine. I'm not sure if it's got the heaviest-duty power train, but that's easily replaced, if necessary. I think I could find some mil-spec stuff from Army surplus." He looked up. "Hey, why is Bart running?"

"Bart never runs." *What's wrong?*

Bart pulled up at the door, bending over to catch his breath. "Roger, there's a fight over at Nellie's. They want you to settle it. Right away, before someone gets hurt."

CHAPTER FIFTY-SEVEN

After leaving the coffee shop, the escapees drove west for a mile or so until SOS spotted a convenience store with several parked cars out front. While Alicia topped off her gas, Tess sat with Heidi. Rebecca went inside to purchase some water and throwaway phones. SOS roamed the parking lot, scanning the license plates.

While Alicia waited for the pump to print her receipt–she had intentionally used her credit card–SOS crawled back in the car sporting a Cheshire Cat grin. "Our little bug is going to Iowa. West of here. If we're lucky, they're starting for home tonight."

Alicia slipped in behind the wheel, started the engine, and made a quick u-turn back the way they had entered. A few blocks away, she pulled in among the cars in the parking area of an apartment complex and stopped. She took one of the phones and told everyone she would be right back. Five minutes later, she returned without the phone. "Don't worry," was all she said. "It's well disposed of."

They continued east until reaching I-94, then entered the moderate stream of southbound traffic. Everyone seemed lost in thought as the Interstate curved east, then crossed into Indiana. They exited south on I-65, while SOS kept turning his head toward the back of the car. "I don't think we're being followed. I saw a few suspicious headlights, but we lost them all when we turned south. So, now would someone like to tell me what's going on?"

Alicia gave SOS his assignment. "Stay with us until New Jersey, where I'll would drop you off with Heidi to buy supplies and equipment you and I will need for our trip to New Mexico. Then I'll drop off Tess and Rebecca at the ship, see them safely on board, then return to pick you up." That seemed to satisfy SOS, who fell noisily asleep.

Driving just under ten miles over the speed limit, they bypassed Indianapolis around midnight, switched drivers to Rebecca outside of Columbus, Ohio, then back to Alicia at the Pennsylvania turnpike just as the horizon they faced showed a gray line of dawn.

A few hours later, they stopped for breakfast at a New Jersey diner, reviewed their plans, gave SOS one of the phones, and dropped him and Heidi in a large industrial shopping area. Although the stores were just opening, the parking lot was full of trucks, as local manufacturers swarmed through the area stocking up just in time with the parts they would need for today's orders.

The exhausting trip behind them now, the three women finally stood on the dock in Jersey City, looking past the bow of the Justice Avenger at a smog-spectacular sunrise behind the Statue of Liberty. The Avenger's captain was a West African man, Themdo Osewa, well-built and rather handsome–as long as he didn't smile to show his missing teeth. Tess was impressed with the amount of deference he showed Alicia. His British-accented English was mostly understandable, at least to Rebecca and Alicia, and his comprehension seemed perfect as Alicia explained what he was to do with his passengers.

The Avenger was not scheduled to leave for three days, but all had agreed it was best for Tess and Rebecca to stay hidden on board until departure. Rebecca, however, had a few reservations. "I hate to be practical, but what we're wearing is all the clothes we have."

Alicia volunteered to shop for them, "… but I don't think it's a good idea for me to come back here, just in case they pick up my trail. Besides, I have to get your man to New Mexico to help with the–" She glanced at Captain Osewa. "–with the project. Captain, it's not that I don't trust you, but the fewer people who know the details of our work, the better."

"I take no offense, Mrs. Silsbury. In my business, it does not pay to be overly inquisitive." He shifted his attention to his two passengers. "If you will provide her with a list of your needs, my wife will be happy to shop for you. She loves the shopping excursions here in the United States. She will be grateful for the opportunity."

Rebecca thanked the captain. "I shall also need ammunition for my pistol. And, if possible, a similar pistol for Ms. Fixman."

Tess backed away, "I'd rather not have a pistol. I'm afraid to use one, and I'm not even sure I remember how."

"Did you know once upon a time?" Rebecca asked.

"Yes, Mel taught all us kids to use the entire armory. Pistols, rifles, shotguns. He was mostly interested in the boys, but I was the oldest, so he had to teach me, too."

"Good. It's not something you forget," said Rebecca. "You do, however, need to practice your aim. We'll have plenty of time once we're under way to shoot at flotsam. Right, Captain?"

"That is correct. Shooting is one of our favorite recreations. We have also shotguns, if you like to shoot the skeet."

"Maybe she'll learn," Rebecca said, implying to Tess that she herself already knew. "Still, I don't see us traipsing around Africa carrying shotguns. It's not ladylike."

"I understand, but my wife enjoys the shotgun."

I think I'll find this captain's wife an interesting traveling companion.

"So, she will shop for a pistol for Mrs. Fixman?"

The captain shook his head. "Purchasing a pistol in United States is not same as purchasing dress. But rest assured. Mrs. Fixman will have choice of all your familiar weapons once we are under weigh." He offered a small bow to Rebecca. "And you shall have adequate ammunition for your practice."

Tess, feeling uncomfortable with this discussion of firearms, was at first relieved when Alicia's phone rang, then puzzled because nobody knew this number. *Oh, no. SOS has it.*

Alicia stepped away, behind an cream-colored shipping container, emerging moments later, not looking her usual cool self. "That was your man. He says he and the dog have been followed. I don't know how, but I have to rescue him."

Tess slapped her forehead. "Stupid, stupid, stupid. I know how they found him. I should have trusted Heidi."

"What do you mean?" Rebecca asked. "You *always* trust her."

"Not this time. When she was chasing her tail, I thought she was goofing off, but she was trying to tell us there was another beacon."

"But where?"

"In her collar, of course. They must have put it there while we were locked up."

Alicia agreed, holding her hand to her head. "Of course. We were all stupid not to check the dog's collar. Well, done is done. I will tell your man to get rid of the collar. Maybe we can use the same trick a second time."

"I hope so," said Tess. "But please be careful."

"I will, rest assured. But now you must follow your own advice." Alicia extended her hand to Tess. "Next time I see you will be in Africa. I hope to have the new Aremac with me, ready to begin our work."

Oh, oh. Alicia used the name, Aremac, right in front of the captain.

CHAPTER FIFTY-EIGHT

Denise drove Roger from the garage to Nellie's. They were met out front by Marna and Nellie, both trying to talk at once. Denise urged them inside, out of sight. As soon as they opened the front door, he could hear the sounds of squabbling from the basement.

Before he could run downstairs, Marna stopped him to explain. "It started right after Bart came downstairs. He had some photos one of the dealers had given him of an old rug. The dealer told him the rug was worth about $4,000 as it was, but it would have been worth a whole lot more if he had the name of the weaver. Apparently he was willing to pay several thousand dollars if Bart could authenticate the piece. Even more if it turned out to be an early work of one of our most famous weavers."

"So what's the problem?"

"Two of the ladies claim it's theirs."

"Who?"

"Yazhi and Nascha." Unlike their granddaughters, these septuagenarian ladies guarded their traditional names, just as they preserved other ancient traditions. Yazhi and Nascha had probably been friends all their lives. Now were at each other's throats.

Roger stopped dead. "Oh, shit. Why do they want me?" Though he barely shared ten words of English or Navajo with the old weavers, he and they had been communicating about their respective arts. He had been teaching the weavers how to make snoods, which they thought were fashion accessories. Or perhaps three-dimensional weavings, works of art. He wasn't quite sure either concept applied, but there was no mistaking their interest in this new form, which they were replicating in traditional wool materials.

Nellie wrung her hands. "They respect you. And you are the only neutral party they respect."

"Why?"

"Because you're a weaver, and probably the only weaver in the Four Corners who has no clan connections on either side."

"But if I intervene, I'll lose my neutrality."

"You'll just have to pay the price. You might save a life."

Each weaver had shown Roger some of their miniatures, whose work was as intricate as his snood-making. They had given him a small loom. They had been teaching him to make a rug, and jabbering back and forth about his unique new pattern. They weren't quite friends, but to his surprise and vast enjoyment, they had quickly become respected colleagues. Genius that he was, Roger had known only a handful of colleagues he could respect, but now that rare, enjoyable connection was at risk. All because of a photograph.

A photograph.

Yes!

Nudging Marna and Nellie in front of him, he started down the stairs with a fresh idea. "Both of you have to translate for me. One of you take Yazhi and the other take Nascha."

They paused for a moment halfway down the stairs, discussing their clan connections until Nellie announced she would translate for Yazhi. Marna seemed to agree.

Downstairs, he closed his eyes and imagined how Tess would handle this delicate situation. He started with a few controlled breaths, then listened to Nellie tell how Yazhi claimed to have made this particular rug when she was a young girl, more than half a century ago. Her story was quite convincing, until he listened to Marna make the same claim for Nascha. When he was sure each had told her side, he asked the other four ladies whether they had anything to add, but none were willing to take sides.

He spoke slowly so Nellie could translate. "I am honored that you trust me to decide the true weaver of this rug, but I am not wise enough to resolve this dispute."

He watched while the women took in this statement with obvious disappointment, then said, "However, I have built a machine that can do so."

This had better work, he thought as the chattering ladies trooped with their translators over to Western Stage. He had confidence in Aremac, but would it work in this culture? He knew that pictures were not universal across cultures, but maybe they were sufficiently universal for his purposes. *Well, I'll know soon enough.*

At the garage, he let the women walk around Aremac, touch it, and ask questions. Then he put the snood on his own head and lay down on the gurney, with Denise at the controls. He touched the snood, saying, "I will show you how I remember making this weaving. You will see my hands, and you will see my fingers making the knots. You have watched me do this, so you can assure yourself that this is a true picture of what I did."

He waited for Nellie to finish her translation, then waited for questions. There were none. He hoped that meant they had understood, not that they were too baffled to frame any questions. "All right, Denise, turn it on."

He heard the reassuring familiar hum. He had already tested this Aremac on himself, so he was confident that this part, at least, would function properly. He brought his mind back to Nellie's basement, to his workbench at the time when the weavers had first come to watch him work. He remembered them trooping down the stairs. He couldn't see Aremac's monitors, but he could hear the oohs and aahs of the ladies as they saw themselves through his eyes. *So far, so good.*

He skipped most of the introductions, going right back to picturing his hands picking up the partial snood and turning it over to inspect his work. Step by step, he went through his memory of adding one nanotube to the complex, checking his work with the microscope, and setting it down on the workbench, satisfied.

"All right, Denise. You can shut if off. Let's see what they think."

The hum stopped, leaving the room empty of sound. Roger pulled himself out of the magnet's gap and sat up. "Do they understand?"

Nellie exchanged a few words with each woman. "Yes, they understand. They are amazed."

"But do they believe that they have seen a true picture?"

Nellie didn't have to ask. "Yes. They watched each step in your process. They missed nothing."

That had been everything he had hoped for, but now came the crucial step. He had heard stories of the Navajo weavers' remarkable memories. The stories seemed plausible because he himself could remember every detail of creating each of his inventions. *But I am much younger than these women.* "Ask Yazhi if she remembers making the weaving in the photo."

Nellie asked, and Yazhi said "*oke'*".

That much Navajo I can understand without translation. "Now ask her if she would be willing to put on the snood and show us her memory of weaving the rug."

This is the key moment. Roger listened to Nellie translating his question, but instead of answering with words, Yazhi simply stepped toward him and reached her wrinkled hand out for his snood. He let out his held breath, trying not to make too much noise.

He sat her down on the gurney while he fitted the snood to her head. He was surprised and relieved that even though she was half his size, their head sizes and shapes matched quite well. He had two other snoods now, but he knew it would be more convincing if she used the one he had worn.

He explained that each person's memory worked differently, just like each weaving was different. Consequently, he would spend some time adjusting the memory machine to Yazhi's memory. She would have to remove her jewelry so it would not be harmed by the machine. Nellie took off a dozen items, then helped her lie down on the gurney. Denise then wheeled the gurney into position in the magnet's gap.

Roger turned on the machine. "Nellie, tell her to visualize her large silver bracelet with the three turquoise stones."

Nellie said a few words, and Roger could see Yazhi clenching her fists in concentration before he focused on his own screen's interpretation of her mental image. He had hoped it would be the bracelet so he wouldn't have a problem calibrating, but immediately saw he had no such luck. The picture was an unidentifiable structure in orange and green.

This isn't working.

CHAPTER FIFTY-NINE

Tess didn't really believe what Birgit, the captain's Norwegian wife, had to say about the danger of pirates, but she breathed a little easier when, after a week of sailing, they finally sighted land on the other side of the Atlantic. Her relief simply demonstrated that Tess didn't really understand pirates.

She'd heard about the pirates the first day out of Newark, at shooting practice. Tess had put herself under Birgit's tutelage. She dressed in one of her new Birgit-selected outfits–all-white jeans and military-style shirt complete with epaulets and seven pockets. White deck boots, and white floatable wide-brimmed hat with chin strap.

Birgit was a forty-something ship captain's daughter and now a ship-captain's wife. She quickly convinced Tess that her experience with weapons was not all theoretical or game-playing. It helped that Birgit looked like a Valkyrie right out of a Wagnerian opera–tall, blue eyes, and blonde braided-hair. All she lacked was a spear and a sword, but the large pistol she brandished was a more than adequate substitute.

"We'll start with hand-weapons," Birgit explained before a single shot was fired. "That way, you'll be prepared when we reach Simbara."

Tess knew that Simbara was their ultimate destination, but this was the first time she'd heard it mentioned on board. She had an impression that Simbara was not the name that had been mentioned to the Port Authority officials before they left, but she thought it better not to ask. Now, however, she did ask Birgit the question on her mind since she first met the captain. "Why all this emphasis on guns?"

"Parts of Simbara are less than what you would consider civilized–which is why our organization is so important in the first place."

"I understand that, but I meant on board Justice Avenger. We're all alone out here in the middle of the ocean, and I imagine you trust your crew or you wouldn't have them on board."

Birgit had a deep, rough laugh. "There are pirates. We were lucky not to encounter any the last few trips, but you must never let your crew become complacent. Perhaps our pugnacious reputation has scared all the pirates away. That's the best type of defense."

"What type is that?"

"Being so repugnant that nobody wants to bother with you."

"Like the machine guns mounted in front and back? They *are* machine guns, aren't they?"

"Technically they are autocannons, but they're just machine guns with bigger bullets. But it's fore and aft, dear, not front and back."

"Aye, ma'am," said Tess, saluting. "And port and starboard, amidships and poop."

Again the coarse laugh. "You've been studying, Lubber. Excellent."

"So the autocannons are what scare away the pirates?"

"That and not carrying cargo that anyone wants. Who wants a lot of pencils and paper clips? Certainly not pirates."

"How would pirates know what you're carrying? All the cargo seems to be sealed in containers, except for some vehicles. And they're completely wrapped in tarps. Though I'd think pirates would be interested in vehicles, at least."

"They have their ways of knowing. It's their business to find out, at least for the more professional pirates."

"And the less professional ones?"

"They'll take anything–including the women–then find some use for it or throw it overboard. Yes, the women, too."

Tess had changed the subject, but now, just minutes after she spotted the silhouette of African hills against the cloudless blue sky, the subject returned to her mind. An undulating siren rising in pitch caused her to turn aft, where two vessels were approaching much too quickly for sailing ships. Within minutes, all twelve crew members were on deck, two each pulling the tarps off the autocannons, several others armed with long-barreled weapons. Birgit herself was armed with something larger that Tess didn't recognize from their practice sessions.

"It's a shoulder-launched rocket weapon," said Rebecca, appearing at Tess's side with pistol in hand. "Used to cripple tanks or bring down planes. Or sink small boats–" She pointed to the two craft which had now separated and were approaching Justice Avenger fore and aft. "–like those."

Birgit was shouting directions to the crew, then stopped and turned to Tess, who stood frozen with fear. "Run to your cabin, now. Get your pistol and be sure it's ready for use."

"I … I don't think I could use the gun. Not on a human being."

"If one of these pirates gets to you, he won't be a human being. Once you have your pistol, climb up to the bridge and relieve the captain."

Confused, Tess stood her ground. ""Relieve the captain? What do you mean, relieve the captain?"

"Just get up there. He'll tell you what to do."

Birgit slapped Tess on the rump. "Now get going. If you're not sure you can fire your weapon, you'll only be a handicap down here. We need the captain's firepower."

Intellectually, Tess wanted to be up top to see what was happening, what the threats were, and how she might counter them. But emotionally, all her instincts told her to hide in her cave the way her ancestors must have done, thousands of years ago–at least the ones who survived to become ancestors.

The ancestors won.

She scrambled up the ladder–the shortest route to her cabin. Though it was described that way, it was not actually below decks, but two stories up in the poop, just below the bridge where only the captain now stood watch.

Chest heaving, she dismounted the ladder and stumbled across the narrow deck to her cabin door.

Inside, it was only after she'd locked the room that she realized the flimsy door would be no defense at all if the pirates did board the ship.

Her cabin had a small round window facing to starboard, but its narrow view showed only choppy ocean. No pirate ships. No coastline.

The rattle of gunshots broke her revery. She remembered Rebecca's instructions.

Her pistol was in its holster, hanging in her locked closet. She fumbled with the simple three-digit combination. *I've hacked some of the world's most sophisticated security systems, so why does it take me four tries to set all three dials correctly. I don't think I'm in any condition to handle a loaded weapon.*

Despite these thoughts, she strapped on the leather holster.

Her head felt wooly. She hadn't been seasick the whole way, but maybe the malaise was coming on her now. She could feel every little roll, pitch, and yaw of the ship exaggerated a hundred times. *I'd better sit down*, she thought, but she was wobbling so much almost missed the bed.

She inched around carefully until she was facing the door, only to realize she was totally exposed to the small window. Turning full circle, she saw that virtually every corner of the cabin would be exposed to a gun thrust through that window.

She stood carefully, stepped over to the window, and closed the dark drapes. Then, using the wall for support, she worked her way around to the tiny bathroom and sat on the closed toilet. *Maybe I should use the toilet before the shooting starts. I've heard that people often wet themselves out of fear, but my body's reaction seems to be to clench my bladder like a miser's purse.*

The sounds of more gunfire brought her mind back to the external situation. *Wetting my pants is the least of my worries.*

She opened the safety strap on her holster and removed the pistol. She steadied her mind to run through the checking procedures Birgit had drilled into her. She steeled herself, placed one boot firmly on each side of the toilet, then released the safety with shaking hands.

CHAPTER SIXTY

Roger asked Denise to bring the bracelet and set it down on top of his monitor so he could more easily compare it to Aremac's output. The screen didn't show much of a picture to start with, but at least there were three distinct orange blobs. *I'm guessing Aremac's got the number right. If so, they represent a color change of the three turquoise stones, even though neither their shapes nor their sizes gave me a clue as to which was which. This calibration is going to be a lot of work–if I could do it at all.*

"Nellie, why don't you let Yazhi out of the machine for now. Denise will explain to you about adjusting the machine for each person, and you can translate it for the weavers. Marna, maybe you can think of something to keep them entertained."

"Don't you need Yazhi in the machine?"

"Not for now, but I'll need her in a little while. Aremac has all her readings recorded, but I'll need new data for a second object later, one with different colors and shapes."

"How about one of my tattoos?" said SOS, who had just appeared at the garage door, followed closely by Alicia. "Or would the ladies be shocked?"

Denise ran to him and jumped into his arms. He lifted her tiny frame easily, then happily accepted a flurry of kisses. The ladies seemed more amused than shocked, tittering among themselves. Neither Denise nor SOS seemed to notice.

Roger, missing Tess even more, pretended not to notice. "You're just in time. I don't think I can do this calibration all by myself." Hearing the words from his own mouth, he remembered what Norton had been telling him ever since he came to New Mexico. He realized he had never done things "all by himself," but when Tess and SOS were gone, he thought nobody else would be able to help him–at least with creative tasks. *I've not yet fully accepted Denise or Marna onto the team. I'll have to make up for that.*

For now, though, there was work to do. "When you're done playing kissy-face, you can put Denise down. I need her more than I need you right now. Hey, you could do some magic tricks to keep the ladies amused while Denise and I work on the calibration."

SOS proved to be a crowd-pleaser with disappearing and reappearing handkerchiefs and coins. Denise proved to be a natural in seeing the adjustments needed to bring the picture of the bracelet in line with the bracelet itself. With one key hint from Marna, the job was done in less than five minutes–at least done to the best approximation they could make without having more sample objects.

Roger asked for more jewelry. When he turned down Yazhi's squash blossom necklace as too similar in color combination to what they already had, Nascha offered her red, blue, and gold bracelet. Roger accepted it. Nascha cast a triumphant glance at Yazhi, who pretended not to notice as Nellie helped her climb back onto the gurney.

Now that the initial calibration of Yazhi's brain was done, the second calibration ought to have been much easier. Ought to have been, but wasn't. To get more data points, Roger had Marna rotate Nascha's bracelet ninety degrees while Yazhi watched, producing a new picture from her brain. It still didn't help.

Roger asked Marna to rotate the bracelet again, but while she did so, Nellie came to him and whispered, "My grandmother's sister doesn't want to look too carefully at Nascha's jewelry."

Roger cursed to himself. *We forgot about culture. We may have to reprogram everything. And what's Tess going to have to deal with in Africa?*

CHAPTER SIXTY-ONE

Tess sat cowering in her tiny bathroom, listening. Shots rang out, then a loud hissing sound and an explosion that sounded far off. *I can't just sit here doing nothing. My friends may be in danger, and I'm supposed to be relieving the captain. What am I made of, anyway?*

Cautiously, she opened the bathroom door a crack.

Sensing nothing but distant sounds of gunfire, she inched the door wider. Her room was empty.

She took three deep breaths headed out of the bathroom to the window. She pulled back the curtains. Two pirate ships were now closer to the Avenger and still moving. *At least they're not getting reinforcements*, she thought, then realized one of the ships had an unfamiliar configuration of sails. *It issn't one of the original two. There* are *reinforcements. I have to reinforce our side.*

The moment she stepped out of the cabin, a staccato of bullets ricocheted off the wall three feet away. She wanted to dive back inside, but knew that the shooter would probably adjust his aim to where she was standing. By sheer force of will over instinct, she moved her feet past the chipped wall to the ladder.

Starting to climb, she heard more clanging impacts around her. Resisting the temptation to stop and look back at her cabin door, she clambered up to the bridge level. When she grabbed the door handle, the captain swung around and aimed his shotgun at her face. The image flashed into her mind–*I have just two seconds to live.*

"Jesus Christos!" the Captain yelled, swinging the shotgun barrel up towards the ceiling. "Call your name before you make a surprise."

He looked her up and down, his eyes halting for a moment on the wet spot on her white jeans, making her aware of her bladder's betrayal. She felt her face flush, but he said nothing, only beckoning her over to the huge steering wheel. He explained how to keep the ship full speed ahead, on course, and that she was to touch nothing else. Then he handed her another shotgun. "If the pirate comes through that door, you shoot first. Understand?"

I understood, but I don't know if I can remember the shotgun's mechanisms. Or shoot even if I could.

Without waiting for her answer, Captain Osewa pointed out the window to the foredeck. "You see pirates boarding, you warn us with the loud-talker." He tapped on a microphone, but left without explaining how to use it.

After a few seconds of hesitation, Tess heard more gunshots and switched into her take-charge mode. She verified the ship's heading, then fiddled with the mike until she figured out how the button on the side worked. *Are there pirates boarding the ship right now?*

She surveyed the full circle of windows, catching her attention on the pirate ship to the north, which was now burning. And listing to starboard. Mesmerized by the sight, she stared until shouts from below recalled her to duty. Two of the Avenger's crew on the foredeck were defending the autocannon from three pirates. Tess pulled her eyes away and ran to check all the other windows.

She saw Birgit operating the aft autocannon, with no pirates in sight. Turning left, she saw a man whom she did not recognize as crew. He was carrying a rifle and appeared to be sneaking toward Birgit's position.

Grabbing the microphone, she shouted, "Pirate boarding on the left ... port. Midship. He has a rifle."

Nobody seemed to be paying any attention. She repeated the message, this time remembering to press the button. The mid-ship man stopped his forward movement. He knelt into firing position, aiming his rifle at Birgit.

"Behind you, Birgit!" she shouted. "Behind you!"

Birgit, firing her noisy autocannon on one of the pirate ships, showed no sign of hearing.

Tess grabbed the shotgun and flung open the bridge door.

Without thinking about whether the shotgun had sufficient range, she aimed and fired.

The recoil slammed into her shoulder and knocked her backwards against the edge of the open door.

Something stabbed into her hip, the pain dropping her to one knee.

She could no longer see the deck, but she could still hear the clatter of Birgit's gun. Then all was quiet.

She tried to see what was happening, but her leg wouldn't take her weight. She fell back to her knees.

Minutes passed. The only sound was the vibration of the ship's engines. *At least they're still running, which is a good sign. Or is it? Maybe the pirates have won and were moving to the bridge to take control.*

Silence. Holding onto the shotgun, she crawled back into the bridge and locked the door. She desperately needed to stand up and look outside, but her hip was burning with pain.

Maybe everyone is dead. Pirates. Crew. Maybe the ship is running full speed out into the empty ocean. Or straight into a rocky shore.

She managed to grab the steering wheel, hoping to pull herself upright, but she heard footsteps out on deck. Someone tried the handle of the cabin door. She let go of the wheel and steadied the shotgun with both hands, ready to shoot anyone and everyone who entered.

Silence again, then a knock. *Shoot through the door, before you lose your nerve completely.*

She fought the temptation, not sure she'd be able to pull the trigger anyway. She yanked her finger out of the trigger guard and flexed it, testing its strength against her leg. *Stupid. You were strong enough for skeet shooting.*

She rested her finger on the trigger again. *But would pirates knock?*

Reason after reason for not shooting flooded through her mind. *Maybe it's the pirate captain–like Errol Flynn as Captain Blood–a civilized man who would treat her like a lady, but take her for his personal concubine.*

Stop dreaming. This is no movie. Her finger tightened a fraction. *The best you can hope for is a quick death. Take some of them with you.*

She steadied the shotgun one more time, and began her breathing exercises, readying herself for the worst that was to come. *Or the worst that I'm about to do.*

She heard a voice, muffled by the door. "Tess. Tess. Don't shoot. It's me, Rebecca. It's all over."

Over? Has Rebecca surrendered to the pirates?

"Come on, Tess. It's all safe now."

"Maybe she's not in there," Birgit's voice boomed, easy to recognize even through the door. "She may be hiding below."

"Maybe, but she was supposed to be here."

Tess heard the latch click. The door banged open, but she saw no-one. From the right, she heard Rebecca's clear voice, calling inside the cabin. "Maybe she went to the loo?"

Tess held the gun pointed at the doorway, her hands shaking. A millimeter at a time, she pried her finger off the trigger. She clicked off what she hoped was the safety. "I'm in here," she squeaked. "Don't shoot."

"Why would I shoot?" said Rebecca, her face appearing as she came through the door. "You're not a pirate."

Tess whooshed out an audible breath. "I think I was telling myself not to shoot *you*."

"Are you all right?"

"I think so." She put down the shotgun, suddenly feeling the pain in her hip. Her clothes were intact, but wet. *Not with blood. Thank God.* "I thought I was shot, but it's just a bruise."

"Let me see," said Rebecca, turning Tess around.

"Where are the pirates?"

"Scared them off," said Birgit. "We sunk one of their ships, then the others tested the range of our cannon. We fired one round from each, and the splashes were impressive enough to make them rethink their plan."

"I thought I saw some of them boarding us."

"Oh, we took care of them," said Rebecca. "Birgit's crew seems to be real professionals at this anti-pirate business."

There had been something Tess wanted to say about that, but she couldn't remember. "Then we're safe?"

"Not only safe, but close," said Birgit, stepping in and grabbing the wheel. "We're no more than thirty minutes from port."

CHAPTER SIXTY-TWO

I'm not up to **this**, Roger thought. *Jewelry is jewelry. Useless rocks and metal arranged in a pattern that's only good for calibrating my invention. Why it should matter to whom it belongs?* The whole matter was beyond him, but he accepted Nellie's explanation. As a hypothesis, a least. "If she's your grandmother's sister, do you think she'll look at *your* bracelet?"

Nellie twisted off her own bracelet, which was a wide silver band inlaid with semicircles of pink and white shell on an ebony background. Roger thought that Nascha's bracelet, with its red and blue, had been a superior calibration template, but at least these inlays were simple geometric forms, which was an advantage at this stage.

In any event, Yazhi seemed to find Nellie's bracelet acceptable. She quickly produced an Aremac image that was recognizable, though off-color. Roger slid his chair back from the console. "Here, Denise, see if you can calibrate these colors. Your eyes have more cones than mine."

Denise pooh-poohed the idea, but took Roger's place. Roger stood, watched what she was doing for a moment, then went to greet Alicia. She had kept in the background, but was scrutinizing every step of the calibration process.

"What are you doing?" Alicia asked. "Isn't Aremac working?"

"It's working, but we're calibrating it for Yazhi's brain. It's taking a while."

"But when you calibrated for me, it took seconds."

"That's because all we had to do was make a few adjustments to Tess's calibration."

"And you can't do that for–what's her name?"

"Yazhi. Evidently not. You're an Anglo female, Alicia, like Tess. Yazhi is not. Your brains don't work the same way."

Alicia furrowed her brow. "Is it genetic or cultural?"

"I have no idea," said Roger. "Not my speciality. Maybe we can do some experiments if you don't take my Aremac away for a few weeks."

"You can try them on the next Aremac, or the one after that. I'm not really interested in the question, as long as it doesn't affect the way Aremac works in Africa."

Roger almost laughed at her claim that she wasn't concerned. "The different culture might make a difference. We never really thought of this effect. It was just by chance that I put a Navajo woman in the snood."

"Why did you? Put a Navajo woman in the snood, I mean?"

"We're trying to settle a dispute about who made an old weaving."

Alicia's entire body noticeably stiffened. "We don't really have time for settling disputes here. We'll have more than enough to settle when we get to Africa."

Alicia's tone made Roger feel like a four-year-old who had just stolen a cookie. "I thought it would be a good test for Aremac. And it was. Better than I had imagined. What if you got to Africa and found out how difficult it was to calibrate for the different ethnic groups there?"

"That's why we sent Tess there." Alicia wasn't yielding even a millimeter.

"I don't know if Tess could have done this alone." He looked over at Denise, who was no longer touching the console, but listening to their conversation. "I know I couldn't. Are you done, Denise?" *No sense trying to win an argument with Alicia.*

"It looks good to me, but we won't know until we have some movement."

"Have Nellie turn the bracelet."

"Oh, we already did that. It worked fine. But now we need some continuous motion."

Roger asked Nellie to ask Yazhi if she was ready for more. She said something short and crisp, then lay down again, ready to be rolled into the gap.

Roger gave Denise a thumbs-up. "Okay. Tell her we want her to remember making the rug in the photo. Tell her to start when her loom is set up, about ten percent of the rug finished."

Nellie spoke at length to Yazhi, who then spoke even longer back to her grand-niece, who translated for Roger. "She says that it's not correct to start the process with a weaving already partway finished. First, she must choose the yarn and set up the loom."

Roger was getting a headache from all the delays, but he kept his thoughts to himself. "Okay, tell her to start where she must. We'll just have to wait until she's got enough finished to compare patterns. Then we'll repeat the process with Nascha and find out who has the pattern exactly right."

He was wrong. Nascha never put her head in the snood. As soon as she saw the pictures of Yazhi's hands selecting yarns, she said something to Marna and quietly left the garage.

"She's seen enough," Marna explained. "It was obvious to her that Yazhi chose the yarns. She said her memory must be failing, because it's certainly Yazhi's creation. She will be glad to tell that to anyone who's willing to listen. And I think the other women have seen the same thing."

CHAPTER SIXTY-THREE

Marna tiptoed into Nellie 's kitchen early on this frosty morning, hoping she might have time to polish some loose ends in her theory before Roger and Denise were awake. Nellie had already been up and out, as evidenced by the half-full carafe warming in the coffee maker. Marna poured herself a cup, sampled one sip, jotted two lines on her notepad, then stopped to think.

She heard a noise outside and glanced out the kitchen window to see her cousin Marybeth hustling across the street, a look of urgency on her smooth, young face. Marna sighed and took another sip of coffee before rising to intercept her cousin and prevent her from waking the others.

She opened the kitchen door, stepped out, and finger on her lips, motioned Marybeth to come around back. "What's up?" she whispered. "You're up early. Weren't you working late last night?" Marybeth, who was barely out of high school, supported her two infants as a night waitress at Best Western's Restaurant in Grants. She usually slept late in the morning, while her grandmother tended the children.

"That's what's up. Something I heard at work." Marybeth panted, her arms folded tightly around her body against the morning chill. "Can I come inside?"

"Okay, but try to be quiet." Marybeth had one of those voices with only one volume setting–loud and penetrating. *Maybe that's why her boyfriends didn't marry her. She's pretty enough to attract them, but too loud to keep them.*

In the kitchen, Marna offered Marybeth the last of the coffee, but she declined, saying, "I drink way too much at work. It's bad for my complexion."

Marna resisted the temptation to feel the bump growing on her cheek, then poured herself a second cup of coffee. "Okay, what did you hear that's so important?"

"Last night, I waited on four FBI agents who were staying at the Inn. I recognized Frank Wesley, but the others must have been from out of town. One was from Chicago, I think, and he had on this really fancy suit–"

Marna laid her palm on her cousin's arm. "You can tell me about their wardrobes later, Beth. What were they saying that's so important?"

"Oh, yeah. Do you want to know what they ordered?"

Marna sighed. "Not now, Beth. Maybe later. What did they say?"

"Well, I didn't catch everything, of course, because I didn't want them to think I was eavesdropping. Though I really was, of course. But, you know, if they thought I was, they might stop saying anything. But you know how they don't see us–"

"I know, honey. They don't respect us. But what did they say?"

"Oh, yeah. It was about, you know, your friend, Roger. The weaver. I think they said his name was Fishman, or Freshman, or something like that."

"Fixman."

"Yeah, that's it. Fixman. I should have remembered, because I tried to think he was the man who fixes things. Get it? Fix man?"

Marna tried to control her impatience by slowly sipping coffee. "I get it. That was good, Beth. A good way to remember. But what did they say about Mr. Fixman?"

"I think they're coming here today to arrest him or something. They said something about finding his wife. At least I think she was his wife, you know. Someone named Tesla? Isn't that a nice name, Tesla? We had Tess Yazzi who was two years behind me in school, but her name wasn't Tesla. I don't think so, anyway. Maybe–"

"Did they say what they wanted with her? Or him?"

"You know, maybe just to question him, but, you know, they think they can do whatever they want to us. Well, you know, not just to us, because he's not really one of us, but he's, you know, your friend, and we're not supposed to tell anyone we know him–"

"You didn't say anything to them, did you?"

Marybeth sucked in her breath, making a small whistling sound. "Oh, no, I knew you wouldn't want me to say anything. I would have left right away and come back here to warn you, but Jodi wasn't working and I was the only waitress, so, you know, I had to stay until closing. Even if we only had two tables. Then by the time I got back here, it was too late and, you know, I didn't want to wake you up."

Marna wanted to tell her cousin she should have called, but there was no point now. "So, they're coming here today?"

"I think so. I woke up as early as I could so I could tell you."

Marna patted her arm. "You did good, honey. Listen, is there someone you could call over at the Inn to find out if they've left already?"

337 • GERALD M. WEINBERG

Marybeth rolled her eyes upward in concentration. "Olive, maybe, at the front desk. But, you know, I'm not sure if she's on this early. Maybe she–"

Marna pointed to the phone hanging on the wall next to the bulletin board. "How about you call. If it's not Olive, maybe whoever is there can tell you. If they ask why you want to know, just tell them … um … you wanted to thank them for the tip they left you last night."

"But it wasn't a very good tip. Those FBI guys never leave a good tip. When–"

Marna threw her cousin an extra-large wink. "We're just pretending, honey. So they won't be suspicious. Okay?"

Marybeth's eyes opened wide as she nodded with understanding. "Ooh. I get it. Like spies!"

"Perfect. Okay, you call. I'm going to wake up Mr. Fixman."

But Roger was already awake, and stumbling groggily down the hall to meet Marna halfway. "What's all the shouting about? We were working half the night."

"Sorry," said Marna, grasping his elbow so he wouldn't wander away while she knocked on Denise's door. "The FBI is on the way here to find you."

Roger's eyes cleared instantly. "Here? This house?"

"Not yet. They may still be in Grants. I don't know if they know where you are in Crownpoint, but at best you have an hour to get out of here. With the truck."

Denise stuck her head out her door, a questioning look on her face, which looked unfamiliar without her thick glasses. Her extra-long sleeping shirt said "Here I Am–Now What Are Your Other Two Wishes?" *How appropriate*, Marna thought. *My*

AREMAC POWER • 338

second wish would be for Tess or Rebecca to be here to handle this mess.

"The FBI is coming?" Denise asked, squinting.

"For Roger, but maybe for you, too."

"And Aremac," said Roger. "That's what they really want."

"You're more important," said Denise. "We can always build another Aremac."

They're going to argue about it, Marna thought. *We don't have time for arguments. I'm not the best person to deal with this–but they're worse than me. I guess I'm going to have to do something.*

She caught herself reaching up to pull a strand of hair into her mouth. "Let's not stand here arguing. Get some clothes on and pack what you'll need."

Roger spoke through his t-shirt, half off over his head. "Need for what?"

"For you, Roger, Africa."

CHAPTER SIXTY-FOUR

Marna spent three days watching over the FBI agents as they searched for Roger. On the first day, she had to make up a lie that wasn't a lie, because she knew the agents were trained in lie-detection. After many trials, she settled on a simple, "Roger was here last week, but I don't know where he is now." True enough, but misleading. He *had* been here last week (and this morning, too, but she didn't say that). And, right then, she didn't know exactly where he was–*just somewhere on the back road, Route 9 to Standing Rock, or heading towards Crystal. Or maybe somewhere else.*

On the second morning, Alicia called from Albuquerque, instructing Marna to call her back from a public phone to avoid wire-tapping. As she left the house for the pay phone at the supermarket, she ran into cousin Marybeth, who reported that a "fat lady" had joined the FBI party last night. "Maurice told me she arrived by train and, you know, rented a car from him. The FBI guys didn't seem too happy to see her, but my boss was pleased. She bought three dinner specials. And, you know, I think she would have had more, but the agents left and she had to rush to follow them. She did wait for me to box a dozen sweet-rolls, though. But we only had eight left over from the morning shift, and that made her really mad. That woman sure can pack it away."

Marna recognized Inga Steinman from the Marybeth's description. On the phone, Alicia confirmed her guess, but didn't seem too happy about it. *More or less resigned*, Marna thought. Alicia had SOS and Heidi with her, and seemed eager to know if Aremac was ready. She wanted to speak to Roger, so Marna told her to drop SOS and the dog off in Crystal, then come alone to take the Aremac truck to Justice For Africa's private airfield in Arizona. The moment Alicia hung up, Marna realized there might be a problem removing the truck under the FBI noses. *There might even be a problem now with them tapping this phone. There aren't that many phones to tap in Crownpoint. I'll just have to take a chance.*

While the FBI, with Inga, was having lunch at the drive-in, Marna slipped over to Western Stage to discuss the problem with Norton.

"Well," he said, standing in the locked garage, "they've been here more than a day and they haven't come to see me, so they probably don't know Aremac is here. Or that it's on a truck."

"But if we take it out, they might recognize it. One of them, I know, used Aremac back East."

Norton sized up the truck with an experienced eye. "I have a tarp that I think would cover the magnet. And we could drive out when they're looking the other way."

Marna walked around the truck, thinking about about the chance that Norton's plan would work. "What's this?" she asked, pointing to a black and orange symbol on the cab door. "What's HollyNav?"

"That's the movie company that used to own the trucks. We never took it off. Hey, that gives me an idea."

"What?"

"Jimmy Gardner. He might actually be good for something."

"Jimmy Gardner? He's twelve years old."

"You've been out of touch, Maralah. You're not the only one to grow up and go off to college."

"You're right. So how's the grown-up Jimmy Gardner going to help us?"

"For two years, he's been salivating after one of these trucks for his movie projects. I can promise him the use of one of the spares if he decorates this one with some of his movie equipment and drives it out of town."

As predicted, Jimmy accepted the job without a moment's hesitation. By the time Alicia arrived to escort him out of town, the Aremac truck was so convincingly festooned with cameras, tripods, lightbanks, speed rings, softboxes, amps, speakers, and other esoteric paraphernalia that Marna could imagine it wasn't Jimmy Gardner driving, but Robert Redford. Evidently, the FBI saw the same image, for they hardly looked up as Aremac cruised past and out Highway 9.

Now, thought Marna, *my only problem is what to do when Denise and SOS come back with Heidi to work on the stove.*

Two days later, Kit Kelly showed up with his disassembled hogan stove.

I guess my "only problem" was just wishful thinking.

CHAPTER SIXTY-FIVE

From her open cabin door, Tess enjoyed the smell of exotic greenery as she watched the land slip slowly by. Justice Avenger hardly made a wake easing through the narrow channel leading to Nurse Bay, home of Simbara's only harbor. A single lighthouse had been the first sign of human habitation, but now Tess saw what looked like an industrial complex pressed close to the shore, with four jetties extending into the water. The perfume of tropical flowers was gradually overlaid with refinery stink. *We're approaching civilization.*

Thinking this complex was their docking area, Tess left her cabin and stood on deck, leaning to one side to favor the huge, purpling bruise on her hip. She couldn't help noticing what a contrast the dry, hot land breeze was to the sea air to which she had become accustomed during the past ten days. Birgit stood at the rail alongside the captain's cabin, twenty steps forward. "Ahoy, captain's mate," Tess called, laughing. She really wanted to ask Birgit what had happened to the pirate she shot—or shot at—but she hadn't been able to muster up the nerve. *Today is my last chance, but here I am, making jokes.*

"Ahoy, yourself, landlubber. Are you happy your voyage is almost over?"

"Yes, but sad, too, to be leaving you." *Not really, since the pirate attack, but I can't bring myself to say so.* She couldn't reconcile this smiling, helpful Birgit with the image of Birgit gunning down human beings. *Or was I thinking of Tess gunning down a human being?* She forced the thought aside. "Is that our dock?"

Birgit laughed again. "You truly are a landlubber. Those jetties are for oil tankers, as any experienced sea woman would recognize."

Tess now saw that all three ships alongside the jetties were oil tankers, "They're bringing in oil? Or taking it out?"

"Out. It's Simbara's principal source of wealth. Come to the upper deck with me. We'll be able to see Port City much better from there."

From the bridge deck, Port City looked to Tess like a small town of some three or four thousand residents. As the ship drew closer, she saw she had made the mistake of estimating the population according to the large white buildings she could see from a distance. From a few hundred meters away, all the "foliage" surrounding the white stucco buildings revealed itself to be a scattering of low dwellings–huts made of green and brown organic matter. "Doesn't look that wealthy to me."

"Oh, Simbara's upper classes do business here, but they don't live here. You have to go up the coast a few miles to Strong Hill to find where the rich people live. There aren't many of them, but they are very wealthy."

Now Tess could see it was indeed a city–in population, if not in wealth. Behind the buildings stood several rows of sawtooth hills, then gray mountains. Coming closer, she could see that the highlands were largely devoid of vegetation of any color except for the green terraced gardens on the lower slopes and green bands striping the higher reaches.

"They are irrigation ditches," Birgit said when asked. "Simbara is a dry country, and every drop of runoff is caught and brought down to the gardens. Do not let anyone see you waste water. It's the greatest sin."

Tess looked around. They were now almost entirely surrounded by land–peppered with brown huts and green gardens, becoming sparser farther away from the white buildings. "But there's abundant water in this bay."

"Too brackish for anything but washing boats and nets," said Birgit. "But it does support a lush population of fish."

Tess could now see the docks, with what looked like hundreds of small boats, nothing even approaching the size of Justice Avenger. "I don't see where we're going to berth."

"We're not putting in. The harbor is strictly natural, and not deep enough for us to use a jetty. That's why the tankers anchor back up channel. " She pointed to a barge, smaller than their ship but much larger than the fishing boats. "They have one floating dock. See the crane?"

Tess looked where Birgit pointed and saw a flat-bottomed boat bearing a derrick painted in red and yellow stripes. "That little thing is going to unload our ship?"

"It's a slow, tedious process, but you won't have to watch. See!" Birgit now pointed toward the white buildings. "There's a motor launch coming out to get you. And me. If Alicia is not there to meet you, I'll give you a tour of Port City."

Rebecca appeared in the stairwell leading up from the passenger deck. "Packing's done, what little there was of it. Didn't Alicia say that if all went well, the Aremac would be here by the time we arrive?"

Tess shaded her eyes and squinting to see if she could make out any of the people aboard the approaching launch. "How could that be?"

"They're supposed to fly it over when it's ready. Still, it does seem unlikely that Roger could build one that fast."

"And Roger will be with it?" Tess looked harder, trying to focus. She wished she had binoculars.

Rebecca seemed to hear the excitement in Tess's voice. "I can't think of any reason why we'd need Roger."

"*I* need Roger," Tess said, turning to Rebecca, fists on hips, but blushing.

"Is he tall, dark, and handsome?" Birgit asked. "And young?"

"Very handsome," said Tess.

"Well, then is that him waving to us?"

Tess spun around. On the launch, now close enough to reveal faces, stood Roger, waving a tan pith helmet. A moment later, the launch was too close to the hull to be seen. She ran down the stairway, sliding her hands down the railings and barely letting her toes touch iron. She reached the main deck just in time to see her husband's thick black hair appear at the top of the ladder.

"Welcome to Port City," he said, laughing her into his arms.

I knew I had missed him, but not this much. She held the hug for minutes, then let him guide her down the ladder to the launch. She didn't let go of him until she stepped onto the small wooden dock facing a whitewashed building with a red-lettered sign reading, "Simbara Customs Office."

Two ebony-skinned, white-uniformed, customs officials greeted her as she disembarked, making her anticipate long, tiresome customs procedures. As she approached, the two men stood aside, revealing Alicia standing behind them. They simply said some words in a language she didn't understand, then Alicia stepped forward and took both her hands and greeted her in English.

Alicia waved at Rebecca, who was still saying goodbye on the launch. "All the paperwork is taken care of. I'm sure you'd like to settle into your hotel, but it's still early. Do you think you could possibly come to the courthouse so we could demonstrate Aremac? People here are ever so eager to see it, but your husband refused to start it up without you here to assist."

"That would be fine," said Tess, as Roger walked up beside her and took her hand. She noticed her hand was already sweating, or his was, in spite of the dry breeze. "The ship was entirely civilized–" *Aside from killing pirates,* her mind cut in. "–and I really have nothing to put away. But I would like to catch up on the news from home."

Roger removed his hand, wiped it on his pants, then took her hand again. "We can walk to the courthouse. It's just far enough for me to give you the headlines."

Rebecca quickly engaged Alicia in conversation about the details along the quay, slowing her down to give Tess and Roger secure talking distance. There seemed to be no sidewalk, but Roger guided her expertly along the red clay street, dodging the melange of brightly clothed pedestrians, bicycles, push carts, donkey wagons, and a few trucks piled way too high with assorted goods. She saw a few men in Western tropical business attire–white suits, Panama hats, pastel cotton shirts–though about half of them were Caucasian and carried their suit jackets folded over their arms.

As they passed an open-air fish market, Tess glanced back to be sure Alicia was out of hearing rang before asking Roger, "First, how is everybody?"

He squeezed her hand lovingly. "Your family is fine. Your brother Thomas won some sort of prize. I have a letter from your mom with all the news from California."

"And your family?"

"All healthy. My cousin Bart is out in Crownpoint, working on rug sales."

A wizened vendor wearing a gray robe stepped into their path waving a colorful woven basket about the size of large suitcase. Looking into his booth, Tess thought it must be his most valuable ware, but she waved him aside. "Rug sales?"

"Most of our customers pay with rugs. Or jewelry."

"Oh. No cash?"

"Some. Bart's doing very well for us. The bank account is in Marna's father's name. In fact, the whole business is, which is a good thing."

"Why?"

"Marna's worried that her husband might try to muscle in on the Hogan Stove money."

They passed a fruit stand, then Tess pulled Roger back to look for a snack.

"Are we protected?"

"Against the fruit?"

She picked up a small melon and sniffed it. "That, too, but I meant our money. And do you have any local money? This smells good."

Roger held out some coins to the purple-turbaned woman tending the fruit tray, pointing to the melon. The woman took two coins, tucked them inside her full-length wrap, and smiled at Tess, saying something incomprehensible.

Roger handed Tess his Swiss Army knife. "Our money is safe, but we may be attacked from other directions."

Tess cut out a slice of the melon, scraped out the seeds, and handed it to Roger. "What directions?"

"I barely escaped ahead of the FBI, but you already knew about them. Marna phoned this morning. It seems one old

Navajo man whose wife bought a stove turned around and traded it to some nosy reporter for a pickup truck."

"How bad is that?" Tess asked.

"We might be able to deal with the FBI, but we definitely don't need to be bothered by swarms of reporters trying to unearth our secrets."

CHAPTER SIXTY-SIX

Tess sat down with her husband in the shade of a broad-leafed tree on a low bench in front of a modern office building. The white paint failed to conceal the building's poured-concrete construction, but from a distance contributed the look of all the older white buildings in the neighborhood. It seemed to house several financial institutions, but the largest sign was for the Central Bank of West Africa.

Their corroded stone bench sat in a small grassy park in front of the building, with a round fountain in which a flock of tiny yellow birds bathed themselves. Assured that there was time to enjoy their melon before they were needed in court, Tess explored Roger's news. "I can understand the reporters' interest in our stoves, but I think Marna's secret is well protected. But what do you think the FBI wants now?"

"The Aremac, of course. JFA is already buying parts for the third one."

Tess looked around for someplace to throw her melon skin. Finding no trash bin, she moved over to the fountain and placed the skin on the ground. As soon as she stepped back, the flock of tiny birds converged on the treasure, making an amazing amount of noise for such small creatures. "Number three is also for JFA?"

"They're paying for it–for the magnet, principally–but I'm hoping we can keep it in Crownpoint for a while so SOS and Denise can try some improvements to the software. Alicia hasn't agreed yet, so I'm glad you're here to handle her." He kissed her on the cheek, leaving splotch of sticky melon juice. "But that's not the main reason I'm glad you're here."

She touched the spot on her cheek, but didn't attempt to wipe it off, giving him a lascivious grin in return for his kiss. "Do you have all the parts you need? We couldn't take anything out of the lab when the feds closed it down."

"The only thing JFA can't buy are the snoods, but I taught some Navajo women how to make them."

Tess was about to ask for more details, but saw Alicia sitting with Rebecca on the other side of the park. She was pointing to her watch. "Looks like it's time to go." She stood and placed the rest of the melon scraps near the fountain. "Any idea what this case is all about?"

Roger took her hand as they resumed their stroll. "Three men are accused of rape. That's all I've been able to find out, other than they want us to interview witnesses using Aremac. But there's the courthouse. I guess we'll find out more soon enough."

They walked to the front of a low white building–the colonnaded arcade of which filled the entire space between two dirt streets running up the slope of Simbara City. The columns were plastered, but in places the plaster was worn. Tess could see the underlying irregular stones supporting the flat, slightly inclined thatched roof. The four stairs up to the arcade were also stone, which seemed to be the predominant construction material of the older buildings. Wood was evidently in short supply.

As she ascended the stairs, Tess was surprised to see that the entrance did not lead inside, but through the building into an inner courtyard. She stood puzzled for a moment, not seeing any doors, until Alicia motioned her ahead. Passing through the entrance, she saw that the courtyard was surrounded by the building on all four sides. All the doors and windows faced inward, under another arcade that ran all the way around the square.

In the center of the courtyard–Tess wondered if this was the original meaning of the word "court"–stood a thatched canopy on aluminum legs supported by guy wires. Under the canopy stood a mammoth table consisting of a thick slab of dark brown, hand-carved wood on four sturdy legs. On the table was one object–a gavel.

Surrounding the canopy were dozens of folding chairs, most of which were occupied by dark-skinned women in maroon or gold sleeveless, low-cut dresses with matching turbans. Even more women sat cross-legged on colorful, patterned carpets on the lawn. All the women had nose rings, earrings, and one or more beaded necklaces. Obviously, this trial was of great interest to the women of the community, but in one area, a few men in gray uniforms sat on chairs. Tess was about to take a chair herself when Alicia took her arm and guided her to one of the few chairs under the canopy. "We sit here. Not out in the sun."

"Because we're foreigners?" Tess asked.

"No, because we're official members of the court."

Tess sat, saving the seat next to her for Roger, who was talking with some western-clad men under the arcade. "I thought these might be for the jury."

"No jury. Just one judge."

Just then, a gold-gowned man emerged from a north-side door and walked toward the canopy. Under the exotic gown, he wore a Western white shirt and black tie, and on his large bald head perched a charcoal straw weave hat about three sizes too small. Even if the crowd hadn't suddenly hushed, Tess would have known by his lordly posture and gait that he was the judge. Roger stopped talking and hurried over to sit next to Tess while the judge took his position standing behind the wooden table. He scanned the crowd, picked up the gavel, rapped sharply three times, and began a speech that Tess could not understand. In the middle of the speech, he inclined his head toward her and Roger, saying something that sounded respectful–or so Tess imagined.

When the judge stopped speaking, he motioned to the gray-uniformed men, one of whom strode over to the south wing of the building. For the first time, Tess noticed that the windows on that wing were barred.

More uniformed men emerged from a door, dragging three men, hands bound and feet hobbled by chains. Their clothes were tattered, but seemed to have once been some sort of cocoa-colored uniform. The prisoners seemed to be trying to show defiance, but all that disappeared when they were pushed to their knees in front of the judge's table. One tried to say something, but stopped when he was struck on the mouth by one of the soldiers.

The judge began another incomprehensible speech. Tess tuned him out, looking instead for any reaction among the spectators. Then, out of the stream of syllables, she heard the word "Aremac," and saw heads turned in her direction.

"It's your turn," Alicia whispered. "Follow the judge out back."

CHAPTER SIXTY-SEVEN

Tess had never seen Aremac on a truck, but the moment she emerged to the street behind the court building, she understood the sound of the generator, the thick smell of diesel fuel and exhaust, and the sight of the makeshift canvas canopy. The electromagnet stood mounted on a flatbed that occupied half of the truck behind an enclosed structure. She assumed that its many cabinets were filled with spare-parts and electronic equipment. Mounted on the side of this structure was a large flat monitor. Based on the crowd on the other side, Tess surmised there must be a matching monitor there, too.

A gurney was mounted on tracks in front of the magnet. At the foot of the gurney, Roger had climbed up to a control station. He beckoned her to follow him, and gave her a hand up the steep, narrow steps. He showed her a few slight changes to the familiar Aremac control panel. "I added these two controls when we discovered how much adjusting we had to do for cultural differences. It's a good thing we tested in Crownpoint before coming here."

Tess peered closely at the new controls. "Have you had time to make the adjustments here?"

"Everyone's been very cooperative. I think I have the gross cultural adjustments made, at least for the cultures we're going to be working with today."

"The crowd seems friendly enough."

"They've seen this demonstrated before, so they know what to expect. They know the difference between truth and lies, too."

The judge strode up to the truck and climbed onto the platform with Roger and Tess. A small man in a soiled white suit stood below him. He was wearing glasses, which Tess now realized were the first glasses she had seen on anyone here. "He's the translator," Roger explained. "Alicia assures me he's quite good."

"He'd better be," said Tess. "I don't think we want to misunderstand the judge."

"He does seem fierce," Roger whispered, "We'd better shut up. He's staring at us like he's ready to start."

The judge said a few words, then waited while those words were translated for the visitors. "We are ready for the first witness. He has called Madame Rachida to place herself in the true-witness machine." He looked at the judge, then at Roger. "The judge did not say so, but she is one of the victims, claiming she was raped by all three of the defendants."

An attractive women of about twenty climbed the stairs to the platform, watched but not assisted by two soldiers. Roger urged Tess toward the woman. "You need to place her in the gurney. I don't think they like men touching their women."

"Or raping them," she said, extended her hands to the woman, hoping she would understand the gesture.

Madame Rachida stepped forward and took Tess's hands. The translator moved to a position beneath the gurney, ready to relay Tess's instructions, but the witness seemed to understand Tess's first gestures. She sat on the edge of the gurney and allowed Tess to remove her maroon turban. Her hair was cropped close to her head, which was convenient, but not necessary. Tess wondered if this was the standard woman's haircut, or if she had been shaved for this occasion.

Rachida's nose ring and earrings looked like metal, so they had to come off. She understood immediately about the earrings, removing them and handing them to Tess. The nose ring was a different story. Tess tried to explain with gestures, but with no success. The witness simply did not understand.

Tess turned to the translator, "The nose ring must be removed before she can put her head in the machine. Otherwise, the machine might rip it out of her nose."

The translator said something to Rachida, who rattled off a long string of words in response. Tess thought she looked frightened.

The translator said something to the judge, who uttered several stern words that made the witness cower. "What's wrong?" Tess asked.

The translator gestured to Rachida, "The ring is a symbol of her marriage–" He pointed to Tess's hand. "Like your ring, but worn differently. If we remove it, she is afraid she will no longer be married."

"I didn't know that," said Tess. "Just assure her that we'll put it back when her witnessing is over."

Glasses said something to Rachida, who shook her head violently in rhythm with another long speech. "She says the ring can only be placed in her nose during a marriage ceremony, and she is afraid her husband will not want to marry her again once he sees how she was raped."

"Can't the judge resolve this?"

Glasses said something to the judge, who barked out orders to the soldiers. They dispersed into the crowd, returning a minute later with a scrawny man in tow. The judge spoke to the man. The man answered, standing proudly.

"What's happening," Tess asked Glasses.

"He says he is no longer married to her anyway, as she has been used by other men. He says he trusts her, and does not need to see the rape to believe her story. He says we should cut the ring."

"Cut it? Why not just open the clasp."

"There is no clasp. The ring is–how you say?–welded into her nose."

Oh my God, Tess thought. *What have we gotten ourselves into? I don't want to force her to lose her husband, but I don't want these rapists to go free, if they really raped her.*

The judge was saying something to Rachida. He didn't sound happy. She lowered her head and started to cry as two of the soldiers climbed up on the truck to hold her arms. A large man in work clothes appeared. Tess had been watching Rachida and didn't see where he came from. He carried a bolt cutter.

"Don't!" Tess shouted, moving between the worker and Rachida. She fixed her gaze on the translator. "Tell the judge to wait. Maybe there are other witnesses we can do first. Then when she sees it's all right, we can try her again. If we need to."

Glasses rattled off several long phrases to the judge, gesturing with his hands. The judge listened patiently, then raised his arms in the air to quiet the crowd of spectators. He gave a short speech, then said something to the soldiers holding Rachida. When they released her, she looked shyly at the judge, then climbed off the truck.

She was quickly replaced by a young girl, also in maroon, but wearing no nose ring. Glasses said her name was Sema, meaning "speak." Tess guessed she was no more than twelve, maybe thirteen, years old. She sat on the gurney without any guidance from Tess, then allowed Tess to remove her turban, necklace, and earrings. She sat perfectly still while Tess fitted her with a snood, then said something. Tess looked to the translator, but before he could say anything, she realized that Sema had spoken heavily-accented English. "I want to touch."

Tess answered carefully, enunciating each word. "What do you want to touch?"

"The true-witness machine."

"Yes. Of course you may touch."

Sema's eyes went wide, her lips tightly closed. She turned toward the three defendants and stared for a full minute. Then she turned to the Aremac and laid her palm on the outside of the magnet while she murmured something, this time not in English. Then she turned again, glared at the three accused men, and lay down on her back.

CHAPTER SIXTY-EIGHT

Marna thought Kit Kelly didn't look like a reporter–more like a native in boots, worn jeans, denim shirt, and a deep tan to go with his dark hair. *But he sure acts like one.*

He'd been sticking to her like a nasty burr ever since Norton told him she was the one to answer his questions about the hogan stove. *Norton will pay for that*, she thought, trying to think of a way to dispose of Mr. Kelly. *On the other hand, it's my fault that he's here, so I guess it's right that I'm the one to deal with him.*

She definitely wasn't going to invite him into her house, or into Southwest Stage, so right now she was sitting across from him at one of the picnic tables at the drive-in, the sun warming her back and the December air freezing her front. *At least he has the sun in his eyes so he can't read my expression. That John Wayne knew a few useful things.*

"–so after I traded the truck to Mr. Black Goat, I had the stove disassembled, but the engineers I hired couldn't figure it out, so I'm here to get an explanation for my readers."

"Why would some TV couch potatoes care about an old clunky stove made out of junk?"

"Because it seems to produce energy for nothing, that's why. Haven't you heard of the energy crisis? Greenhouse gases? Global warming?"

"Haven't *you* heard of solar power?" She held up her palm to the sunlight, as if it might be a solar panel. "You can feel it right on your own hand."

"Yeah, I saw the solar panel, but what's this?" He drew the core cylinder out of his pocket and smacked it down on the table, right next to his Navajo taco. "When they tried to open it up, it melted the insides into a lump."

Marna could see the heat-blackened patterns on the otherwise polished exterior shell. "That was foolish, tampering with the regulator."

"Regulator? What's that?"

"It just evens out the power when the sun is too bright. This is New Mexico, after all, not Seattle."

"So how does it work?"

Marna slid the napkin out from under his taco and started scribbling equations as fast as she could write, keeping up a meaningless physics chatter to accompany her writing. After a couple of minutes, he raised his hands in defeat. "All right, let's skip the equations for now. How are you involved in all this?"

He poised his pen over his notebook, making no attempt to copy the equations. Marna put a hurt expression on her face. "I was brought on the project to supply the heat transfer equations, but you don't seem interested."

"All right, I'm sorry, but I'm just no math whiz. Can you translate that for a dilettante?"

Marna picked up the napkin again and reached for his pen. "But they're really simple. And quite elegant."

He pulled back his hand so she couldn't take the pen. "Okay, maybe some other time. Why here?"

"It's the only place in town to get a decent lunch."

"I mean, why is the project here on the Navajo reservation?"

"Because this is my home. Why else?"

"I don't know. You tell me, Marna."

Marna felt herself blushing at the familiar use of her first name. "It's Dr. Savron, please."

He nodded, half frowning, half smiling, then pushed on with his questions. "All right, Dr. Savron, so why else is the project here?"

"Well, I wouldn't agree to participate if they weren't going to help my people, so they brought the project here. And I came along to act as translator for the Dineh."

Kelly reached into his pack and brought out a large camera. "Okay, how about you let me take some pictures of you for my story?"

"I'd really rather not have my picture in the paper."

"Could I have one just for my own pleasure?"

Now she was flustered. "Not really." *Why would he want a picture of me?*

To her surprise, he put down the camera and didn't press. "Okay, then let me take some pictures of the factory where you make these gadgets?"

"Oh, Mr. Begay would never allow that. I think he has some secret manufacturing methods." As soon as the words were out of her mouth, Marna realized that saying "secret" to a reporter was like saying "meat" to a hungry dog. But it was too late, and any attempt to retract the word would only make it more enticing.

"How about I talk to Mr. Begay myself?"

"He's, uh, out of town. Gone to Phoenix to buy some parts, I think."

"When will he be back?"

"Oh, I don't know. I think he has a lady friend down there." *Maybe that will distract him*, she thought.

But it didn't work. He packed his camera away, crumpled his napkin in his hands, dropped it on the ground under the table, and stood. "I'll be back in a couple of days. Maybe he'll see me then. And sell me another regulator."

Marna bent down to retrieve his discarded napkin. "Littering is a serious offense here."

"Sorry." He handed her his card. "If you've got something to tell me before Mr. Begay comes back, give me a call. Collect."

CHAPTER SIXTY-NINE

Much later, after a seemingly endless parade of younger and younger rape victims, Tess realized that Rachida must have been first to testify because she was the oldest. The younger girls had all been nearly as defiant as Sema, but had Tess been the judge, she would have stopped the trial after watching just thirty seconds of Sema's first-person rape scene. In fact, she did stop the trial temporarily, bending over the side of the truck to vomit the half-digested melon.

As it was, the judge gave every rape victim her turn to tell her story in pictures, pictures that Tess couldn't watch, but which the spectators seemed to take in with unreadable expressions. Nor did their expressions change when the last witness was dismissed.

To Tess's great relief, Rachida was not called back to the truck. She wondered if there would be defense arguments, but there seemed to be nobody to speak for the defendants–not that there was much to say after seeing their crimes through the eyes of their victims. Nor were the defendants allowed to speak in their own behalf–not allowed, or not wanting, for their own reasons. Instead, they were yanked to their feet and marched back inside the courtyard to once again face the judge's table.

When Tess climbed down from the truck to follow them, the interpreter explained that the judge would declare his verdict at the traditional table of justice. When the spectators had all settled down on their chairs and mats, the judge made a small speech, translated simply as "guilty."

From Tess's knowledge of American courts, she had assumed the prisoners would now be taken away for later sentencing and possible appeals. Instead, the judge spoke to the leader of the soldiers, who stepped forward and handed him an elaborately carved stick the size of a broom handle, but thicker. The judge then spoke to the spectators, and all the witnesses stepped forward in a line.

First in line was Rachida. The judge stepped out from behind his table and held out the stick to her, but when she reached for it, he pulled it away. He then moved to Sema and handed her the stick.

Suddenly, to her horror, Tess remembered the poster in Alicia's booth at the entrepreneur's convention in Las Vegas. Sema stood quietly with the stick in both hands, one end resting on the ground while the soldiers ripped the tattered clothing off the now-convicted defendants. When they were all naked, the soldiers stepped away.

Tess knew what was about to happen, but she didn't dare cover her eyes. She saw Sema walk over to the kneeling rapists, raise the stick, and swing it swiftly and deliberately at the head of the closest man. He ducked to one side, the stick catching him on the neck with a sickening sound. He swayed, but didn't fall.

Sema then stepped in front of the second rapist, raised the stick, and–having apparently learned from the first–struck him across the back. He grunted, but remained steady.

When Sema approached the third rapist, he tried to stand but was tripped and pushed by two soldiers. With his hands chained, he couldn't break his fall, and landed squarely on his face in the dirt, raising a small cloud of dust. Sema didn't wait for him to stand, but stepped forward and used both hands to drive the end of the stick into the back of his skull. The blow resonated with a sound like Roger thumping the melon that now burned in Tess's throat.

Sema stepped calmly back, handing the stick to the next victim in line. One by one, the women–girls, really–directed one blow to each of the rapists. At first they bravely grunted at each strike, though the third rapist lay unmoving, face down in the dust. After half a dozen blows, however, they seemed to lose their courage and began groaning, then screaming, then moaning as they lost even the energy to scream.

As the last, and youngest, girl struck her last blow, Tess hoped the punishment was over. Now, she thought, the men will be taken to jail, hopefully for long sentences.

But when the girl–she couldn't have been older than eight–returned to the victim line, she handed the stick to a spectator, an old woman dressed in gold and emerald green and decked out in at least a dozen gaudy necklaces. The woman looked feeble, but managed to strike three rather solid blows, after which she handed the stick to another woman from the crowd. One after another, never hurrying, women stepped forward and took their turns beating the rapists.

After a dozen women had taken turns, the second man collapsed on his face, but like the first to collapse, continued to receive blows to all parts of his body. The last rapist held out somewhat longer, but eventually, he, too, fell. He tried to roll away, covering his bloody skin in gray dust, but the woman with the stick simply followed him and administered her blow to his crotch. He stopped moving.

At last, Tess thought, or hoped, it must be over, but the beatings continued. A shadow passed over the courtyard. Tess looked up and saw a dark cloud, perhaps a symbol of this entire proceeding. She felt a drop on her hand, then another. She moved under the canopy, and a moment later, the air was filled with drops. Surely the rain would end this butchery.

But the beatings continued. Nobody fled for shelter. Every woman stood in the downpour, waiting her turn with the stick or, if she had already taken a turn, watching the others, blow after blow. Part of Tess remembered Aremac's pictures and wanted to stand out in the rain with them. For a moment, she even felt her hands grasping as if yearning for her turn with the stick. She looked for Rebecca, found her standing in the rain, and wondered if she would take a turn. Alicia stood under the canopy, dry and unruffled, her face expressionless.

The rain stopped. The three rapists' blood temporarily washed away, Tess could see the broken skin and swollen bruises covering their bodies. As each new woman stepped forward, she directed her blows at the few remaining unwounded areas of skin.

The rain began again, washing away the blood for a second time. Tess saw no new blood flow from the wounds. It took her a minute to realize what that meant, but the blows continued. Finally, a young woman finished her task and could not find another woman to take the stick. The captain of the soldiers took the stick from her, took a large rag from his uniform pocket, dipped it in a puddle, and carefully wiped the blood off the stick. When it was clean, he handed it to the judge, who turned and left by the way he had entered the courtyard.

The crowd turned their backs on the three dead men, quickly emptying the courtyard. "What will they do with the bodies," Tess asked Alicia.

"You don't want to know," Alicia said. "I believe court is over for the day. Let me take you to Simbara's finest restaurant. It's way past dinner time."

CHAPTER SEVENTY

Tess turned down Alicia's invitation to the restaurant. She could barely stand up without Roger's assistance. He wasn't too steady himself. *Even if I was capable of standing alone, I certainly wouldn't be able to force my churning stomach to hold down food.*

Rebecca, though shaken, seemed to be taking events more stoically. She whispered to Tess that she would go along with Alicia to find out more about what was going on. Tess didn't have the energy to stop her, though she already knew more than she wanted to about how naive she had been.

Their room was in the Palace Hotel–thirteen rooms with three baths, one on each floor, and a small restaurant downstairs. It was the dinner hour, but Tess found the odors from the restaurant nauseating, so they quickly obtained their key from the front desk and headed for the antique two-person elevator. Their third-floor quarters were called a deluxe suite, which apparently meant that it was next door to the bath and had French doors leading to a small balcony facing the harbor.

For the next few day, whenever she and Roger were not at the courthouse, reluctantly training the local operators in Aremac operations, Tess slumped on that balcony, feeding her meals to the squawking seagulls and looking with longing out across the pink flagstone terrace to the blue waters of the Gulf of Guinea, imagining the shores of America, far across the Atlantic. Roger would order food from the restaurant, but most plates were sent back untouched except by the gulls.

Luckily, the rest of the trials that week were for relatively minor crimes. The theft of a beaded basket from the market was shown in the video produced by the market owner. The thief's Aremac session produced a different version of the transaction in which he paid the owner, but Aremac spotted the fabrication. The thief was punished by ten lashes on his bare back with a thin rod–plus seventeen days of street-sweeping.

Joy-riding on someone else's moped earned a young man twenty lashes and unspecified work in the sewage treatment plant. The rider claimed mistaken identity, but Aremac produced four witnesses showing him on the machine in question.

Tess felt slightly consoled when some cases acquitted the innocent, avoiding the grotesque punishments and partially fulfilling her aspirations for Aremac. One young woman claimed that an older man with a jewelry stand in the market had promised her a necklace and two rings if she would let him fondle her privates. She produced an Aremac video of the transaction, but Aremac caught the lie. The woman asked for another chance, producing a milder version of the same fondling. Aremac accepted this version.

The man was willing to show his version, but the judge simply asked him if he had fondled the girl as seen in the video. He admitted that he had, but that he had only promised her one ring. The judge made him give her the ring, after which the man and girl left the courtyard holding hands. From the looks on their faces, Tess thought the girl would have more jewelry before the day was out.

At the end of the week, Alicia announced that they were to travel north to administer justice among some of the remote tribes in the savannah. Tess didn't want to go, but Alicia insisted, and Roger argued that the change of scenery would be good for Tess's depression–and his. Rebecca heard that the region was engaged in what some called an armed rebellion and others called a civil war. She insisted that all three of their party travel armed, though Tess kept her pistol in its holster packed in her duffel.

With a small military escort, the Aremac truck made its way north over roads that often disappeared as they crossed stony ground. Farther north, the hills became wooded, then lost most of their trees and gave way to an endless grassy plain. Around noon, before entering the plain, the convoy stopped about a mile away from a small town. Alicia drove the Aremac truck into the town, leaving Rebecca, Tess, and Roger to make camp. The afternoon passed with no sign of Alicia and her escort.

When the sun caressed the tops of the distant trees, Rebecca decided not to wait any longer. She began preparing supper and wouldn't accept any help. Tess and Roger sat on camp chairs in front of their tent, watching Rebecca's silhouette working in the distance against the broad, sweeping violet and goldenrod background of the sunset.

Tess decided it was time to talk about the topic they had been avoiding. She took her husband's hand in both of hers. "I haven't been sleeping well."

"I know. Not talking well, either."

She kissed his palm. "I think I'm ready to talk now."

"About your dreams?"

"Yes, my dreams. Every time I doze off, I experience those rape scenes. Feel them, like it's me being violated. I'm utterly blazing with rage, and then I'm standing over those naked men with that stick in my hands, beating on them. And then I'm paralyzed with shame. Which is worse, Roger, the rapes or the beatings? Which is worse?"

"Maybe they're both worse. Maybe we're all just evil monkeys."

The sun was now a huge, flattened ball of flame, sinking below a layer of magenta clouds. "Are we evil because we think about what we do?"

"Probably. I don't think monkeys are evil. They never tasted the fruit from the tree of knowledge."

"But we have. That's where it all starts." She looked away from the half-sun and into his eyes. "Like in the Garden of Eden."

They could see irrigated rows of small fruit trees at the edge of the town. A cloud of dust moved through it. Probably Aremac returning to the campsite. Roger pointed to the orchard. "Should we walk into town? Maybe there's an apple on one of those trees. You could pick it for me, then we could slip into our tent and play Adam and Eve."

She couldn't help but giggle, the first time she had laughed since the rape trial. "Oh, Roger, I know you're trying to cheer me up, but I don't want to be cheered up. Wherever we go, whatever we invent, we bring trouble."

"We didn't cause those rapes. And they would have beaten those men even if we hadn't brought Aremac here. Would you rather–"

The Aremac truck skidded to a stop a few feet away, raising a billow of choking dust. "This damn thing didn't work, Roger," Alicia screamed as she jumped down from the cab. "The damn thing didn't work!"

Tess remained seated, but Roger stood. "Calm down, Alicia. Tell me exactly what didn't work. Here, take my seat."

"I'd rather stand. Your damn Aremac didn't work! It just shut down and nothing my crew could do would get it going."

"I'll have to look at the logs," Roger said. "In the morning, when it's light."

"No, look at them now. I have to have go back into the town tonight, and it has to be working."

"All right," he said, ducking into his tent for a flashlight. "I'll take a look now. But if something's broken, it could be risky to try fixing it in the dark."

"We'll set up floodlights. Whatever you need."

Roger emerged from the tent. "Right now, all I need is this flashlight. Why don't you shut off the engine? We don't need to run the generator now. I work better when it's quiet. We can run off batteries."

Roger walked over to the truck. Alicia went to the cab and shut off the engine, then started to follow him. "No, I need Tess. I don't need you looking over my shoulder while I work. Why don't you go get something to eat? If you're in such a hurry, you can bring back something for me and Tess so I don't have to stop."

Alicia stood her ground for a moment, as if she was affronted by Roger making her into a waitress, then turned on her heel and headed for the glow of the cooking fire. Tess climbed up beside him at the console. "What do you think is wrong?"

He powered up the screen and tapped a few keys. "I don't think anything is wrong," he whispered. "I think Aremac is working exactly as it should."

"Then why is Alicia pissed? I've never seen her like this."

He pointed to the screen. "She's pissed because she was in town trying to torture someone in Aremac. Evidently, she doesn't know Aremac is rigged to reject involuntary testimony."

371 • GERALD M. WEINBERG

CHAPTER SEVENTY-ONE

Tess looked at the monitor for confirmation, but her heart immediately knew Roger was right. *I've been tricked. By Alicia. By my own optimism. From the beginning.* "They're just like the FBI," she gasped. "Torturers!"

Roger raised his finger to his lips. "Don't let her hear you. Didn't you tell her about the anti-torture system?"

"I don't remember. I must have assumed she knew."

"It was never publicized. How would she know?"

"Well, she knows now, and she doesn't like it."

Roger shook his head. "But she doesn't know. She thinks Aremac is broken. That's the way we designed it, so it would just shut down with a fake error message."

Tess squeezed Roger's hand. "We have to leave this place. This awful place."

He returned her reassuring squeeze. Then Tess saw Alicia and Rebecca coming toward them. Rebecca knew about the anti-torture system. Hopefully, she had the sense to say nothing about it. "It's a broken thyristor," Tess said loudly, before Rebecca had a chance to say anything.

"How long will it take to replace it?" Alicia asked.

Rebecca said nothing, but Tess saw her wink. She'd kept their secret. "That's a problem. Thyristors never break. Never before anyway. We don't carry a spare."

"So fix it."

AREMAC POWER • 372

"I can't fix it with what I have in the truck," said Roger, picking up the scam. "We need a new thyristor."

Alicia muttered something and smacked her palm with her fist. "All right. Write down the exact specs. I'll send one of the soldiers back to Port City for it."

Roger jumped down from the truck, directly in front of Alicia. "They won't have it in Port City. I checked everything when we were there, just in case something like this happened."

"So why didn't you order one?"

"I didn't think it would break. There are lots of parts like that, parts we think are reliable. If we kept spares of everything, the truck would be overloaded. Besides, when you get your second Aremac, you'll have a sort of built-in spare parts system."

"That's not good enough. We need the information now."

"What information is that?" Tess asked, lowering herself from the truck and hoping to sound casual.

Alicia seemed to realize her slip. "It's, uh, just for the trial. The people in town are eager for this trial to be over with. But that's not important right now. What is this broken part? And why is it so important?"

"It's a CNZ4134 thyristor."

"What the hell is that, in plain language?"

From the way he wrinkled his forehead, Tess saw that Roger was about to launch into one of his famous tech-talk snow jobs. It came naturally to him.

"Oh, sorry," he said, all apologetic seriousness. "It's a solid-state semiconductor with some number of layers of alternating N and P-type material."

"That tells me nothing. What does it do?"

"It's a kind of switch. It conducts if it's forward biased."

"That doesn't mean a thing to me."

"Well, that's probably because I oversimplified. This one is actually an SCR–oh, sorry, that's a silicon controlled rectifier, but it's not really different from a thyristor, so I didn't want to get too technical with you. It's just a matter of definition, but the IEEE hasn't yet finalized the standard–"

"Enough. Can't you substitute some other part?"

"Oh, sure. If we had a CNZ4136, we could probably cobble it in. Different pin configuration, but yeah, I could probably make do. It would be a little harder with a thirty-eight, but–"

"So in other words, there are any number of these thyristor things you could use?"

"Yeah, but they don't have any of them in Port City."

"Any idea where they do have them?"

Tess felt the urgent push of the impatience in Alicia's voice, but Roger remained unperturbed. "Sure. I looked it up. We get surprisingly good web reception out here. Of course, I don't know this area like you do, but according to the web, Nigeria is the nearest place that would have CNZs. A town called Ilorin."

"Ilorin's no good."

"Why not? Sounds like a nice town. City, actually."

"I can't send someone there. Simbara soldiers can't go into Nigeria."

Roger shrugged one shoulder. "So go yourself."

"I can't leave the soldiers without someone in charge. You saw what unsupervised soldiers can do in these villages."

Tess gasped. "You mean those were Simbara soldiers, the rapists?"

"No, of course not. But they were military. From some little rebel group that terrorizes these villages up north."

And I can guess who you were torturing in town today. A "little rebel group" that has uniforms and has somehow gotten all the way to Port City. "Well, *we* could go. That way we'll be sure Roger can get exactly what he needs." *And if we do go, you'll never see us again.*

Alicia shook her head, casting moving floodlight shadows on the truck. "No, I can't let you leave the country. Once you're in Nigeria, they might not let you come back to Simbara. They might think you were spies. No, we'll go up there in one of the cars and find a trader who can go across the border for us."

Tess tried to hide her disappointment. It wasn't going to be that easy to get out of Alicia's hands. She was trying to think of what to do next when Roger spoke up. "Sounds like a plan. But we'd better take Aremac with us."

"Why?" said Alicia, sounding like she didn't approve of the idea.

"There's a lot of manufacturing variance among those CNZs, so we won't know if we've got a good one until we try it out. If you're in a hurry, you wouldn't want to have to drive back up there a second time. Or a third."

"All right," Alicia agreed. "Leave your tent and supplies here. If we start driving now, we can be at the border before the stores open and be back here in time for the–" Her lips moved silently, groping for the right words. "–next court case."

Tess went around to the front of the truck, but Rebecca caught up with her before she could climb up. "Bring your passport. And your gun."

CHAPTER SEVENTY-TWO

There were four of them, the FBI men, plus the enormous Inga, not really enough to find someone who didn't want to be found, even in a town of fewer than three thousand inhabitants. Not when none of those inhabitants lost any love for federal agencies of any kind, least of all the Federal Bureau of Investigation. Not when the unexpected early snow had first slowed traffic, then bogged it down in the snow-melt mud roads.

Still, Marna thought, *the FBI has certain advantages.* When their mission leader, Don Capitol, first questioned her, she learned that he knew SOS and Denise by sight. (He knew Roger and Tess, too, but they were safely out of the country.) Later, Al and Tom told her they saw the agents unloading night-vision goggles and other hi-tech detection equipment. Standing in line at the market, she overheard that Inga was offering money to cooperating informers–none of whom were taking the bait. *Not so far, anyway, but someone might weaken at any time.*

And, she thought as her phone rang, *they can tap phones and emails.*

She checked the caller ID, but it was blocked. Very few people had this number, and most of them were now in Africa. It had to be SOS or Denise. *If I pick it up, can they trace where it came from?*

Before she could decide, the ringing stopped. *If it's SOS, he can hack the phone network. Either he knows they can't trace the origin, or he has a way of blocking the trace. I could just not answer, but I have to tell them about Kelly taking the stove apart. Next time it rings–*

As if telepathically, the phone rang again. Before the other party could speak, she said, "Don't call. I'll come see you as soon as I can." She hung up, hoping that it was indeed SOS, and that he was still in Crystal.

Now all I have to do is get there, and not be followed. Rebecca would know how–but Rebecca's not here, so it's up to me.

She dressed warmly, with heavy boots. Though the snow was melting now, the air was cold enough that more snow was a threat. She left the house and strolled as casually as she could over to the Southwestern Stage garage. As far as she could tell, she wasn't followed.

Norton wasn't around, but Louis agreed that he'd want her to have his four-by-four pickup if she was taking the shortcut to Crystal. "The snow tires are in pretty good shape, but if you run into mud, stop and put on the chains. They're in the tool chest. Key's on the ring."

She didn't know how to put on chains, but she was in a hurry to leave before the FBI showed up, so she didn't ask. *It will be obvious, I'm sure.*

She knew she should take food, but she didn't want to be seen loading up at Basha's. *There's a market in Twin Lakes. It's a couple of miles out of my way, but I can top off the gas there, too.*

All the way along Highway 9 out to Standing Rock, she kept looking back to see if she was being followed. She stopped a few times, pulling into a forest road and waiting behind the undergrowth to see if somebody trailed. In ten minutes, she never saw another vehicle. Back on the road, she had to stop looking over her shoulder to concentrate on the driving. The road was wet but firm, with scattered patches of slick snow where the piñons cast their shade.

From Standing Rock to Coyote Canyon, the forest was so thick that the snow hadn't melted at all. She stopped to engage the four-wheel-drive, pausing for a few moments to listen to the chattering piñon jays discussing her presence. She considered putting on the chains, but she figured that just a few miles would take her to Highway 491, which was paved.

At Twin Lakes, she bought cokes, a couple of turkey and cheese sandwiches wrapped in plastic, filled the tank, and asked about conditions on road to Crystal. The geezer behind the counter said, "I ain't heard no complaints ... but I ain't heard of no one coming that way, neither."

She decided to take the shortcut. The long ways around were both twice the distance, and risked the chance of being spotted. She asked the attendant if he would put on the chains, but he complained that his back didn't allow him to do that kind of work anymore. It was growing late, and a few flakes were touching her cheeks. Rather than waste any more time listening to boring stories, she jumped in the truck and drove off north up 491 to the Crystal cutoff at Tohatchi.

Ten miles later, in the growing darkness, she swerved to avoid a crossing porcupine. The truck skidded into the right-hand ditch. There didn't seem to be any damage. Unfortunately, the pickup was now stuck up to its axles in the mud—and the snow began to fall in earnest.

CHAPTER SEVENTY-THREE

The thyristor convoy was packed up and on the road–if you could call the rutted cow path a road–in less than five minutes. *It's a blessing that we can't see the pot holes in the dark. Feeling them is bad enough. Anticipating them could lead to accidents.*

Roger had insisted on driving the Aremac truck. Out here, nobody cared that he had no international license, but Alicia did seem to care about protecting her investment in other ways. Tess and Rebecca shared the cab with him, but two soldiers rode along on the flatbed in back. Alicia's car led the way in front. A second fully armed car brought up the rear.

Before they left camp, the team really had no chance to discuss plans, but as soon as they were safely alone, Roger spoke up. "I persuaded Alicia to go north because I figured we could just run across the border into Nigeria."

No need to discuss the agreement to leave. We all know what we have to get the hell out of Simbara, with or without Aremac.

Rebecca didn't take her eyes off the passenger side window, where the the gray-on-black landscape sped by. "A good idea, but it won't work. From what I've heard, anyone trying to sneak from Simbara into Nigeria without proper papers is likely to be shot. Besides, don't you want to take the Aremac with us? I thought that's what you had in mind when you convinced Alicia to take it."

"No, I was only thinking of a way to keep the three of us together, without anybody else along to listen in." Roger took his eyes off the road for a moment to look at Rebecca. "If it was a bad idea, why didn't you stop me?"

"Well, it was a good idea. And now we can use it to drive right into Zezanika, where I think they'll welcome us."

Tess craned her neck to check on the guards out back. "I don't believe Alicia would like that."

Rebecca checked the guards, too. "Maybe, but I think she put the guards there more to protect the truck from the rebels. It seems to be touch-and-go about who governs this northern region. We may have to worry more about the rebels than Alicia's troops."

The truck slammed hard into an unseen pothole, then two more in quick succession. Roger struggled to keep on the road. "Do they mine these tenth century freeways?"

Tess rubbed her head where it had hit the overhead light fixture. *I knew I wanted a middle-seat seat belt. Now I know why.* "I don't think they have to mine them. Anybody crazy enough to drive this cow path in the dark is not likely to survive. At least they could slow down."

"They could slow down," said Rebecca. "We'd still reach the border with Ilorin in plenty of time. But then they'd expose themselves to a rebel ambush. We should be happy if they break a spring or two. That would make it much easier for us to outrun them. Our truck is far more rugged than their cars, isn't it, Roger?"

"It is, but they're faster than we are. They can just shoot us if they see we're running away."

"They won't shoot at the truck because they're afraid to damage Aremac." Rebecca rapped her knuckles on the rear window, as if she were knocking on wood. "And they won't shoot at us because Aremac is no use to them without us to repair it."

"And to remove the software protection?" Tess said.

"She doesn't know about that, but she will want you two alive to fix the broken part."

"And not you, Rebecca?"

"I'm dispensable. That's why I have two guns."

The mention of guns silenced Tess. As the kilometers passed by, the first faint daylight revealed the gray outlines of a dry but sporadically irrigated landscape. As they neared Ilorin, the road actually improved a bit, probably because of lack of rain to make potholes. When it was light enough to reveal colors–mostly sand and green–Rebecca gave them the details of her plan and told them to check their weapons one more time.

A few kilometers after the road became patchy asphalt, Rebecca pointed out the city ahead and to their right. "There's about half a million people here, but only a few thousand on the Simbara side of the border. Mostly this side consists of a market for goods that aren't taxed in Simbara, but are in Nigeria. At least that's what I've been told."

"You've been busy," said Tess. "I thought you were playing the tourist while we worked."

"More like the spy. I don't have much experience playing tourist."

But you do playing spy!

The Simbara-side market, when they arrived a few minutes later, was not at all what Tess had envisioned. There were no buildings, but only a grove of widely-separated large trees. Under each tree, a family sat cross-legged on the ground with their wares spread out in baskets, on blankets or on the bare soil in front of them.

"I can read those signs," said Roger, surprise in his voice. "Some of them are in Arabic."

"At least half the population here is Muslim," said Rebecca. "Including the rebels."

"If I can converse with them in Arabic, it might be easier to persuade them to trust me."

Up in front of them, Alicia's car stopped near a grove of trees more tightly spaced than those they had seen previously. As Roger pulled to a stop behind her, he left room between the truck and Alicia's car for a quick turnaround.

Rebecca began to roll down her window, stopping suddenly when a small stone struck the door. "I think they don't like the looks of the army uniforms," she said. "That's a good sign. Okay, Roger, see what you can find."

Tess saw Alicia step out of the lead car and begin talking with some of the merchants, mostly with hand gestures. One of her troops had accompanied her as interpreter, but the rest remained at their posts, guarding the vehicles. Roger climbed out of the truck and approached a merchant selling pastries, breads, and some kind of liquid refreshment in corked bottles of a dozen unmatched colors and sizes.

I hope Alicia thinks he's innocently buying refreshments.

At first, the merchant eyed Roger suspiciously, but as soon as he greeted the man and his family in Arabic, the man's frown twisted into a friendly smile. After a while, the man stood, waved his wife and two small sons away. He surreptitiously took some bills from Roger, then casually walked over to speak with some of his neighboring colleagues. Soon, they, too, waved their families away. Except for Alicia's negotiations, which had attracted a small crowd, the entire market had became quiet.

Tess watched Roger's merchants, one by one, drift over to surround Alicia. *I hope they're careful. I don't want anyone risking their lives for us.* A group of tourists dressed in shorts and t-shirts entered the market and were immediately attracted by the crowd. When two of Roger's merchants started yelling at Alicia and making threatening gestures, the soldiers left their posts and ran to her aid.

Rebecca swung open her door and jumped out. "Now! Tess, take out the car behind us, then get back here in two seconds."

Tess had already slipped out the driver's door. She didn't hear Rebecca's last words clearly over the commotion in the market, but she knew her assignment. Her pistol was still in her holster because she couldn't see if all the soldiers had left the trailing car. As soon as she cleared the rear of the truck, she saw that everyone had gone forward to join the brouhaha. She drew her pistol.

The rear car had pulled close to the truck, almost too close for safety. She stopped and planted both feet. She flicked off the pistol's safety, aimed carefully, took three deep breaths, and put two spaced shots between the slats of the rusted grille into the car's radiator.

Without waiting to see leakage, she holstered the gun, turned, and walked deliberately back to the truck, hoping nobody had seen her or heard the shots.

Roger was already inside with the engine running, ready to drive.

Rebecca stood on the passenger side running board, holding the door for her.

Tess jumped inside and slid over to make room for Rebecca. Roger was already rolling into his u-turn by the time Rebecca was seated.

Tess held her breath, listening for the sound of shots, hoping the merchants could delay Alicia's crew long enough for their Aremac truck to speed out of firing range.

A little girl dressed in green and yellow escaped from her mother's hand and ran into the road in front of the truck.

Roger slammed on the brakes and spun the wheel.

The mother screamed and the little girl fell down in the dust, just inches away from the huge right front tire.

There's sure to be bullets now. Hit us if you must, but please don't hit that little girl.

CHAPTER SEVENTY-FOUR

The pickup's interior light switch didn't work, so Marna checked her watch by opening the door for an instant. She'd been stuck here almost two hours since she'd barely avoided hitting the porcupine creeping across the road. She had a slight nose bleed from the abrupt stop. *Lucky this old truck doesn't have seat belts.*

Her shoulder throbbed from the seat-belt bruise, but otherwise her body seemed intact. Certainly her bladder was working at high efficiency, forcing her to make risky trips out onto the wet, cold, slippery mud. *Grandfather said my nose would bleed if I killed a porcupine. I didn't kill this one, but my nose is bleeding anyway. Maybe it was scared to death. I know I almost was.*

Neither moon nor stars shone through the thick grayness above. The windshield was covered with an inch of snow, but it didn't really matter. Not a single car had passed since Norton's pickup had slid off the road and dropped the two right wheels into the mud-thick ditch. *And, at this late hour, no car is likely to come until morning–if then.*

Her phone didn't connect, either inside the truck or out in the cold and wind. Protected from the wind, she was marginally warmer in the truck, but frigid enough that she was tempted to run the engine and heater. *Not yet. Wait until I really need it. If nobody comes in the morning, I'll just have to hike out. I should try to figure out which direction would be best. I'm right between nothing and nowhere. If I could see a light, I could walk to it now, but there's not even a candle flame–assuming I could see it through this blizzard.*

The flakes were now driving almost horizontally against the left side–the south side–of the truck. She was glad now that she'd scavenged the tool box for anything useful while there was still some dim light. She'd found a flashlight almost the size of a baseball bat. Also, there was a blanket covered with gray and brown dog hairs. The blanket was now wrapped around her, and the flashlight lay, off, on the passenger seat. *I could use it as a weapon, if there were the slightest danger of another human being coming up here–but there isn't. But if someone does come, it will be my beacon. I could leave lights on, but I don't know how long the battery will last.*

She knew from old stories that people simply fell asleep when they froze to death. *As long as I can keep doing interesting equations in my head, I won't fall asleep.*

Despite this theory, she must have dozed off because she snapped awake at the sound of an engine coming down the hill from the direction of Tohatchi. She grabbed for the flashlight in the dark. She missed her mark and knocked the cylinder on the floor. She groped around for it, but felt nothing. *It must have rolled under the seat.*

The sound of the engine came closer, not moving too fast, but fast enough to pass her before she found the light. She sat erect and opened the door, blinding herself momentarily with the dim overhead light.

She shut the door, then opened it again. *I don't want to step out in the road. They might hit me. Or they might swerve and wind up in the ditch, too.*

She opened and shut the door three more times as the car approached, then left it open so they could see that she was alone. *That might be bad, but my weapon is under the seat somewhere. Too late now.*

The car rolled past. It's not going to stop, she thought, and started waving her arms. Just past the truck, their brake lights flashed red.

The car half slid to a full stop about a hundred feet down the hill. A dark shape emerged, carrying a light. Then another, and another.

The dark silence was broken by a female voice. "*Yah-ah-deh.*"

Marna let out her breath, not realizing she'd been holding it. "*Yah-ah-deh.*"

"*Ha-tde-la-ha-den-ne-eenh?*" (What are you looking for?)

A woman approached. Though she was about her own age, Marna didn't recognize her. Nor did she recognize the other women, which made sense when they explained in Navajo that they had come all the way from Nageezi, far to the west. A fourth woman, still in the car, had brought her sick infant to see a famous medicine man who lived in the woods near Mexican Springs.

"Is the baby all right now?"

"He's sleeping comfortably. Finally. We were reluctant to stop because we might wake him, but Isabel saw you. She recognized Norton Begay's truck and said we must help her cousin's friend."

The women set to work, mindless of the cold and mud. Two of them put on Marna's chains while the third retrieved a tow line from their trunk and hooked it to the front of Norton's truck. In less than fifteen minutes, the pickup was out of the ditch, but the women insisted they follow Marna until she reached Crystal.

Crystal was out of their way, but they quashed Marna's protests. "The road is very treacherous. There was another car stuck in the ditch, just like you, about half a mile back. Two men. Anglos, I think. Government plates, so we did not stop for them. They will find their way out in the morning."

Marna blanched. *Somehow, the FBI has been following me.*

I was leading them to my friends.

CHAPTER SEVENTY-FIVE

According to the estimate Rebecca gave Tess, it was fifty klicks from Ilorin to the Zezanika border, where a bridge crossed the Niger River. None of the three said anything until the skyline of Ilorin vanished behind them and Tess broke the silence. "I still think we should have shot out their tires. Are they behind us?" She had heard no bullets, though she had imagined every dust devil in the side view mirror was one of Alicia's cars about to capture them.

Rebecca craned her neck so she could see in the side view mirror. "Nobody. At least not yet. If we had shot the tires, Alicia would have seen the damage right away. She would have found new cars, probably stealing them at gunpoint. This way, if we're lucky, they'll start pursuing us and break down when they're well out of town."

Rebecca had tapped on the windshield, indicating the sparse habitation scattered on the squalid agricultural landscape. "Look out there. Do you see any cars to steal?"

"None," said Roger. "That's the problem."

"Why?" asked Tess.

"Because we don't have enough fuel to make fifty kilometers, and no cars means no gas stations."

"Maybe we'll see one," Tess said, but after ten klicks, her optimism had turned inside out. Not only were there no gas stations, there were no villages. She thought of stopping at one of the rare houses and trying to bargain for some diesel fuel, but none of the thatched-roof buildings displayed even a junked car. Not even a motorbike.

"Are you sure we don't have enough fuel, darling?" Tess asked for the fifth or sixth time.

"The needle's resting on the pin already."

"What are we going to do? We can't abandon Aremac to that monster."

Rebecca pointed to a wooded area far to the right. "We could hide it in the trees, but I don't like our chances of walking the rest of the way. Even if Silsbury's rotters don't find us, we could be gored by buffalos, trampled by elephants, attacked by warthogs, torn to pieces by hyenas, or maybe eaten by lions. It's a zoo out there, and they're not in cages."

Tess blanched at Rebecca's bestiary. "I thought lions were rare around here."

"It only takes one–" Rebecca cut her comment short when Roger suddenly swerved right onto a faint track heading into the woods. "What are you doing, Roger? It's not that kind of zoo, and we don't have time for sightseeing."

"You've given me an idea," he said. "Check behind us. First thing we have to do is get deep in those woods without anybody seeing us."

Rebecca turned around to look. "Then I suggest you slow down. You're raising a dust cloud that could be seen in Derby."

He eased off on the accelerator. "Is that better?"

"A mite more," said Tess. "There, that's sufficient. Now, why are we hiding in the woods? They might not see us, but you're only postponing the inevitable. We'll have to come out sooner or later."

"Later. Once we have fuel."

Tess watched them pass the first trees, which were widely scattered, with very little underbrush between them. "Darling, I know this diesel can run on butter or axle grease, but you're not going to find any oil in those woods."

"Just watch out back and tell me when we're in deep enough to be hidden from the road. We already have the fuel we need."

Tess offered Rebecca a puzzled shrug. "Alicia took our spare fuel. What am I missing?"

Rebecca returned the gesture. "There might be a bit of clotted cream in the fridge. That might move us a furlong or two."

Roger ignored both women, concentrating on finding a path between the trees. After a long silence, where the only sound were the rumble of the engine and the scraping of the thicker underbrush, he braked to a stop. "This is as far in as I can go, if I want to be able to get out again. I think we'll be safe in here, as long as they didn't see us leave the road."

Tess peered back anxiously. "We'll know soon enough."

Roger opened the driver's door. "No hurry. This will take a while. Rebecca, do we have enough food and water to hide out for a couple of days?"

Tess recognized his tone. "You're going to invent something, aren't you, darling? Something that's going to save us."

"Actually, I've already invented it, but it will take some time to modify it. Mostly, I want to wait until they give up searching for us."

Rebecca climbed out of the truck. "I'll check the provisions. We have a few nibbles, but if you want a real nosh-up, I might have to go hunting." She waved her pistol towards the deeper woods.

Roger ambled back to the rear of the truck, but Tess pursued him. "Are you going to keep us in the dark, then? What invention are you talking about?"

He turned toward her, looking genuinely puzzled for a moment, then his face cleared. "Oh, I forgot. You weren't there."

"Roger. Stop it. I wasn't where?"

"On the reservation. When Norton told us about the trucks."

"Told you *what* about the trucks?"

"That they're hybrids. Or at least this one was before its battery failed."

Chapter Seventy-Six

It was after midnight when Marna found SOS, Denise, and Heidi tucked away in a hogan a few miles outside of Crystal. The snug little building was well off the beaten track, and she noticed with satisfaction that her tire tracks were almost covered with snow by the time the trio finished hugging and ducked inside to enjoy the warmth of the tiny fire.

Heidi showered Marna with shaken snow while she explained about Kit Kelly and the FBI tail. "That's why you have to leave right away," she concluded.

SOS didn't buy her argument, and wanted to stay. "If your reporter is reverse engineering stoves, our secrets may not be safe."

"But you've built plenty of protection."

"Nothing is ever absolutely safe," said Denise.

SOS nodded his agreement. "If enough people focus on the problem long enough, someone could crack it. We have more work to do, and I can't do it here." He spread his arms to show how he could almost reach two opposite walls of the wooden building at the same time.

"You can't stay here, anyway," Marna pleaded. "But you can't come back to Crownpoint, either, or they'll find you."

SOS shrugged, stooping over so his head wouldn't hit the ceiling. "They found me before, in Chicago. They couldn't get a thing out of me."

Denise pulled him down to sit beside her on the red and black wool blanket covering the sagging bed. "Last time they thought Tess would give them what they wanted. It will be different this time."

Marna was pleased to hear that Denise was on her side. Heidi, lying with one paw covering her feet, seemed to accept her, too. "Maybe you two should just go to Africa with the others."

"I can't leave until we solve the stove problem."

"Yes, you can. I'll take care of it, somehow. I'm getting pretty good at software."

"I don't think so. I think I know what to do, and it's a matter of both hardware and software. Maybe you can do the one, but I'm the only one who can do the other. Though I'd much prefer Roger did it."

Denise nodded agreement, but said, "I think he'll have his hands full in Africa right now. How about you show Marna your ideas? Don't underestimate her."

They stayed up while SOS explained, not daring to risk sleeping too late and being found by the FBI in the morning. Every so often, Heidi would alert to something outside. Each time, Marna's heart jumped, anticipating the FBI. Then Heidi would relax and walk back to lay down at, or on, her feet.

Around five, they wrapped it up and decided that Denise and SOS would drive their car to Phoenix, or possibly Los Angeles, to shop for retinal and voice recognition hardware. Marna would return to Crownpoint with Heidi to keep an eye on the agents, fend off reporters, and start building software for owner-identity verification, so stoves wouldn't work except for the original owners.

"Will your people accept the identity device?" Denise asked. "We've had some cultural surprises already."

"I don't see why not," Marna said. "We are a practical people, Everyone's used to registering their trucks and putting identifying marks on their jewelry. But if someone doesn't want to have one, then we'll sell the stove to someone else. Norton has a waiting list as long as a rattlesnake."

"What about retrofitting the stoves we've already sold?"

"We can work something out, but it's getting late. Or, I should say, early. You don't want to be here when the FBI manages to extract themselves from the mud."

It was still dark, but no longer snowing, when they finished packing and stood outside to say goodbye. "Maybe I'll see you next time in Africa," Marna said.

"Maybe the time after next," SOS said. "First I'll have to come back to Crownpoint. I have to fetch some things from the garage and do the final integration tests of the security system."

"But the FBI–," Marna protested.

"Don't worry. Maybe they'll be gone by the time we get back."

CHAPTER SEVENTY-SEVEN

Tess watched Roger enter the combination that unlocked the truck's tool drawers and parts cabinets. He was in his inventor trance, so she knew there was no point in interrupting him. Still, when he pulled out one of the quantum displacement cylinders, she couldn't restrain herself. "You're going to drive the electric motor with one of those?"

He cocked his head to one side, studying the device. "Not exactly. I may need a couple." He rummaged around in the drawer. "It looks like we only have two. I think I can modify one to raise the power output. I think. I wish I had Marna here to do the calculations."

That hurts. "You don't think I can handle it?"

"Sure, I guess so. In a pinch."

He still didn't seem to notice her upset, which aggravated her even more. *Get over it, girl. You know he's like that, and it usually doesn't bother you. This time, you're anxious because we're in deep trouble. And that means no time for pouting.* "I'll get my computer. Just let me know what you need." *But it still hurts.*

Tess allowed herself to be distracted by their pattern of work. Roger, outside, focused on the mechanics. She sat in the cab performing computations, or came outside to act as her husband's gofer or extra pair of hands.

Rebecca, the only one with outdoor experience, set up a camp–inventorying food and water, digging a latrine, arranging the tarp over the magnet to divert rainwater into a jug. Seeing

Tess moping around, she sent her on a scouting mission. "Don't go out of sight of the truck, but look for signs of human activity–trails, cut wood, artifacts, even trash."

Tess found all of those things. A trail ran within throwing distance of the truck, but it was littered with leaves and looked as if it hadn't been walked on this season. Branches and stumps showed smooth cuts, but aged by the weather. She found a short length of broken chain, rusted almost beyond recognition, and a faded piece of day-glo survey ribbon tied to the trunk of a young eucalyptus tree.

As for trash, she found a scattering of bones–bleached white or still holding shreds of soft connective tissue, all showing indentations she decided were tooth marks. When she finished her survey, she reported her findings to Rebecca, bringing her the largest fresh bone. She thought it might be a human femur, but Rebecca assured her it was from some animal. Somehow, Tess wasn't convinced.

Sitting in the cab with nothing more to do, Tess grew even more cranky as the sky clouded over, threatening rain. "Just our luck. We've got no spare clothes, and now we won't be able to work outside."

Rebecca grabbed her shirt sleeve and tugged her out of the cab. "Stop whining. We need the water, and we're not helpless. I think we can rearrange the tarp so Roger will have a dry workspace."

Twenty minutes later, they had almost finished when the first drops wet Tess's cheek. She tied down the last corner of the tarp, then ducked under to watch Roger at work. *He's marvelous. All this time, he never once looked up at us working above his head. He'll get us out of here, and Rebecca will keep us safe while he's doing it. But me, I'm overwhelmed and incompetent. I guess I'm no Albert Schweitzer.*

Roger continued to work the rest of the day, as long as the natural light was still adequate. All the while, Tess kept an anxious eye toward the road, but nobody appeared. When the rain intensity increased toward twilight, Rebecca insisted he stop for the night. "Come into the cab where it's dry. We'll have a cold supper and then grab some sleep."

Roger squeezed inside. "I'll have to keep working. I could have been done by now if I had all the tools and parts I need. The rain isn't making it any easier."

Rebecca used her Swiss Army knife to open a can of peaches packed for the lunch they had skipped. "The rain is our friend. It gives us water–I have no idea how far the nearest water is. And it will wash away our tracks. But you can't work at night. Even if our batteries hold out, any light out here can be seen for kilometers."

Tess took a slippery peach slice between her fingers and fed it to Roger. "Can you roll down a window, at least? It's going to be hard to sleep in here with the musty smell and the dampness, with us all crowded together.'

"One of us can sleep under the tarp, on the gurney. Not you, Tess. You've served more than your time on that bed."

I wonder which feels more helpless, my months in a persistent vegetative state or a single night trapped in this truck, surrounded by night sounds of roaming predatory animals and putrid odors of their dead prey. I'm definitely a city girl. And a coward.

She sat, awake, with Roger sleeping innocently, head on her shoulder. She continued to refresh her cowardice with every gasp, grunt, growl out in the dark, until sometime early in the morning, when she finally dozed off. When she awoke, suddenly, it was full daylight. She was alone in the cab, but she could hear Roger tinkering outside. *Well, I guess a complete coward couldn't have gone to sleep here sitting up in a truck. Gods, my back feels like it's baked in clay.*

She came outside, used Rebecca's latrine, then returned to offer her help to Roger. "Where's Rebecca?"

He didn't look up from the cylinder he was studying with a magnifying glass. "I don't know. She went somewhere. I think I heard shots a while ago."

Tess looked around, seeing no sign of their partner. "She shouldn't go off by herself."

"She's got her guns, and she knows how to use them. Better than you can say for us."

"Then she should stay close to protect us."

"Protect us from what? What could–?"

Rebecca came crashing through the undergrowth, dragging a deer-like animal. "What's that?"

"An impala."

"You shot it?"

"No, I stole it from the hyenas. Of course I shot it, silly boy. But the hyenas tried to steal it from *me*." She turned to show her right side. Wet blood smeared her cheek. Her sleeve was ripped and soaked with more blood, perhaps from her face or from the arm itself.

"My god," Tess gasped.

Rebecca mopped blood off her face with her left sleeve. "It's all right. I shot one and the other attacked it. Now we won't starve."

Tess swallowed hard. "You want us to eat it?"

"That's the idea."

"Are we supposed to eat it raw?" Tess asked. "If we try to cook it outside, the hyenas will come after it. Won't it have

worms or parasites?" *I'm babbling. Stop it.* "Roger, how long
are we going to stay here? Maybe we don't need the extra food."

From the woods came a sound like twenty people
screaming, giggling, and whooping all at the same time. Tess
went rigid. "What's that?"

Rebecca cocked her head, staring into the woods. "I think
it's my hyena friends come to take this meat away from us. With
reinforcements."

Over the eerie wailing came a roar and a snarl. Tess
jumped into the cab. "And what's *that*?"

Rebecca pushed the impala away from her and joined
Tess. "Sounds like the king of beasts has come to take this meat
away from *them*."

CHAPTER SEVENTY-EIGHT

Marna drove back to Crownpoint with Heidi for company, avoiding the shortcut for easier roads. As the days passed with no sign of SOS, she kept hoping the FBI would give up and leave the reservation. To her dismay, they kept hanging around in a maddening pattern. One day they would snoop around town, then they would disappear for one, or two, or three days before showing up again unannounced.

To avoid the chance that Inga Steinman or Special Agent Capitol might recognize Heidi, Marna spent most of her time in the Southwest Stage office with the dog at her feet. She buried herself in work on the identity software, all the while fearing the next phone call, the next problem. *My strength has always been focus–working on one problem at a time. Now I'm juggling dozens, or so it seems.*

She decided to do what Rebecca would do: make a list. *SOS coming to town, the FBI lurking in wait to kidnap him, reporters trying to unlock the stove's secrets, keeping stove production moving forward, developing a retrofit plan, worrying about what's happening in Africa without any word, and now the wind has knocked a tree onto Nellie's garage roof. All I need now is for Karl to show up.*

But it wasn't Karl banging open the door, it was Jimmy Gardner, squatting down to ruffle Heidi's ears. With his acne and dyed hair, he looked all the world like a petulant teen-ager. "Is the truck ready?"

"What truck?"

"You said I could use one of the trucks. I need it for today's shoot out on the mesa."

Oh, no, another one for the list. What would Rebecca do? Or maybe Tess. She slipped around the desk, put her arm around his shoulders, and tried to imitate Tess's tone. "I'm sorry, Jimmy. Norton's out of town, and his crew hasn't had time to get it ready. We've got quite a few more immediate problems."

"Like those FBI thugs?"

"Like those FBI thugs." She took a deep breath, steeled herself, then tugged on his long black braid. "Come on, Jimmy. Give us a few more days. Until Norton gets back."

He returned her smile, looking as if he were about to cry. "But I'm shooting a movie. Every day that goes by, I have expenses."

Looking at the elaborate silver jewelry on his wrists and neck, Marna doubted that Jimmy spent even a cent on anything else. "What kind of expenses?"

Jimmy fiddled with the palm-sized natural turquoise squash-blossom on his necklace. "Um, like film."

"I don't think so, Jimmy. You don't use film if you're not shooting." She patted his cheek. *I can't believe I'm flirting with this kid.* "Wait a minute. You use a digital camera."

His blush was obvious, even through his dark skin. "Well, I meant mag tape."

"Come on, Jimmy, you can do better than that. Tape is reusable, so don't jerk me around. I don't have time for this. You don't have any expenses, so you can wait a few days for the truck."

"Uh, well, I'm paying Emily to sew costumes and do makeup. I have her on a retainer."

Emily Nez was proprietress of Hair Today in Thoreau, another distant cousin of both Marna and Jimmy, better known for her skill with a needle than with clippers. "We both know Emily wouldn't take your money for–."

She slapped herself on the forehead. "Did you say costumes and makeup? What kind of costumes?"

Jimmy puffed with visible pride. "Spanish conquistadors. Priests. Old-fashioned stuff. I mean, she's not really making them all from scratch, just altering stuff from her great-grandmother. Well, actually, she's my great-aunt, too. And, besides–"

Deliberately, Marna laid a calming hand on his arm. "Jimmy, my cousin, if I get you the truck, can I borrow Emily for a while?"

CHAPTER SEVENTY-NINE

They couldn't see the lion yet, but Tess urged Roger to climb into the truck immediately. "We still have enough diesel fuel to get away from here. Just throw your tools in the bin and crawl up here."

He raised one hand in protest. "But I'm not finished."

"Finish later, when we're safe."

"But I'm all set up here. And I haven't finished testing the upgraded battery."

Tentatively, at first, the small head and rounded ears of a hyena appeared among the trees. *It's kind of cute, with all those spots*, Tess thought, until she saw the second and third start ripping apart the impala carcass.

She was paralyzed with fear, but Roger kept calmly arranging his tools in their proper slots, ignoring her pleas to retreat to the cab and drive away.

More hyenas joined the feeding frenzy, more than Tess could count, but certainly more than they had ammunition to shoot. Stiffly, she managed to put her hands over her ears to drown out the growling and snarling, but she couldn't take her eyes off the primitive feast.

When she managed to shout over the ruckus, Roger called back, "They're busy. They have no interest in me. I'll be finished in a few minutes."

Tess bit her lip, counting the seconds. Suddenly, most of the hyenas looked up from their meal. It took a moment for her to realize that they were responding to a sound–a deep roar from within the trees.

"A lion," Rebecca said unnecessarily, just as the massive maned head showed itself.

The hyenas hesitated, shrieking, then bolted as two female lions appeared alongside the male. Tess was so hypnotized by the lions that she was startled by the pressure of Roger's body squeezing into the driver's seat beside her. "Hyenas, yes," he said as he twisted the ignition key. "Lions, no. I can always replace the tools."

"Where are you going?" Tess asked. "Aren't we safe in the truck?"

Rebecca grasped her shoulder. "He's right, dearie. It's not likely, but if a lion decides you'd make a slap-up dessert, he could rip off that door as easily as you'd crack a soft-boiled egg."

Tess leaned away from the door as Roger backed the truck cautiously away from the lions.

"How far away will be safe, Rebecca?" he asked. "I need a few more minutes to be sure of the electric motor, but I don't want to use more diesel fuel than I have to."

Tess watched the hyenas creeping just as cautiously, toward the jungle royalty. "I'd feel better if we couldn't see them. Then by Fermat's principle, they couldn't see us."

Rebecca was also watching the interplay among the forest creatures. "I'd rather keep an eye on them. I think they're interested in the meat more than in us."

"Unless they decide *we're* the meat," Tess said.

"All right, if you've lost your bottle, we'll stay out of sight. But I'm more stuffed about our other pursuers, Roger, so find us a place where we can't be seen from the road."

They eventually parked in a deep dry wash. Rebecca worried about possible flooding, but even after yesterday's rains, the ground was merely damp. Once Rebecca's wounds were tended to, Tess spent the rest of the day helping Roger test the electric motor and calculating adjustments for the quantum battery. They restricted Rebecca to lookout duty, and forbade further hunting, though Tess's empty stomach protested vigorously and caused her to make clumsy mistakes in her calculations.

After another restless night, Tess heard Roger awake at first light, tinker with the electric motor for about fifteen minutes, then declare the truck ready for the road. She noticed how silently the truck was running, but Roger stopped twice in the first hour to make further adjustments. Though they were now more than half the distance to the border, Tess still watched anxiously behind. "Maybe they've given up on us," she said hopefully. "Or maybe they don't know which way we went."

"There aren't very many directions to go around here," said Rebecca. "Plus, there aren't many trucks like this on the road. They would probably find somebody to tell them about us at every intersection."

"No," Tess sighed. Her back was beginning to throb in new places from the washboard road and stiff suspension. "Not many vehicles of any kind."

Roger took one hand off the wheel and pointed out back with his thumb. "Not many. But something coming up behind us is raising an enormous dust cloud."

"Alicia's cars?"

"With all the dust, I can't be sure. Could be her."

Rebecca checked the odometer. "About as good as I hoped for."

"They're still some ways back. Maybe I can outrun them. How far to the border?"

"I wish I knew," Rebecca said. "I wish there were road signs. My best guess is somewhere between eighteen and twenty-two klicks."

The truck bounced high in the air, the wheels juddering as they hit the ground. Roger struggled to keep the clumsy vehicle on the road. "The potholes slow us down, but overall I think they slow them more. If the road stays like this, I'd guess it will be another eight or ten klicks before they catch us."

"That's ten or twelve short," Rebecca said. "Any way you could go faster?"

"To get the maximum, I'd probably have to readjust the cylinder, and that would risk an accident like the one that took off SOS's ear. I could go faster now, but I can't risk more speed on this rough road. We're top-heavy, and we could easily tip over. If we'd dumped the magnet, we could probably match their speed, but it's too late to stop for that."

Tess could hear the strain in her own voice. "So what can we do?"

Rebecca took one of her pistols out of its holster. "Keep driving. Check your ammunition. Too bad we have no rifle. They have the range on us. Hard cheese on us."

"I thought you said they wouldn't shoot at us."

"They can shoot at the tires."

"At these speeds," Roger said, "that could amount to the same thing."

Rebecca reached across Roger's chest and unholstered his gun, handing it to Tess. "You just worry about the driving, Roger. If any shooting starts, we'll take care of it. Do not stop for anything. And Tess, if they get close, shoot for their radiators."

We? thought Tess. *How do I keep getting into these shooting situations?*

Klick by klick, the trailing cars edged closer. The odometer read in miles, but by doing the conversion in her head, Tess tried in vain to keep her mind off the possibility of shooting. *Radiators are one thing. Human beings are quite another. I can easily forget about shooting a radiator.*

Roger was doing his best to maintain speed while keeping the truck on the road, in spite of the jarring and swaying from the potholes. Tess had become so adapted to the rough ride that she twisted her back when the road suddenly smoothed out. "Asphalt," Roger cried. "There goes our advantage."

Rebecca looked in the mirror, then at the odometer. "But maybe it means we are closer to the river than I thought. And traffic is picking up. That might slow them down."

"There's a lot of green on the horizon," Tess said. "Maybe that's the river."

Now that the road was smooth, Roger risked pushing up the speed as far as he could without stopping to adjust the cylinder. "It's still not close enough. I can almost smell Alicia's perfume. I never liked that stink."

"Bulgari Pour Femme. Perfect for the ascetic charity worker. Makes me want to chuck." Rebecca held her nose to emphasize her revulsion with her countrywoman.

Tess heard a chattering sound that drowned out Rebecca's further opinions of their pursuer. "Is that the truck? My God, what could be worse than a breakdown now?"

Rebecca laughed sardonically. "What could be worse? How about the perfumed lady shooting at us with automatic weapons?"

CHAPTER EIGHTY

MaryBeth's mother came in person to tell Marna her daughter had phoned. The FBI men were safely back at the Inn.

Marna swung into action. *I don't know where Inga is. I'll have to watch for her. At least she'll be easy to recognize. Besides, I'm not really sure what she's up to. Sometimes she seems to be working with the FBI, but sometimes she seems to be undermining them.*

Marna quickly walked the four blocks through the cold, clear night to Louis Tsoh's house, thinking how the FBI agents were no longer just "men." The local agent, Frank Wesley, had been replaced by a young woman from Los Angeles. *Of course, Inga is a woman–but, no, she's really not part of the team.*

So why did they change the team? Evidently our locals aren't good enough, though Frank was the only one who understood three words of dineh bizaad. *Inga certainly didn't. So much the safer for us.*

Louis emerged from the front door before Marna reached his porch. He tossed a small suitcase tied with rope in his Chevy pickup and gave Marna a high sign. Thirty-five minutes later, they pulled up in Thoreau at the back door of Hair Today. SOS was already inside, watching Emily put up Denise's long ebony hair in "Dineh fashion."

Emily, a large middle-aged woman with perfectly proportioned features except for her conspicuous overbite, finished up the hairdo, then spent a full half hour tracing SOS's face with her pudgy fingers before announcing to Marna, "I can do it. I'll give him a bigger nose, dye his hair, darken his skin. I can't do anything about the eyes, but nobody's going to notice if he wears sunglasses. You have sunglasses, Louis?"

"I do. Let me get the suitcase."

While Louis was out, Emily told SOS to take off his shirt, shoes, and socks. "I've got to do any skin that might show. Jimmy says that's the kind of detail that can ruin a movie."

As soon as his shirt was off, Emily grabbed his hand and twisted it to expose the LOVE tattoo on his forearm. "That will never do. No decent Dineh would decorate his skin. Can you keep your sleeves rolled down all the time? No, that's not good enough. Just a minute."

She disappeared into the salon's tiny bathroom, emerging a few moments later holding up a white plastic first-aid kit. "We'll bandage over it, once your skin is done."

Louis returned with the suitcase and opened it on the counter for Emily to examine. She tossed a pair of jeans and a blue and black plaid shirt to Denise. "Here, put these on him while I get the face putty ready. If they need alteration, you can do that while I fix his nose. There's thread and stuff in the cabinet next to the Singer."

Denise looked helplessly at Marna. "Can you sew?"

Marna shrugged. "I made doll dresses when I was ten. Let's hope these clothes are the right size."

The sleeves were little short, but Emily decided nobody would notice because "Louis isn't that well dressed anyway." Louis took no offense, and was rather amused by Emily's rendition of his nose on SOS's face. SOS wasn't that pleased with his new hair color, but thought his new haircut was an improvement over his half-grown-out original.

When Emily pronounced her work finished, she gave Denise a bottle of skin stain along with touch-up instructions. Louis handed over the suitcase, and he and SOS exchanged car keys, saying he would stay with his mother's sister's oldest daughter in Ramah until he heard SOS was finished with his stove work and ready to leave for Africa. In the meanwhile, Marna's plan had SOS and Denise taking care of Louis's house. SOS would work at the garage, but Denise would stay out of sight.

"It's not so much the FBI seeing you I'm worried about," Marna explained. "It's Louis's reputation. If people see he's living with a strange woman, they'll all be talking about it. Something might leak back to the FBI."

"That's all right with me," said Denise, studying her lover's new face up close. "The disguise is risky enough."

CHAPTER EIGHTY-ONE

Tess tried to picture the military escort to their original convoy. "I'm no expert, but I didn't think Alicia's men had automatic weapons."

Rebecca stared intently into the mirror. "Sorry, but I *am* an expert, and they do. They must have stopped for new weapons along the way."

Roger swerved the truck to pass an oxcart. "Well, if they did, they didn't take time to practice. They haven't hit us yet."

"It's a bumpy road," Rebecca explained.

"I don't think so. Compared to what we were on before, this is like driving on glass."

"This isn't the cinema, Roger. It's not that easy shooting from a moving vehicle."

Roger laughed. "Especially when you've turned around and are driving the other way."

"What?"

"Look in the mirror. It wasn't Alicia shooting. It was someone behind her, and they weren't shooting at us."

Tess hit Roger on the arm. "Better look ahead. I think someone's blocked the road."

Roger decelerated, allowing their new pursuers to gain ground. "Our rescuers seem to be soldiers. See the uniforms?"

Tess put her hands over her face. "Oh, no. Those are the same uniforms the rapists were wearing."

"Same color, that's for sure," said Rebecca. "Probably rebels."

Tess's head spun with pictures of the rapes Aremac had shown. "So the frying pan is gone, but the fire is determined to catch us."

"They might be friendly," said Rebecca. "You know, the enemy of my enemy is my friend."

"Do you want to risk it? You saw those Aremac videos. We can't take a chance."

"What other chance is there?" said Roger. "They've blocked the road."

"That barricade looks quite flimsy," said Rebecca. "But if you're going to crash it, you'd better decide NOW."

Roger pressed down his foot. The truck jerked forward, picking up speed.

The two barricade guards starting waving their rifles. The truck kept accelerating. The guards vaulted out into the ditches, one to each side.

Roger peered intently ahead. "I don't know if it's that flimsy. They're concrete road dividers–designed to flip us over. Maybe I should stop."

He started to ease off, but Tess pressed her foot against his, holding down the accelerator. "No stopping. We can make it. I see a bridge ahead."

Roger aimed for the tiny space between two concrete road dividers. "Tuck your head between your knees."

Tess bent over, first peeking at the speedometer. Sixty, then sixty-five, then edged up toward–.

The truck smashed into the barriers, sounding like bones snapping.

Feeling like bones snapping.

The front end soared upward, then plunged with a massive jolt.

Bounced twice.

Shots crackled.

Windshield spiderwebbed.

But the truck kept rolling forward.

So did the cars behind them.

Tess shook away her blurred vision, shouting over the racket. "Ha! Conservation of momentum really works."

The collision seemed to have knocked the steering out of alignment. Roger fought to keep the truck straight. "Don't give Newton all the credit. The barriers were set up backwards."

Rebecca kept shifting her eyes from the mirror to the bridge in front of them. "What did that sign say?"

"What sign?"

"The one on the barrier?"

"It was in Arabic, but I didn't really pay much attention."

Shots sounded behind them. Roger took one hand off the wheel and slapped his forehead. "Oh, shit."

"Oh shit, what?"

"It said the bridge was out."

CHAPTER EIGHTY-TWO

According to Marna's informant network, the FBI was checked out of the Inn in Grants. SOS's disguise wasn't put to a real test until three days later when they returned. To her dismay, Inga recognized SOS the moment she encountered the three of them at the drive-in. Marna was already thinking of a quick escape when Inga assured her she wouldn't tell the FBI team as long as she could talk with SOS confidentially. Marna was confused, and didn't entirely trust Inga, but she agreed—and kept planning an escape.

Even if Inga didn't talk, most of the Crownpoint locals who knew Louis had seen through the disguise. Marna could tell because people kept dropping into Southwestern Stage to have a look at Emily's work. Jimmy was one of the first, offering SOS a bit part as Alvar Núñez Cabeza de Vaca in his new movie. (Marna later learned he had asked Inga to play the part of Mad Queen Joan.)

SOS was intrigued by the offer, but Marna and Denise kept him focused on finishing his identity-verification work as quickly as possible. "We need to leave the FBI surveillance behind."

Later, Marna caught her indefatigable colleague surfing the web, exploring every type of information protection—passwords, key cards, fingerprints, palm vein analysis, retinal scans, iris scans, odor identification, hand geometry, face recognition, signature, plus a variety of voice analyses, and other less well-known systems. After a couple of days of this endless surfing, Marna dragged the culprit over to Louis's house so she and Denise could gang up on him.

Denise went first, removing her thick glasses as if preparing for a fight. She didn't hit him, but she laid down a verbal barrage that attacked all his weak points. "We've been lucky so far, Sweetie. The FBI seems to be on vacation, but our luck could run out any day." She peered around at the four close walls of Louis's shabby single-wide trailer. "The secret technology of Marna's energy generator is probably adequate for now–and, besides, I'm tired of being cooped up in here."

"I've given you lots of algorithms to work on," he whined. "And you know more about security than I do."

Denise snapped back, hands on hips, "If I know so much more than you, how about listening to my advice for a change?"

I think I will stay out of the middle of this for a while, Marna thought. *I like the way she stands up to him.*

"What advice? I don't remember any advice." He looked genuinely puzzled, and hurt.

"That's exactly what I mean. You aren't listening."

SOS stared out the window, saying nothing. Marna decided it was time for her to step in. "Maybe he would hear you better if you didn't talk."

"Huh?" Denise shook her head, "How can he listen if I don't talk?"

"I think he pays more attention to the written word, especially on technical problems. What did Tess say? He's not primarily auditory, but visual?"

SOS kept staring out the window, as if to prove Marna's point. Denise stood motionless, which Marna took to mean she was thinking deeply about possibly refuting the theory. Finally, she said, "Maybe. That might explain a lot of things."

"Then let's test it out. Do we have a flip chart somewhere?"

"You're kidding, right? Louis doesn't even have a colander. Don't Navajo eat spaghetti?"

Marna giggled. "Actually, in my family, pizza was the preferred native cuisine."

"Well, he doesn't have a pizza slicer, either. Can we just use pencil and paper?"

"He has that?"

Denise put on her glasses and reached for her briefcase. "*I* have that."

"All right," said Marna, dragging SOS by his elbow away from the window to one of the two kitchen chairs. "You sit here. Denise, you sit in the other one and see if you can write down what you want to get across, as simply as possible."

Denise sat. She pondered for a long time, uncharacteristically chewing on her pencil's eraser. All of a sudden, she printed PASSWORDS on the top sheet of her yellow pad. She held up the pad about two inches from his face and nodded with a questioning look.

He nodded back, though Marna thought he looked as if he were about to cry.

Denise took back the pad and printed EASY TO FORGET, EASY TO STEAL underneath PASSWORDS. When she held it up to him again, he shrugged, which gave her pause. Then she slapped the pad on the table and printed, NOT ALL CUSTOMERS ARE LITERATE.

This time, he nodded his understanding. She slashed a large X through PASSWORDS, tore the paper in half, and dropped it ostentatiously on the floor. He made no objection.

One by one, she repeated the procedure for the other candidate technologies. Key cards were too easy to lose or steal. Fingerprints required a costly reader, as did palm-vein analysis, retinal and iris scans, face recognition, and hand geometry. Odor identification was undeveloped technology, which seemed to fascinate SOS. It took Denise more than ten minutes to persuade him to set it aside.

He threw in a few obscure biometric methods, but Denise quickly wrote RESEARCH, NOT DEVELOPMENT on the first two, then simply pointed to the words as he tried to raise each new method. After half a dozen, she wrote: ENOUGH. GET THE POINT?

With a reluctant nod, he agreed.

She picked up the VOICE RECOGNITION sheet and was about to write on it when she stopped and turned to Marna. "I think I see why he didn't just pick this one right away. It seems obvious to me–cheap, off-the-shelf hardware, easy-to-program correlation filters, and we already have the necessary processing power. But he's not into voice as a method of communication, is he?"

"Seems not," Marna agreed.

"Hey," he objected. "I may not *prefer* auditory, but I can hear. And I heard that."

"Well, hallelujah," said Denise, leaping up, plopping herself in his lap, and throwing her arms around his neck. "Now I know why I love you. Did you hear that?"

He was about to kiss her when someone knocked on the door. Marna motioned them to hide in the bathroom. When they were out of sight, she called out in Navajo, "Louis isn't home. I'm just his house-sitter."

The only reply was more knocking, so she tried English. "Louis isn't home."

A male voice rattled through the door. "We're not looking for Louis. We want to talk with Stephen Spencer."

"I don't know any Stephen Spencer."

Another male voice said, "We know he's in there. We're here to help."

The second biggest lie, she thought.

"We have to talk to him. Don't make us knock down the door."

Okay, there's at least two of them, and they've seen through the disguise, so what's the point. "Okay. Hold off. Anyway, the door's not locked."

The doorknob turned with suspicious deliberateness. The door opened a crack and someone peeked in.

Marna showed her open palms. *No point in getting shot by mistake.*

Two men wearing suits entered. As far as Marna could see, they carried no weapons.

The shorter of the two scanned the room with a professional eye while the tall, skinny one focused on Marna. "Where's Spencer?"

She wasn't quite ready to give up all control. "First tell me what the FBI wants with him."

"You've got it wrong, Dr. Savron. We're not the FBI. Inga Steinman told us Spencer was in trouble here, and Alicia Silsbury sent us to help you out."

CHAPTER EIGHTY-THREE

The damaged Aremac truck crested a small rise, revealing the broad, shining expanse of the great River Niger. Tess could see that the road led to the remains of a bridge. *It must have been bombed.*

Of the ten or twelve spans, four were entirely missing. The span closest to the shore was bent into a V, with the point stuck down in the broad marshland. "That's it," said Tess. "End of the line. The only question now is whether we should shoot ourselves before the bad guys get us."

Roger slowed the truck. "That's for the movies. Maybe they were just trying to warn us that the bridge was out."

"So they shot at us? Get real!"

"Maybe they thought we were part of the Simbara army. That Aremac was some new weapon. Maybe we can explain."

"Dammit, Roger, you're not the one that's about to be raped."

Rebecca reached across and shook each of them by a shoulder. "Stop it, you two. This is no time for your first quarrel."

"It's not our first," Tess snapped.

"I said stop the ding-dong, and do not try to draw me in. First of all, Tess, make no assumptions about whom they want to rape."

She stared Roger in the eyes. He turned white.

"Second of all, cut this suicide bull." She let go of their shoulders and touched her twin pistols. "If we are about to die, I intend to take as much company as I can."

"I can't … do that," said Tess, her voice cracking.

"Be quiet. You're so scared you're not thinking–either of you." She pointed to their left. "Third of all, and most important, I can see another bridge, upstream."

Roger didn't look. "Why would they have two bridges at the same place?"

"How about you stop speculating and just drive over there and see? That army behind us seems to be getting their act together."

Roger opened his mouth to say something, then looked to his left, turned the wheel and started the truck moving parallel to the river. A short distance ahead, the road ended at a marsh full of tall grass. "What now?"

"Go left, away from the river until you find a dry patch."

Roger obeyed Rebecca's instructions, skirting the marsh until the land rose and put them in a position to look back and see the entire bridge. He turned to the right along the crest of a ridge, then looked down. "Damn. It's a *railroad* bridge. We're sunk."

Tess's engineering mind overrode her panic. *The bridge design is deceptively simple. It's totally flat, only a few feet above the water, built on closely-spaced concrete pilings spanned with straight sections on steel girders, no guard rails, no service road, just tracks on a bed of umber gravel.* "It's a totally minimal bridge. Maybe we can abandon the truck and run across. If the other side is really Zezanika, they can't follow us there."

"They can follow us halfway," said Rebecca. "Or just shoot us from the shore. And if you trip, you will fall in the river. If you do not drown, the hippos will crush you and the crocs will eat the pieces."

Roger brought the truck to a full stop. "That's not helpful, Rebecca. I can't drive across that. It won't hold the truck."

"Now I know you've lost your brain. If it will hold an entire train, it will hold one miserable truck. If you're afraid to drive, move over and let me take the wheel."

Rebecca's challenge seemed to restore some of Roger's courage. "I can drive it, but how do I get up on the track?"

"Looks like a service road, over there, to your left."

"That's back towards the troops."

"Sometimes you have to go backwards before you can go forward. You know that. Just stop talking and drive."

"But they're coming toward us."

"The longer you wait, the closer they come."

"What if a train comes? There's only one track."

"Enough!" Rebecca opened the passenger door and jumped out. She ran around the front of the truck, opened the driver's door, and pushed Roger into Tess. "Move over. Now! And hold on."

She climbed in under the wheel, put the truck in gear, and goosed it down the hill. They bumped up onto the service road, then back in the direction of the cocoa-uniformed troops. "Keep your heads down," she shouted.

She raced the truck closer to the troops until they raised their rifles and started shooting. She slammed the brake, then whipped the truck into a sudden u-turn and accelerated back along the service road parallel to the tracks. "Now hang on."

With a jerk, she swerved the truck up the graveled embankment toward the tracks. The truck leaned perilously, skidding in the gravel, dropping one centimeter for every two it climbed.

Tess was sure they would tip over, but with a lurch, they were on the tracks juddering along over the railroad ties. She saw the last of the land slide past beneath them, then the tall grasses shading dark shallow water. As the marsh thinned to open water, she saw smooth gray slick rocks breaking the surface.

She caught her breath, then forced lungs to draw in air.

Calm down. We're safe now—as long as we don't tip over. Or the bridge doesn't collapse.

CHAPTER EIGHTY-FOUR

Though the two Justice-for-Africa men were inside Louis's trailer home and didn't seem to be armed, Marna did not invite them to make themselves comfortable. *I have no idea why Inga would send these thugs to "help" SOS, but if he and Denise stay quiet in the bathroom, maybe I can convince these two to leave. In case they're cooperating with the FBI. They've already looked at what's in plain sight, and they don't seem curious about what might be hidden.*

The men introduced themselves as John–the tall one with a buzz cut and heavy five-o'clock shadow–and Mac–the short one with what sounded like an Eastern European accent. Marna didn't offer her name, but they seemed to know who she was. "Dr. Savron," said Mac, "we have bad news. Your associates have been captured by rebels in Simbara."

Marna swallowed hard to suppress her instinct to say something. *They could be fishing for information. Just keep still and let them spill their story.*

Mac seemed annoyed by her lack of response. "Doesn't this news concern you?"

Don't answer. Don't let him control the situation. "What associates are you talking about? Someone from Los Alamos?"

Mac's annoyed tone intensified. "Please, Dr. Savron, this is not a game, and we're here to help you save your associates. We're talking about the Fixmans and Miss Solomon, as I think you know very well."

"What makes you think those people I'm supposed to know have been captured by these so-called rebels?"

Mac pressed his lips together, and his pock-marked face grew red. Before he could speak, his partner put a restraining arm on his biceps and said, "Let me explain. You don't know us. You have every right to be suspicious."

He drew some papers from his breast pocket, unfolded them, and held the top one up under the light of the bare bulb above the kitchen table. "May I set this down on the table, so you can see it better?"

Marna didn't reply, but he set the paper down anyway. He smoothed out the folds and motioned Marna too look closely. "These are satellite pictures taken over Northern Simbara. You can recognize the Aremac, I think."

Where did they get these? What are their connections?

"You can see they are cut off from the South by rebel forces."

The picture seemed real, but Marna wasn't ready to concede anything. "Assuming you're right and these are pictures showing they're really in trouble, why haven't you rescued them? You certainly don't believe that I could help."

"No, that's exactly what we do believe. We need your help in *finding* them. After that, we can take care of their rescue, as you suggest."

"Finding them? You can *see* where they are. Why would you need me?" She almost slipped and said "us."

"We can see where they *were*, but now they've disappeared. It's thick jungle up there near the river. They could be anywhere, and it's hostile territory. We need to know exactly where they are so we can make a precise incursion, in and out."

"So? I can't help. I've never even been to Africa."

Mac couldn't restrain himself any longer. "We don't need help with geography. We need help interrogating some rebel captives, who do know where they are."

Oh, oh. I think I see where this is going.

John shoved his partner aside and placed his own finger on the picture. "You can see that Aremac has been captured. We need another Aremac to question the captives. You need to come over and build another one."

"That would take weeks."

"No. We are already buying all the parts except the software and the snoods. We need you to supply those."

She couldn't conceal her surprise at their speedy acquisition. "You have a magnet?"

"Yes, we have the magnet and all the parts from the bill of materials. But we don't know how it all goes together."

"Where are they?"

"Most of them are already on our plane, ready to go to Simbara."

"Most?"

"The magnet is on its way. Two days, max."

In spite of herself, Marna was beginning to believe their story. "What about the truck?"

"This particular plane isn't big enough for your trucks, but there are trucks in Simbara we can adapt. Or we can bring the truck over later. For now, you can set up a stationary installation in Simbara City where the prisoners are."

Now came Marna's key question. "And what if these prisoners don't want to cooperate?"

Mac grabbed his left hand in his right and made a twisting motion. "It doesn't matter. The Aremac can show us what they saw."

She could almost feel the pain in her own arm, but tried to look calm and rational. "Not really. You've apparently been misinformed. Aremac has built-in safeguards against coercion."

"But *you* put them in, right?"

Marna said nothing. Mac pushed ahead. "So you can take them out." It was not a question.

I don't like the sound of that. What are they really after? "We might be able to remove the controls. I'm not really sure."

Mac strode over the the bathroom door and tried the handle, which was locked. He turned back to Marna. "Your friend in here would know, right?"

Before she could say anything, the door opened. SOS stepped out, leaving Denise concealed. "Yes, I'm the one who would know, but I'd still have to do some research to see if it's feasible. But in any case, even if it's technically feasible, it's against our policies."

John showed no surprise at SOS's appearance, speaking to him in a carefully modulated tone, in sharp contrast with Mac's anger. "Oh, of course, Mr. Spencer, the change would just be temporary. Until we rescue your colleagues. Then you can put the controls right back in."

Sure. Now Marna knew where this was going. She had to communicate with SOS before he revealed too much.

"Su'wI," said Marna, then repeated herself, hoping the JFA men didn't know it was Klingon for "hide." To her relief, SOS nodded his understanding.

"What did you say?" Mac demanded.

"Oh, sorry. I'm always slipping into Navajo. Stephen doesn't understand, either. Stephen, I asked you to tell them how long it will take you to be ready."

Marna held her breath. SOS appeared to be thinking deeply. "I would have to make those control modifications here, where we have our dongle burner set up. It will take a couple of days."

John spoke before his partner could object. "That's fine, but we need to be ready when the magnet arrives."

"I'll get on it first thing in the morning."

CHAPTER EIGHTY-FIVE

Halfway across the bridge, in the middle of the vast Niger River, Tess felt the bumping stop. The truck slowed to a halt.

"What happened?"

Rebecca released a short, low whistle. "We have a little a problem."

"More than those troops behind us?"

Roger pointed along the tracks. "I think she means those troops ahead of us."

Tess saw a swarm of pea green uniforms near the end of the bridge. "Oh, no, not again."

"From what I hear of the Zezanikans," Rebecca said, "I think we are safe. At least I think they will talk before they shoot. One reason I stopped. Must not look aggressive."

Tess picked up on her exact wording. "*One* reason? Is there another?"

"Actually, about thirty reasons, not counting the crocodiles. You cannot always see the crocs."

Tess stretched her neck, trying to see up ahead through the wisps of mist rising off the river and beginning to fog the inside of the windshield. "Any other reasons?" *As if that isn't enough.*

"I think a tie rod could be coming loose. I cannot be sure of the steering."

"Terrific. What else?"

429 • GERALD M. WEINBERG

"There seems to be a tight little island up ahead, supporting the bridge. It looks like a car park, but instead of cars, it's parking a whacking great bloat of hippos."

Roger wiped a circle in the windshield fog, but the dust on the outside was now turning to runnels of mud. "I can't see them, but I believe it's called a *raft* of hippos."

"Thanks, Roger, you're a real brick. An *American* brick. How about climbing out and clearing the mud off the windscreen?"

Ignoring Rebecca's sarcasm, Roger nudged Tess to move so he could climb out. "I see them now. And I think the Zezanikans see them, too. They're stopped well on the other side."

While Roger clambered out, Tess twisted so she could see out back. "Well, the rebels don't see them, because they're moving up."

"But they see *us*. And we're on the wrong side of the hippos. So, do we do a runner?"

Tess ran her tongue over her dry lips. "Through the hippos? The tracks are laid right on the island, and some of the hippos are on the tracks."

"Better them than the rebels," said Roger, slipping in alongside Tess and slamming the door. "The hippos don't have AK-47s. And they're peaceful animals. Herbivores."

"They may not eat you," said Rebecca. "But they have large feet, and they weigh four tons. And then there are the crocs."

Roger dried his hands, then folded his muddy handkerchief. "So we'll drive through, nice and slow."

"Even if I could steer reliably, I would not want to risk bumping one of them. You startle them and they could knock this lorry right off the bridge."

Roger spread his hands. "So, we just sit here? Do nothing?""

Tess checked ahead, then behind. "The Zezanikans are moving again. A few of them. Maybe they know what to do about the hippos. So let's wait and see. If the rebels get too close, too fast, we'll try driving through the hippos. Slowly."

Roger fidgeted in his seat, trying to put his handkerchief in his back pocket. "It's hard for me to sit here and do nothing."

She patted his shoulder. "I know, dear. This might be a good time to think about what we've done wrong, in case we get out of here."

"So you won't strike another bad deal." There was no blame in Roger's voice, only regret.

Tess thought for a minute. *He's absolutely right.* "I did, didn't I."

Roger put his arms around her. "Anything wrong, we did together. You couldn't know."

"I don't think it was lack of data. I think it was because I–we–have been solving the wrong problem."

Roger released her and took her hand. "What do you mean?"

Before she could answer, a loud explosion erupted in front of them. They saw the hippos begin to stir, then another explosion started them running for the water.

For a moment, several hippos headed up alongside the track towards the Aremac, but another explosion ripped up dirt and grass in front of them.

"It's grenades," Rebecca shouted. "The Zezanikans are using grenade launchers."

Clumsily, the hippos stopped and turned toward the water, disappearing in great splashes. The water churned mightily for about thirty seconds, then the smooth current took over.

"They're gone," said Rebecca. "The Zezanikans are moving this way."

Tess looked out back. "So are the rebels."

Roger ignored them both. "What did you mean, 'solving the wrong problem'"?

The green-clad troops had almost reached the hippo island. Rebecca began checking one of her pistols. "Let's continue this little debate outside. We'll look less threatening that way. In fact, leave your weapons in the cab."

Tess was more than happy to hide her pistol in the glove compartment. "So you trust the Zezanikans?"

Rebecca scrunched down and put her pistols under the seat. "I don't know. But I know I don't trust those rebels."

"Do you trust the hippos?" Roger asked.

"The hippos? Why do you ask?"

"Because a few of them are coming back."

CHAPTER EIGHTY-SIX

At five the next morning, Marna noticed that SOS didn't even protest when she sent Heidi to wake him and Denise. *I don't think he's ever been up this early in his life. I guess he realizes this is no game.*

They dressed quickly, skipped breakfast, and reached Southwest Stage well before six. To their amazement, Norton was already there–and trying to fend off reporter Kit Kelly. Norton literally pushed Kelly into Marna's care, suggesting she take him out back to see the junkyard where they salvaged parts for the stoves. She was half annoyed, but half pleased–telling herself the pleasure came solely from helping remove Kelly from the premises. Free of him, Norton and SOS could work on the voice recognition while Denise was carrying out some mysterious hacking, guarded by the ever-watchful Heidi.

After a tour of the junkyard, she stalled even more by suggesting that she and Kelly have breakfast over at the drive-in, where they had a pleasant tete-a-tete over biscuits, gravy, and sausages. By the time the sun came up and warmed the air enough for them to move to an outside table, brothers George (Gaagi), Al, and Tom arrived for breakfast.

She knew her brothers were looking Kelly over, the way they used to grill her rare high school boyfriends. When they found out that the reporter was an ex-marine, though, they fell into exchanging war stories. Marna sat back and watched two squirrels chasing each other in round-tree spirals, letting the boys accomplish her distraction work for her.

An hour or so later, while George was fluttering his hands in mock dogfights, telling his fifteenth or twentieth flying story, Heidi came rushing up to sniff her hand. A moment later, Denise appeared, her long braid flying out behind her. The men invited her to join them, but she whispered Marna away. "Marybeth called. She says the FBI is coming to arrest you. With a warrant."

Marna moved away from the table, trying to stay out of hearing distance of Kelly. "Arrest me? What for?"

"Marybeth wasn't very clear, but she thinks someone called Karl told them you had stolen national security secrets from Los Alamos. He said you're using them to build the hogan stoves."

Marna went limp at the mention of her husband, sagging in Denise's arms. *He'll never let me out of his clutches. I can't deal with this. Not now. Tess needs me.*

Denise dragged her to a bench. "Are you okay?"

"No. But don't say anything to my brothers. I don't want them in trouble with the FBI."

"We've got to hide you somewhere before they get here. Can you walk back to the Stage?"

"It's you we have to hide, Denise. And SOS. I don't know enough about Aremac to help them–though don't tell JFA that. They have to think I'm essential."

"We can't keep running away. We need a plan."

We need Tess, that's what we need. She's our planner. "How about we run to Africa? We're needed there."

"If we're going to Africa, we have to move, and fast."

When Marna remained rooted to the bench, Denise took her by both hands and pulled her upright. "Come on, girl.

Remember Old Chinese proverb: journey of ten thousand miles to Africa begins with a single step."

Marna took three wobbly steps, but then Kit Kelly caught up with them. "I heard that business about the FBI being after you. Did I hear right? Where are you going?"

Denise spun around, stared at the reporter for a moment, then snatched something out of his ear. "You bastard. Mind your damn business." Heidi alerted at her tone. Marna feared she might attack the reporter, but Heidi merely stared menacingly.

Denise held on to Kelly's ear like a schoolmarm chastising a gum chewer. She called out to Marna's brothers. "Hey, guys, come over here and beat the crap out of this sneak. And his camera, too."

As the brothers raced over, Denise dropped the earpiece, grinding it into the pavement with her heel. Kelly tried to stop her, but his "stop that" was way too late.

Al arrived first, immediately pinning he reporter's arm behind his back. "What's he doing, Shideezhi?" Before his little sister could answer, George had Kelly's other arm, and Tom had his massive fist cocked ten inches from the man's face.

"He was spying on us," Denise said coldly. "Listening in on our private conversation."

Marna couldn't help admiring the way Kit did not whine or flinch, even though he was totally at the mercy of her three brothers. "Hang on to him, but don't hurt him. Yet."

She moved alongside Tom and coaxed his fist away from Kit's face. "I have a proposition for you, Mr. Reporter Man."

"I won't be coerced," he said defiantly. "I was just doing my job, but if you want your brothers to beat the crap out of me, well, I've taken beatings before. I'll heal eventually."

"Let him go, Al. George. He can run if he wants, but he'll be missing the story of his short journalistic career."

Chapter Eighty-Seven

Tess watched, half-frightened, half-amused, as the hippos lumbered, dripping, out of the river, causing the Zezanikans to beat a Keystone Cops retreat from the island. "What do we do now?"

"We wait for more grenades," Rebecca said.

"I don't think so," said Roger. "The grenades don't work."

"Of course they work. As soon as they throw some more, the hippos will leave, so we can cross the island."

"What about the crocs?"

"What crocs?"

"The big ones who didn't budge when the grenades went off."

Rebecca removed her glasses and took another look. "Oh. *Those* crocs."

How could you miss them? "The grenades scared off the hippos, but they weren't the real problem. We could probably have walked past them without any trouble, but I wouldn't care to challenge the crocs."

"There you go again," Roger said.

"About what?"

"About solving the wrong problem."

"What I meant was we've been trying to be sure Aremac gets only into the right hands, and stays out of the wrong hands–"

"That's not the problem I'm trying to solve," said Roger. "I don't think we can keep it out of the wrong hands. I'm trying to see that when it does fall into the wrong hands, it can't be used wrongly."

Tess nodded her agreement. "Sure, but we've seen how hard that is to do. Heck, we've seen how hard all of it is to do. We've been kidnapped, shot at, bribed, threatened, tricked, spied on, and who knows what else."

"Nobody said inventing was easy."

"Actually, that's what you always say, but you're wrong. How come you can invent things with a snap of your fingers, but when it comes to seeing that your inventions are used properly, the finger-snapping doesn't work?"

"Lots of times they work."

"All right, you two," Rebecca said, exasperation filling her voice. "Can you continue this later? Roger, if you ever made an invention that worked, now is the time. How about inventing something that will get us safely through those crocs. And hippos, too, while you're at it."

Roger seemed to ignore her, reaching behind the seat for his laptop instead. He opened the machine, waited for it to wake up, then started typing at high speed.

Tess pinched his neck. "Roger? Did you hear what Rebecca said? We need an invention. Now."

"I heard her, but I don't want to repeat the mistake we made last time. I know nothing about crocodiles. I need data."

Knowing there was no way of stopping her husband once he descended into his invention trance, Tess turned her attention to the rebel forces inching up behind them. *Thank God they're moving really slow, but Roger could take forever. Maybe we should just surrender and offer them Aremac.*

Thinking of Aremac reminded her of the pictures from the rape trial. *Maybe it would be better just to throw ourselves to the crocodiles.*

She noticed Rebecca removing one of her pistols, checking the clip. She absent-mindedly placed her hand over the glove compartment, as if sealing it against temptation, then opened it and took out her own pistol. *I'm not going to shoot anybody, but at least it would keep my mind from these nightmares.*

She watched Roger close his computer, jump down to the side of the truck, and begin opening equipment drawers. *What's he doing? Never mind. Don't let yourself be distracted.*

Turning the semi-automatic over in her hands three or four times to mount her courage, Tess checked both the chamber and magazine for live rounds. She left the safety catch on. *I can be ready to fire a warning shot or two to slow them down, but I don't want an accident.*

She was about to check everything again when Roger's voice interrupted. "Do we have any more gum?"

"More guns?" said Tess holding up her ready weapon. "Just what you see."

"Not guns. Gum?"

"Gum?"

"Chewing gum."

She saw now that his mouth was chomping on a large wad. "What for?"

He held up a breadboard about the size of a box of tissues and attached to a small speaker with two wires. "To protect your ears while I test my sound generator."

Rebecca recoiled in mock disgust, making exaggerated chewing motions with her mouth wide open. "You're the only one with that unsavory Colonial habit."

"Then this will have to do. Three sticks apiece."

He handed out the silvery sticks, instructing the women to chew quickly, then plug their ears. That accomplished, he threw a switch on the board and began twisting a dial. Even with the gum in her ears, Tess could hear the changing pitch as the dial rotated.

Tess saw his lips move, but she couldn't hear him clearly. She pointed to her ears and shook her head.

He climbed up on the truck and put his mouth close to her ear. "Watch the crocs. I need to find a frequency they don't like."

"Be careful you don't find one they find appetizing." Tess saw one of the big crocs begin to stir. *Maybe it's just a coincidence.*

No, there's another. "Around that frequency, Roger. They're moving."

"But not leaving," Rebecca said.

Roger opened the door. "I have to get closer. Intensity diminishes with the square of distance. Minus an air friction factor, which is–"

Tess ruffled his hair and pointed back away from the crocs. "Never mind the friction factor, dear. The rebels are getting closer, and I'm scared."

He put his hand over her hand. "No need to be scared. Just think of it as a three-d video game."

Chapter Eighty-Eight

Denise, her arms full of groceries, watched helplessly as the FBI team drove one car in front and one behind Marna's truck, trapping her in Basha's parking lot. She wanted to protest as Marna was dragged away, but she couldn't risk being detained herself. She returned to the store for a shopping cart, loaded it with her bags, and wheeled it away to Southwest Sage.

Norton made a few phone calls and determined that Marna being held incommunicado at Nellie's while the FBI executed their search warrant, Their warrant didn't seem to cover Southwest Stage, so Denise sat herself down in the office and took over responsibility for implementing their plan.

Evidently, the FBI was less well-informed than JFA's John and Mac, who dropped into the garage's office late in the afternoon. Her hacking unfinished, Denise wasn't at all happy to see them. "Could you please leave the door open like you found it. We like to take advantage of a warm day like this. We won't have many more now that winter's here."

John took the lead while Mac eyeballed the premises. "Then you'll be happy to know how warm it is in Simbara. We have word that the magnet has arrived ahead of schedule. Are you ready to leave?"

She blanked both her computer screens as Mac slipped around behind her. "We're not going anywhere until Dr. Savron comes with us."

"But the FBI has her. And you don't need her to set up the Aremac."

They definitely know more than the government. "But we do. You seem to know so much about our work, so you should know about recalibration."

"What's that?" said John.

So their information doesn't come from any of the weaver ladies. Good. That narrows it down. "We've learned here that we have to recalibrate Aremac for each different culture, not just for each individual. Dr. Savron is the only one who can do that."

Mac put down an engine part he was examining. "You're exaggerating. Roger Fixman did it."

How do they know? I have to be careful how they're playing me. How do they know anything? Despite her puzzlement, Denise pressed ahead. "Right. And he's available?"

"You know he isn't," John said. "We get your point."

"So, how about you use your influence to get Dr. Savron released?"

Denise expected opposition, but the two men exchanged a significant look. Mac left, saying he'd look into it. "Assuming we can have her released," asked John, "how soon will you be ready? Our plane is all set to go."

Now comes the critical part. "We discussed that. You can take the Aremac parts, but we'll go on regular commercial flights."

"The only commercial flights—if you could get reservations—will take you two days."

"If you can get the FBI to free Marna, I'm sure you can get us a few airline reservations."

"Nevertheless, I insist you go on our private jet. It's faster. And safer. We don't want you kidnapped, too."

"Simbara sounds like a dangerous place."

John raised his hands assuringly. "Don't worry. Now that we know the threat, we'll supply you with personal bodyguards. We should have done that for the Fixmans. We're paying for our mistake."

"Sounds more like *we're* paying for your mistake. So, if we're going to have bodyguards, we'll bring our own. Do you have room for six of us? And a dog?"

John pondered the question for a few moments. "A few of our people will have to fly commercial, but, yes, I think that will be fine."

"All right, we"ll be ready as soon as you get Dr. Savron." She sat down and activated her screens. "Why don't you go take care of that while I finish up some last minute details."

As soon as John left, SOS slipped in from the adjoining office. "Did it work?"

She swiveled around to face him. "Just a minute. Are you finished with the voice recognition?"

"Norton will have to do some more testing, but I think it's good enough for the time being. It doesn't have to be perfect to keep them from selling their stoves."

"Still, if you don't have anything else to do, then keep helping him with the testing until we leave. None of your usual shortcuts."

"Okay, okay," he whined.

"Then get back to work."

"First tell me, did you bring it off with Mutt and Jeff?"

"I think so, but I find it hard to believe they can free Marna from the FBI's clutches."

He peered past her at the screens. "Then we'll have to hope Plan B works. Have you hacked the lab's computers yet?"

"Of course. Even *you* could have done it," she said, but she was smiling.

"Thanks." He was smiling, too. He bent over to kiss the top of her head, casting a glance at her screens. "What are you doing there? Hacking the FBI's files?"

"No, that was the first thing I did, to find out what evidence they had. Turns out that Marna's husband did tell the FBI she was stealing secrets from Los Alamos. That's about all the so-called evidence they needed to get the warrant."

"Shit. He's must be a true patriot, to turn in his wife."

"Especially since it's all a lie."

He changed his viewing angle and took a closer look at the screens. "So what are you hacking now?"

"I figured that if JFA could access our military spy satellite pictures, so can I."

"But we already have the pictures," he said, puzzled.

She sighed. "As usually, babe, you're way too trusting or naive. We don't know if those have been doctored. And we don't know if we have *all* the pictures. Here's another in the sequence, much later than the JFA pictures. And farther north."

"They seem to be in the middle of a bridge across this big river."

"That's the Niger."

He slid a visitor chair over next to her, sitting down for a closer look. "I recognize some of the vehicles on both sides, but what are those dark ones on the little island north of them?"

"I don't think they're vehicles. I think they're hippos."

CHAPTER EIGHTY-NINE

Tess was ready to start moving, but Roger ignored her and busied himself tearing the non-skid rubber mat from the truck bed. "Come on, Roger. What are you doing?"

He tugged the last corner of the mat away from the truck with a slight pop, then began cutting the long brown strip into pieces. "My theory is that the crocs will move away from the sound, but I always like to have a backup system."

Rebecca waved her pistols. "We can always run back to the truck. There are just a few rebels, so maybe we can fight them off.

Tess didn't like that idea. "Why not forward? Maybe we can dodge the crocs."

"According to my information, they're very fast," said Roger, shaking his head. "But also they tend to avoid bigger prey. That's why the hippos are so casual around them. So take one of these mats to make yourself look as big as possible."

Tess took a mat and tried to extend it with both arms outstretched. "It's awkward."

Rebecca lifted her arms, then began to stagger. "And it's acting like a sail. If the wind picks up, it could blow us right into the river."

"Okay," said Roger, rolling his mat. "Do this. You can unroll it when we get closer, if they start to stir. They're supposed to be nocturnal, so if we're lucky they'll just sleep right through our passing. I won't start the sound generator unless I see signs of movement. But I only have the one, so stick close to me."

They secured their holsters and climbed off the truck. Roger helped a shaken Tess step down. There wasn't much room between the door and the edge of the bridge–between the bridge and the river below.

They moved around cautiously to the front of the truck. "Just a minute," said Rebecca. "I want to take a souvenir from under the bonnet. I've always wanted a fuel injector."

Tess waited helplessly while Roger helped Rebecca remove the small but essential box. *I don't really care right now if they take Aremac. Or dump it in the river, for that matter.*

Finally, they began their slow advance, Rebecca walking backwards to keep an eye on the rebels, and Roger constantly checking his sound generator. Tess advanced one unnatural step at a time, from one railroad tie to the next. Her hip was hurting again. The small muscles in her legs went rigid as if she were walking on ice. She concentrated on putting one foot in front of the other, but always fixing her eyes on the largest, closest crocodile.

When they were about ten meters away from this frightening monster, they stepped off the tracks and onto the grassy soil of the island. The big croc raised his black head and began to hiss.

Tess froze.

"Open your mat," Roger whispered. "Then keep moving at a steady pace."

Easy for you to say, she thought, but dutifully unrolled her mat and spread it wide, just below her eyes. She tried to start walking again, but her quivering legs wouldn't obey.

She heard the high whine of the generator, then saw a smaller croc stand on its stubby legs and slowly move a body length away from them. *Maybe it's working, but the big sucker isn't buying it.*

Rebecca turned around and opened her mat, as if she were no longer concerned with the rebels or the breeze. "Stay away from the ones that are moving. Size does not matter."

Sure, thought Tess. *Does yawning count?* The big boy's mouth opened wide enough to swallow a camel. Or a person. The rows of large yellow teeth forced the poem from her childhood into Tess's mind:

"How cheerfully he seems to grin.
How neatly spreads his claws,
And welcomes little fishes in,
With gently smiling jaws!"

Just take one step, Tess told herself. Her left foot inched forward.

Now another.

One step at a time, she followed Rebecca's winding path among the drowsy crocks. Without warning, a roar rumbled out behind her.

She fought the urge to turn around, but she must have paused because Roger bumped her from behind. "Keep moving. If he attacks, he'll hit me first."

That's not a comforting thought, you numbskull. What would I do without you? But she kept moving, now past all but two small crocs hanging around near what looked like a family of hippos.

Maybe when we reach the hippos, we'll be safe–from the crocs. Or maybe they've got their eyes on that baby–which is bigger than me. But he's got his family protecting him.

When she was about five meters away, the hippo family seemed to take notice. The daddy hippo–at least he was the biggest–started vocalizing, deep, resonant, staccato grunts. *I don't know whether they're a warning or a greeting, but I have no intention of finding out.* "Maybe the sound is annoying them, Roger. Could you turn it off now?"

"And risk the crocs?"

Tess turned. A few crocs were stirring, apparently rearranging themselves according to some unknown crocodilian pecking order. From this distance, they seemed less of a clear and present danger than the hippos. "Stay far away from the baby," she whispered, thinking of what she'd been warned about grizzlies.

"But she is so adorable," said Rebecca. "I have to hug her."

"Don't be–" Tess warned, then realized Rebecca was teasing, which meant she felt the danger had passed. She allowed herself to become aware of her legs, which felt like jelly. "I have to sit down."

Rebecca took Tess's hand and led her a dozen steps along the tracks past the end of the island. "They won't come out here. Let's just set and let our legs dangle until the Zezanikans come for us. Now you lovebirds can argue to your heart's content."

CHAPTER NINETY

As far as Marna could see from her vantage point, handcuffed on the sofa in Nellie's living room, Don Capitol's FBI crew had spent a full say accomplishing nothing. They had mess up her sister-in-law's neat house–breaking a few dishes in the process. So far, they hadn't found any of the warranted "government secrets"–neither papers nor computer files. The frustration on Don's face as he came into the family room seemed to confirm her conjecture.

"I suppose you sent the key data to Africa with Roger. You should know that action merely compounds your felony."

"I told you, there's no felony. I didn't steal any secrets." She spoke gently, not wanting to rile him up any further. He seemed a nice enough guy, concerned over her comfort, but still intent on fulfilling his search mission. "I know you're not finding anything, so how soon are you going to let me go? Nellie will be home in a few minutes. She's not going to be happy about what you've done to her house."

"I'll see that she's compensated for anything we broke, but you're not going to be free any time in the near future. As soon as we wrap up here, we'll take you somewhere more secure."

Marna's cell phone rang. "Don't answer that," Don commanded.

"I can't, not with my hands cuffed behind my back. But I think you may want to answer it yourself."

He seemed to be considering the idea, then made up his mind and answered the call. He moved to the far side of the living room, so Marna had no chance to hear the other end of the conversation.

"Who is this? ... Why? ... Listen–"

He closed the phone. "Some idiot telling me to turn on the TV news. If he keeps calling, I'll put on a trace."

"Why would you want to do that?"

"It's a serious crime, interfering with a federal investigation."

"Maybe he was trying to help?"

Don laughed. "Very funny. How is watching TV going to help?"

It will let you see the interview I made with Kelly before you arrested me. I hope this works. It was awfully rushed. "Maybe it will help keep you out of any more trouble. Why don't you humor me and turn on the TV for a few minutes. You're crew isn't ready to leave yet anyway, and I'm bored."

Don huffed, but picked up the remote and tuned to channel 4. The picture showed Kit Kelly interviewing Marna in Nellie's living room, the same room Don and Marna sat in now. "–solar stoves for poor Navajo," the TV-Marna was saying.

Yuck. I sound awful. And look worse. Marna closed her eyes so she wouldn't have to see her own dumpy image on the screen.

"And how did you happen to wind up doing this kind of work?" TV-Kelly asked.

TV-Marna: "I was working at Los Alamos National Laboratory, on energy conservation, which I consider much more important to American security than some new hydrogen bomb."

The camera zoomed in on the interviewer. "Dr. Savron is a Native American, a Navajo from a family that includes a long line of patriots."

The camera panned to the array of photos above Nellie's fireplace as Kelly stood and began pointing to one picture after another. "This is her great-grandfather, Samuel, who as a Navajo code talker in World War II. He was awarded the Congressional Gold Medal for his service–"

This wasn't part of the interview. What's he doing?

TV-Kelly touched another picture, a group of old Navajo men with George W. Bush as well as three young marines in full dress uniform. "–as did more than four hundred of his compatriots, including two of Dr. Savron's great-grandfathers."

Agent Capitol slipped down on the sofa next to Marna, his eyes fixed on the screen. Kit Kelly had moved on to a collage holding more than a hundred medals mounted on a red-white-and blue cloth background. "Both her grandfathers served in the Marines, as did her father and her seven brothers."

Out of the corner of her eye, Marna saw the other three agents standing in the archway watching the program as Kelly pressed on. "We are now in the living room of Dr. Savron's oldest brother, who earned *two* Silver Stars for gallantry in action."

The narrator moved on to a picture of two young Navajo men in uniform, arms around each other's shoulders. Marna turned around to check the real picture, here in the room, then turned her attention back to the screen, where Kelly was saying, "Here he is on the left, with his brother George, who *also* earned two Silver Stars, one for saving the lives of two fellow marine pilots in a daring rescue."

Kelly walked away from the picture gallery and sat down again across from Marna's screen double. "But what about their little sister, Marna Savron herself? No, she didn't join the

Marines. She wanted to, but because of a childhood accident, she could not pass the fitness test."

Gods. Who told him about that? I certainly didn't in the interview.

Kelly paused for effect. "Instead, she went to college to study physics, graduating first in her class, and going on to earn a PhD, with distinction, at one of America's finest universities. She then went on to serve her country as a researcher at the top-secret Los Alamos National Laboratory."

He's laying it on too thick, Marna worried. *My part of the lab isn't secret at all.*

The screen changed to show Kelly back next to TV-Marna, looking at her with with pitying eyes. "And what does she receive for her service?" He held up two printed pages.

Don leaned forward, trying to read the writing, just as Kelly said, "In my right hand, I hold her final personnel report, written by her boss just before she left the laboratory to pursue her charitable work of bringing warmth and electricity to the less fortunate among her people."

The screen switched to a picture of the inside of shabby hogan where an old Navajo couple sat huddled around one of the hogan stoves. Marna sighed and blushed at his words. *He's giving me far too much credit–but I suppose it's necessary for the effect. What a production!*

The picture switched back to Kelly. "In my left hand, I hold a series of emails from that boss to one of his colleagues concerning Dr. Savron."

Marna felt her body loosen with relief. *He didn't actually have those in the interview, but Denise must have gotten them. And more. I didn't know about the emails.*

"Let me read you from this so-called evaluation," said Kelly while white words on a black background began to scroll down the screen. Some of the words were highlighted in red, like "lazy bitch" and "ignorant savage."

He's better than I thought. He makes it look like this was part of the interview. Is he making this up, or did they really say those things about me?

He then proceeded to read the parts of the evaluation that berated her because her work was theoretical and had absolutely nothing to do with national security.

Marna felt Don Capitol fidgeting next to her as Kelly's face again filled the screen. "Let me just read that last part again. '*Nothing* to do with national security work.'"

As he said the words, they appeared spelled out on the screen, then faded, slowly replaced by a video clip of Don Capitol handcuffing Marna and leading her away.

The video began to repeat, then shrunk into a small window above Kelly's shoulder. "This deplorable action took place this morning, just after my interview with Dr. Savron. FBI Special Agent in Charge, Donald Philip Capitol, arrested Dr. Savron and searched her heroic brother's home on a charge of stealing national secrets. Secrets, I remind you, that she never could have had in the first place–" He waved the paper in his right hand. "–because her work HAD NOTHING TO DO WITH NATIONAL SECURITY."

The small window faded as the camera panned to TV-Marna, sitting humbly with hands folded in her lap. Kelly's voice, now slow and quiet, enunciated every syllable. "Now I ask you, listeners, decide for yourself. Is this the way our government should treat a great American family of patriots? A great American woman? I'm sure your congressional representatives would like to hear your opinion."

Don Capitol's cell phone began to ring.

CHAPTER NINETY-ONE

Tess thought Rebecca was teasing again, but Roger took her invitation to argue seriously, not as if they had just escaped three kinds of mortal danger. Roger was incapable of joking about his inventions.

"I've done the best I could, Tess. Look how many protections we've built into Aremac. It detects falsified pictures, and won't take pictures at all from someone who's afraid or being coerced. We've buried the code so that it can't be modified without destroying the machine, and the same protections are built into the hardware."

Tess, now aware of the cold, wet sweat coating her skin inside her clothing, welcomed the opportunity to stop thinking about wild animals and feral humans. *The last month has taught me a lot about myself. What's inside. More than all my years of theory in graduate school.*

She shivered, then leaned onto Roger's protective shoulder. "You've just proved my point, darling. Not to minimize your marvelous sound generator, but all your brilliant inventions and inventions on top of inventions haven't solved the real problem."

"I don't think that's accurate. Or fair. We've slipped once or twice, but we've corrected those slips quickly. And other than that, nobody's been able to misuse Aremac."

The Zezanikan troops paused on the shore, now split into two groups. Tess counted a group of ten advancing cautiously toward them along the tracks. *We need to work this out before they get here, or we're out of the frying pan into the fire. Again.* "Maybe misuse is the wrong measure?"

He seemed unaware of the Zezanikans. "What's wrong with it? We don't want people hurt, do we?"

"Of course not, sweetie, but what about the people who are hurt because we've been so cautious that hardly anybody gets to use Aremac? What about people who are wrongly convicted of crimes for which Aremac could clear them? What about people with brain defects that could be detected by Aremac so they could be repaired? Or just people who have lost something important but can't get access to Aremac to recall the picture of where they put it.?"

Absentmindedly, he stroked her hair. "But we don't restrict access. Anybody with a lost object can use our services for a very reasonable fee. And if they can't afford it, we give the service free."

Tess could now make out facial expressions on the approaching soldiers. They weren't smiling, but they didn't seem angry, either. *Careful, girl. You've already made too many cross-cultural assumptions.* "But we have only one Aremac we can use–assuming the Zezanikans can recover the truck. There are thousands of people who can't use it simply because supply can't match demand. Maybe millions."

He spread his palms. "So what do you want me to do?" Make another Aremac? I've got one in the Crownpoint garage, but it's hard enough to control the use of one. Two will be twice as hard." His brow wrinkled. "No, that's not right. More than twice as hard. With one, we can pretty much watch it all the time–one of us. With two, we'd have to start hiring other guardians, and who could we trust?"

She sat up, creating some distance between them. "So you're just going to let thousands of people go without our help? Just because a few people might misuse Aremac? Wouldn't it be better to balance the losses against the gains?"

"And how would you propose equating a coerced conviction against, say, a found wedding ring? You can't do it."

Rebecca approached, clearing her throat. "Um, listen you two. This is an interesting rap session, but our friends up ahead have stopped. I think they're waiting for some move from us."

"How about you go up and see if you can talk to them?" Tess said, willing to drop the discussion at this critical point, but fearing that Roger needed a conclusion.

"Roger should go. I don't speak Arabic."

"Maybe they don't either. Give it a try. They probably speak French, Rebecca, and your French is better than mine. And certainly better than Roger's."

"Roger doesn't speak French."

"Exactly." Tess waved Rebecca ahead. "If you can't communicate, yell for Roger."

Rebecca snorted, then turned and walked toward the soldiers, pistols holstered and arms to her side with palms out. When Tess saw the Zezanikans weren't going to harm Rebecca, she turned her attention back to Roger. "You're right. You can't balance gains against losses." She smiled lovingly at him, hoping to tone down the argument.

"Just like that? You're giving up? Letting me win the argument? Something's fishy about that smile."

She took his hand and gave a sincere squeeze. "Nothing's fishy. I'm not letting you win. In fact, I'm smiling because you've just made my case, out of your own mouth."

He looked at her suspiciously. "I don't see it. You've just admitted that it's impossible to balance gains against losses."

"No, I didn't."

"Yes you did. You said, and I quote, 'You can't balance gains against losses.'"

Before she responded, Tess turned away and looked at where Rebecca and the soldiers were still talking. *So far, everything seems to be going well.* "Yes, those were the words, but you didn't pronounce my sentence quite right. I said, and I quote, 'You can't balance gains against losses.' *You* can't, and I can't either. But *society* does it all the time."

She wanted to press her argument, but Rebecca was shouting something over the murmur of small waves splashing against the bridge pilings. "They know who we are. I think I convinced them that we could work out some mutually advantageous arrangement. So it's going to be okay. But they say we have to get off the bridge because the rebels may be bringing up a train. The Zezanikans can stop it at their end. They have a barrier, but they can't prevent the train from reaching the truck."

Roger's eyes acquired a vacant look. "I've got a way to derail the train before it reaches the truck–"

Tess pinched his arm. "No more inventions, darling. Not until we're safe on the other side."

"But, the truck–"

Rebecca tweaked his nose. "Don't worry about the truck. If they can, they'll retrieve it later. If not, they'll push it into the river. Just take the guts out."

Roger stood and reluctantly gathered a few parts to carry inside his shirt. He pulled Tess up close to him, protecting her from the growing wind. As they walked toward the shore, they passed two of the Zezanikan soldiers. They exchanged smiles.

Once the soldiers were behind them, Tess spoke again. "We Americans have an incredible political system. Maybe others do, too. I sure hope the Zezanikans do."

"Our system isn't perfect."

"It doesn't have to be perfect, only workable. Capable of balancing gains against losses. In America, we have laws and courts and markets and schools and an adversary system that allows both the ACLU and the NRA to make their case for what's good and what's bad."

"That sounds lovely, Tess, but look what that system has done to us so far."

They reached the shore, but the Zezanikans had moved further inland. There was no more open water beneath them, just marsh, much like the other bank of the river, but trampled by the hippos. "Is it really what the system has done, or what we have done, through the system?"

He stopped to plead with her. "What else could we have done? Just given up and let people steal Aremac to use for whatever they want?"

"Yes. That's exactly what we should have done." She pointed to the marsh. "I don't think those gray things are logs. I think they're why the Zezanikans have moved away from here."

Surprised at her answer more than by the crocodiles, he started walking again. After a few quick steps, he said, "Well, I don't accept that, but for the sake of argument, suppose you're right, and we should have given up Aremac to the FBI's torturers, the thieving corporations, the terrorists, the religious fanatics. We didn't. In fact, we've worked our butts off to prevent that. So that's where we are, and we can't go back in time. So what do you propose we do now?"

"There's a saying my riding instructor used to have: 'If you find yourself in a hole, the first thing to do is stop digging.'"

"So we stop fighting and just let the bad guys take over?"

"No. I didn't say that, either. I said that the first thing we do is stop digging. The next thing we do is give everybody a shovel."

They were only a few steps away from Rebecca and the soldiers, but he stopped short. "Huh?"

"Aremac is the shovel. We give it away. To everybody. If everyone has one, anyone who's tortured could show how it was done through another Aremac–one of our trusted ones. " She watched Rebecca coming back towards them, a broad smile on her face, accompanied by one of the Zezanikan soldiers.

Tess took her husband's hand and urged him forward. "And I think we'll start with Zezanika. For better or worse."

Chapter Ninety-Two

Minutes after Don's call from Washington, Marna was free of handcuffs and out of the house gathering three of her brothers with Heidi, Denise, and SOS. As they piled into a van driven by JFA's John, she saw Mac standing in the shadows talking with, of all people, Inga Steinman. Marna took the empty passenger seat and tried to pump John about the relationship between JFA and Ms. Steinman. He refused to say anything, so when they reached Interstate 40, she gave up and climbed between the seats into the back.

Marna's plan had assumed they would turn west, but John whipped the van onto the East ramp, which wasn't the direction to Arizona. Her head spun with all sorts of new possibilities, but she remained alert. When they turned south on Highway 117, about five miles past Grants, she relaxed a bit and studied the black lava lunar landscape of Malpais National Monument for reassurance. *If my ancestors could cross this desolate terrain and survive, surely we'll be able to survive this trip to Africa. If that's where they're really taking us.*

Half an hour later, the lava petered out, giving way to vast grasslands and distant snow-capped mountains. Marna tried to use the gentle panorama to relax, but there were too many unknowns stirring in her mind. During the next hour, the only event of note was turning west on Highway 36 and crossing the continental divide for the second time.

I haven't seen a town since we left the Interstate. I wonder if that was for a reason. If my memory serves me right, we could have reached the same spot by driving a more heavily traveled route through Gallup. So, John doesn't want to be seen. Why not?

They barely slowed for the dozen or so buildings of Fence Lake. *I have an ominous feeling this was the last American culture I will see for a long time.*

There weren't many more remote places than Fence Lake, but a couple of miles later, they turned off the paved highway onto a gravel road which took them out of sight of any sign of human presence–save for a few wispy vapor trails in the otherwise clear blue sky. *At least it's good flying conditions.*

Marna knew that somewhere ahead of them was the border between New Mexico and Arizona, but when the gravel disappeared in favor of dirt, she realized she would see no sign of a border crossing. *If we're actually going to Arizona as promised.*

The grasslands around them made it seem that you could see forever in any direction, but they were actually traversing low wavy hills–which Marna realized only when they crested a wave and saw the plane's silvery body. A small white shed stood nearby. In the field, a green fuel tank perched on legs, but she couldn't distinguish the grass landing strip until brother George pointed out the boundary markers.

"What sort of plane is that?" she asked. "Do you know it?"

"Don't worry," he said. "I can fly anything. It's French, so some of the controls will be peculiar, but I can handle it."

John pulled the van to within a few feet of the plane. Two men stood at the top of the stairs that extruded from an oval door in the fuselage. With no wasted motions, John organized a bucket-brigade to relay their luggage from the van to the plane, then parked the van in the shed and slid the door closed. Marna called Heidi, who had wandered over to the fuel tank and was marking the territory. Without further ceremony, they all boarded, strapped in, and took off. *Now there are three of them to contend with. Not good, but there's nothing I can do about it now.*

The passenger compartment was comfortable, but not luxurious. It had seats for 8, a small kitchen and a single toilet. Most of the fuselage was given over to a freight area where Marna could see the Aremac magnet strapped down with red and yellow cords, surrounded by dozens of sealed wooden crates similarly fastened. Just in front of this cargo were two low cots, the sight of which made Marna aware of just how exhausted she was from her long day.

She commandeered the left-hand cot, took off her shoes, and strapped herself in. Heidi commandeered the second cot, but nobody objected. The last thing Marna remembered was Tom covering her with a light-blue mesh blanket.

* * *

The bumps of a landing awakened her. She sat up, rubbed her eyes, and looked out upon a dark jungle barely illuminated by flares that raced past as they braked to a stop on the runway. John wouldn't tell them where they were. He strongly suggested they not leave the plane, even to stretch their legs. In spite of the warning, Tom stepped out the door and stood on top of the steps so he could get a GPS reading.

Back inside, he told everyone the airfield was in Colombia. "South America," he said. "Not the shortest route to West Africa."

They stayed on the ground only long enough to offload six of the crates and add two dark-skinned armed men. Marna could only imagine who the men were, or what the crates contained.

They took off in the dark, but within the hour, they could see dawn's purple margin ahead of them, gradually revealing the verdurous Amazon basin below. From time to time, Marna caught a glimpse of the brown water snaking its way east, until finally the mother of all rivers became too wide for the jungle to hide. She thought their next stop would be somewhere in Brazil, but John informed her that their next stop would be in Africa–Simbara. That was the signal she'd been waiting for. Her stomach twisted in knots. The emotional reality was nothing like she'd planned.

She struggled to pull herself together and assemble her team–yes, she was now thinking of them as *her* team. *And I'm responsible for their lives.* They huddled in the cargo area, leaving Al and Heidi to keep John occupied up front. It was their first opportunity to study Denise's data privately.

They all pressed close as Denise opened her computer. "This is the last picture we have with them in it, out there in the middle of the bridge. On the satellite's next pass, they were gone, and so were most of the troops on both sides. We don't know whether they crossed the bridge or not. If they didn't, we'll have to go into Simbara and find them."

"And if they did …?" Tom asked.

"Well, then we'll find out what Zezanika is like," said his brother.

Denise called up a new screen. "I can tell you something about that. It's a former French colony that gained independence at the same time as Simbara, but not by fighting. It seems that there was nothing there that the French thought was worth bothering with."

"Poor, in other words," said SOS.

She put her finger over her lips. "Keep your voice down. Not exactly. Long after independence, someone figured out that pretty much the whole country was sitting on top of an enormous pool of oil. You can imagine how popular Zezanika became overnight, but by that time, they had a strong, democratic government committed to independence and preserving their unique ecology."

SOS glanced toward the front of the cabin, then whispered, "So who got the oil?"

"Nobody," said Denise. "That's where the Zezanikans are unique. All the big powers have been wooing them to get a crack at the oil, but so far they've all been refused. A dozen years ago, a US oil cartel tried to bribe government officials to grant them drilling rights, but the plot was exposed. The US was expelled from the country. Same thing happened to China three years later. Now the other Big Powers tiptoe around the country like kittens in a dog park."

"So, we Americans might not be welcome there?"

Tom checked, then rechecked, the magazine of his Model 31. "We'll deal with that if it happens. So who has the oil now, Denise?"

"Nobody. The country is still holding out."

"For what? They could be rich."

"The official position is that the oil will be much more valuable years down the road, when it can be used for something other than burning." She clicked on a few links, then peered closely at a screen full of tiny numbers. "According to polls, the people seem to support the government's position by a large margin. A growing margin. Their biggest fear seems to be that someone will just move in militarily and take over their oil."

"Sounds like they have a reason to be afraid," said Tom. "They're awfully small, with an awful lot of oil."

"For now, they're letting the big powers keep each other in check while they guard their borders against their smaller neighbors–like Simbara."

"And against rogue planes dropping in unexpectedly?"

"That remains to be seen," said Marna. "Are we ready for Phase Two?"

"Ready to fly," said George, as he and Tom unholstered their pistols and crept forward. Marna waved them back and took the lead. Plopping down in the seat next to John, she said, softly, "We've changed our minds. We'd like you to take us to Zezanika first. After we check things out there, we'll move down to Simbara and help get the Aremac running."

"Why Zezanika? Your colleagues are in Simbara, held by the rebels."

Is he lying, or maybe he just doesn't know? "We have evidence they might be in Zezanika. It won't take long to check."

"If they're in Zezanika, you can forget about helping them. It's a vicious country, run by a ruthless dictator. We wouldn't live for ten minutes if we landed there." His voice hardened. "You're going to Simbara. End of discussion."

Marna nodded to her brothers. "In that case, we'll have to be more persuasive."

To back up her words, Tom and George moved into the pilots' cabin. John raised his hand to protest, but Al waved his pistol in warning.

Before she could move, one of the armed guards grabbed Marna, holding the point of a large knife to her eye. "*Eu cortarei sua cara.*"

"He says he will cut her face," John said calmly. "If you want your sister to remain beautiful, you will put down your weapons."

Beautiful? Marna froze, praying that the plane didn't hit turbulence. *Now why did I register that, when there's a knife about to blind me?*

When she felt the wet spot in her pants, she began to giggle uncontrollably, hysterically. She almost failed to hear the clunk from the forward cabin, followed by Tom's voice. "We've knocked out your pilots. Nobody is going to fly this plane until you put away that knife."

Marna held her breath. *If one of the others can pilot this plane, they'll call his bluff.*

Tom stepped through the door and saw that the second guard had pulled his pistol. "And that gun, too."

The knife wavered an inch from Marna's face. It looked as big as a plow blade. It wasn't moving away. *Stalemate.*

"*Pode você voar o plano?*" John asked the guards.

It was close enough to Spanish, Marna thought. *Can you fly the plane? If one of them can, we're cooked.*

Marna's guard shook his head, causing the knife to vibrate. Marna watched the knife so carefully she didn't see the other guard's answer.

Evidently, Tom did. "Put down the weapons."

"You're bluffing," John said, confidently. "You wouldn't let the plane crash."

"Why not? You'll probably kill us anyway."

"Why would we kill you? We need your expertise?"

"Stop stalling!" Tom shouted. As if in response, the plane suddenly dropped ten feet, throwing everyone off balance.

Marna felt a cold slash across her forehead.

Sticky blood on her face.

She began to wobble, but the knife stayed close.

Denise ran to help her, but her guard's threatening look drove her back. She stopped about five feet away, towel in hand, looking at Tom for directions.

"I'm not going to say it again," Tom demanded. "Put down the weapons."

John held up his open hands, face pale green. "They don't understand." He flicked his gaze back and forth between Tom and Marna's guard "*Colocar as armas!*"

The guards didn't move, but looked at John questioningly. "*Colocar as armas!*" he repeated, more forcefully.

Ever so slowly, too slowly, the knife withdrew from Marna's view.

Tom stepped forward and took the blade, while Al easily disarmed the second guard. Denise ran to Marna, using the towel to stanch the blood flow.

"Find something to tie them up with," Tom said to nobody in particular, then, to Denise, "I just hope you're right about Zezanika."

Chapter Ninety-Three

A month had passed with no word from the missing Aremac team. After searching for the entire month, Inga Steinman couldn't believe she was finally in this god-forsaken cesspool of a country, about to make contact. As her translator escorted her into the Zezanikan Ministry of Justice, she wondered if she'd brought enough cash to bail out the naive kids.

After thirty days in jail here, they should be more than ready to make any kind of deal I offer. So far, though, I haven't seen a lot of respect for the American dollar.

Puffing and sweating up the stairs, she wondered why this had to be the only two-story building in the city, maybe in the entire flea-bag country. *And why they don't have an elevator. I never would have come here in a thousand years, if there'd been any choice.*

Her translator, a tall, well-dressed man who certainly weighed less than half of her own bulk, put his hand gently on her elbow to give at least moral support to her exhausting climb. *That's the one good thing about this country–the men seemed to love big women, the bigger the better.* She'd been off the Niger boat less than an hour, yet she had received even more squeezes on her ample bottom than she gathered when she was an anorexic beauty queen. *I love it.*

But that's the only thing I love about this trip, which wouldn't have been necessary if it hadn't been for those pesky Aremac kids. They've cost me substantial income from my clandestine connection with Justice for Africa and their web of cousin companies. They've almost killed my government job, and still could if I can't bring this trip to a successful conclusion. But maybe that wouldn't matter if I could conjure up a really successful conclusion. It would serve that Silsbury bitch right for screwing up the sweet deal.

Once she had convinced her government superiors that she was the one for this current assignment, she would have vastly preferred to do it in the United States–at home in D.C. if she could. But these damn kids had been in Zezanika for four weeks now and showed no signs of coming out. In fact, when the agency's computer robots spotted Denise May Yao and Stephen Orem Spencer flying to Lagos with his mother, Inga knew the Aremac team might be setting up operations in the region.

Though Inga traveled with all the highest credentials, the United States had no embassy in Zezanika. The best she could do was fly to Abuja where the embassy supplied a limousine to take her to the Niger where she could catch a boat to Zezan, the capital. She wanted to have the limo drive her all the way–she liked boats even less than planes–but the ambassador said some of the countryside in between was too dangerous. He gave no details, and she didn't ask. *It's dangerous enough just being here, in this land with no elevators.*

She paused at the top of the steps to catch her breath and control her anger before the meeting. If she was to pull this off, the Fixman family had to think of her as an old friend, all sweetness and light. She saw a sign, in French, but she knew enough to translate "Prison" without the aid of her handsome guide. The arrow pointed right, so when he tried to guide her to the left, she resisted. "*A droite,*" she insisted.

Surprised by her use of French, he responded in kind. "*Pardon, Madame, mais non.*" Then he recovered his translator role. "The Aremac office, he is to the left."

"The Aremac office?"

He misunderstood her objection. "Excuse me, Madame. I, myself, lacked precision. The Aremac *offices*, they are to the left. And the laboratory, also."

"I didn't know they had offices. When I heard they were in the Ministry of Justice, I assumed they were in prison." *And I was going to rescue them. And earn their gratitude.*

He laughed. "Ah, the *plaisanterie*. Very good, Madame. Yes, honored guests in the prison–very *amusant*."

Inga decided to drop the subject and follow where he led. She soon found herself passing six doors whose translucent windows bore freshly painted signs saying Aremac, and directing the reader further down the corridor. As they approached the door at the end of the corridor, it opened, revealing Tess Myers Fixman, whom she barely recognized as the same woman she had first seen lying comatose in a hospital bed. *Now she looks fully alive, alert, and–damn her–pretty and petite. And, for Christ's sake, flanked by that damned dog and wearing a sidearm.*

Inga raised both hands, palms out. "Don't be afraid. I'm not here to arrest you."

Tess produced a sparkling chuckle. "Oh, I'm so relieved. Heidi, down!"

Why does everyone think I'm joking, Inga thought. "No, I've come to warn you, and to make an offer you can't refuse."

"Well, that sounds interesting. Why don't you come inside. Would you like something to eat? To drink? You must be tired from traveling."

Inga stepped into the room, smelled something delicious baking, and automatically looked for a suitable chair. To her surprise, there were two huge black leather chairs and a matching sofa. Just to be safe, she took the sofa. "You may wait outside," she told her translator. "I won't need you now, but I will later. *Plus tard*." She handed him a ten-dollar bill. "Buy yourself a cup of coffee, or whatever it is you drink here."

He left the room staring at the money and looking confused. Inga put him out of her mind. "Yes, I'll have iced tea, if it's not too much trouble. With sugar. And whatever you have to eat."

"I thought you might," said Tess, opening a warming oven and removing a tray heaped with pastries which she set in front of her guest.

Inga took two pastries and decided a bit of small talk would be good sales technique. She noticed a chart on the wall. *Get her answering an innocent question or two.* "That's an interesting chart, with all those countries and numbers. The numbers look important."

"They are. Maybe the most important numbers we have."

"Are they secret?"

"Not at all. The countries have brought people here to use Aremac, and have ordered one or more machines to be shipped as soon as our manufacturing is in full swing."

Inga's mind automatically began to multiply the number of countries by the price per Aremac. The dollar amount almost distracted her from the pastries. "What are the numbers?"

"The first number under each country represents the number of innocent people Aremac has freed."

Inga could hear the pride in Tess's voice, but dismissed this number as irrelevant to her own purposes. "And the second?"

"The number of guilty people Aremac has helped convict. But speaking of convictions, why would I think you were here to arrest me?"

"It's a crime to do business with an illegal arms dealer, but perhaps you didn't know that about Justice for Africa. They are well disguised." She could see from the expression on the young woman's face that she did not, in fact, know. *Well, good. JFA reneged on my deal, so they deserved whatever they got.*

"Fortunately, we don't do business with them any more. It was a mistake, even though I didn't know about their illegal activities. We've arranged to return their money, but you couldn't arrest us anyway. The US has no jurisdiction here."

She sounds serious. Maybe she realizes it wasn't a joke. "You may be happy to know you don't have to give them back their money, since their business is illegal." *If I can screw Silsbury and her bosses, so much the better. They owe me ten percent of that money, but they will never pay, even if they recover it all.* "They're just crooks, plain and simple. If you wanted honest dealings, you should have dealt with your government–who I, of course, represent."

Tess said nothing. Instead, she broke off a piece of Danish and tossed it to Heidi, who snapped it out of the air while remaining in a down position.

Inga tried to interpret the smile on Tess's face, but failed. "Anyway, I'm here to give you a chance to correct that–at a very nice profit, too."

Chapter Ninety-Four

By this time, Inga had devoured half the pastries, so Tess took another tray out of the small refrigerator and slipped them into the oven. *I hope I don't run out.* "This batch should be done before the first ones are all gone. Aren't they nice?"

"Very nice," said Inga, dabbing her lips with a linen napkin. "May I have some more tea?"

"Of course." Tess brought the pitcher to the coffee table. "Zezanika is a poor country, but they have wonderful bakeries. And restaurants. And people. We're very happy to have been invited to become citizens here."

Inga choked on a mouthful of apricot Danish. "Citizens? But you're American citizens. Whatever happened to patriotism?"

"Zezanika doesn't mind if we have dual citizenship. I hope that the United States feels the same way."

"Hmm. I don't think that's the usual practice–" She gulped down half a glass of tea. "–but maybe I could arrange that for you as part of the package."

"Oh, tell me about the package. You said something about a very nice profit."

Inga set down her tea, brushed pastry crumbs off her hands, and interlaced her fingers in her lap. "Let's just say we're talking about eight figures, more or less."

Tess gave a convincing whistle. "Who would we have to kill for that amount of money?"

"No killing required," Inga laughed. "All your government wants is the Aremac, with a few simple conditions."

Tess stood as if to leave, and Heidi followed her, but when she merely looked in on the pastries in the oven, the dog took one sniff then returned to her reclining spot. "We've already turned down your conditions–in spite of your agents' coercive tactics."

"I don't understand why you people are so stubborn. Well, that doesn't matter. Whatever your reasons, I'll concede we were probably too harsh. That's why I've been given this assignment to apologize and try a different approach. We need Aremac for national security, and we're willing to pay a king's ransom for it. I would think you'd want us to have it as your patriotic duty."

Tess used a potholder to extract the pastries and set them on a trivet in front of Inga. "Be careful. They're hot. You know, Ms. Steinman, we've always said you can have Aremac. We're just as patriotic as the guy next door, the guy with NRA bumper stickers on his car." She tested the temperature of the pastries with her fingertip, then let Heidi lick off the warm sugar. "Besides, you already have our first Aremac. You just took it when you kidnapped me."

"I'm shocked. Nobody told me you were kidnapped." She pointed her finger at one pastry after another, as if she weren't going to eat them all, eventually. "I'm sure that was simply a misunderstanding. In any case, Aremac is no good to us with all the built-in shutoffs. Whenever our people try to use it, the tiniest amount of pain shuts down the machine for two hours. We need those shutoffs shut off." She smiled at her own joke.

"Well, that's just what we can't give you."

"Just listen to my offer before you say no. The president himself has authorized us to pay you $100,000,000 for the device–without the shutoffs. Actually, that's nine figures, isn't it."

"That's the only condition?"

"You would also have to give us all copies of the digital record of your own session in the Aremac, just so there's no misunderstanding about the so-called kidnapping."

You don't want the evidence of your crimes floating around. Tess stared at the new platter of rolls, which was already one-third empty. She was afraid to look at Inga, lest she give away her feelings about Inga's latest condition. "And?"

"Nothing unreasonable. Of course, your government would want exclusive use of the Aremac."

Tess pointed to the sales chart. "We've already signed contracts with other countries."

"That's not a problem as long as they have the shutoffs in place and you continue to keep the software secret. No patents or copyright, of course. Instead, it would be put under the legal protection of the Espionage Act–"

"What does that involve?"

"Just makes it a federal crime to reveal any of the software. And anyone who works on it would have to have Q-clearance." Her hand hovered over the pastry platter, making a decision.

I wonder why the decision is so difficult, since she will eventually eat them all. "I'm not familiar with Q-clearance."

"It's like top secret, but for civilians. That could be a problem for your husband, being an Arab and all, but that's my job to brush aside little obstacles like that." Her hand swept a few crumbs off her lap.

"And if he didn't pass the security screening, wouldn't that make it rather difficult for us to operate, given that he's the inventor?"

"I'm sure we could work something out, if that happens. He'd be on the payroll in any case, as you all would, and paid a generous salary, though you probably wouldn't need it."

"Anything else?"

Inga shook her head dismissively. "Just some minor details for the lawyers to work out. So what do you think?"

"It's certainly a generous offer. I'll have to discuss it with my colleagues."

"Of course."

We won't be discussing what you think. Our biggest problem is how to get you off our backs, permanently.

Tess offered her best smile. "Why don't you take a break? The Banadoora restaurant downstairs and on the corner to your right has a bountiful buffet. I'm sure you'll enjoy it."

CHAPTER NINETY-FIVE

Using the security cameras Denise had set up a month ago, the Aremac team watched Tess's entire session with Inga. The moment Inga left for the restaurant–snatching the last two sweet rolls to fortify her on her walk down the block–they all streamed into the lounge. Before anyone was even seated, SOS said, "That's a lot of money."

Norton, who had traveled to Zezanika to teach the locals how to make Hogan Stoves, corrected him. "No, that's a *whole lot* of money."

"Is it before or after taxes?" Rebecca asked.

"I forgot to ask," Tess sighed. "I didn't think there was any chance you'd go for it."

"Probably not," said Norton. "But it's still a whole lot of money."

Marna said nothing, but agreed with a nod.

Marna had seemed distant from the discussion, and Tess wondered if she was feeling ill. She kept looking at her watch, so Tess decided it must be some appointment she was eager to complete. She let it go without comment. If Marna had something to say, she would say it, so Tess went on. "Are any of you really tempted?"

Denise sat with her hands in their lap as if they were discussing which spoon to use with tea. "Actually, it's not a matter of quantity, but of quality. A hundred million dollars is a different dimension, a different universe. I suppose it would be logical to discuss if we could use some of the money to address our concerns."

"That's why I didn't just turn her down cold," said Tess. She knew that every one of them had unbreakable personal reasons for detesting the idea of their work being used for torture. Denise's parents had been tortured in East Asia. Norton had been a prisoner of war. Roger's mother had been tortured in Syria, and SOS's mother had been "tortured" in a mental hospital. Neither Marna nor Rebecca would talk about their experiences, but Tess knew Marna's husband had treated her like a prisoner of war. As for what had happened to Rebecca, she would never talk about her wartime experiences. Tess could only conjecture, based on her emotional reactions to the whole subject. *They're not going to accept this offer, but we have to discuss it now, to put it to rest once and for all.*

Tess slipped into her facilitator role, standing and writing "pros and cons" on the blackboard. Zezanika didn't seem to have whiteboards. "Maybe we have to rethink everything in terms of what we could do if we had that different dimension at our disposal. Denise, would you like to play Devil's Advocate, just to be sure we're not overlooking anything?"

Denise nodded. An instant later, they all seemed to realize that Roger hadn't said anything about the offer. When Tess touched him lightly on the cheek, he emerged from his thinking trance. "What we have to offer is genuine guaranteed tamper-proof, coercion-proof Aremac. That should be worth something to honest people."

Roger kept talking while she wrote. "We also have an essentially infinite supply of practically free energy."

While Tess wrote notes on the board, Roger looked around for someone to say something, but they all waited patiently for his next words. "So, since we are inventors, I propose we invent ways of using the laws of our own new universe. If we can't think of ways to do that, what makes us think we would be able to think of ways to use their money?"

Tess bent down and threw her arms around her husband. She kissed his ear while everybody else applauded. "So you were listening to me on the bridge."

Marna raised her hand. "I'm totally confident you're not going to change your minds and accept torture for any amount of money." She checked her watch. "I have to meet someone. Can you go on without me? I'll agree with whatever the team decides."

Tess nodded her assent, her conjecture about Marna's appointment confirmed. "Sure. We'll tell you all about it later."

As soon as Marna closed the door behind her, Roger picked up where he'd been interrupted. With quite a bit of back and forth, he laid out some alternative plans for Aremac's future without massive outside funding. Tess took a break to relieve herself of all the tea she'd been drinking, glass for glass, with Inga. When she returned, Denise was framing objections to Roger's plan.

"But all people won't have the same chance. A working Aremac is a million-dollar item, so it would be available only to the rich and powerful. Poor countries like Zezanika would be even worse off than before." She paused to look at SOS for agreement, then seemed to have second thoughts about her own idea. "I guess we could use some of our money to rectify that." Then she paused again. "But I don't like the idea of charity. It demeans people."

Tess didn't disagree. "It can, but I think we could invent a way around that."

As the back and forth continued, Tess raced to write all their ideas on the blackboard. The squeak of the chalk reminded her of just how low tech Zezanika was. "Okay, we'll table these rich versus poor questions for now. What else?"

Roger's hand shot up. "I don't think we should table them quite yet. As Denise reminded us, Aremac is a high-tech invention, requiring a large capital investment. But SOS pointed out that it requires an advanced technological capability to maintain. No matter how you slice it, it once again favors the rich nations over the poor nations."

Roger inclined his head toward Norton, who picked up his hint. "But the Hogan Stove is not high-tech."

Roger didn't agree. "Its quantum core is about as high-tech as it gets. We're the only people in the world who know about it. For now, at least."

"*Aoo'–*" Norton said, then seemed to realize he was so excited he was speaking Dineh. "I mean yes, but it's cheap, and sealed, and requires no maintenance. The rest is purposely low-tech, and it provides cheap energy. Very cheap. So it favors poor nations–or at least doesn't disfavor them." He pursed his lips in thought. "That is, if I can find more auto graveyards. Their cars here are even older than at home."

Tess wrote "auto graveyards" on the blackboard, then looked at her watch. "I suspect even Inga has to stop eating eventually, so we'd better wind this up. We're not finished with inventing our new universe–"

"–not by a long shot," said Roger.

Tess gave him a knowing smile. "–but I think we have explored enough to give Inga her answer. Do we need to vote?"

Every head shook.

"Okay," said Tess. "Here's what I think we've got so far. When we turn down the American offer, we won't have the money to provide Aremacs to poor nations, but there are alternative ways to finance them. We can earn enough money from the snoods and the dongles to finance Hogan Stoves for this entire country and the Navajo nation–and other poor countries all over the world."

Denise stretched and pointed to the slogan on her t-shirt,: "I'd Kill for a Nobel Peace Prize." She waited a moment for the message to sink in, then said, "Something we been avoiding in this discussion: the quantum displacement technology could also be used as a weapon. We haven't dealt with that at all."

Having anticipated this objection, Tess walked to the counter. "True, and there's not much we can do about that." She opened a drawer and held up the bread knife. "This can be used as a weapon, too. Should we stop slicing bread?"

CHAPTER NINETY-SIX

As she walked from the Aremac office to her apartment, Marna passed the new hospital the government was building with the promised funds from Aremac and Hogan Stove profits. A rush of pride filled her chest, but she fought it down so she could practice how she would open her encounter with Karl. *What are you doing here? No, that was a stupid question. It's clear that he's here to see me, and there's only one reason for that.*

The main street was busy, as usual during shopping hours. A few merchants greeted her, and she was tempted to stop and buy something to hold in her hands, but she resisted the temptation. *Why don't you leave me alone? No, that sounds too much like begging.*

She turned up the side street at the tourist information bureau, which was closed, as usual. *Maybe a question isn't the right way to start. Hello, Karl. Whatever brought you here, you're not wanted. Please leave me alone. No, that's just as bad, begging. What happened to that pride in yourself?*

She slowed down in front of the cobbler's shop to watch the shoemakers at work through the open door. She heard a siren in the distance and resumed her walk. *If you don't leave immediately, I'll call the police. But if I threaten him, what will he do?*

She rounded the final corner and saw Karl waiting outside her front door, holding a small suitcase and a large packing tube. She stopped a few feet in front of him, but he stepped forward and tried to kiss her. She turned her head so his kiss landed awkwardly on her cheek. She stepped back out of his reach.

"Let's go inside?" he said. "I'm broiling out here."

"I like the heat," she said, making no move toward the door.

"Well, it's killing me. Let's go inside."

"All right," she said, but instead of moving toward her door, she headed across the unpaved street.

"Where are you going," he called after her.

"You said you wanted to get out of the heat." She pointed to the small cafe on the other side of the street. "The Camel's Nose is air-conditioned."

He grabbed his suitcase and packing tube and ran to catch up with her just as a middle-aged man in white robes opened the door for her. She exchanged some words with the man, then took a small table–one of five–near a Hogan Stove on which two kettles were steaming. When Karl joined her, he asked, "What did he say to you? I couldn't understand a word."

"We were speaking French. I haven't mastered much Arabic yet."

"But what did he say? He looked like he knew you pretty well."

"I ordered us some cold drinks, then he was just thanking me again for their air conditioning. They think it was a gift, but I was just being selfish. It's nice to have a cool place right across the street."

"That's all he said? Seems like you talked longer than that."

"Do you really want to know?"

"You're my wife. I should know what other men are saying to you."

"Okay. He wanted to know if you were the man who used to beat me."

Karl half stood from his chair. "I never beat you." He looked over at the table where the man was sitting with two other men, similarly dressed. He hesitated for a moment, then slowly sat down again. "Besides, I hear that Muslim men regularly beat their wives. It's their right. Their duty."

She shook her head, slowly. "Your knowledge of Islam is sadly deficient, Karl. It's true that a man may strike his wife, gently, under certain circumstances–"

"See!"

"–but never in the face."

"I never hit you in the face. If you told them that, you're lying."

"Here, now, when there's a dispute about who is lying about a crime, they use Aremac. Do you know how that works?"

A young girl, not more than thirteen, came out from behind a beaded curtain in back and set two glasses in front of them. Karl ogled the girl's back until she disappeared behind the curtain, then mumbled. "Inga explained it to me." He reached across the table and stroked her cheek. "Anyway, that's irrelevant. If I gave you a love tap some time, it was because I was drinking, but now I've stopped drinking."

Unbidden, a thrill of hope rose in her throat, familiar hope from their former relationship. "Good for you." She lifted her glass a few inches, saluting him sincerely.

"And I'm painting again." He reached for the cardboard tube he'd been carrying and set it on the table in front of her. "I brought you one of my new paintings. As a gift."

"How thoughtful." Eager to see his new work, she tore the tape off one end of the tube and slipped out the rolled canvas. She stood and spread the canvas on the next table. Her heart fell as she recognized it as the painting of Black Mesa that had been sitting in his studio from before they were married, one of the paintings that had made her fall in love with him. She said nothing as the three men in white came over to admire the work.

He watched her intently, as if looking for a sign that she recognized his deception, but she gave none. When the men stopped talking about the painting and returned to their table, she changed the subject. "You mentioned Inga. Is that Inga Steinman? You know her?"

"She brought me here. She wants me to bring you back to the US, where she will pay us a fortune for the secrets to some invention."

He stopped abruptly, as if realizing he might have said too much. "Of course, I told her I didn't care about the money. I just wanted you back with me, where you belong. But, still, once we're rich, everything will be perfect. I can paint, and you can play with your theories. You know, you're emotionally unstable. You need me to manage things for you."

Ignoring the put-down of her work, she laid her hand on his and said, softly, "That's not going to happen, Karl. I'm glad you're making some changes in your life, but I've been making changes, too. Our lives are now on separate paths, and we're no longer married. If I had any money, which I don't, and won't, none of it would be yours."

She lifted her hand, but he grabbed it tightly in his. "You're wrong, Marna. Maybe the news didn't reach you here in the boondocks, but our divorce is not final. You're still married to me, and our official residence is in New Mexico, so half of all your property is rightfully mine."

Marna pulled her hand away, so firmly that it surprised him into letting go. She placed both hands in her lap and looked out the cafe window at the whitewashed buildings, the packed clay streets, and the old men sitting on a bench under twin palm trees. "Look around, Karl. I know there are superficial similarities, but we're not in New Mexico now. We're in Zezanika, where they probably don't even recognize our marriage in the first place."

"They have to recognize it, by international law."

"Perhaps. I'm a physicist, not a lawyer, but we've been hanging around Islamic courts here. And in Simbara. Laws here are different." She stood. "Come on. I'd like to show you the local court. It's quite quaint."

"I'm not interested in their damn court." He picked up his glass, tasted the tea, then slammed it down on the table. "What is this swill? I could use a real drink."

"Oh, I thought you'd given it up?"

"I have … for the most part. But I'm hot, and I could use a cold beer. One beer isn't really drinking."

She was tempted to point out that he'd just said he wanted a real drink, but instead said, calmly, "I'm afraid they don't have Goose Island India Pale Ale here."

"That's okay. In this heat, I'd even settle for a can of Coors."

"Oh, they don't sell any kind of alcohol here. Not legally. I suppose I could find you a bootlegger, but if they catch you drinking alcohol, you'll get eighty lashes."

"That's ridiculous. Lashes? Come on, Marna, this is the twenty-first century."

"Oh, but it's true." She took his elbow and urged him out of his seat. "Come on, you'll really want to see where they do this." He didn't resist.

As she led him outside and back to the center of town, she asked him about news of all their old acquaintances back in Los Alamos. When they arrived at the stone courthouse, she led him through the building, past the offices, and out into the courtyard. "See that wall on the far side? Let's take a closer look."

She drew him closer. "Notice that the stones are different than the stones in the courthouse itself. I'm told this wall is much older–so old that nobody can put a date on it. Anyway, those iron rings are for tying up the drinker while he receives his eighty lashes."

Karl's hands were trembling, though Marna could not tell if it was from fear or from need for a drink. "Most of the time," she said, "the wall is used for lashes, but from time to time, it's used for adulterers."

"You mean they whip people just for having a little extra-marital fun?"

"Oh, it doesn't matter whether you had fun or not. And it's not whipping. Under Sharia law, adultery is considered a crime against humanity. Punishable by lapidation."

"Huh? What's that?"

"You mean you've never seen a stoning? It's quite awful. They tie them to the wall, then the family and friends of the offended party choose the type of stones that will prolong the agony. It can take hours before the adulterer dies."

Karl looked around the courtyard, then whispered, "That's barbaric."

"I agree. But it's their culture, which we have to accept if we live here." She laid her arm gently on his. "Still, I want you to know that in your case, even though it's my right, I wouldn't throw any stones. Not after all we've meant to each other."

"I'm no adulterer."

"But you are, Karl. I saw you. In the casino."

"You can't prove that. It's just your word against mine."

"No, Karl, it's just your word against Aremac's. Would you like to try your lying prowess against our technology?"

He studied the stone wall, but said nothing.

She chuckled and elbowed him in the ribs. "Not to worry, though. You always said I throw like a girl." She twisted a strand of her dark hair and put it between her lips. "Hmm. I supposed I'd have to hire a capable man to be my surrogate."

He grabbed her wrist and yanked her hand away from her mouth. "What's wrong with you, Marna. Have you gone nuts? Don't you care about me, after all we've meant to each other?"

She didn't attempt to pull her hand away, but simply turned her head and nodded toward a passing man carrying a live chicken. When Karl let go of her hand, she said, "I don't know if I care about you, Karl, so much as feel sorry for you. That's why I showed you this wall and told you about lapidation. I truly hope you can sneak back out of Zezanika before someone in authority realizes you're my ex-husband."

He tightened his grip on her wrist. "Not ex. I told you, our divorce is not final."

"Oh, here in Zezanika it is. I filed an adultery complaint against you just after we arrived, and you were tried in absentia. In fact, that man with the chicken was my lawyer. He was very good, and my complaint was honored. So, there's an outstanding charge against you. If they catch you, it's up against that wall. I hope Inga bought you a return ticket, but if she didn't I may be able to scrape up enough to help you out. I owe you that much, after all we've meant to each other."

Chapter Ninety-Seven

On her way downstairs, Tess ran into Marna returning from the courthouse. Remembering the concern on her face when she had left the meeting, she asked, "Is everything all right?"

"Just fine," Marna smiled. "I had a surprise visit from Karl."

"Karl? Your ex? Here in Zezanika?"

"Inga paid for his trip. She thought he might have some claim over our inventions. But you're on your way out. I'll tell you about it later."

"But it came out all right? He didn't hit you?"

"Oh, no. I just took him on a tour, before he left. He was very interested in the wall at the courthouse where they tie up the camels."

Tess knew from Marna's mischievous smile that there was more to the story, but it could wait until she'd finished her meeting with Inga. She hugged Marna goodbye, then rushed to the Banadoora restaurant. Though the restaurant was packed with diners, she had no trouble locating Inga by the stack of used plates on her table, the closest one to the buffet.

She sat down and told Inga their decision, preparing herself for Inga to raise the ante. She hoped Inga would not attempt to pressure her, but her fears of an awkward situation proved groundless.

"I suspected you might not accept," Inga sighed. "And I was prepared to offer you more, but I don't think it will make any difference."

"You're right," said Tess. "Even ten times as much money wouldn't change our minds."

"I understand perfectly." Inga dipped her fingers in the flowered finger bowl, then wiped them on her flaxen napkin. "This baklava is delicious, but the honey gets into everything." She leaned over with a grunt and picked up her briefcase. "I did some financials of my own on the way over here." She extracted a single piece of paper and laid it in front of Tess. "I've done some market research, and I think your business has a lot more potential than the government was offering you."

Tess ignored the sheet, but fixed her eyes on Inga's face.

Inga tapped on the paper. "To realize the billions on this spreadsheet, what you need is an executive who can build a marketing organization. Someone with extensive experience dealing with government and hi-tech."

Tess pressed her tongue against her palate to keep from smiling. "You mean someone like Alicia Silsbury?"

Inga made a spitting sound. "That snob. If I were you, Tess, I wouldn't trust her. She's too skinny."

Tess covered her mouth. "Gee, Inga, I would think that other than Alicia, a person with those qualifications would be hard to find. Did you have someone particular in mind?"

Inga looked around the restaurant, her eyes resting on the waiter restocking the tiered buffet. "You know, I rather like this part of the world. For the right price, I might be available."

"What an interesting thought, Inga. Tell me more."

Inga proceeded to sketch out a grand plan for making billions from selling Aremac to governments–and non-governments–all over the world. Tess listened attentively, always ready to gather ideas from any source. *With her weight behind us, I believe we actually could make billions.*

Don't be nasty, her other inner voice chided. *She may be able to sell sand to camels, but she probably can't do anything about her weight.* "And what would you need from us?"

"Just remove those silly controls. Everybody says they're just an impediment to proper use. You take them out, and I can do the rest. Your people would be free to continue your research. To invent new things."

"That sounds just wonderful, Inga …" Tess lifted a crocodile-shaped chunk of halvah off her plate and placed it on Inga's. "… but it's not going to happen."

Inga had already bitten off the croc's head. "I could really do it, you know."

"I know. You're very good at what you do.

Inga beamed. The croc's tail disappeared.

"I am puzzled by one thing, though."

Inga already had another piece of halvah at her lips. "What's that?"

"Whatever happened to patriotism?"

THE END

CPSIA information can be obtained at www.ICGtesting.com
Printed in the USA
BVOW03s2300131014

370690BV00024B/533/P